Holly Bush Road

An Angelica Barrister Story

by

A. A. Valentine

DORRANCE
PUBLISHING CO
EST. 1920
PITTSBURGH, PENNSYLVANIA 15238

Dorrance Publishing Co
585 Alpha Drive
Suite 103
Pittsburgh, PA 15238
Visit our website at *www.dorrancebookstore.com*

ISBN: 978-1-4809-8614-5
eISBN: 978-1-4809-8595-7

Special Thanks to the Following:

Mom: For being an amazing parent. I miss you every day.

R. Dale B.: Thanks for reading my drafts and offering your feedback as well as being a father figure.

P.J., Steve, Matt and Jordan: Thanks for being there for me during rough times.

S. Baker-Martin: Thanks for helping me become a better writer in Freshman English.

And finally Dr. Andrew Becker, for helping with translations.

One

Miller's Run was small and agriculturally focused town that always seemed a little different from its neighbors. One could use certain clichéd words like "quaint" and "picturesque" to describe it while passing through. Despite large swathes of otherwise boring farmland lying on its perimeter and peppered throughout the interior, there were areas of rocky outcrops that hid large cave systems beneath that would give spelunkers ample reasons to make a pilgrimage at least once in their life. The caving club at the local high school always kept a fresh stock of students interested in exploring these, but on at least one occasion in the past, bred a disaster. Two younger children, after "borrowing" their two older siblings' gear, trekked out inexplicably on their own and were lost to the bowels of the earth. They erected a small statue in front of the Town Hall in their memory, but there was something vague about the inscription beneath it. "To the Children Who've Been Lost." The names of the boy and girl depicted in the bronze effigy were not mentioned, nor did they really resemble the previously mentioned casualties.

It was on a chilly day in late spring that Angelica Barrister found herself sitting atop a large wooden bridge spanning more than sixty feet across an offshoot of Miller's Run (the small river/large stream after which the town was named), on the family's newly acquired property. She kicked her feet as she stared down at the small school of silvery minnows darting back and forth in formation. Her parents were not far away walking in the tall grasses, but they'd might as well been a hundred miles away as she was lost in her own new world now.

Edward, her father, had his arm wrapped around his wife's shoulders as they gazed at the sea of new foliage before them. "Wow, this place got overgrown quickly!"

Rosanna replied, "No kidding! You think they would've at least had someone come and mow this stuff before we got here."

He sighed. "We'll have to get someone with a big mower to come out and take of this until I get something bigger."

She wrapped her arms around his waist and smiled. "We knew there'd be bumps in the road on this little adventure of ours. The best thing is, we can't even see our neighbors' houses from here. Our yard doesn't have to be the best on the block."

He looked to his left and right, then back at her. "Hey, you know, you're right! Since I'll be working from home now, I won't have to shower or shave...."

Playfully cutting him off, "Oh, no, you will! We still have to put up with you!"

"Oh, yeah, I totally forgot about that. I *am* going to grow a beard, though."

She sighed lightly and smirked. "All right, I guess I'll let that slide." She kissed him, then looked over at her daughter, who was laughing quietly. "Sweetie, be careful up there!"

Angelica didn't look back as she said, "I know, I'm being careful." The fish continued to move in unison. She glanced back after a short pause. "Daddy, there's fish in the water!"

He smiled. "Oh, yeah? Maybe I'll teach you how to fish someday!"

Her eyes lit up. "Really? Cool!"

As her attention turned back to the water, Edward said to his wife, "And I'll let *you* bait the hooks!"

She raised her eyebrow. "Ew! No way am I lancing a bunch of worms with hooks!"

He chuckled. "Okay, okay, but you do have to gut the fish we bring back."

"Hah! If you think you're going full on Grizzly Adams out here, you're nuts!" She couldn't help but laugh at his faux surprised face.

"And here I thought we'd be going 'off the grid' and starting our 'prepper' lifestyle in earnest."

She kissed him. "I do love you. We can do this." The nearby thorny vines then caught her attention. "Hey, are those blackberry bushes?"

"You know… I think they might be. That or raspberry, mulberry… hard to tell now, though."

"Looks like I'll have to learn how to make pie then. Of course, you'll have to wait a few months for it."

Suggestively, "But I want your pie now!"

She was raised by a strict Catholic mother and even though they were married, they were within earshot of their daughter. "You behave, Mr. Barrister! You may have to wait a few months on that too if you don't mow the lawn!"

Still coy, "Hey, your personal grooming is your business."

Feigning shock, she playfully slapped his chest. "Keep that up and I'll make sure you take a cold shower!"

"Only if you join me…."

She started to giggle, but they found their attention ripped toward the bridge. They had heard a sharp yelp, a large splash, and their daughter wasn't sitting on the handrail of the bridge any longer. Both of their hearts immediately jumped into overdrive and they sprinted toward the bridge with Olympian speed.

He cried out, "Ange!? ANGE!?"

He could see his daughter submerged in the frigid and quickly flowing stream. She was in over her head and struggling with some sort of unseen force that was keeping her held down.

Rosanna screamed, "Get her, Ed!"

He'd already jumped into the water and was soon completely under himself. The icy water that rushed into his ears stung mercilessly as he swam to the center and grabbed his daughter's arms. He was a strong swimmer and in relatively good shape, but there certainly seemed to be something pulling against him. It wasn't his daughter, he soon found out, as the gulp of water that had infiltrated her lungs essentially incapacitated her. His paternal instinct, stronger than ever, did manage to free her from the unseen grappler holding onto the other end. Rosanna, watching the scene helplessly from the bank, ran across the bridge to the other side, "Oh, God, please! Please save her!"

There was only a small sigh of relief, however, as Edward took in a loud gasp of air upon surfacing. He trudged toward the opposite shore as his wife ran toward them. Angelica's black irises had rolled partially back into her head, her lips having taken on an unsettling light blue shade.

"Angelica!? Ed, she's not breathing!"

Edward draped her over his knee and raised her feet into the air. As he wrapped on her back to try and coax the water out, "Ange! Breathe, baby girl, BREATHE!"

Several agonizing seconds passed as Rosanna watched on in horror. Her eyes were completely saturated with tears.

"Please, God! PLEASE!"

The tears of pain, however, were soon transmuted to tears of joy as Angelica began to cough up mouthfuls of water onto the ground.

"Thank you!" Her hands then felt the deathly chill of the water that covered her daughter completely. "Ed, we have to get her inside! She'll freeze to death!"

The fight for life was clearly not over as they took flight toward the house. They were soon in the bathroom.

"Hon, get her out of those wet clothes so she can warm up!"

He dashed to a box in the hall and retrieved a towel for her. As Rosanna toweled her off, Edward sprinted to the family Subaru and desperately searched the boxes for a warm set of clothes.

Meanwhile, Rosanna embraced her daughter closely to keep her warm. "Angelica, you're okay now. Mama's here."

Through deep and painful coughs, "Someone... pushed me in...."

Her brow furrowed. "Honey, it's okay. You probably just leaned over too far. No one was on the bridge but you."

As the screen door slapped shut at the back door, she looked at her mother, clearly frustrated. "No, Mom, I *was* pushed! I felt two hands push me!"

Edward had heard her exclamation from the hallway. He handed off the clothes. "Baby girl, Mom and I were right there. We didn't see anyone else. You're okay now, that's all matters."

Scowling, "You don't believe me either!?"

Her tone more forceful, "Angelica! You were just too close to the edge! There's no need to lie about it!"

Seeing the two clearly agitated with one another and not backing down, "Ladies, please! There's only one way to settle this!"

They both looked at him sternly.

He then said in a lighter tone, "I'm going to have to teach you how to swim, Ange."

The comment did its job. The situation was temporarily diffused. He would, a few months later, teach his daughter how to swim. This event, however, was just a bitter omen of things to come.

Two

With physical pain still stinging her lungs throughout the evening, Angelica was not looking forward to the inevitable darkness that day. The sun had already set, but she felt as if a longer and more dreaded war was coming after her brief battle with death earlier that day. She wasn't really paying attention as she passed her parents' bedroom in her plain white pjs. Edward's voice, however, snagged her attention. "Ange, baby girl, if you need to sleep in our bed tonight, we understand."

Her mother echoed the warm smile of father.

Angelica, stone-faced, replied, "I can't sleep in your bed forever." She wasn't sure why she was resisting the temporary solace being offered, but she felt compelled to stand up to her lingering fears. For a couple of weeks prior to their arrival, Angelica had been experiencing recurring night terrors every single night. She hadn't experienced these before and they were undoubtedly remarkable. Waking up every night screaming at the top of her lungs and drenched in sweat became commonplace. *They're trying to kill me!* were the only cogent words her parents understood during her largely incoherent rambling.

No..., was all Angelica heard in her own mind, in an oddly foreign voice then and there.

Her mother continued. "Honey, it's okay. We want to make sure you're safe. You're still coughing a lot and...."

This new, raspy, yet forceful voice sounded off again in her mind, *"Tell her to shut up and go to bed!"*

Edward noticed her eyes shift to each side before she returned to looking into his own. It pulled on an uncomfortable nerve that had been wriggling its way to the surface since they first started looking into the property.

Angelica replied in a dull tone, "I'm okay. Goodnight."

They returned the expression as she quietly shut the door to their room, then hers. Rosanna couldn't help but feel familiarity in the exchange. There was always a gap between her and daughter. It quietly reminded her of the one with her own mother. She thought on it for a few moments before looking over at her husband. He'd been quiet since Angelica disappeared into her room and was clearly bothered by something.

"What's wrong, hon?"

Mildly surprised coming out of his thoughts, "Huh? Oh, nothing. I'm just worried about her."

"I am too, but you know how she gets."

It wasn't his daughter's brooding that was bothering him. He was used to that. "I know. She was so insistent that someone pushed her, though. Do you think...."

He was calmly cut off. "Ed, we were right there. There's no way someone pushed her, then ran away without us seeing them."

He was hesitant to say that it wasn't a physical person he was pinning this on. He'd converted to Catholicism for his wife before they wed, but he grew up with a different set of beliefs different than those his wife held. "I know, we hardly took our eyes off her. I mean... what if it was something else?"

Understanding his implication, she put her hand on his shoulder. "Ed, I thought you stopped believing in that sort of thing when you were a kid."

He then heard the same voice speak to him, although he didn't know it was same as the one Angelica heard. It was straining but still steady.

"Oh, she was pushed. You know it."

Rosanna looked at him, confused, as he seemed to snap uncomfortably out of the small trance he was in listening to the words. They troubled him. He hadn't heard a voice in years. "You're right, hon. She was just so insistent, that's all."

"You okay?"

He was aware of his awkwardness now. "Yeah, yeah, I'm fine. I'm just tired. It's been a long day."

He returned to staring blankly at the covers on the bed, hoping certain beliefs he'd covered years ago would have no reason to surface. Trying to buoy his spirits, "Hon, you need to relax! You saved our daughter's life today! I can't even swim!"

He sighed and kissed her forehead. "You would've done the same thing regardless."

"Thank you, Mr. Modesty, but you get the gold medal today."

"You know, I should teach both of you how to swim."

Despite having her own uncertainty when being in water over her head, "Yeah, okay. I'd like that. We can have a picnic lunch and make a day out of it."

He reached over to turn off the lamp on the table next to the bed, "Well, that sounds like a plan. It'll have to wait a couple of months, though. The water's way too cold right now!"

She yawned. "No kidding!"

Angelica, meanwhile, stared at her teddy bear atop her mattress pressed against the wall. She looked at the stitched smile which brought a strange sort of comfort now that she thought about it. Its innards were cotton, its eyes and nose a handful of plastic bits sewn on in some distant factory halfway around the world. She didn't understand why it comforted her, but she didn't care at this point. She felt compelled to weather the coming torrent of negativity that was on the horizon and she would take any comfort she could get. And even though part of her wanted to get up and sleep in the next room with her parents, she stayed.

Three

3:00 A.M.

Angelica, alone, was crouched along the edge of the stream bisecting her family's property. The sun warmly kissed her cheeks as she stared at the large school of small fish lurching to and fro in the current before her. She couldn't quite figure out the strange pattern of the school. They seemed to be evading some unseen predator... but what?

Suddenly, the school came to a stop directly in front of her. The tiny silver fish seemed fixated on her and her alone. Leaning forward and practically hovering directly over the fish, she didn't notice the sun, which had been fixed at high noon, was suddenly plummeting to the horizon. It was the sharp drop in temperature that caused her to stop staring at the water and turn her gaze to the black sky dotted with many red stars. Her face contorted with perplexity, knowing full well that several hours didn't just elapse in seconds. She quickly looked back down the school of minnows, with their eyes reflecting yellow light back at her. Or were they glowing? She couldn't tell. The images startled her, causing her to fall flat on her bottom. The ground then began to faintly rumble in the distance, unnerving her as she tried to rise to her feet. All around the property, large fountains of black fluid started erupting here and there, emitting the foul smell of sulfur. Overwhelmed by the stench, she stumbled and dropped to the ground again. Now her feet were being pulled into the earth and held there without relent. The minnows from below then leapt from the water and latched onto her legs, burrowing small holes into her flesh. She cried out in pain, but no one was there to rescue her.

She desperately swiped the fish from her skin and they, one by one, fell to the ground, wriggling and flopping around. Angelica pulled and pulled attempting to free her slowly sinking legs from the thick tar-like mud beneath her. The erupting liquid from the ground was now starting to flood every square inch of terra firma. As the black sludge spilled over the banks of the stream from the land, she felt a sudden surge of frigid black water crashing down the stream toward her and past. She looked to her right and was struck dumb by the growing black fog being emitted from the stream and slowly taking a humanoid shape. As its form solidified, it stood towering above the land by nearly ten feet. The creature's glowing yellow eyes seated in its dog-like head commanded her gaze. It slowly trudged through the swiftly rising liquid toward her, each step causing a crescendo of squishy thuds. It paused a few feet in front of her, looking down with contempt and pure malice. It stretched its arm-like appendages out and quickly clapped its hands together. The resulting explosion of thick black fluid from every angle quickly over-took Angelica. Within seconds, the water was several feet above her head. It invaded her mouth despite her best efforts to hold her breath. The pain felt as hot as fire, stabbing her lungs completely through. The liquid covered and infected every inch of her body, then infiltrating every cell of her being. Fire… fire from fluid. The last gasps of air bubbled from her struggling lips….

The pain was still real when she awoke screaming like a banshee. Something else was also still too real: The black humanoid mass with the glowing yellow eyes and a canine head was looming over her at the foot of her mattress. Its perceived height caused it to have to lean to fit in the room with an eight-foot ceiling. Now closer than in the dream, she could see that its body resembled a grossly deformed person, only much taller than anyone she'd ever seen.

Angelica was clinging tightly to her teddy bear as she scrambled to the edge of the bed and bailed out. She hit the floor with a loud thud before regaining her footing. Without hesitation she ran through the charged and frigid area that the black figure was occupying and into the hall.

The door to her parents' bedroom was forced open with the power of a charging bull. All of the recent sounds had awoken her parents, but Angelica beat them to the punch. Edward tried to get up, but Angelica's momentum knocked him back down.

"Ange!? Are you okay?"

She gripped her father tightly with no intent to let go. She turned her head toward his face. "Something tried to kill me!"

Rosanna immediately *knew* that the only possible explanation for this was some type of dream brought on by the recent trauma. And given that parents usually write off all unperceived fears as "overactive imagination," she wanted to try and control this situation as much as possible to restore the peace. Concern did manage to color Rosanna's words, but they were not the dominant tone.

"Angelica, dear, it's okay. You just had a nightmare, that's all."

Edward gripped his daughter snuggly as she looked up at her mother.

"You weren't there! It was in my room! I SAW IT!"

He kissed Angelica on her forehead. "You're okay now. We're here."

Rosanna cut in on their moment. "Angelica, what have we told you about lying? You just had a nightmare, that's...."

Gritting her teeth and nearly growling, "I KNOW what I saw!"

She tried to snap her daughter out of her state of mind, but was cut off.

"YOU weren't there! You never believe me!"

Edward stepped in with his own calming words for both of the fighters chomping at the bit. "Babe, it's okay. Let's just calm down. I've got you, Ange."

She put her face against her father's chest, turning away from her mother.

Rosanna snapped out sharply, "Just go to sleep, Angelica."

No more words as she turned her back to them and lay on her side to try and get back to slumbering.

Edward comforted his distraught daughter as best he could before turning his back to his wife and placing a protective arm over his pride and joy, Angelica.

Four

Angelica had managed to slide out from her parents' bed without waking them. She was sitting on the front porch in the large swing chair for two as the sun was just starting to peak over the horizon. The rosy fingered dawn was majestic, especially with so much unspoiled land in front of her as far as she could see. The dew was light on the grass that morning. The birds had only just begun to chirp far off in the distance. The only one close by was a crow clicking loudly and alone. It was perched rather prominently on an old fence post next to the driveway.

After staring at the horizon for a minute or so, she noticed that the clicking sound from the crow was becoming louder and more insistent. As she turned her head to look at the crow it began to caw. She looked at it curiously as it repeated the sound three more times before taking flight toward the road at the end of the driveway. Her eyes followed as the crow then went to a loan oak tree across the road at the edge of a neighbor's property. It was then that she noticed something truly bizarre. With the light from the sun still in its daily infancy, she could faintly see the form of what looked like a man materializing from the asphalt itself. Unlike other living beings, however, his shape seemed unnaturally dark, almost jet. As it rose fully to its feet, she could only guess that it seemed like a fairly tall man. It then started to slowly shamble down the road and toward the driveway. Unable to accept what her eyes were perceiving, she suddenly believed herself to be dreaming. She remembered hearing the phrase that instructed her to pinch herself awake, but it didn't work. She then slapped her own cheek with her hand, but still she was there and the humanoid figure was still lumbering down the road. She watched on baited breath as the figure drew closer and closer to the driveway. Her eyes grew large as she then saw a car zipping down the road and having just rounded a fairly acute curve. The headlight's sheen, rather than reflecting back the features of the figure, only seemed to be absorbed by it. With only a second to react, she opened her mouth to yell something, but no sound came out. Either the realization of the figure not being able to hear her voice from so far away, or the pure dread she was now feeling. The car, however, only drove on down the road without missing a beat. It seemed to go through with no physical reaction from the figure.

The apparition, after staggering along the road, suddenly walked onto the driveway. Angelica had grabbed her blanket and started to get up to leave. Before she could, however, the humanoid sank, almost melted, back into the earth from where it came.

The sun was noticeably higher up then as she continued to watch for any other strange sightings. Soon her father would awake, and she would be able to speak with him about it.

What Angelica didn't know was that only two weeks prior to their arrival at the new home, a local man by the name of "Fetch" Price was killed in front of their home on the same road she had been staring at. "Fetch" was a nickname, obviously, that he had gotten pretty early on from his friends. He didn't like it at first, but it grew on him and so he kept it.

The scene of the accident was gruesome. A car, zipping around that same acute curve, did not see Fetch in time to stop. He was walking, intoxicated, from his own minor fender-bender just up the road. The only casualty of that, however, was a fence post. The sheriff of the county was even taken aback, his reaction justified by the new guy on the volunteer rescue squad that puked his fresh chicken pot pie dinner all over the neighbor's land upon seeing the mangled corpse strewn across the road. The distinct smash of the tire over the head sprayed Fetch's cranial cauliflower with red streaks in a memorable pattern that would make an abstract artist drop to their knees and the muses, one by one, for such grandeur. It was neither beautiful nor artistic, however, as it only reminded everyone there that death humiliates all in the end.

Angelica also didn't know, and was never told about, the encounter that would come soon to Rosanna when she went to check the mail one day. Being home alone and wanting to take a break from the house painting, Rosanna would go to check the mailbox, only to have an unknown Ford pickup truck pull to a stop at her mailbox. The old grizzled man inside, his flesh tanned and wrinkled from years of work on the farm, clearly showed his scowl upon coming to a stop. Rosanna greeted him as politely as possible, but he had no intention of returning it. He only went on about how his son was now damned for eternity because he died in front of her "goddamned" house, which he meant rather literally. She had no sense of how to respond—who does? He would curtly pull away, the old truck chugging faithfully along with brown smoke gurgling from the tailpipe.

Fetch died quickly there on the road, but his journey afterword afforded him no rest. Angelica had the inkling of an idea that he was lost, mindless… bound. She didn't like thinking about it.

Five

Not long after, that same morning, Edward stirred groggily from sleep, not finding Angelica under his arm or on the bed at all. His stirring caused Rosanna to shift, but only long enough to read the clock and see 7:45 A.M. staring back at her. She pulled the covers up to her chin and tried to reenter the position she was sleeping in, her husband rising slowly to his feet. He looked around the room one more time, checking for his daughter. He then tiptoed out into the hallway and toward the door of Angelica's bedroom. Gently he pressed the door forward, peeking in but not wanting to wake her. Seeing her bed empty, he entered the room only to see that no one was there. A small shot of panic came over him, awakening him completely. He quickly glided back down the hall and passed the open bathroom door. No one in there either. He checked the box-littered living room after a cursory search of the empty kitchen. Motion from the corner of his eye quickly caught his attention: The swing on the long porch wrapping around the house was arcing back and forth. On that swing, much to his relief, was Angelica.

He made his way to the door and walked out onto the green planks of wood covering the entire span of the platform. Angelica was sitting with her arms wrapped around her knees, still wearing her thermal pajamas and wrapped up in her favorite blanket. Her attention was fixated on the hill not far in the distance. The small dirt path leading from the porch went off at an angle and through a now overgrowing patch of weeds and wildflowers.

Something seemed to be playing a strange game of peekaboo, appearing and reappearing in the tall flora and fauna. She snapped out of what seemed like a trance as the sound of the screen door slapped quickly behind her father. Even Edward jumped at the sound, still not used to the house's quirks.

Seeing Angelica jostle a bit, he said warmly, "Hey, baby girl. Didn't mean to scare you." He sat on the swing next to her, putting his arm around her shoulders and kissing her forehead.

"Hey, Dad." Her response was a little distant still as she quickly looked back at the top of hill.

Edward noticed and asked, "What are you looking at, babe?"

Angelica looked back at him and said with some hesitation, "I thought I saw someone up there... probably nothing."

He looked at the top of the hill but did not see the figure to which she was referring. Edward saw a small air of frustration around Angelica, she knowing he wasn't seeing it. He asked, "Where at, hon?"

She pointed to the area at the top of the hill and said, "Right up there." She looked back at him as his eyes looked the hill over. "I guess you can't see it, can you?"

Angelica sighed as Edward has a temporarily unspoken moment of understanding and familiarity before saying, "What does it look like?" He saw an image flash quickly in his mind, what he thought might be the "something" to which she was referring.

She hesitated again, for a moment, not sure if she wanted to bother explaining what was happening. "It's hard to see, but I think it was a man."

He squeezed her in his arm again before asking, "Do you know if it's a bad man or a good one?"

Angelica started to pick up that her father might be understanding her situation more than he was letting on. "I can't tell. I've just seen him going in and out of the weeds there. I think he's lost and confused. I keep hearing the word 'fetch' in my head."

"Fetch? You mean like a dog?"

"I don't know... it's weird."

He looked at her and smiled, lowering his voice and head to her level. "I'll tell you something if you promise not to tell your mother."

Oh, a secret! Angelica couldn't pass up gaining inside knowledge. She eagerly accepted his pinky swear.

"I used to see things like that a lot when I was a kid. I don't so much now that I'm grown up, though."

Angelica looked off the side for a moment, trying to wrap her head around what exactly what was happening. Looking back at him, "What are they?"

"It depends, really. Sometimes, when people die, their ghost might hang around a place. Sometimes people get so attached to things in life that they can't let go even after they're dead."

Her eyes widened with some shock. "Mom always said that ghosts aren't real, though."

He looked back at the kitchen door that remained closed. Satisfied with their security, "Your mother doesn't believe things like that exist. I don't think she's ever seen one before."

Angelica pondered this new information before asking, "So why don't you tell her what you see? Maybe she'll believe you then."

Edward chuckled for a moment, replying, "You know your mother. She's hard to convince."

That answer just seemed too simple for Angelica's racing mind. "Why does she have to be so mean about it, though? I don't call her a liar when she says she saw so-and-so at the store and I wasn't there."

He laughed aloud before replying, "I wish it were that simple." His smile slid away. "Your mom was brought up to believe that ghosts and spirits aren't real."

Angelica's lip snarled a bit before she said, "Mommy can be real dumb sometimes."

Edward couldn't help but laugh before taking on a semi-serious parental tone. "Angelica! Don't say that about your mother!"

Seeing his reaction, she shrugged any concern away before replying, "Well, she can be. Even she says that smart people do stupid stuff sometimes, too."

Still smiling warmly at his daughter, "I guess you're right about that." He stared off at the morning sun as its disc became fully exposed in the sky, lost in its beauty. Moments later his air became a little more serious. "Hey, remember—not a word of this to your mother. If you see anything else, you come to me, okay?"

Father and daughter swung on the porch for another ten minutes or so, enjoying the still air of the morning.

Rosanna suddenly appeared at the door, rubbing her eyes and stepping outside. "What are you two doing up? Aren't you cold?"

Edward then realized he hadn't been wearing any socks, and his feet were getting cold now that he thought about it. He replied, "Morning, hon, we were just talking, enjoying the sunrise."

Completely oblivious, she said jokingly, "Well, as long as you weren't trash-talking me...." She looked over at his somewhat coy face and raised a distrustful eyebrow.

He attempted to spare himself. "Nah, why would we want to talk about you? We were just talking about life." He seemed to have succeeded for the most part, even if she didn't fully trust his answer. "Okay, you two."

Angelica then asked, "What's for breakfast?"

Rosanna was hit with a sudden realization, her mouth contorting in frustration. "Well, I have some bad news: just toast and Coke. I haven't gone to the store yet and that's all we have right now."

Edward and Angelica shrugged off the inconvenience before she continued.

"Oh, and it's just warm Coke. I forgot to put it in the fridge last night."

Angelica rolled her eyes noticeably and sighed before her father stood and picked her up. He then said with a smile, "Ah, it's okay. We can have a crappy breakfast for one morning, I guess."

Six

Later that morning, Angelica was going through the boxes in her room, trying to find her favorite toys and clothes. Meanwhile, in the kitchen, Rosanna and Edward were talking. Rosanna was writing notes on a pad of paper.

"Okay, so we'll need milk, eggs, cereal...."

Edward responded with a playful tone, "And more coffee! The big grizzly bear needs his coffee in the morning!"

Looking up momentarily, then back down, "Coffee.... What do you guys want for dinner tonight, anyway?"

He responded, "I don't know." Looking back down the hall toward his daughter's bedroom, "Ange, honey, come here a sec."

She called from her room, "I'll be there in a minute!"

He continued. "Spaghetti maybe? That's easy to make."

Angelica made her way into the kitchen now. "What, Daddy?"

"What do you want to eat for dinner?"

She pondered the question for a moment, then answered, "Let's get pizza!"

Edward nodded his head in approval as Rosanna asked, "Do they have any pizza places around here?"

Her husband replied, "I thought every town in America had a pizza place."

As far as the three of them knew, he was right. What kind of town doesn't have a pizza place in the twenty-first century?

Rosanna answered, "Ugh, we don't have a phone book yet, or an internet connection. I'll have to look while I'm in town. The usual toppings?"

Edward responded, "Yes! Extra anchovies!"

Angelica playfully slapped his leg before replying in the most obvious you-can't-be-serious tone, "Dad! Gross!"

He and Rosanna laughed.

"I know, hon, I'm kidding. Onions and mushrooms."

Rosanna wrote a couple more things down on her notepad, then said, "Okay, I think that'll about cover the food for a few days. Are you staying here, Ed?"

"Yeah, babe, I have to make sure one of us is here when the moving van shows up."

She looked down at her watch. "Right, I guess they'll be here soon." She took her purse from the kitchen table. "All right, you two, behave while I'm gone." She kissed her husband, then looked down at her daughter. "And be careful outside, Angelica. Stay off the bridge."

Angelica replied, "I will." She disappeared down the hall again without another word.

Rosanna pointed at her husband before opening the door. "And *you* make sure she stays off the bridge."

He looked at her with a particularly dumbfounded expression. "Do you think you have to remind me of that?"

The effect of her words was just now sinking in inside her mind. "Ed, I'm sorry. I didn't mean you wouldn't...."

He hugged her. "I know what you meant. It's okay, we're both going to be guarded about that."

She lowered her head onto his chest as he placed his hand on the back of her neck and kissed her on the top of her head. "I'm still scared. I just don't want anything to happen...."

Edward said gently, "I know, neither do I. I won't let her out of my sight."

Rosanna kissed him once more before going out the door and heading to town.

He then walked down the hall toward Angelica's bedroom. "Hey, Ange, you want to go out and check out the barns?"

Her response was giddy with excitement. "Yeah! I'll be out in a minute!"

"Okay, just don't wear your nice shoes."

A few minutes later, Angelica ran into the kitchen, where her father was unpacking and putting up a few dishes.

"Hey! You ready to go?"

She eagerly nodded and was scooped up into her father's arms. She hugged his neck tightly, but his new whiskers were way too ticklish. "Why are you growing a beard, Daddy?"

He smiled. "We're on farmland now. I gotta blend in with the locals and look manly! Grr!" He flexed his free arm and took her outside.

They walked up the path leading from the back of the porch and up over the hill. The sun was shining brightly overhead in the near cloudless sky. Angelica didn't see the same entity atop the hill as they approached, and she was glad of it. It seemed like, at least for now, she was able to put all of the bad things that had recently happened out of her mind. As they crested the hill and started heading toward the clearing that separated two moderately large barns facing each other, however, an all-too-familiar dread snuck into the back of her mind. One of the structures seemed more forbidding than the other. Despite being nearly identical and at the same state of needing repairs, the barn on the left was far more intent on keeping them out.

Edward stopped at the crossroads as Angelica said purposely, "Let's see *that* one," pointing to her right. She then pointed to her left. "*That* one feels bad."

Understanding her meaning, he looked at her and said, "I agree, baby girl. Let's go to this one."

They walked to the barn on the right and stood at the doorway. He put Angelica on the ground and started to dig through his pockets for the keys. She looked at the left barn nervously as he rifled through the keyring.

He paused for a moment to pat her on the head lovingly. "Just try not to think about that one too much."

Angelica turned her attention back to the barn door in front of her as Edward tried a couple of keys before finding the correct one. He then opened the rusty Masterlock and put it in his pocket. He raised the rusty, squealing metal bar latched across the metal rails before pulling the doors open. The inside let out a gust of air that was perfumed with the smell of old wood, some mold, and a small surge of ammonia from the pests that were no doubt living inside and had been for years. Suddenly a startled possum darted out of one of the stalls and ran past them. Edward and Angelica backed away quickly, giving it plenty of head room.

Angelica grabbed her father's leg and jumped behind him. She peeked around at the critter wandering off into the tall grass nearby. "What was *that*!?"

He pulled her forward gently. "That's just a possum. They like to stow-away in buildings sometimes."

The image of the large black eyes on the grayish white fur, the needlelike teeth and hairless tail, still sharp in her mind. "They're ugly!"

He laughed. "They are a little ugly. Not everything can be as pretty as you."

Edward messed up her hair a bit with his hand.

She didn't seem to notice, now staring into the dark corners of the barn. "Are there any more in there?"

He picked her up again. "I don't know, hon, but I doubt it. They usually run away when people are around." He tickled her chin and she giggled.

He then looked around the relatively empty wooden structure. The oc-casional odd piece of hay and straw were strewn here and there. A large white ladder near the door led to the upper storage area. The stalls inside were once used to contain various farm animals but not much evidence of them remained, other than a couple of metal buckets and a pitchfork. Small animal droppings also littered the floor in different areas of floor throughout.

Edward, noticing this, said, "We'll have to clean this thing up before we can use it."

She then asked, "What are we going to use it for?"

He was saving this surprise for a few days now. "Well, I figure since we're on a farm now we can get you a pet. How does that sound?"

Angelica's eyes widened as she covered her agape mouth. Bursting with excitement, "Really!? Any animal I want?"

With a little reserve and caution, "Well, one you can take of yourself. How about a rabbit?"

She shook her head.

"Okay, then how about a piggy? You want a pig?"

She smiled and shook her head again.

"Well, what did you have in mind, babe?"

Her answer was quick. "A goat!"

Laughing at the request he didn't see coming, he responded, "A goat? My Angelica wants a goat? Why do you want a goat?"

Giggling again, "Because they're funny!"

Edward beamed a smile. "I guess you do always laugh at goat videos on TV." He did his best to imitate a goat sound and gently bumped his head on hers.

She laughed and he replied, "Yeah, I guess we can get you a goat. We'll have to see when the 4-H Club is going to do a show or something."

She clinched her fists with bubbling excitement. "Really!? I love you, Daddy!" Angelica kissed him on the cheek. She then looked confused. "What's 4-H Club?"

He thought a moment, not having been a member of it at any point or knowing much about it. "I think it's an agriculture club. They get schoolkids involved in animal care and stuff."

Angelica tried to repeat this new word she was processing. "Agruc...."

Smiling, "Agriculture. It's just a fancy word for farming."

Their conversation was interrupted by a large moving van starting to roll down and up their long gravel driveway.

Edward then started to walk back toward the house. "Well, sweetie, it looks like we get to unpack some more boxes." He knew this idea wasn't nearly as thrilling as the previous news. He tried to get her interested. "Yay!"

Angelica stuck out her tongue and frowned, then replied, "Boooo!"

Seven

Later that evening, the three of them were sitting at the table, the only piece of furniture or decoration in the room besides the chairs. The half-eaten pizza from the only local pizza shop awaited its fate as dinner. Edward held back a burp from the Coke, but only partially, causing Angelica to giggle. His wife wasn't so impressed. He decided to tell her what he was sensing won't be good news to his wife.

"Rose, Angelica and I were discussing something. *We* have decided that Angelica needs a pet."

This definitely raised her eyebrow. "What kind of pet?"

Her daughter didn't wait to finish chewing and interrupted, "A goat!"

Rosanna's eyes widened in surprise at her daughter. "Don't talk with your mouthful." Then to her husband, "Ed, a goat!?"

He knew this was coming. Edward could only hope that his wife was just having a knee-jerk reaction because of her own lack of experience in working with animals. Of course, he couldn't claim much other than having a dog when he was growing up. "Yeah, I think they're fairly easy to take care of. She'll get to learn some responsibility, too. Besides, we can have fresh goat's milk every morning if we get a female."

Both Angelica and Rosanna were shocked for different reasons.

Before the latter could speak, however, her daughter jumped in. "I thought milk came from cows."

Edward answered his daughter, "Lots of animals make milk. People just usually drink milk from cows. In some parts of the world, people drink goat's milk every day."

Rosanna scrunched up her face in disgust. "Gross! Have you ever even tried goat's milk?"

He replied, "No, but I'm willing to give it a taste. I'm sure there's a farm *somewhere* in our area that has goats."

His daughter eagerly added, "I wanna try goat's milk, too!"

Rosanna started to respond without thinking, "Ange...." She let out a quick and sharp sigh. "Ed, do you even know how to take care of a goat?" She knew he didn't with firsthand experience, but he was always willing to learn something new. It was one of the things that she admired about him. She wasn't willing to let down her poker-face just yet, even though it was a novel idea. They *were* living in rural country now, and thinking the two of them wouldn't want a pet of some sorts was outrageous.

He cheerfully responded, "Well, dear, there's this thing called the internet. Some people also still read ancient tomes called 'books.'" Edward's tone changed to a more serious one, knowing his wife didn't care for heavy doses of sarcasm. "Besides, I'm sure the 4-H Club will have plenty of people who are willing to teach. Angelica might also make some new friends."

She looked back and forth at them a few moments, hesitating to let her protest go quietly. Her daughter interrupted her defensive maneuvers. "I want to vote! I vote for goat!" She raised her hand and Edward soon reflected the gesture. Seeing her mother hesitating to cast her ballot, "We win! Two turds!"

Edward burst out laughing at what he knew was an intentional mispronunciation. Rosanna was not as amused, but didn't want to spoil the good air.

"I guess you're right: You're two *turds*." That smile her husband loved had finally started to show again.

Later, as they were ending their doughy feast, Edward was picking up the dishes and Rosanna was looking for the trash bags that were still unpacked, Angelica having disappeared down the hall into her room. Soon enough Rosanna found one and met him at the trashcan near the sink area. He dumped what little remained from the plates and put them in the sink. She turned on the water and started the cleanup.

Edward wrapped his arms around her waist and kissed her on the ear. "Thanks for going along with the pet idea. I know it's probably not the best idea we've had."

Any tension over the matter seemed trivial now, but she was willing to string him along just a bit longer. "A goat... what on Earth is Angelica thinking?"

"She's always laughing at those videos on TV. I'm not surprised."

"Well, let's hope she doesn't get bored with it. If that happens, *you'll* be the one feeding it and shoveling its poop."

In a relaxed and reassuring tone, "We'll be fine. If it doesn't work out, I'm sure there will be someone in the area willing to take it off our hands."

She shrugged and replied, "I suppose.... Just one thing: Don't expect me to drink any goat's milk."

With feigned shock, "What!? I was going to give you first dibs!"

"Ha! Not going to happen."

They kissed each other's lips warmly before she stepped back and looked down the hall, making sure they were alone. He looked confused for a moment, not sure about the need for secrecy.

She then said in a low whisper, "Ed, something weird happened when I was in town today getting groceries. I went to the *only* grocery store in town. Everyone knew I was an outsider right away."

He responded during the pause, "Well, this is a small town. I'm sure everyone knows everyone. We'll meet most of them in time, I'm sure."

She nervously looked down the hallway again. Feeling that Angelica was well out of earshot, "It's not that. When I told them we just moved in here, they looked at me like I was crazy."

"What do you mean, babe?"

"They said something like, '*That* house? Why *that* house?'"

He still had those uneasy and tense feelings deep inside, but wasn't going to let on. "Well, the real estate agent said the house hadn't been lived in for like twenty years. Maybe they were just surprised."

She continued. "It's not just that: One or two older ladies there just walked away from the conversation when I mentioned that. Not a polite word between them. Then there was this old man who came up to me and said out of the blue, 'Keep an eye on that kid of yours!'"

Still remaining elusive, "It's a small town, like I said. They probably haven't seen new people around in decades. Besides, they were probably just jealous of how good you look."

He smiled and kissed her again. Most of the immediate apprehension in her demeanor had started to retreat into the darkness.

She stared at him right in the eyes and said playfully, "I'd think *you* would know something about spooky feelings."

Yeah, he knew that she knew that he knew, but he was tired. He grinned. "Come on, honey, we'll be fine. We just have to get settled in. And apparently the town will have to get used to *us*."

She leaned in and said, "You'd better be right, turd...."

Eight

Angelica continued to have the same dream every night, the same as the night before, for the next two weeks. Edward knew there was something deeper going on, but he didn't know enough to come to any definitive conclusions. Rosanna was convinced that it was just her daughter's near brush with death that brought them on. They were both used to their daughter making her nightly trip to their room where she would get at least *some* sleep.

Edward was also in the process of acquiring a used truck from one of the locals. He contacted the farmer after finding a good deal in the trading post. All that was left of the process was to take it for a test drive and discuss it with his wife. They reasoned that they would have to be sharp and ask questions, not wanting to be taken advantage of "some rube." The three of them were going to have to reach out to their community eventually, and maybe even learn to trust a few of them. That, however, would take time and effort. There really isn't a way to rush through those sorts of things.

Edward had also managed to find out when the next 4-H Club show was going to be: The Miller's Run Spring Festival at the local fairgrounds. Today he was going to take his daughter to that fair, with Rosanna staying behind to do some needed painting....

"Babe, I wish you would come with us. We've all been working hard and need a break."

Rosanna was determined to finish the tasks she had set out for herself. Her mind simply couldn't let go of the idea. "Ed, I have to finish painting the walls in our room. Then Angelica's room needs to be painted and...." He responded as she trailed off, "Okay, okay. We'll put in a good word for you with the locals."

Rosanna sighed. "Okay, you two. Behave!" She kissed her husband before he and Angelica headed outside to the family car.

Once inside, Edward paused before starting the car. "Seatbelt!" Angelica didn't get to ride in the front seat much and was fine with buckling up. "Ready to go look at some animals?" She eagerly nodded.

"Then let's go!" He pressed the accelerator and they were off down the long gravel driveway.

Soon enough they were on the paved road and heading toward the fairgrounds. Minutes into the trip, Angelica's excitement seemed to fade out.

Edward, noticing it, asked, "You okay, Ange?"

Her face had become groggy. "I'm tired. I didn't sleep long enough."

"I know, baby girl. Why don't you try and catch a nap while I drive."

She quickly agreed and rested her head against the door, falling asleep in a few short moments.

A little over half an hour passed and Edward saw the large sign for the town's fairgrounds. Angelica started to awaken as the car slowed for the turn.

Smiling, "Ange, wake up. We're here!"

She stretched and yawned, but was quickly brought to life at the sight of a large gray horse being led from a trailer and toward the entrance of a long metal building. "Look at the horse! It's so pretty!"

He laughed at her excitement. Still grinning, "We're going to get to see all kinds of animals today!"

Squeezing her teddy bear tightly, she exclaimed, "Goats! We want goats!" She even motioned her arms and the arms of the teddy bear in a demanding manner.

Edward pulled the car to a stop in a grassy field nearby that served as the makeshift parking lot. He put the Subaru into park and said, "Do you know which color you want?"

She started to unbuckle her seatbelt, his question making the experience ever the more real. "I don't know! Brown... black... gray... no, white. I can't decide!"

He took the keys out of the ignition and locked the doors behind him with a click of the remote. Angelica ran up to his side and took his hand as they strolled toward the entrance of the grounds. The faint smell of manure and other barnyard aromas were wafting in the breeze. Angelica crinkled her nose and clasped it with her fingers. "Eww! Something stinks!"

The smell didn't seem to bother Edward as much. "You'll have to get used to that, sweetie. Of course, there are probably a *lot* of animals here."

"Do you have to give goats baths?"

Laughing, "I don't think so."

The words didn't discourage her much. "I'll have to give it a bath if it stinks this bad."

They walked around the patchwork of buildings for a while, checking out some local stalls with homemade jams and jellies, pickles, and all other manner of goods made before winter to preserve their produce. It was also the time Angelica was introduced to the glorious taste of funnel cake. She and Edward needed a couple of napkins each to clean up the powdered sugar from their faces.

After having stuffed themselves with who-knows how many calories, they made their way over to one of the metal buildings bearing a "Livestock" sign above its main entrance. Angelica nearly pulled her father's arm out of socket, dragging him to the threshold.

He couldn't help but beam a grin at her enthusiasm. "How about I just carry you."

She hesitated for a moment, knowing good and well he wouldn't be able to keep up with her desired breakneck speed. She could, however, see over the neatly placed guardrails and half-walls separating the animals. Angelica leapt up and was caught. From her new vantage point, she could now see the same horse she saw on the way in. It was in the far corner of the building munching on a feedbag of oats. Pointing toward it, "Look! There's the horse we saw!"

"You want to go check it out?"

She clapped her hands excitedly and nodded her head.

"All right, let's go look at the horse."

The two of them waded through the crowd of locals and out-of-town visitors, eventually getting to the horse stall. They stopped and looked over the animal. Angelica was in awe, having never seen one up close like this. The gray mare was well behaved, and seemed to enjoy the attention she had been getting all day.

Angelica then pointed at the sign hanging over the steel restraining fence. "What's that say, Daddy?"

He almost told her outright, but remembered that he and Rosanna were teaching her to read. "Let's see if you can do it. What's the first letter?"

She was able to identify the letters, one by one, but had a little trouble putting it together. "G, E, R, T, I, E." She hadn't seen this word before. "Gear...."

"Ger, as in Grr!"

She finished the rest. "Gertie? That's a weird name."

Gertie's owner had stood up from her chair to greet them. The older woman, in her late fifties, was somewhat rotund, dressed in bibbed overalls, a flannel shirt, and a circular straw hat, (for special occasions, of course). She extended her hand to him. "Hi there. My name's Ethyl."

He shook her hand. "Hello! My name's Edward Barrister. And this little troublemaker is my daughter. Introduce yourself, hon."

Ethyl smiled and extended her hand.

Shaking her hand, "Hello, I'm Angelica."

"Angelica! What a pretty name. Do you like horses?"

"They're pretty, but Dad said I'll have to wait a couple years."

Ethyl laughed along with Edward, then saying, "That might be a good idea. I'll tell you what, though: Since you seem like a nice girl, how about I let you sit on her back?" She quickly looked over at her father. "If that's okay with your dad, of course."

"I don't see why not."

Angelica was giddy with enthusiasm as Ethyl said, "Okay, dear, first thing you need to know about horses is that they don't like to be startled. You have to be calm and gentle when you approach them. They can scare easily."

The five-year-old's face became more serious. "What do they do when they're scared?"

Ethyl said calmly, "Sometimes they'll kick their hind legs. We don't want her kicking that steel wall there." She noticed the continued concern on Angelica's face and said reassuringly, "But I'm going to introduce you two first." Ethyl stepped away from the fence and back to a wicker basket on the ground away from the stall. She took one of the carrots from inside and brought it to Angelica. "I'm sure she'll be fine with you if you feed her this," winking her eye.

Edward looked at his daughter and smiled as Ethyl gently tugged on the rope holding the horse to the sturdy metal support beam in the middle of her pen. She removed the feedbag from the horse's face and placed it aside.

Leading the horse to the edge of the fence in front of them, "Now Angelica, hold the carrot out in front of Gertie's mouth and let her pluck it out of your hand."

She gingerly extended her hand and sure enough, Gertie snatched it from her grasp.

Ethyl scratched the white blaze on Gertie's forehead. "There. Now give her head a good scratch and she'll be your friend."

Ethyl removed her hand, Angelica now stretching and slowly scratching the relaxed beast's forehead.

Edward also scratched the horse's head a couple of times as well. He said with genuine gratitude, "Thank you for letting her pet your horse."

Ethyl responded, "No trouble at all. Are you two visiting from out of town?"

Angelica replied, "We just moved here from Johnston City."

Edward picked up the conversation. "We moved into the old farm on Holly Bush Road. I think the last person to live there was named Harris."

Now, it seemed, they were going to get similar reactions to what Rosanna had encountered on her first trip into town.

Ethyl said with courteous disbelief, "The old Harris place? I guess they were selling it for pretty cheap?"

"Yeah, it was a good deal. You know, my wife was saying that people were really surprised when she told them we were moving in there. Bad land?" He was withholding all of the feelings they had on the property, and certainly the downright scary things that had happened just a couple of weeks before.

Ethyl hesitated a moment, looking at Angelica's probing eyes staring into her own. Turning back toward Edward, "Well, let's just say that the last owner fell on hard times."

He knew she was hiding something, but was content with just leaving it be. He didn't feel it was a conversation worth having in front of Angelica and adding to her growing list of problems with their new home. Edward changed the subject. "Well, we're actually here today to look at getting Angelica a goat."

Ethyl's smile returned. "Ah, does she like goat's milk?"

He said, "No, but we're looking to try some. We mainly want to get her a pet to take care of. Know of anyone here selling any?"

"That's a good idea! Teach her some responsibility early." Looking over toward Angelica now, "And it'll make you a better person in the long run."

Angelica smiled. "How will a goat make me a better person?"

Edward fielded this one. "You'll learn how to be an adult faster."

Even though Angelica was enjoying being a kid, for the most part, she wanted to take on more adult-type things. She was already, at her young age, becoming annoyed at the answers adults give kids when they think they're too young.

Ethyl then said, "That's right! Nothing like some work on the farm to make you stronger on the inside and the outside." Looking back at Edward now, "If I'm not mistaken, the Kelly family brought a couple of goats in with them today. You should go and ask if they're selling."

She pointed to a stall at the other end of the building. A man in his thirties, next to an enclosure with a handful of goats inside, waved at her, and she waved back.

"That man down there in the green hat that just waved at me is Jonathon Kelly. You tell him I sent you and maybe you two can work something out."

Edward responded, "Thanks a lot! Angelica, tell her thank you for letting her pet her horse."

Angelica replied quickly, "Thank you for letting me pet your horse. Didn't you say I could sit on her, too?"

The conversation about the house had certainly distracted her. Ethyl replied with some shock, "You know you're right! I did say that. You want your dad to put you up there?"

Angelica nodded as Ethyl stepped aside to open the metal gate. He carefully placed his daughter on the horse's bare back. She did her best to contain her excitement as she scratched the side of Gertie's neck. "She's such a nice horse, Daddy."

"She sure is." He reached into his pocket and removed a small digital camera. He put it up to his face, but quickly asked, "Is it okay if I take a picture of her?" Ethyl agreed and he said to his daughter, "All right, baby girl, smile for the camera!"

She did as Edward took a quick couple of photos.

"I think Mommy will be jealous when she sees this picture." He then took Angelica from the horse's back and continued to carry her. He shook Ethyl's hand once again. "Well, it was nice to meet you. We're going to go and see the other animals."

"Nice to meet you, too. Have fun," waving at them as they turned to adjacent animal stalls.

Just as he turned around and started walking away, Ethyl spoke up again. "Oh, Mr. Barrister! One more thing."

He stopped and turned back toward her.

"Just a word aside, if you don't mind."

He placed Angelica on the ground told her to wait. She did. He then walked over to Ethyl, who directed him to the far side of the stall.

Seeing her lower her head for secrecy, he asked politely, "What is it?"

She looked over at Angelica, who had her back turned to them. She then said to Edward in a hushed tone, "Be extra careful with your kid there. Don't let her wander off or anything."

His face showed confusion. "You mean here at the fair?"

Ethyl replied, "Well, of course that, but I mean at home or anywhere in town."

"We always keep an eye on our daughter. What do you mean, exactly?"

"Well, life on the farm, especially here, can be dangerous. Just don't let her wander off is all I'm saying."

Not showing most of his unnerved emotions, "Okay, thanks, Ethyl. I'll keep an eye on her." He then stepped away and picked his daughter up once again.

They stopped several feet down at the fence around a pen. On the straw-covered floor a large female pig was lying on her side with her eight new piglets fighting for milk. There was enough for all but they squirmed and squiggled nonetheless, the dominant ones looking to secure the best teat.

Angelica giggled at the tussle. "They must be really hungry!"

Edward replied, "That's a lot of bacon!" He looked down at a blue ribbon displayed on the top of the fence. "And look, it won first place."

"First place in what?"

"I don't know. Maybe for being the biggest. She probably weighs more than you and I put together!"

Soon enough they reached the enclosure with the goats inside. Angelica leapt down as they approached and ran straight for the gap in the galvanized metal fencing. She was quickly enthralled by the five goats inside.

Edward walked over and shook the hand of Jonathon Kelly. "Hey there! My name's Ed Barrister and that's my daughter Angelica. Ethyl down there said you might have some goats for sale."

Jonathon adjusted his trusty, and dirty, John Deere hat. "I suppose we could let a couple go for the right price."

Edward replied, "That's sounds fair to me."

"Are you looking for a milk goat?"

"Well, my daughter wants to get one as a pet, but we haven't really tried goat's milk. We'd love to try some if you know of any...."

Jonathon jumped in quickly. "I've got just the thing." He walked back to a cooler set up next to the table they had set up. He pulled out a Mason jar filled with fresh milk and handed it to Edward. "Go ahead and try it if you like. It won first place today!"

He unscrewed the brass lid and took a small drink. Somewhat surprised, "You know, that's actually really good." He looked over at his daughter, who was still looking at the three adult goats and the two kids walking around. "Hey, Ange, come here and try the milk. It's really good!"

Reluctantly she pulled away from the fence and approached her father. He handed her the jar and she took a drink.

She then took a second drink. "That tastes good!" She handed the container back to her father and went back to her vigil at the fence.

Edward screwed the lid back on. "Well, I guess we could use a milk goat, then."

A young girl with shoulder-length blonde hair and blue eyes, Jonathon's daughter, made her way over to Angelica now and introduced herself.

Jonathon continued. "Is this your first goat?"

"Yeah, we're pretty new to the farming thing. We just moved here from Johnston City. I worked there for several years as an architect. My wife and I thought it would be a nice change of pace to move here." He intentionally left out the part about the farm to which they'd moved.

"Well, first thing is, they're herd animals, so they shouldn't be alone. I have a milking goat there that just had two kids a couple of weeks ago. They've been dehorned and all, so you don't need to worry about that. I've given them some of the shots they need early, but you'll need to follow up with the vet for the rest. I can give you a list of what they've already gotten." He could see the look on Edward's face that revealed he felt like he was in over his head. "It sounds like a lot, but once you get the basics down, they're really easy to take care of."

Meanwhile, Angelica was talking with the girl, Abby. "Did you grow up here?"

Abby replied, "Yeah, me and my brother live near the edge of town. You just moved here?"

"Yeah, we came from Johnston City. It's a few hours from here."

"I'm starting kindergarten this fall. Have you started school yet?"

"Not yet, I just turned five. I'm going to start this fall, too."

Angelica liked Abby right away. "Cool! Maybe we'll be in the same class." Angelica didn't yet know that her mother had already been planning on her going to the Catholic school about an hour from their home. Abby was going to be attending the town's local school instead.

Edward and Jonathon had come to an agreement on price and now he and his family were the proud new owners of one adult goat and the two kids. He called over to his daughter, "Hey, Ange, we own three goats now!"

Her smile told the story. "Really? Cool! Thank you!"

Jonathon called over his son, John Jr., along with Abby. He looked at his ten-year-old son. "Little John, these folks here, the Barristers, just bought three of our goats. I want you and your sister to help them learn how to take care of them."

Edward responded, "Ah, your kids don't have to worry about that."

John Jr. answered in a confident tone, "Mr. Barrister, we've grown up taking care of goats. My sister and I know a thing or two. It's why we're in the 4-H Club. It'll help us learn more if we teach you."

Jonathon Sr. said, "Believe me, Mr. Barrister, they know what they're doing."

Edward replied with a little bit of surprise and amusement, "Well, okay then. I guess we have a deal."

Little John then asked, "Where's your tow trailer, Mr. Barrister? We'll walk 'em out for you."

That made Edward suddenly remember two key problems. "I completely forgot: We haven't gotten the truck we're looking at yet and we don't have a trailer."

Jonathan chuckled at the greenhorn, but decided to be merciful. "Don't worry about it, Mr. Barrister. We can deliver them to your farm for you. You do have a barn, don't you?"

The momentary apprehension was eased a bit. "Yeah, we have two of those. At least we have that."

Jonathan laughed out loud. "Good. I tell you what, I'll even throw in a couple of bags of feed for you." The price of the feed was included in the price the experienced farmer had set. He rightly understood that they probably didn't have a clue what they were doing, judging from their spotless clothes. The near perfect condition of Edward's jeans and flannel shirt were a dead giveaway. "Where's your farm at? We'll deliver them as soon as we're finished here."

I suppose Edward was seeing this inevitability. "We live out on Holly Bush Road."

Little John then turned his head away from their conversation and went to introduce himself to his sister's new friend.

Jonathon Sr. said, "The old Harris place, huh?"

Edward lowered his voice a bit. "Yeah, we've heard it's got a bad reputation. No one really says why, though."

Big John was wanting to avoid the conversation altogether as well, but said, "Just local tragedy. Nothing to really concern yourself with."

He knew now that he was poking around in things the townspeople would rather forget. "Well, I hope we don't encounter anything like that." The uncomfortable silence only lasted for a few seconds, but seemed like an eternity. Deciding to focus on the business at hand once again, "So what time do you want to bring the goats by?"

He looked at his watch and said, "We'll be getting out of here at around 4:30. We can probably make it to your place around 5:30 or so."

"That sounds great. We'll try and clean up the barn a little before then."

Nine

Meanwhile, back at the homestead, Rosanna was upstairs getting ready to paint one of the guest bedrooms. When they had moved in, each of the ten rooms in the house was painted in a faded off-white shade. Whether it was this color due to age or choice, she was looking to brighten things up. As she spread out the painter's tarp over the hardwood floors Rosanna's feet were finding all of the creaky floorboards. She quietly laughed to herself. "No wonder they think this place is creepy."

After setting up the primer can and paint can, she double-checked the paint sample she'd picked up at the hardware store. The bluish gray color looked great on the walls in her mind. It was only then that she noticed the name of it. "Stormy Sky... that's a gloomy name." Rosanna shrugged off the notion and fastened the paint roller to the long painting rod. Turning it as tightly as she could on the final twist, "There...."

A faint sound suddenly caught her attention.

Tap, tap, tap.

To the best of her ability, she determined it must be someone knocking on their door. "Who could that be?"

Clueless as to who would be visiting, she headed downstairs. Once there she made her way to the front door in their living room. Rosanna couldn't make out anyone through the curtains, and so opened the door. She then stepped onto the porch holding the screen door. To the left, to the right, no one. No one on the porch, no car in the driveway, nada.

"Hello?"

No one answered back.

Not waiting much longer she shut the door again, making sure to lock the deadbolt.

Tap, tap, tap.

Rosanna's head was slung around one hundred and eighty degrees. "*Back* door?" Another close guess as to the source of the sound. She was a little hesitant then, as it seemed she couldn't hear anything. The birds and even the bugs had gone quiet. Rosanna couldn't explain the cold shards of fear slowly creeping across her mind like ice.

Several apprehensive steps through the living room and down the hall, she heard it again.

Tap, tap, tap.

Her ears were sure the back door was being knocked upon by a local wishing to welcome them. But how? Did they walk across their forty acres of land instead of using a car? As she approached the back door, however, she couldn't discern a figure through those curtains either. Rosanna then unlocked the door at the handle and peered outside. The same thing as before: a vacant porch. She slowly stepped outside and walked atop the small hill leading to the area of the barns. From here she could see the majority of the house, as well as the previously cleared land surrounding their home. No one was there. It was this that caused a thought that led to a small epiphany: *You're alone.* This thought was certainly her own, but it seemed to be assisted into the forefront of her thoughts by something unknown. The realization briefly chased her to a corner of the house where she tried to find the door-knocker. The only thing she saw, however, was the sunny sky shining down on the grass and against the white wooden paneling of the house. She reassured herself, "Probably the wind. Hopefully not some punk kids trying to mess with me." Both of these answers seemed plausible and comforting. After all, the wind is just the wind. The kids are just annoying brats, as always. Back at their old house in the suburbs of Johnston City, certain neighborhood kids would get the inclination to play pranks. The most common of which was "ring and run," tormenting the Barristers with their own doorbell. Once a year, on a certain night of revelry, they could even expect a T.P.

job or two or three dozen egg bombs. On one year, Rosanna was even gifted with a flaming bag of… you know what. Needless to say, she wasn't happy at hall that night when she was cleaning up her feces-laden sneaker.

Mrs. Barrister gave a couple of cursory glances to and fro before heading back inside. She closed the door and secured the deadbolt before heading back upstairs. Dead set on finishing the primer coat before her husband and daughter returned, she walked straight to the guest bedroom. There she kneeled and took a screwdriver and opened the primer can. Setting the lid aside, she poured enough primer into the painting tray to get started. She went to stand and took up the roller in her hands when…

Tap, tap, tap.

Whatever was making this noise was really starting to press her buttons. Instead of running downstairs, however, she ran to the windows overlooking the backyard area. Not a soul to be seen.

Tap, tap, tap.

She darted to the room across the hall overlooking the front yard. Still, no one there. *Tap, tap, tap.*

Clearly annoyed and confused, "That came from the side of the house!" The tapping sound, in groups of three, now struck the opposite side of the house. Now standing in the hall, she looked up and back. Again, three taps, now from the roof directly over her. "What the heck!? Is the house falling apart!?"

The sounds then ceased, but only for a few seconds.

TAP, TAP, TAP.

The considerably louder rapping was perceived from downstairs.

TAP, TAP, TAP again from the guest bedroom wall. The sequence was repeated, seemingly hitting every door, window, and wall inside the house. Rosanna ran to the window of the bedroom again. Still no one in sight.

Once again, the sounds ceased. Suddenly she couldn't discern which was more frightening, the sounds, or their sudden departure. She put her forehead against the glass, trying to see around as much as possible. The wind wasn't blowing, and there was scarcely anything outside to indicate that she wasn't looking at a still landscape portrait.

THUD, THUD, THUD.

The three slams against the wall to her right kicked her instincts into flight as she lurched away from the wall, falling on her bottom.

THUD, THUD, THUD.

Now it was as if something was smashing on the window itself. She could even see the glass panes vibrating with each hit. Even though her mind raced for a rational explanation, nothing of the sort was found. Only the primal fear welling up and spilling over inside of her was doing her thinking for her. Another round of sickening thuds against the opposite wall in the room caused her to quickly scramble to her feet and out the door.

With her adrenaline sending her body into overdrive, she felt lucky that she didn't trip on the way down the main staircase. Rosanna made it into the kitchen with a specific thought in mind: the baseball bat she kept propped up at the back door. She wasn't surprised to see no one through the white curtains as she leaned against the sturdy wooden door with her shoulder. Quickly the Louisville Slugger was in her hands and she felt ready to hit anything with the force of a Major Leaguer.

THUD, THUD, THUD again the sounds came from upstairs, then the sides of the house, the roof. The last three came from the door upon which she was leaning, causing her to turn and face it. "What the hell do you want!?" She wasn't sure why she was yelling this, but rational thought was still not in control.

Rosanna then quickly darted at the door, trying to escape. She fumbled with the deadbolt but managed to get it open. She then burst out onto the back porch, the bat cocked to her side and ready to strike. With no one in front of her, she ran to the patch of weed-choked grass adjacent to the house. Gritting her teeth and breathing heavily, she charged the corner of the house and emerged on the other side to the same situation as before: not a being in sight. The fear, anxiety, and anger were now bubbling to a head inside. This emotional soup was ready to explode.

"You damn kids! If I find out who you are I'll make sure your parents know about this!" This sounded a lot more intimidating in her mind. Now that she was yelling it to seemingly no audience, it was nakedly absurd.

She managed to get her breathing under control and started back toward the covered back porch. Mrs. Barrister called out in her best stern parent voice, "Knock it off! Stay off our land!"

The silence was the only thing that responded. No giggling and nothing scurrying away, just the still air of their acreage in every direction.

Now content that the harassing party had been scared away, she went through the backdoor once again, making double sure to lock the handle and deadbolt behind her. With the bat still in hand, she walked back upstairs to paint, hearing no other sounds. Once inside, the tension started to slowly dissolve. The fear was now being processed more coherently and gave way to rational thought. While instinctively clutching the rosary around her neck, she tried to persuade herself into believing that nuisance kids were the problem. If kids were causing this event to happen, they were the best damn ninjas in the county. The thought, *You're alone,* relentlessly resounded in her thoughts as she began applying the coat of primer to the walls.

Ten

Rosanna had been diligently painting for about an hour and finally, the primer coat for the room was finished. She wrapped the roller in a plastic bag and set it aside. The work was satisfying, but still laboring in its own way. She stepped back and double-checked her work, sipping on a water bottle and enjoying the gentle classical music being broadcast by a local station on her simple plug-in radio. Wiping the sweat from her forehead, "We are going to need air conditioning in here. Spring and it's already too hot." Rosanna had considered opening the windows, but the one in the guest bedroom was being stubborn. Apparently the previous owner had painted over the sill, and it was stuck shut. And guessing by the age of the home and its last known occupants, it had been several years since it had been opened at all.

Accepting her progress, she decided to go back downstairs and get another cold bottle of water from the fridge. After acquiring the refreshment, she headed to the bathroom to clean the sweat and primer specks from her forehead. She checked herself in the mirror. Her deeply brown eyes staring back at her long, black, curly hair remind her of Angelica. They did share many of the same traits in appearance. This resemblance reminded her to check her watch. "They should be back by now...." Rosanna didn't dwell on the concern and decided to return to the guest bedroom to finish cleaning up for the evening. The primer coat would need to dry overnight, and she was getting worn down by all of the chores required with moving into a new home. Whether she would ever admit that to her husband and daughter would remain to be seen.

Rosanna then trudged back upstairs, ready to call it a day. She kneeled down to turn off the radio. "Thank you, Berlin Philharmonic." The brief silence, however, was broken.

Tap, tap, tap.

She was more than ready to catch the tormentors in the act now. She quietly snuck out of the room and toward the stairs, the baseball lumber in hand. In a sly whisper, "I'll catch you this time, you little punks!"

TAP, TAP, TAP.

Now that she was downstairs, the sound was quite distinct and obviously coming from the backdoor. Creeping like a cat burglar in her own home, she approached the kitchen. The thick white curtains over the windows of the back porch only allowed the image of two distorted and muffled shadows. *You're mine now!* she thought to herself. She unlocked the deadbolt without a sound, surprising herself in the dexterous motion. The shadows still didn't move, but the lock on the door handle was now opened. Rosanna gripped the door handle and ripped it open with a flash of vengeance. Her war cry was loud and sure. "I got you, little sh…." The image had now processed in her mind. "Damnit, Ed! You scared the crap out of me!"

Angelica had ducked behind her father, caught off guard by the sight of her mother threatening them with a baseball bat. Edward had also backed away. Seeing her tension dissolve gave him reason to step forward again.

With a nervous chuckle, "Whoa there, hon! It's just us, your family."

Rosanna apologized and hugged him.

He reassuringly put his hand on the back of her head. "What's wrong, Rosy?"

"Ed… I think some kids were messing with me after you left. They kept knocking on the door and running. They were even beating on the side of the house!" It was the explanation she was sticking with, but saying it aloud and comparing it to the events that occurred seemed nonsensical. "They were throwing stuff at the roof, the walls…."

Angelica was now staring at Rosanna with her eyebrow raised. She knew her mother wasn't "in her right mind," as she thought of it. Inquisitively she decided to question the witness. "They were on the *roof?*"

Rosanna didn't like her tone. "Angelica, I said they were throwing stuff on the roof." This didn't satiate her daughter's curiosity.

Looking back to her husband, "Ed, you might want to check the roof to see if they damaged anything."

Edward responded, "I'll check the roof tomorrow. Did you see them? Maybe we can tell the police to watch out for 'em."

"No, I didn't see them. They were sneaky."

Edward and Angelica were both aware of how easily they could see the majority of their land from the house. The only areas that were obstructed from view were the barns, somewhat at least, and the path leading across the bridged stream and the forest beyond. He thought for a moment before responding. "Maybe they were hiding behind the barn. Did you check there?"

Now her story was starting to sound more and more plausible. "You know, I didn't check there! I bet that's where they were hiding. Those little devils were driving me crazy!"

The three of them headed inside to the dining room. Angelica, still not buying the story, caught her mother's gaze again.

Rosanna decided to preemptively shut down the inquisition. "Did you two have fun at the festival?"

Edward eagerly replied, "Yeah! The funnel cake was phenomenal!" He wasn't sure how well she'd take the news about the acquisition of their new livestock. "I got a few pictures of the animals. I even got a couple of Ange on a horse."

Rosanna wasn't clear on the wording. "You let her ride a horse? She could've been thrown off!"

Her protective instinct, although slightly insulting to him as a parent at the moment, reminded him of how much Rosanna really cared for her daughter. "She just sat on a horse. It was tied to a post. It was a really gentle mare."

Angelica didn't care much for her mother's nagging, especially when she was grating on Edward. "Dad's not stupid, Mom."

Knowing full well this may start a battle between them, Edward softly scorned Angelica's tone. "Baby! Mom's just looking out for you, that's all. She doesn't want you to get hurt." He was blocking the space between them and now reached down to kiss Angelica on the top of her head. "And neither do I."

Angelica didn't pay any more attention to her mother and headed down the hallway toward her bedroom. A vein was protruding from Rosanna's forehead now as she clinched the bridge of her nose with her thumb and forefinger. She closed her eyes and quietly muttered, "If I talked back to my mother that way when I was a kid...."

Edward knew good and well that Rosanna's mother was strict and heavy-handed, quite literally. Corporeal punishment was the norm. Rosanna would often get "rosy cheeks" as a result of this, although they were never confused as blushing in the slightest. He also knew that she would repeat, in perverse zeal, *Turn the other cheek, Rosanna!* This would go on for several repetitions: left-right, left-right, left-right. He hugged her warmly, speaking softly. "We're just under a lot of stress right now. We'll all mellow out after we get through moving in."

He had managed to cool her temper enough. Playfully frustrated, "You and your smooth-talking. How'd I end up with you, anyway?"

Smiling, "You were the only one that fell for my 'smooth-talking.'"

They shared a quiet laugh and kissed one another.

"We'll be fine."

Some of the worry had crept back into her voice. "She's just been so difficult these past few weeks."

He rested the side of his face on her lowered forehead. "After what happened on day one, I'm glad she's dealing with it as well as she is."

She sighed. "You're right." She hugged him tightly for a few seconds before looking up and asking, "Didn't find a goat at the fair?"

Hesitation filled him momentarily and gave way to evasiveness. "We did!"

"Well, where is it?"

"We don't have a trailer yet, so the owner said he would bring them by after he finished up there."

She almost missed a detail in that sentence. "Wait... *them?*"

No way out now. "Yeah! They're herd animals. You can't just buy one. They won't do well that way."

Since she had already decided that Angelica and Edward were going to take care of them, Rosanna didn't let it bother her. "I guess two goats isn't too much. One for both of you."

Edward backed away and headed toward the fridge for a cold drink. He casually answered, "Oh, don't worry, Rosy; we got you one, too."

Rosanna's eyes now widened with disbelief. "*Three* goats, Ed!?"

He cracked open the fresh can of beer in his hand. "Honey, it's a mother and her two kids. How could we live with ourselves if we split up their family?"

Edward's smile was still disarming to his wife, but he was really pushing it. "Three goats is a lot to take care of, especially with two young ones!"

He took a drink from the cool can and replied in suit, "It's okay, honey, the owners are going to show us the ropes. Their kids are going to teach us how to take of them. It's for school." She was tilting her head to the side and he wasn't winning this one as easily as he'd hoped.

"Ange even made a friend there!"

Rosanna rolled her eyes but without much genuine antipathy. She folded her arms and shook her head. "I can't take my eye off you two for a minute. Always doing crazy things I get dragged into."

He put his arm around her shoulders. "We'll even let you milk the mama goat in the mornings if you want."

Now her eyebrow was raised in gentle reproach. "No way am I milking a goat! You two will have to work out that little problem."

Edward laughed. "Who knows, you might like it!" Seeing her shake her head while turning toward the oven, "Babe, I'm going to go out and tidy up the barn a bit before they bring the goats over."

"Okay, hon." As he neared the back door leading from the kitchen, Rosanna turned from the open cabinet doors and said, "Oh, ha! Very funny, Ed!"

He looked back at her in confusion. "What do you mean, babe?"

Swinging the cabinet doors open wide, her eyebrow raised. "Rearranged the dishes behind my back, I see!"

Edward saw the odd zigzag shape in which the plates were stacked. Rosanna was always very organized in the kitchen: a place for everything and everything in its place. "That's odd."

Not convinced by his perplexed face, "Sure, the dishes did that themselves, I guess." She then opened another door only to see that the bowls there were arranged in a strange and delicate wall structure in which they were upright and the one above it inverted. The rows and columns repeated in shape two rows deep. "You two were having a lot of fun, I see!"

Shaking his head and genuinely baffled, "Honey, I have no idea how they got that way...."

"Come on now! You and Ange...."

He cut her off. "Ange and I were at the festival this morning. How could we have done that? You've been here all day."

"Yeah, but... *I* didn't stack them that way! Maybe it was those kids who were harassing me."

Now raising his eyebrow, "A bunch of kids snuck onto our land, broke into the house and rearranged the dishes, delicately I might add, then got away without disturbing you."

She felt the absurdity in her brief theory. "Ed, you don't need to be sarcastic. If that's not it... I don't know."

He stepped closer and hugged her. "Don't worry about it, babe. Sometimes we forget when we do things."

This hit a sore spot in Rosanna, even though Edward wasn't intentionally pushing it. "I *know* I didn't do it! And don't even mention my mother's condition...." Rosanna's mother suffered from dementia and was currently being cared for at a nursing home out of town.

Now he felt remorseful for being a little careless with his words. "No, babe, I didn't mean that. I didn't mean it that way at all. I didn't think for a second there. I would never try and dismiss something you say because of that! I apologize."

Her tension dissolved a bit. "I know, Ed. I get paranoid about that sometimes."

He kissed her on the lips. "I'm with you until the end, remember that."

A smile crept back to her face as she sighed again. "Fine. I'll sort the dishes out. You go shovel those chocolate-covered raisins in the barn!"

Understanding her euphemism, "Only if we get to share them for a snack!"

Crinkling her nose, "Eww!" She smacked his bottom. "Get to work, Mr. Nasty!"

Eleven

Around 5:15 P.M., Angelica and her father were trying to tidy up the barn a bit before their new animals arrived. Rosanna didn't want any part of cleaning up the literal former pigsty and the enclosures in the barn. Angelica was using a rusty old rake to pull out any rocks and unidentified animal left-overs from the stalls. Edward was picking up heavier debris and placing it in a dilapidated wooden crate.

Stretching her back, she asked, "Do goats sleep on hay?"

Now she was thinking of problems even he'd neglected. "You know what, I bet they do. Maybe Mr. Kelly will have some to sell. Hey, is your new friend coming along?"

"Yep!"

As she was speaking he was leaping up trying to knock a few cobwebs down. Satisfied, "I think they'll like their new home. What do you think?"

She looked around the room at the only two lightbulbs inside that still worked. "It's kinda dark in here. I hope they don't get scared."

Edward placed his hand on her hair, messing it up a little. "I tell you what: We'll go the hardware store in town tomorrow and get a whole bunch of lightbulbs. Does that sound good?"

Angelica showed some relief, but was still forlorn. "I hope they can sleep better than I can."

He knelt down in front of her, getting at eye-level. "Ah, listen, baby girl, I know you're still having those nightmares. They won't last forever."

Only partially satisfied with his answer, "I hope so. You and Mommy snore a lot."

He couldn't help but burst out laughing. "I'm sorry about that, Ange. Maybe I'll get us some of those strips you put on your nose."

She giggled as he loudly imitated his snoring.

Soon her mind went to another topic, however, and her face went neutral again. "Do you think kids were really out here knocking on the side of the house?"

Her incisiveness still didn't cease to amaze him. "I haven't talked to her about it yet. I'm still not sure exactly what happened."

Angelica responded in a matter-of-fact tone, "I don't think it was kids doing it. She would've seen them. You can see almost everywhere from here."

Edward's face was also serious, speaking to her as if she were an adult. "Well, what do you think happened, sweetie?"

She looked out the barn's open door toward the house, making sure her mother wasn't lurking around. "I think it was...," she peered out toward the doorway again, "some of *them*."

"Them. So you think there's more than one out there?"

"Yeah. She said they were knocking all over the house."

He tried to ease the tension with his tone. "Maybe it was just one... a really fast one."

His attempt was unsuccessful. "No, Daddy, I know there's more than one. You know what I mean... *I know*."

Edward was reluctant to admit that he felt the same way, but she wasn't kidding or exaggerating. Somehow he knew it, too. "We'll figure out what we need to do. Don't worry...."

Their conversation halted as they hear the distinct sound of tires crunching on gravel slowly making its way toward their house.

Angelica seemed to snap out of her melancholy. "I think the goats are here!"

He watched her run out the door in front of him. "I think they are."

As he got outside, Angelica was waving at her new friend Abby, who was sitting next to her brother in the approaching truck. Rosanna had also heard the vehicle and was making her way out of the kitchen and onto the back porch. The truck came to a stop as the three Barristers finished their waving. Mr. Kelly and his two children got out and shut the doors behind them.

Edward extended his hand again. "Mr. Kelly, thanks for bringing the goats out."

Shaking his hand, "No problem, Mr. Barrister."

"This is my wife, Rosanna."

She greeted him and was also introduced to Little John and Abby.

The latter quickly walked over to her new acquaintance. "Hey, Angelica."

She smiled. "Hey, Abby. Want to see the barn?"

Abby had seen a barn every day of her natural life as far as she could remember, but she was eager to spend time with her. "Sure!"

They raced off into the poorly lit building.

Once inside, "It sure is dark in here."

Angelica was happy that someone else felt the exact same way, even if not to the depth of darkness she knew. "I know! That's what I said! We're going to get more lightbulbs tomorrow."

She and Abby walked around the barn, Angelica appearing as proud as if she'd built the thing herself. They stopped for a moment at one of the stalls near the doors leading out to the driveway, Abby's face becoming grave.

"Do you know about what happened here a long time ago?"

Angelica shook her head no, but before she could speak, Abby's father entered with the mother goat led by a rope. His tone was sharp and direct.

"Abby! I told you not to go on about that! What's in the past is gone now."

Angelica was feeling more and more confirmed in her suspicions, given the terribly obvious and clumsy cover up.

Abby's head dropped. "I'm sorry. I won't say anything." She went to her father as she handed off the light brown-and-white furred mother goat to her.

Rosanna was standing and watching over, quite happy that Mr. Kelly didn't want to feed her daughter's imagination with unnecessary fuel. Suddenly one of the kid goats was audibly bleating loudly. Rosanna approached Edward, who was carrying the crying culprit. The small frame of the animal and its cries for mother even tugged at her heartstrings.

"Aww, be careful, Ed!"

He laughed as he walked by her.

Mr. Kelly then said in a reassuring tone, "Ah, he just wants his mama. They can make all kinds of noise when they're young."

Rosanna now felt a little uncomfortable with the new pets being offloaded onto their property. "They don't make a *lot* of noise, do they?"

John Kelly replied, "Nah, not unless there's something wrong. As long as you keep 'em safe and sound in the barn at night, you shouldn't have any trouble with them. Probably won't hear a peep out of them most nights."

This brought her some relief. "Well, that's good to know."

The previously loud goat quieted immediately when placed on the ground next to its mother in a stall. Little John, meanwhile, had brought the second kid in. This solid white goat joined his mother and solid caramel-colored sister. Still uneasy with their environment, they stayed close to one of the two working lightbulbs overhead.

Soon the two bags of feed and thankfully for the Barristers, three bundles of straw, were unloaded.

Little John walked over to Angelica and Abby. "Hey, Angelica, you wanna help make the straw beds for 'em?"

She agreed and the three started spreading the cut straw over the ground in one of larger stalls.

They finished within a few minutes.

John Kelly then said to his son, "All right now, John Jr., go ahead and tell them when to feed 'em and how much."

Little John went into his familiar lecture on goat care basics. Feeding amounts, directions on how to use Diatomaceous Earth as a supplement to help prevent bloat, and pretty much everything else he knew about goats was taught to the Barristers. Whether or not they could remember everything had yet to be seen.

Edward and Rosanna were genuinely impressed. The former said, "Well, thank you, John Jr. You know a lot about goats."

His wife was still concerned about the level of work they'd be expected to do. "Can we have your number in case we have any questions?"

John Sr. laughed and gave them his cell number.

Mr. Kelly then called his children over and they headed toward their truck. Edward remembered to ask where he could pick up a trailer and equipment to maintain their large property. Kelly wrote down a couple of phone numbers and addresses, and advised him on which store to avoid. By painful experience, John Sr. had learned about their inflated prices and gouging payment plans they'd offered him in the past.

As she got to the truck, Abby stopped and said to Angelica, "Hey, you want us to come by tomorrow and show you how to milk the mother?"

She enthusiastically accepted the offer. Angelica and her parents then all wished farewell to their new acquaintances. John Sr. started the truck, drove it around the dirt clearing in front of the barns and rolled on down the driveway.

Angelica and Edward headed into the barn to top off the makeshift container of water on the ground.

Rosanna walked toward the house. "Don't stay out long, you two. Dinner is in the oven."

"Okay, hon, we'll be in in a minute." His attention turned back to his daughter, who was laughing at the kid goats jumping around. "I didn't know they could jump so much!"

She laughed and had an epiphany. "I'll call that one Pop Tart!"

Edward pointed to the other caramel-colored goat with a small white blaze on its forehead. "And we can call her Coffee. Does that sound good?"

Angelica agreed.

"And the mother already has a name: Agnes."

Now she'd heard two strange names today. "*Agnes?* What kinda name is that?"

"Hehe, I guess it's a goat name."

Several minutes later the three of them were seated at the table getting ready to eat the meatloaf and vegetables that Rosanna had prepared. Before any food was put on the table, however, they looked at one another as Rosanna said, "Angelica, would you lead us in grace?"

She replied, "Sure. God is great...."

Her words were cut off, however, as they heard the sound of some of the silverware in the nearby drawer being jostled about.

They looked at one another again before turning toward the drawer.

Seeing and hearing nothing else, Rosanna said, "Not sure what that was. Continue, Angelica."

"God is good...."

The sound of silverware jingling and clanking sounded again.

Rosanna looked more concerned now. "What on Earth?"

Edward shrugged. "Mice maybe?"

Angelica scrunched her nose. "Eww, gross!"

Rosanna looked at her once again. "Just keep going."

"Let us thank Him for our food."

The next jumbled sounds of metallic clanking were much louder. Whatever was making the noise now made the drawer thud loudly and shake for a few seconds.

Wide-eyed, everyone stared at the drawer as Edward said, "Rats?"

Rosanna replied, "Oh, gosh, I hope not! You should get some traps in the morning when you go to the store."

Angelica heard an unfamiliar voice say in her mind, *"That wasn't a rat... ."* She looked at her parents, thinking it was maybe one of them. This thought was quickly, however, thrown away.

Edward rose from the table and reached out for the utensil drawer handle as it briefly jolted once again. He looked back at his family apprehensively before slowly taking the handle in hand. Upon opening the drawer he was dumbstruck by what lay inside. No rat, no mouse, no mammal of any sort. The utensils were all neatly arranged but not in any way the method to which Rosanna would use. The forks were arranged lengthwise in an arched configuration with the teeth of the forks locked at the apex. The spoons underneath were arranged neatly into a strange pattern beneath that in which the mouth of the spoons lay atop one another to form a similar shallow arch underneath.

He then said, astonished, "Whoa! Look at this, Rosy!"

She and Angelica both walked toward the drawer and were shocked at the neat and tidy patterns.

Rosanna noticed something missing. "Wait, where are the case knives?"

Edward didn't see them, but felt an uncanny need to check one of the cabinets overhead. As he opened the door they all saw a stack of bowls still arranged as normal. On the apex, however, the case knives were all spread evenly around the bowl's mouth in what looked like a silver and alabaster sunflower.

"What the...?"

The site of the utensils rattled in Angelica's mind in the similar manner in which they sounded. It was unsettling to her. It tapped right back into that distant dread skulking around the property and her subconscious.

Rosanna, despite having a similar uneasy feeling, didn't want to dwell on it. "Well, let's go ahead and eat. Food's getting cold."

They all returned to the table and made an effort to not discuss the obvious.

Later that evening in bed, Edward was browsing over some old floor plans he was reviewing for work. He was going to be working at home now thanks to the company he had been employed with for keeping him on part-time and in an advisory position. Plus he had also managed his money wisely all his working life, so time on the farm so far was not as bad as it could've been otherwise.

Rosanna finished reading an article from a home-improvement magazine she'd picked up in town. Setting it aside on her nightstand, she noticed her small Bible placed on the shelf below. She turned and looked at her husband. "Hon, I think we should go to Mass next Sunday at St. Mary's. Angelica's going to be going to school there and she'll need to get to know her classmates."

This conversation had come up before, in different forms, throughout their relationship. Rosanna would ever so often, but consistently, try and get her husband to attend Mass. There were certain aspects of the religion that he agreed with in principle, but he wasn't ready to buy in one hundred percent.

"I'll try. I don't know if I'll be busy on Sunday or not. The office expects me to start going again soon and there's still a lot of work to do on the property."

"You know, I prefer that we all go." He was presenting valid reasons, but her need for comfort in her faith wasn't letting go. "Besides, Angelica is going to need to get ready for her first communion here in a couple years."

"That's fine. You two can spend some time together."

She knew he wasn't committing to the process of conversion. "I want all three of us to go. We're a family and it's very important for us to do this."

He removed his glasses and placed them on his nightstand, his way of saying the conversation was over and it was time for bed. "I'll do my best to come along when I can. As soon as Angelica starts school we're all going to be a lot busier."

Rosanna received his kiss, but grabbed his arm as he attempted to roll over and turn off the light next to him. "Edward, this is for all of us. I only want the best for you two."

The fatigue was really causing him to tune out her concerns. "Babe, I know. We'll work this out."

She was not satisfied with his answer, but relented as she knew how tired they both were. "All right, goodnight. But hey, one more thing: I want the priest to bless the house. It'll make me feel a little more at ease."

Edward acknowledged her, but was quick to give in to sleep.

Twelve

Angelica was pulled to the plane of nightmares again that night. The dream would start off as the rerun dream she'd been experiencing every night since her near-death experience. The sun would suddenly drop from the sky, the school of minnows would be staring at her. The eruptions of thick tarry liquid would be there. The stream would begin to flood, and the entity would coagulate out of the mist. This time, however, the creature trudged toward and stopped momentarily in front of her. She tried to scream, but her voice had inexplicably ceased to function. A smile could be seen forming on creature's face. Towering over her, it laughed maniacally. Despite the relatively flat land in her dreamscape, the voice echoed and reverberated for several seconds. As the sound reached a deafening volume, she attempted to cover her ears. Once she placed her palms to mute the sound, however, they were ripped away and to the side by small jet-black tentacles emerging from the streambed. The entity then leaned in close to her face. She could feel the heat emanating from its mouth and eyes, which looked like brightly glowing coals in an insane furnace. As it began to speak, the heat from within it caused her to turn her face away. Hissing malice built to rage. "That bitch of a mother cannot save you! Your pathetic father is helpless! I will savor your blood, your tears, and your souls for all eternity!" The words echoed throughout the now void of light terrain. A hundred times over she heard the words stab her ears. The only source of light, at this point, was the blazing energy emanating from the black mass. Its mouth opened wide and prepared to devour her whole....

Angelica woke up with tears streaming down her cheeks. Her scream was choked out by what appeared to be a thick black smoke filling the room. She fell off of her mattress and to the floor, grabbing her throat. Soon enough she caught her breath, but collapsed onto her face, sobbing loudly.

By the time Edward made it into her room, the dark mist had retreated from the space via some unseen portal. He knelt on the floor next to her, turning over. "Ange, baby! Are you okay?"

She struggled to subdue the cough. "The dream... it was different this time! There was smoke in the room. I saw it when got up!"

He hugged her tightly and looked around the bedroom. "It's okay, it's okay. There's no smoke in the room now."

She clinched him and was finally able to weep freely. With neither of them noticing, Rosanna was now standing in the doorway with her arms folded. She didn't seem too torn up about the scene. Again, as Rosanna *knew*, it was only "overactive imagination and maybe a sprinkling of PTSD."

Without a word, she watched Edward pick his daughter up and carry her toward the door. He nodded that she'd be fine and so they headed back to their bedroom with child in tow. Once inside, Rosanna walked over to an old vanity mirror and removed a small rosary from one of the drawers. At the bed, Edward had already turned onto his side to sleep, Angelica following suit at his back.

"Angelica, hold on a second. I have something for you."

Rosanna placed the rosary around her neck. She was only somewhat familiar with what it meant, but accepted it nonetheless. The three then, one by one, headed back to sleep.

Thirteen

Rosanna got up early that morning and was planning on making a trip to the library. Edward and Angelica stayed behind at home to make the recently purchased goats as comfortable as could be.

The library had only been open for ten minutes when the family Subaru came to a stop in the empty parking lot of the modestly sized book shrine in town. It looked quaint and cozy to Rosanna from the outside and she was ready to indulge in one of her personal hobbies: history. She wanted to know all about the town to which they had recently moved and this seemed like the perfect time and place.

Upon entering the building she immediately saw the front desk and an old lady behind it. She seemed pleasant enough in her face and couldn't have weighed more than ninety pounds soaking wet. Her white hair was tied back in a bun and she wore a stereotypical librarian sweater and plain dress. Even on summer days like this she couldn't help but feel cold.

As Rosanna smiled and approached the desk, the old woman gestured the same and said, "Well, you must be Mrs. Barrister."

Shaking her extended hand, "Yes! How did you know?"

"Well, this is a really small community and when someone decides to move in up *there*, everyone finds out pretty quickly."

Rosanna's smile had dropped. "That makes sense. What do you mean up *there*? Do a lot of people come and go?"

Looking over the small rimmed glasses lowered on her nose, "For a while, many families moved in and out, but no one stayed for long." Seeing Rosanna nod and not content with her answer thus far, "You know… *ghost stories*!" She wiggled her fingers and made a 50's B-movie impression of a ghost moan. "It's surprising sometimes what people will believe. If someone says it or it's written down, it *must* be true. Right?" The two sentences were laden with obvious sarcasm.

The smile had returned to her face. "Well, I'm glad to meet someone with grounded ideas in town. I thought I was the only one for a while there." Seeing the old woman smile and chuckle, "By the way, what's your name?"

"Oh, heavens, where are my manners? My name is Lily Lindemann."

"Nice to meet you, Mrs. Lindemann."

"Please, call me Lily. You make me sound old the other way."

"All right, ma'am. I don't suppose I could trouble you for a library card?"

She winked and said, "You know, I thought you might want one of those." She then reached down and pulled out a paper card. "Just fill this out with your information and I'll get one printed and laminated for you."

Rosanna then picked up the pen and began writing.

Lily continued. "So what sort of literature are you looking for today, Mrs. Barrister?"

Glancing up, "Oh, I actually wanted to learn more about Miller's Run. I love history and this town seems like it has a lot of stories."

"Oh, history. I hate to say it, but the history here can be very boring at times. Not much crime or drama. And, unfortunately, the original library burned down in 1906. We lost everything in the fire that year. Books, newspapers, you name it."

Looking up again, she said with genuine remorse, "Oh? That's a tragedy!"

"Don't you know it! So much information and history lost in one day. Thankfully we haven't had any tragedies like that since then." The old lady then knocked on the wooden desk three times. "Don't want to invite bad luck, now do we?"

She chuckled at the superstitious gesture as she handed her the completed card. "So do you have your newspapers from back then on microfilm?"

"We do. We just recently copied the data from them into digital format so we can print out paper copies as often as we want. It's amazing what technology can do these days, isn't it?"

"It is. Where can I begin?"

"The computer and viewer are right over this way. Let me show you. What are you looking for in particular? Maybe I can point you in the right direction."

Pulling the chair out from the small table bearing the computer and microfilm reader, "Well, I wanted to just browse the town's newspapers as far back as I can. Nineteen-oh-six and on, if possible."

Lily's face didn't seem as friendly as before in an odd way. "Mrs. Barrister, I can get those for you, but if you want to see *everything* you'll be here for days and bored out of your mind. And like I said, we don't have much crime in this town and most days the paper is just farming news and the like."

Confused by the change in airs but still insistent, "Really, it's okay. Like I said, I love history. I want to learn all I can."

She quickly glanced at her up and down, sizing her up with disapproval. "Very well. It's your time, after all."

The old lady then walked back to a nearby storage room as Rosanna turned on the computer and microfilm reader.

Around a minute later, Lily returned with boxes of film. Placing them on the table and letting them intentionally thud, "There you go. *Miller's Run Gazette* from 1906 to 1946. There's more if you get through all of this."

The librarian then turned and left the room as Rosanna said aloud, "Thank you."

No response. The librarian returned to the front desk in view of the computer station.

She glanced over at the desk and back, rolling her eyes before opening one of the boxes in front of her. She thought to herself, *Did I say something impolite?* Unable to think of anything, she fed the first roll of film into the reader. After some adjustments to the lens and scale, she read the headline on the first newspaper: *"Town Library Destroyed by Fire!"*

After perusing the article, she could summarize that they weren't sure how the fire started. Subsequent articles in the following days reinforced this.

She eventually browsed ahead about a month before seeing another headline catch her attention: *"Local Boy Missing and Presumed Dead."* She read the article carefully but not many details stood out. From what she could tell it was a farm well on the other side of town and nowhere near the Barrister home.

Scanning ahead another week she found another headline that grabbed her attention: *"Mayor Thrown from Horse in Recompense and Bounty Parade!"* She gathered from the article that something unknown suddenly spooked the horse on which the mayor was riding. The mayor was thrown to the ground, breaking his neck on impact and ending his life.

Rosanna stretched her arms over her head as the poignant stories raced in her mind. She looked over at the front desk and, to her surprise, the librarian was glaring at her. Despite feeling uncomfortable with her, she asked, "How much are printouts?"

Curtly, "Ten cents a copy."

Nodding her head, "Okay, thanks."

The librarian hardly acknowledged this as Rosanna looked back toward the computer screen. She decided to print out the two recently read articles and laid them next to the printer.

It was nearly five o'clock when Rosanna leaned back in her chair and rubbed her strained eyes. A stack of printouts were sitting in front of the printer.

She suddenly heard a voice from the front desk call out in a direct tone, "Mrs. Barrister, I'm closing the building in ten minutes."

Blinking a couple of times, she looked up at the clock on the wall which verified the closing time. She quickly returned the film to its box and turned the equipment off.

At the desk, she carefully placed the boxes down and said, "Sorry, I lost track of time. I believe I owe you $3.50."

Lily took the four dollars Rosanna placed on the desk and quickly returned two quarters to her. She then slid the laminated library card she'd recently made and said in curt tone, "Thank you, Mrs. Barrister."

Pausing awkwardly for a moment before saying, "Well, okay then. Goodbye."

Walking into the storage room with the reels of film she called out over her shoulder, "Goodbye."

Fourteen

Angelica was out in the unoffending barn when Edward walked to the open double doors leading inside. He smiled as he watched her wipe down the walls of the stalls with a soaked rag. He asked, "Whatcha doing there, baby girl?"

Reaching as high as she could to get the dirt off the back wall, "I'm trying to make it not smell so bad in here."

Seeing her on her tiptoes, "You know, I'm awfully proud of you, Ange. You're taking the responsibility seriously." He walked closer and motioned with his hand, "Here, I'll get up higher if you want some help."

"I was going to use the stool over there to…."

She was cut off by Edward's phone ringing. He pulled it from his pocket and wasn't pleased with who was calling. He rolled his eyes and said, "I gotta take this call: It's the office. I'll be back in a minute, okay?"

She nodded in reply as he put the phone to his ear and walked outside. "Hello?"

"Hey there, Eddie-boy! It's your old pal Mark!"

Rolling his eyes but maintaining a civil tone, "Hi, Mark. How are you?"

It's worth mentioning that Edward never cared for Mark all that much. Sure, he worked with him for years at the office, but he was a pest. Perhaps an outsider might see some of the random acts that Mark performed as helpful, but the trained eye would see that he usually had a personal gain in mind also. He would think to himself, *Oh, I see you're having a problem there. I*

might be able to help you out, but only if I get this little teensy thing in re-
turn. "Teensy" was not always as proportionate to the recipient as it seemed to Mark.

Money, that was what made Mark tick. Money and the often unabashed catering to his many physical whims. Sure, he maintained the façade of respectable to most, but to those who really knew him, he didn't shine so brightly. But hey, sometimes we have to work with assholes just to put food on the table. And Mark, let's just say he was a proctologist's dream (or nightmare) with the level of "pain in the ass" he could be.

"I'm doing great. Hey, do you have a minute to talk?"

"I've got a few minutes, but I'm helping my daughter clean up the barn."

"Hell, I don't know why anyone would want to live that kind of life."

He knew Mark thought his idea of a happy life was bunk, but he forced the politeness still. "Yeah, it's a lot of work, but it's satisfying. What's on your mind?"

"Well, you know my friend at my financial advisor's office. He just let me in on a juicy land deal that's getting ready to go down. Turns out there's a rumor going around that they're considering building a new golf course in the area, and the land prices are still good."

With no surprise at the subject of the call, "Uh-huh. How much are you wanting me to chip in?"

"Straight to the point as always. I like that about you, Eddie-boy. I was thinking you could buy in for $75,000 to $100,000. Being that several of us are going in together, it certainly helps mitigate the risk."

Edward shook his head. "Mark, there's no way I can fork over that kind of money right now. We're already in neck-deep on the house and property costs and farming equipment isn't cheap."

In a lightly mocking tone, "Eddie-boy, come on now! I know you're a skinflint with your money, but we're talking about at *least* a 20-percent return! You just can't pass up deals like that! Hell, you could use the money to grow Angelica's college fund!"

Clearly annoyed at his tactic of dragging his daughter into the argument, "Mark, I'm not going to go and spend Angelica's college fund on speculative real estate. Plus I'm saving to retire one day. What if this whole deal ends up tits up?"

Now sounding disappointed, "Ah, Eddie-boy, I was hoping you'd be more open to the idea, but I'm not surprised. You've always been a low-risk kind of guy."

"You make that sound like a bad thing. I have what I need now because of it. One day, when I retire, I'll have even more because I play it safe and smart."

Frustrated, but still sounding somewhat pleasant, "Well, shit, Eddie-boy, I guess there's no convincing you. I'll give you a call from the bank when I go and withdraw my profits."

"I wish you the best of luck, Mark. Do give me a call if you benefit wildly from the investment!"

"Oh, you know I will!"

Edward knew he would call if fortune went his way, but he really didn't care. He soon returned to helping his daughter wipe down the walls of the barn. Edward didn't hear another word about the deal from Mark. It was a flash in the pan and Mark's impatience cost him thousands of dollars on a golf course that never was.

Fifteen

It was around six in the afternoon when Rosanna pulled into the driveway and returned home. As she entered the kitchen through the backdoor with the stack of printouts under her arm, she saw her husband and daughter waiting for her.

Angelica was washing her hands up for dinner as Edward said, "Hey, there you are! We were starting to get worried. Did you read everything they had there?"

She didn't return his smile, but masked a feeling of uneasiness she had had all day at the library and it was bubbling and boiling inside all the way home. She looked down and said, "Angelica, could you go outside for a few minutes? Mommy and Daddy need to have an adult talk."

Her daughter shrugged and walked nonchalantly out the door.

As she was still in earshot, "It won't take too long, sweetie, I promise."

She called out while walking toward the barn, "Okay!"

Edward's face had gone serious also. "What's the matter, babe?"

She glanced out the kitchen window again before placing the stack of printouts on the kitchen table. Thumbing through the pages, "Ed, there are a *lot* of odd things about this town's newspaper. Start at the top and you'll see what I mean."

Looking down at the stack, "Let's see what we have here...." As he was glancing over the first page which headlined the first missing boy story she read, "Oh, man. Nineteen-oh-six…." Not seeing any details standing out, "Did they ever find him?"

Leaning against the counter next to the sink with her arms crossed, "No. I tried to find something else about that case, but nothing further was written." Seeing him continue to read, "That's just the beginning. Keep going."

He turned the page and saw Rosanna's next printout. He read aloud, "'Local Girl Missing and Presumed Dead.'" The lack of detail was also evident in this article. "Nineteen-ten?"

She nodded her head as he looked up at her. "Keep going."

He then turned to the next page and read aloud, "'Local Boy Missing and Presumed Dead.' Nineteen-fifteen? What the hell?"

"Exactly!" She walked back over to the pile of papers and continued. "Look: 1925, 1929, 1932, 1933, and 1936!"

Edward was baffled.

"Look here, though. This is where it gets really strange." She then showed a printout of an article from 1939, only most of the text was blacked out.

Perplexed, "Why'd you mark through these?"

Raising her eyebrows, "I didn't! That's the thing that worries me even more! They were like that on the microfilm which means someone edited these out *before* they copied them over."

He rifled through the rest of the papers to see all of the missing person's stories completely blacked out by ink from the past only showing the headline. "Why would the town's paper edit these things out?"

Throwing her hands up, "I don't know! That's what I've been trying to figure out. Seems like people go missing on a regular basis around here and they don't want anyone to know about it. When I asked to see the newspapers from that time the librarian looked like she wanted to rip my head off!"

Still trying to process all the information suddenly placed on him, "I don't know. Maybe they don't want bad publicity for the town."

"Who's going to come reading the newspaper of this hick town?"

Her words made too much sense to him. "I'm clueless, babe." He looked down at the stack for a moment before saying, "Maybe John Kelly knows more about this."

"You'd think he would've mentioned something by now. '*Oh, by the way, people go missing here every few years. Good luck!*'"

His trepidation about the property seemed to be justifying itself before him. He muttered, "I knew we shouldn't have moved here."

Now slightly annoyed, "Ed, now's not the time. You know we sank a lot of money into this dream plan of ours."

Gripping the bridge of his nose between his fingers and squinting, "I know... I know... Look, you're right. Now's not the time to start coming unglued. We'll figure this out."

"And we're going to have to keep an eye on our daughter. We can't let her end up a news headline."

More emboldened now, "I'll *never* let that happen. Go ahead and call her in and we'll eat."

Sixteen

5:30 A.M.

Angelica had managed to sneak out of her parents' bed and into the living room. Unable to sleep any longer, to which she was becoming uncomfortably used to, she flipped through the channels of the large television in their living room. Within a minute she found a show she'd never seen before. She knew it was an old production due to the black-and-white images. The men acting out the scene were making funny noises when they hit one another. The giggles came on quickly, giving way to laughing aloud. A stocky bald man began barking like a dog. Another man with dark hair and a bowl-cut waved his hand in front of the bald man's face, raised it high, then dropped it low sharply. The stocky man's face followed the action and jerked downward, snapping him out of his barking fit. The third man, a balding middle-aged sort with a long nose, told the bowl-cut man to "Cut it out!" He was promptly slapped for his insurrection.

Meanwhile, back in her parents' bedroom, Edward stirred from sleep, hearing the laughing coming from down the hall. He turned and checked the bed, seeing Rosanna also twist and turn. He decided to get up and check on his daughter who was still chuckling.

Suddenly his wife groaned, "Shut the door, Ed...."

Once he slid into his slippers, he closed the door quietly behind him, then making his way into the hall. Shuffling his feet, he entered the living room and saw something he'd been missing: a genuine smile on Angelica's face.

She pried her eyes away from the screen for a moment. "Hey, Daddy. These guys are funny!"

"Morning, baby girl." He sat down on the couch next to her and kissed her on the forehead. Now looking at the screen, he immediately recognized the show. As if she'd picked a fine wine from the best stocked cellar. *"The Three Stooges.* Nice choice!" He put his arm around her and enjoyed the fine slapstick comedy.

A few minutes later, at a commercial break, he stood up. "I'm gonna make some coffee. You want anything to drink while I'm up?"

"Orange juice, please."

"One orange juice, coming up!"

He then walked into the kitchen and started the coffee maker. The rich smell quickly permeated the air. Even though Angelica had yet to try coffee, she enjoyed the smell of it in the morning. As he was going to the fridge for the orange juice, the show resumed. Angelica quickly erupted into laughter again. He couldn't help but smile, finally sensing some joy in the house.

He returned to the living room and handed her the glass of orange juice before sitting back on the couch. The next scene had poor Curly blocking an eye-poke, only to be punched in the gut, and then slapped across the face. Angelica laughed more loudly than ever. Despite the enjoyment, Edward needed remind her that the bear was still sleeping in her cave. No one wanted to wake the bear known as Rosanna before it was time proper.

The show came to a close and was followed by an infomercial. Apparently this was the time of day when people who have trouble chopping up vegetables with a knife would be most likely to watch. And what kind of monster only shows two episodes of the Stooges in one day!? Seeing her disappointment, "You want to get some breakfast going?"

She nodded.

"How about some cereal?"

Edward prepared her favorite: Cheerios. Filling the bowl with cereal then milk, he placed it on the table in front of her. She eagerly picked up the spoon and started to eat. He then poured himself a cup of coffee and added the preferred amount of cream and sugar. He sat and indulged in the warm vitalizing drink, savoring each careful sip.

With food still in her mouth, Angelica looked at the cup in his hand. "What does coffee taste like?"

He looked down for a moment, thinking. The only answer he could come up with was, "It's got its own taste." Looking down the hall for Rosanna to suddenly appear, as she often did at their moments of mischief, he was relieved to see no one. He lowered his voice and leaned toward her over the table. "Can you keep a secret?"

She nodded her head.

"Here, don't tell anyone," motioning with his head toward the bedroom. Angelica knew who the easily offended party was.

"Here, try some. Careful, it's hot."

He slid the cup across the kitchen table to her. She instinctively looked over her shoulder. The coast was clear and now it was time to try the previously forbidden beverage. Angelica took a cautionary sip. The warm liquid filled her nose with an even stronger smell of the bean concoction. The caffeine was fast-acting, much faster than the far tamer amounts in sodas, causing her eyes to shake away any sense of sleepiness. Mostly due to her recent harvest of nightmares, she was now understanding why her parents would instinctively drink this every morning. Edward reached for the cup, but it was pulled away as Angelica took a full and complete drink from the cup. She had her fill, albeit small, and allowed her father to snatch the cup away.

He chuckled. "I guess you like it?"

Way beyond fully awake, her eyes beaming with an over-the-top energy, "It tastes really good!"

He couldn't help but feel a momentary guilt, something like a pusher getting a new addict hooked. It did, however, seem to snap her out of the sleepiness and fatigue she was now carrying every day. "Just remember: Don't tell Mommy."

He winked and she responded with a thumbs-up. Edward then watched as his daughter's hands clap together almost on their own several times before she resumed eating her cereal. He then thought to himself, *Please don't tell Rosanna I just gave you coffee.*

After finishing their breakfast and getting dressed for the day, Edward and Angelica headed to the backdoor and outside. Immediately they could hear the mother goat bleating frequently along with her two kids. It wasn't full-blown distress, but the urgency inherent in the tone made it obvious that they were uncomfortable in some way.

Looking down at Angelica, whose face was already laden with concern, "I guess they're ready for breakfast." Once again, he was hoping to keep the mood lighter than what he sensed was the appropriate tension.

They walked toward the barn with muffled urgency. Edward was quick on the heavy iron latch holding the doors shut, allowing Angelica to step in and assess the problem. The bleating stopped immediately upon their entry. All three of the goats had been stressed, but were now visibly calming down. Edward opened both doors wide, allowing as much light in as possible.

Angelica walked to the edge of the pen and scratched the head of the mother goat. "What's wrong, Agnes?"

The goat suddenly let out a forceful sneeze. Tiny projectiles splattered all over the small denim vest that Angelica was wearing over a t-shirt. It was terribly out of fashion, but Angelica had relegated it to farm duty. It used to belong to Rosanna, who probably looked more "hip" wearing it at her age. Her father laughed at her as she recoiled and shook her hands free of the mucous and who knows what else.

Angelica's face was distorted with confusion and surprise. "Bless you?"

"I guess she doesn't like the vest either."

Looking down at the offending slime, "I guess not."

Without having to ask for a reminder on how much to feed her new friends, she took the plastic cup next to feed bag, filled it accordingly, and poured it out into the feeding trough. Agnes was quick to start chomping on the meal.

Meanwhile, Edward was taking notes on a small pad of paper. "Let's see, a dozen lightbulbs will be more than enough." A fallen piece of wood here and there caught his eye as well. "I have nails. Need a couple of two-by-fours...." He trailed off, and continued writing.

His thoughts were soon interrupted by his daughter's words.

"Ow! Don't do that!" Angelica wasn't really injured, just surprised. "Coffee is head-butting everywhere."

"Can you think of anything we need at the store?"

She pondered for a moment but was unable to think of anything.

"Okay, Mr. Kelly said they would be over around 11:00 A.M. today to show us how to milk Agnes. Let's get going so we don't miss them."

The two of them headed back into the kitchen, where Edward grabbed the keys to the family car from the pegs next to the door. Rosanna barely raised her head as she too entered the room.

"Hey, hon! Good morning." Edward's enthusiasm wasn't music to her ears.

Her eyes still only half open, she waved at him. "Ugh."

He maintained his upbeat attitude. "Need anything from the store while we're out?"

Rosanna only glanced toward the coffee pot, her eyes still adjusting to the morning light. "Did you make me coffee, too?"

Smiling, "Don't I always?" He watched her take a cup from the cabinet. "Do you need anything from the store?"

It was just past 7:00 A.M., and she was in no mood to talk. She merely grunted and shook her head.

"All right, we'll back in a bit."

About thirty minutes later, Rosanna was dressed in a white t-shirt and blue jeans, standing just in front of the goat stall inside the barn. She took a sip from the cup of coffee in her hand, staring directly at the goat known as Agnes. The goat, meanwhile, was chewing her food, her lower jaw smoothly moving to the left and the right to grind the grain between her lower teeth and hard pallet.

Rosanna gulped a swallow of the invigorating beverage, her face showing obvious confusion and contemplation. "I don't get it.... Why do people think goats are cute?"

Agnes didn't lose this staring contest. Whether or not Agnes was really trying to understand the human, the human was trying to figure her out. Rosanna leaned in a bit closer to the railing, really trying to figure out the puzzling creature before her.

"No offense, but you're *kinda* ugly."

Agnes continued to chew, only then she also let a few dark-colored pellets drop to the ground behind her without missing a beat. Rosanna glanced over behind the goat, then back to staring at her face.

Raising her eyebrow at what she reflexively considered rude behavior for an animal, "And you just drop those whenever you please...."

Agnes only broke her fixation long enough to ingest another bite of feed.

Having nearly finished her drink, the remainder of which was getting way too cold to enjoy, she tossed the last remnants out onto the dirt covered turnaround between the two barns. The second barn, having yet to be opened since they moved in, drew her attention to its doors. A heavy iron latch, identical to the fixture on the other barn, was locked shut. Rosanna took the heavily rusted Masterlock in her hand. The decay of the metal seemed ominous for some reason. She tugged on it, then dropped it.

"I wonder how long it's been since anyone's been in here."

She then made her way to the windows, hoping to see inside. Covered in years of mold, mud, and other miscellaneous crud, only a workbench and blurry images of what she guessed were tools could be seen. Rosanna's need for cleanliness then managed to reassert the position at the front of her mind. There was reluctance hiding in her resolve, as they had already spent many days cleaning. It was taxing, but it had to be done. "Can't have Father Anderson thinking we live in filth." There were certain things that just had to be done before a priest would be able to comfortably, for Rosanna anyway, see how they lived. This was going to be her new spiritual guide and faith leader. The right impressions had to be maintained if her family was going to be taken seriously. It was hard-wired into her mind since she was as young as she could remember.

Inside the kitchen, she rinsed out her coffee mug and left it out to dry. She then grabbed a hammer Edward had left on the counter nearby and took a copy of the barn keys from one of the pegs before heading back to the locked away building. Once at the door, she tried both keys before finding the one that fit. The locking mechanism ground painfully to the left, but didn't open. Rosanna figured this would happen with the rust nearly devouring the steel padlock. Hammer in hand, she bashed it several times before it popped open. She took the lock and put it in her pocket, only to see another obstruction: three nails driven into the door. They were only halfway in, but bent deliberately to act as another warning to anyone determined to see inside. Unabashed, she pried them loose, one by one, and tossed them aside in the overgrown grass nearby.

The heavy iron latch across the door was the third and final barrier. The handle itself needed to be pounded into submission before it would give way.

"Come," *bash,* "on," *bash,* "you piece of," *BASH.*

The handle soon gave up. Rosanna flung it open and was hit with an overpowering and pungent aroma. She covered her nose immediately and backed away from the threshold.

"Argh! Something's dead in there!"

Even though it offered little help, she covered her mouth and nose with the front of her t-shirt. The sensation of the smell bled into a pool mixed with the scene in front of her. Flies were swarming in the rafters, the upper storage area, and around every window. Only a step inside, she saw writhing chains of maggots undulating around the borders of the windows and in clumps on the ground. They appeared to be feeding on something unseen or looking vigorously for a source. She then felt a sharp blow across the back of her knees. She could literally feel the electrical sensation of her nerves firing in agony as she lost her footing fell to her knees. As she stopped herself from falling flat on her face with her hands, she looked side to side to try and see her attacker. No misbehaving kids, no tall man in a hockey mask. As her mind quickly processed no visual assailant she felt yet another unseen attacker grab her hair from behind and force her face toward the undulating larvae. Her hair lightly touched the writhing mass but her face was held in place only an inch away. She then heard a distinctively animalistic voice, one with which she was not familiar, say in her mind, *"Look at what you are to me!"*

Although only a few seconds transpired, it seemed like an eternity to her. Eventually the invisible hand did release her hair and seem to vanish. She quickly stood up. The blood in her head seemed to evacuate to her stomach as she became heavily nauseated. As she stumbled backward into the turnabout, the breakfast and coffee she'd hope would stay immediately left and colored the dirt with a rainbow of orange, brown, and yellow. Rosanna hated vomiting, even more so than was expected from most people. She wiped some of the saliva soup from her mouth. Despite her best efforts, the dry heaves that followed expanded into another full ejection of anything left in her stomach.

Slowly she regained control of her senses after wiping the throw-up tears from her eyes and slinging a dollop of spit from the corner of her mouth. The disorientation was fading and she could now make out a sound that had been blaring in the background the entire time. The goats in the other barn were bleating loudly, clearly distressed. Ignoring them, she stood back upright and headed to the house.

After a quick cleanup she emerged from the house once again, this time with a dish rag covering her mouth. Rosanna peered into the open doorway, determined to overcome the rash of damaging sensations that coursed through her body. She could scarcely contain her displeasure. "What the... what's in there!?"

Her eyes searched the different clumps of writhing maggots and mobs of flies, but she didn't see a carcass. Upon trying to proceed inside a coughing fit broke loose. Between the diaphragm spasms, she could see the large work-bench and rack of tools she'd seen before. The upper floor that covered only half the length of the barn revealed a small set of stairs leading up from the ground. On the top floor, the only thing she could see was an old wooden chair sitting upright. The way the chair was positioned, obviously years ago because of the cacophony of cobwebs, brought to her mind the illusion of it positioned that way to oversee the rest of the barn. In her mind, however, she *knew* that wasn't the case. She was just becoming paranoid and uneasy again due to being left all alone here. It wasn't that she didn't think she could protect herself, but it always felt better to have someone else around.

Rosanna looked over the insect and larvae swarms again. "What are they eating?" She was no entomologist, but she couldn't see anything to be fed upon where they were. Having sensory overload returning, she resigned to just slamming the door closed and living to fight another day. The voice she heard was filed away under "imagination while under stress" despite being a fully grown adult.

Seventeen

10:00 A.M.

Edward turned the car onto Holly Bush Road. Making their way up the long driveway, both he and Angelica could see the obvious reason for the name. Holly bushes were thick along the edge of the gravel-laden scar running toward the house. The holly, however, was being invaded from its flank by the encroaching weed army that went unchecked for years.

Angelica suddenly lost interest in the botany battle happening on the property. Her face went grim, her gaze fixated on the recently opened barn. The seriousness of her face even scared Edward for a moment, who'd yet to see this reaction from her for himself.

"Hey...."

No answer.

"Baby girl, what's wrong?"

Her tone was robotic and even more distant than her gaze. "She opened it...."

Somehow, despite his best efforts, the sensations of dread were trickling into the recesses of his own psyche, "Opened what?"

The trepidation in his voice didn't sway her answer. Angelica's reply was as direct as a punch in the nose. "The other barn."

Maybe Angelica was stunned by its obvious effect, but he was still trying to evade the issue he knew he couldn't. He could see the door on the "other" barn was shut. "She must've closed it back."

Her jet eyes stared directly into his. She didn't even need to say a word and he knew.

He let out a quick sigh, unable to lessen the effect on his daughter. "I know what you mean, baby girl."

Edward put the car in park. Before they could exit the vehicle, Rosanna was already making a beeline from the backdoor to the Subaru. He tried to say "hello," but was cut off.

"Ed, there's something dead in that barn. We have to clean it out."

He knew that "we" was code for "you" in this case. Edward, once again, was cut off before he could speak. The "look" her parents never wanted to see had come over Angelica's face hard. The disappointment and scorn radiated from her scowl.

"Why did you open it!?"

Rosanna had never heard her daughter lash at her so fully before. It caught her off guard, but she wasn't going to take that tone for a second. "Angelica! Don't you *ever* speak to me that way!"

Edward had instinctively stepped between them. His wife, however, was standing on her tiptoes, looking over his shoulder.

"You do *not* speak to your parents that way!"

Angelica could feel the heat coming off of her mother's anger, but was unafraid. "You knew that place was bad! Why did you open it!?"

Edward was more than aware that this was about to boil over into a war. Ever the peacemaker, he turned to his daughter, still blocking Rosanna. "Angelica, go to your room!"

His daughter stormed off, keeping a piercing, scornful glare on her mother until she reached the porch. After she headed inside, she slammed the door violently behind her.

Rosanna was nearly speechless, partly from anger but also shock. He placed his hands on her shoulders, snapping her briefly out of the river of rage.

"Ed... what is wrong with her!? I've never heard her talk back to me like that!"

He tried to edge a few words in. "Hon, I know."

Her normally pale skin was still flaring red blazes on her face. "What has gotten into her!?"

Edward was starting to sense her cooling down, if only slightly. He kissed her on the forehead, although she was in no mood for it. Edward then placed his hands on top of her head. "Hon, please relax. You're right, she shouldn't have spoken to you that way. We'll handle it. Just try and calm down."

Rosanna managed to take a few deep breaths and regain control of herself. She looked back into her husband's eyes. "What was she talking about, anyway?"

He knew this conversation was probably going to get dicey fast, as opposing beliefs would inevitably come up. "She knew you opened the barn door."

She checked the door on the barn and sure enough, she'd shut and latched it back. Raising her eyebrow in disbelief, "How could she possibly know I opened the barn!?"

Edward decided to water down the words he was wanting to say. "She just knew. I'm not exactly sure how, but she just knew."

Still highly skeptical, she looked over at the door to see the lock was gone and still on the table in the kitchen. Now she had this figured out. "Okay, I get it. The lock's gone. I know she's smart: no magic trick."

He knew Angelica had revealed that her mother had opened the door long before any locking mechanism was visible. In the best interest of peace, he relented, "That's probably it, hon. You know you can't slip anything past her. Mind like a steel trap."

Despite being what she wanted to hear, there was something inside telling her that the explanation was not complete in the least. Staring directly into Edward's eyes, she was hoping to break a confession out of him. "And what's so bad about opening *that* barn?"

He looked over at the windows and doors, which now seemed to be bleeding flies. That unmistakable smell was also in the air. Deciding to slide right on out of this conversation with his cunning, "Because it smells like death...."

Rosanna rolled her eyes, knowing her husband's tricks all too well. "That's the only reason?"

Thankful she'd decide to give up the chase, inherent in her tone, he said with a smile, "Isn't that reason enough?"

Her long sigh almost gave him the impression that the conversation was over. But there was one more matter to settle. "Angelica's grounded for a week and *you* are going to tell her. I'm not going to be the only disciplinarian here."

Edward reluctantly agreed.

Once inside he headed to Angelica, who was shut away in her room. He closed the door behind him, his daughter sitting on the edge of her bed with the same scowl on her face. Kneeling in front of her, "Ange, you can't speak that way to your mother. For what you did, you're grounded for a week."

The scowl was now doused in flammable outrage. "Bull crap! You mean *Mom* said I was grounded!"

She was starting to become a bit much even for his normally smooth temperament to handle. "Ange! You can't speak to either of us like that!" Realizing his own tone of voice showing agitation, he sighed. Continuing in a normal "inside" voice, "Ange, whether or not you agree with what either your mother or I say, you can't yell at us. Is that clear?"

Angelica's expression didn't change. "Fine."

Edward knew she wasn't going to be compliant and this was the best answer he could hope for. "Now stay here and cool down. Do you understand?"

She was now starting to wonder why she had gotten so angry at the situation. The staggering emotions just seemed to come from out of nowhere. She hadn't ever erupted at her mother or father like that. Somehow, however, the anger wasn't fading as quickly as it had come on. Angelica relented, "I understand."

His guard had been lowered a bit. He kissed her on the forehead. "Just stay here until one of us comes to get you. Can you do that for me?"

She nodded.

"Good." Without another word he turned and left the room, calmly shutting the door behind him.

Angelica did lie on the bed, her mind still swimming in a torrent of emotion. The fear, the anger, the dread, the doom, were running amuck inside of her. She had felt relatively tepid versions of these before, but now they were yelling through an amplifier at a metal concert. Edward was right: Her mind was a steel trap. For whatever reasons, ones she couldn't discern yet, that steel trap was doing its best to snap the feet, hands, or face off of anyone without a moment's hesitation. Any answers, however, were not ready to surface. They would continue to stay in the thick fog of the unconscious for much longer.

Not long after, the Kelly family would stop by to demonstrate how to milk a goat. Edward learned pretty quickly, and even Rosanna got her hands marginally dirty trying. Angelica, however, was still confined to her room. Neither her mother nor father would let her spend time with Abby that day. Despite wanting to let his daughter learn this skill and enjoy the company of her friend, she had crossed a line.

While there, John Sr. was as polite as possible about not mentioning the strong smell coming from the "other" barn. Rosanna was quick to apologize for the problem, but was told, "Critters get into barns and die all the time. Sometimes finding and removing them is the hardest part." After all, "You're not going to flush out a dead rabbit."

Before leaving, John Kelly also recommended that Edward build an enclosure outside of the barn for the goats. It would be cheaper than buying feed all the time, and the goats would also do a good deal of "mowing" for him that he'd rather not deal with on top of the large expanse of land.

Edward and Rosanna watched as the Kelly family left, waving to them for a few seconds before walking back toward the house.

 Rosanna was suddenly overtaken by an impulse she could neither explain nor ignore. "We have got to clean that barn out, Ed. It stinks and I don't want Father Anderson to have to smell it when he comes here to bless the house."

He thought he knew where this was going: another item on the honey-do list. "I'll try and find the... whatever is in there."

Rosanna's face became stern. It was strange, however, as a small hint of pleasure peeked out from behind. "No, you're not. *Angelica* is going to find it. We'll make *her* clean it up."

The faint sadism in her voice was unsettling enough, but he knew this would almost certainly bluntly traumatize his daughter. "Hon, it's okay. I can...."

"I *said* Angelica is going to do it!" She was raising her voice for seemingly no reason, no reason comfortably explained in the light of day.

Even though he'd helped Rosanna through bouts of her temper before, there was an overwhelming drive to follow through with this idea in her eyes. He wasn't going to stop her for a second. "All right, if you...."

Before he could finish the words, she stormed into the kitchen and down the hall. *THUD, THUD, THUD* on her daughter's bedroom door. Before Angelica could reply, Rosanna burst in.

"Angelica, since you've insisted on misbehaving today you're going to go and clean out that barn!"

The pouty expression on Angelica's face dropped sharply to wide-eyed fear.

Before she could utter a syllable of protest, "That's an order! I'm not asking you!"

The punishment before seemed harsh: one week of being grounded for talking back. Now asking her to clean the fly-and-maggot-infested barn was just cruel. The very thought of being forced to go in there, much less spend time in there, sent her into tears. Angelica's tone quickly turned to pleading. "Mom, please! Don't make me go in there!"

Edward could hear his daughter crying as he walked down the hall. He was impeded from entering the room by the charged up taskmaster.

Nearly growling, "I said get out there and clean up that barn!"

She turned and blazed out of the room, knocking Edward aside without a thought. Edward was nearly brought to tears himself at his daughter's all-too-real pleading in fear.

Through sniffles and tears she uttered, "Daddy...," as he knelt in front of her.

From the kitchen, Rosanna's voice thundered, "I SAID NOW, ANGELICA!"

Edward whispered to his daughter, "I'll go with you."

They left her room and headed toward the back door.

Rosanna, seeing Edward close to Angelica, shouted, "I said *she* has to clean it up. Not you! Stop sabotaging my parenting!"

He had never seen his wife this angry before. Unwittingly, "Jesus, Rosy, calm down! I'm just making sure she goes."

Edward had lied about this, but she only seemed to care about one mistake he'd just made. "Don't you dare commit sacrilege in this house!" Her accusative finger would've killed him if it were a gun.

He knew good and well she couldn't tolerate taking her Lord's name in vain. "I'm sorry, Rosanna. I made a mistake."

The apology seemed to throw a whole mess of confused thoughts through her head. Unable to process them, she lashed out by smacking a plastic cup from the kitchen table across the room. Without missing a step she pushed through the kitchen into the living room, then out onto the front porch. She slammed the door behind her and began pacing back and forth in front of the front windows.

Edward put his arm around his sobbing daughter, doing his best, but failing, to comfort her. The sentence from this hanging judge was anything but unclear.

Once outside, Edward paused at the door and looked solemnly at Angelica. "I'm sorry, baby girl."

Angelica cautiously approached the threshold as Edward tugged sharply on the bolt. Once open, she was immediately overwhelmed and stumbled backward. As if the flies, maggots, and smell weren't bad enough on their own, Angelica saw a disturbing shape near the rafters. The site nearly took her breath away.

"Daddy, there's something up there!"

Quite distressing to the both of them, Rosanna stepped down from the front porch and walked toward them. Her voice resembling that of a harpy, "What's the matter, Angelica? Do you see a ghost?" Any hidden sadism was now baring itself completely. "There's no such thing as ghosts, Ange! Clean the damn barn!"

Angelica cried harder than ever before as she looked inside and saw a large black humanoid shape hovering near the top of the barn. It didn't move, it just hung there.

Seeing her hesitation, her mother ripped back at her, "Get in there, you little...!" Rosanna suddenly cried out and grabbed the sides of her head in agony. She let out a hissing growl, then turned and stumbled her way back toward the front of the house.

Edward ran toward her with genuine concern as she began to cry out in pain. Angelica, however, stayed stun-locked in between this proverbial rock and a hard place. *Something* in the barn to her right, and *something* that once resembled her mother were two of the choices. She decided to back away and toward the other barn where her goats were bleating as if their lives were at risk.

Rosanna, meanwhile, had fallen to her knees on the grass. The rage seemed to disappear as quickly as it came. All that remained now was fear and genuine remorse. This wasn't her and she and Edward both knew it.

Crying nearly as hard as her daughter, "Ed... what just happened!? I don't know what came over me!"

He had an impulse to chastise her about the barn, but he snuffed it out quickly before it could take hold. "Rosy, are you all right now? What's wrong?"

Her right hand still clasping the side of her head, "I don't know!"

He embraced her, looking over and seeing his daughter equally distraught. "I'm here. You're okay now."

"What's wrong with me? I don't know why I did that!"

Angelica, seeing her mother now under some semblance of control, ran straight toward the backdoor and on to her bedroom. Edward helped Rosanna to her feet, slowly coaxing her to go back inside with him.

Not long after, Rosanna was still trying to get her mind in order. Edward had stepped outside to shut and lockup the doors on both barns. Feeling overwhelming remorse, Rosanna headed down the hall calling Angelica's name. She got no response.

At the closed door to her daughter's room, she pleaded, "Angelica, baby, open the door. I'm sorry I snapped at you like that." Her mother's tears didn't move her to the door. She had even locked the door from the inside. This revelation really struck Rosanna hard. Not only had she lashed out at her, but now her daughter was genuinely afraid of her. "Please... honey, I'm sorry."

It wasn't until Edward had returned and began knocking that Angelica considered opening the door. After a few words from her father, they heard her quietly unlock the door. They carefully pushed on the door and were shocked to see Angelica run to the corner of the room and curl up into a protective ball posture. It would take nearly half an hour before Rosanna's daughter would let her embrace her once again.

Eighteen

The family Subaru came to a stop in the parking lot of St. Mary's School for Girls and Cathedral located in the neighboring county of Cedar Hill. Rosanna had wanted to come to Mass before this first meeting with the assistant principal at the school, Sister Francis, but they were so consumed in unpacking and fix-up chores around the farmhouse that they were exhausted.

The Cathedral itself was fairly grandiose in its Gothic reimagining of the great cathedrals of Europe. The spires and flying buttresses were not on the exact same scale, however, as their attendance was not the same, as say, the mighty Notre Dame of Chartres. Nonetheless, it was a prominent and majestic landmark surrounded by open fields near the edge of town. It was on the same road that led to the highway connecting Miller's Run and Cedar Hill if one were so inclined to avoid the scenic route.

The school building attached to the church was fairly modest in its appearance but large, nonetheless.

Along with the school was an attached quarters where the handful of nuns still taking up residence would turn in for the night at the end of the day. It too was utilitarian and lay in stark contrast to the splendid appearance of the cathedral proper. The nuns there would sometimes refer to it as "the barracks" for its no-nonsense design.

As Rosanna and Angelica approached the front of the school building, the former said, "Isn't this place beautiful?"

Only half interested, mainly from uneasiness about starting kindergarten, "Yeah, it's nice."

Seeing her reaction, "You'll get used to it in no time. Come on, let's go meet Sister Francis."

Once inside the school, they were greeted at the front desk by a woman dressed in a standard habit. The nun smiled and greeted them, reaching over the waist-high wooden barricade separating them and shaking their hands in turn.

"Hello there, I'm Sister Gillian."

Smiling, "Hi, I'm Rosanna Barrister and this is my daughter Angelica. We had a one-o'clock appointment with Sister Francis."

Pleasant and upbeat, "Oh, right! It's nice to meet you two. Angelica, I hope you're ready to start learning!"

The positive energy was too much to keep Angelica withdrawn. She cracked a smile and said, "Yeah, I hope I'm ready."

As Sister Gillian snickered, Rosanna said, "We just moved here from Johnston City several days ago. We live out on Holly Bush Road in Miller's Run."

Gillian wasn't from Miller's Run, so she hadn't heard about the place's history herself. "Oh, okay."

Seeing her unaware, Rosanna replied, "I'm so used to everyone knowing where that place is. I guess if you're not from there the name doesn't mean much."

"That's okay. I've driven through Miller's Run a few times. Beautiful pasture land and rolling hills." She then glanced up at the hands of the electric clock on the wall. "Oh, it's one o'clock now! I don't want to keep Sister Francis waiting. Right this way."

She led them to the wooden door with an inset window pane of fogged glass that bore the words "Assistant Principal" in plain black letters.

As Gillian was still knocking, a nasally and curt voice called out from within, "What is it?"

She cracked open the door and said, "Sister Francis, your one-o'clock appointment is here."

Hardly looking up from the paperwork she was scanning, "Right, send them in."

Mother and daughter entered the office as the former extended her hand. "Hello, Sister Francis, I'm Rosanna Barrister and this is my daughter...."

She was cut off. "Angelica Barrister. I have your application here." The nun saw her hand extended and only returned the lukewarm gesture without getting up. "You may sit down." The tone was more indicative of her allowing her guests to sit down rather than a gratuitous pleasantry.

A brief and awkward pause ensued before Rosanna said, "I hope we aren't interrupting any work you're doing."

Angelica had remained silent the entire time and all at once began to find the appearance of Sister Francis to have a certain quality about it. The normal outline of her was not as defined as everyone else she'd met in her life thus far. She stared.

Sister Francis' tone was still cold and authoritarian. "You're not keeping me from anything. I'm simply looking over your application. Tell me, can the girl count and read?"

Angelica kept staring, her mouth going slightly agape and her left eyebrow raising slightly. She was seeing the blackness from Sister Francis' habit radiating out and mixing with flickering red flame-like emanations here and there. It made for an unsettling aura, even if Angelica didn't know the word yet. The young girl now tilted her head to one side and continued to stare silently. A distant and constant noise began to fill her ears. The sound of a black and vacuous wind began to howl softly as the abyss of her nebulous aura seemed to be staring back.

Rosanna replied, "Well, she can count to a hundred and my husband and I have been teaching her at home with readers we got online. She's doing great so far."

The nun looked up at Rosanna now. "Good to know." Her gaze then quickly shot over toward Angelica. Like a bird of prey her eyes were locked onto Angelica's. "Don't stare, girl, it's impolite!"

For a moment, when Francis turned to Angelica, the latter could've sworn she saw eye shine, like in a photograph. It was gone in an instant, however, as she shook her head and blinked her eyes repeatedly. The noise was also gone.

Her mother then said, "Angelica! Mind your manners."

Looking back and forth at the four eyes looking at her scornfully, "I'm sorry...."

Now looking back at Rosanna, the nun said in short manner, "Very well, here's the itinerary for the first grading period. I also included a standard preschool list of objectives to be taught and learned before the schoolyear begins. Do you have any questions?"

Rosanna replied, "No, ma'am, we understand."

"Very well, that'll be all."

The mother and daughter looked a bit confused and stood up.

The former said, "Thank you, Sister Francis. Have a nice day."

Looking up from her paperwork in annoyance, "Yes, goodbye."

Nineteen

Rosanna placed her phone on the kitchen table after a short conversation.

Edward, who was now standing next to her, asked, "Who was that, babe?"

Looking mildly perplexed, "It was John Kelly. He said that he and his family were coming over to discuss the town's parade that's coming up this weekend."

"Oh, yeah, I think I saw a sign for that when we were at the store earlier."

"Yeah, so did I. He said we have things to do beforehand and that he would help out."

"Hmm, I wonder what we'd need to do to just to watch a parade."

Her eyebrow still raised, "I don't know. I guess we'll find out shortly."

Angelica heard them speaking and was standing in the hallway now.

Seeing her, "Angelica, the Kellys are dropping by again. Make sure your room is straightened up."

She nodded her head and disappeared into her room.

Rosanna then looked up at her husband. "Okay, I'll straighten up in here and you can get the living room."

Several minutes passed before Rosanna heard a brief tap on the Kelly family's truck horn as it rolled up the driveway.

The three Barristers were soon standing in the turnaround between the two barns and waving at their guests.

As the truck came to a stop, Abby was the first to get out of the passenger side. As her brother and parents got out in turn, Mrs. Kelly handed her daughter a wicker basket with a closed top and calico cloth lining.

After greeting one another, Mr. Kelly noticed them eyeing the basket. He said warmly, "We come bearing gifts! Since it's your first year here in the community we wanted to make sure you followed the yearly custom at the parade this weekend." He motioned to Abby, who approached them with the basket. "There's a dolly in there for each of you."

Abby then opened the basket and revealed its contents. Three handmade dollies, of sorts, were fashioned from dent corn (the body and head), hay and straw for arms and legs, and finally blue and pink fabric for simple coveralls and dresses, respectively.

Rosanna looked at them fondly. "Oh, Ed, they're so cute!"

Seeing them hesitate to reach for them, Abby said, "They're yours now, Mr. and Mrs. Barrister. The 4H Club makes these every year."

Mrs. Kelly then said, "Yes, they did a fine job on them this year. The only thing left to do is sew your initials on their clothes. I put some fabric in there for you to use." Looking up at Rosanna now, "You do have a needle and thread, don't you?"

Nodding her head, "Of course!"

"Great! Like I said, each of you need to cut out your initials and sew them onto the dollies' clothing."

Angelica now noticed another detail. "Look, Mom! They even have our hair!" It wasn't their real hair, obviously, but yarn instead.

Edward looked at the straw hat on his effigy and smiled. "Do I need to get a hat like that?"

John Sr. chuckled. "No, that won't be necessary. You *must*, however, sew your own initials onto your own doll."

His stress on the last part of the sentence made Rosanna feel slightly uncomfortable. She couldn't understand why that was so important, but she stayed polite. "Okay, I'll make sure these two don't shirk their responsibilities." There was a slight pause that followed, but Rosanna was quick to fill in the gap. "Oh, I made some sweet tea earlier today. Would you all like a glass?"

They each replied that they would.

She then said, "Great. Angelica, come and help me carry the glasses."

John Jr., however, was quick to jump in. "Don't worry, Mrs. Barrister, I'll help you!"

She agreed as the eager ten-year-old followed her inside. Abby had asked that Angelica show her the goat pin again as Edward talked with Mr. and Mrs. Kelly by the truck.

Inside, Rosanna had two small trays upon which she divided up the glasses.

Still smiling, John Jr. said, "Oh, Mrs. Barrister, I wanted to tell you that if you need any help around the farm, and I mean *anything,* don't hesitate to ask! I'll come running if you need help!"

Oblivious to his clumsy attempt to hide his feelings, "Well, that's sweet of you, John. I'll tell you what, when you turn sixteen and can legally drive, I'll consider that."

Not missing a beat, "Oh, I'm sure Dad wouldn't mind driving me over here. Besides, I already know to drive. I have for years!"

Chuckling, "Well, I appreciate the offer. I'll call you if anything comes up. Plus, when you start looking for a job later in life, you can put me down as a reference for 'agricultural consultation.'"

His cheeks suddenly blushed a little as he backpedaled. "I mean, I'm not trying to say that you can't handle yourself. I'd never want to make you upset or anything... do you know what I mean?"

Still in the proverbial dark, "I know what you mean, Junior. Here, let's get these out to everyone."

Once they stepped outside onto the porch, Junior looked up and could see Abby whispering something into Angelica's ear. The latter looked up in disbelief as the former laughed away. Junior could somehow sense it was at his expense.

Saturday was quick to roll around. The Barristers met the Kelly family at a predetermined spot in a small local bank's parking lot. The streets were lined up and down with what seemed like most of the citizens in attendance. The smells of a few small food carts patrolling up and down the street piqued everyone's appetite, even if the contents therein might cause instantaneous arterial clogging.

Angelica, who was standing next to Abby, looked down at her doll with the initials "AEB" sewn neatly on the front and said, "I wish I could've picked the color of the dress. I don't like pink."

Abby shrugged. "It's tradition. All the girl dolls wear the same clothes and all the boy dolls wear the same clothes."

Abby then looked away as a woman across the street caught Angelica's attention. She starkly stood out from the crowd by posture and clothing. Her solid black dress, somewhat antique looking but with a modern energy, ran the full length of her body to the tops of her shoes. The shoes, dark leather and laced tightly, also were a throwback to a bygone era. In her right hand she rested a cloth parasol that extended over her head. Her dark brown hair was tied back into an elaborate braid with a black ribbon on top. The sun glinted off the circular lenses of her reflective sunglasses. Two small earbuds ran from her ears and down to an iPod she was holding in her left hand. She looked up and down the street as Angelica looked at the dolly also in her left hand. It was wearing a black dress and had the initials "SCG" stitched across the front in white. Angelica also noticed that the people around her seemed to give her a little extra space.

Angelica, then unaware that she was staring for several seconds as she said quietly, "Hey, her dolly isn't wearing pink...."

Even though she was not in earshot, the young lady in her twenties seemed to sense she was being spied upon. She looked up deliberately and cracked a smirk.

Abby, seeing this, said suddenly, "Don't stare at her! She's a witch!"

Angelica snapped out of her gaze and looked at her friend in disbelief. "What?"

Neither of them saw the young lady roll her eyes and walk back into the crowd.

Angelica looked over at Abby and was about to say something when they heard a drum cadence start up in the distance. The local high school marching band was kicking things off and everyone turned to watch. The rank and file of green and gold uniforms, all forty of them, brought their respective instruments up and began to play the high school's fight song. Angelica was impressed with their orderliness as the green plumes atop their gold and green shakos went by with hardly a bounce.

Edward looked down and saw his daughter wanting to see more and picked her up. Holding her up to his eye level, he said with a smile, "You think you'd want to play an instrument in the band?"

"Maybe. It looks like fun."

She watched for a few more seconds before spotting the young girl in the black dress once again a little farther down the road. She was looking on and had removed the earbuds from her ears. It didn't take long before the girl seemed to somehow sense that Angelica was looking at her once more. As she looked up at the curious five-year-old, she subtly smiled. In a restrained manner, she raised her right hand slightly and waved while wiggling her fingers.

Angelica was stunned for a moment, but soon cautiously raised her own hand and waved back. The pale young woman in the black dress didn't look like any witch she'd ever read about or saw on television.

The parade was beginning to wind down after only a brief stint. The attraction at the end, a horse-drawn wagon, was now the focal point of everyone's attention. The wagon was as plain as plain could be and lined with straw. There were two people sitting at the front. Two nuns, one recognizable to Angelica and Rosanna and the other not, rode stoically along. Rosanna waved politely at the older nun whose hands were folded in her lap, but she only looked at her briefly before returning her gaze forward. Rosanna frowned in mild disappointment.

John Sr. then said, "Okay, Barristers, time to give the dollies back."

They were confused for a moment, but upon seeing him and his family step forward and place their effigies in the wagon, they followed suit. Everyone in attendance was doing the same, one by one, in a strange orderly fashion. This wasn't the first time they'd performed this act. As Edward stepped forward he gingerly placed his in the back of the wagon. As Rosanna did the same, Angelica looked down one last time at the felt eyes and smiley face glued to the dent corn before also putting her lot in.

As the wagon slowly moved down the road, Angelica watched as everyone carefully placed their likenesses inside the back of the wagon. Not far away, however, she noticed that the young lady in black simply chucked her dolly in nonchalantly from a distance. This caused the nun she'd recently met, Sister Francis, to look over at her sharply. Angelica didn't need to see the old lady's face to know that she was upset. Strangely, she saw the young lady staring unflinchingly right back at her.

John Sr. then looked over at Edward and said, "Okay, Barristers, now we head to the town hall for the end."

Only a couple of blocks up the road, after a leisurely stroll, the families came to the front lawn of the quaint granite town hall. Most people were standing around on the closed streets and talking amongst themselves quietly. The marching band was not too far away putting their instruments away and placing them next to the school bus that brought them there. It also seemed that now everyone was giving the food vendors more attention. The smell of hotdogs, sausages, and funnel cake filled the air as the families were then waiting in line at a larger vendor cart that had parked on the sidewalk just opposite the town hall.

Rosanna took in a large waft of the flavorful air. "I knew I should've eaten breakfast this morning."

Suddenly, the girl in the black dress came up next to them in line. She looked forward as Edward replied, "Eh, I'm sure there's enough meat here to fill you up."

He wasn't intending on the words coming out like that. They caused the young lady to snicker audibly as Rosanna raised her eyebrows. She smacked him on the arm. "Ed!"

It had just hit him, literally and figuratively. "I didn't mean it like that!"

Angelica certainly didn't get the joke, but was more focused on *not* staring at the intriguing person next to her. She only returned her attention to Edward when he asked what she wanted from the vendor. She vacantly replied, "Hotdog."

As Edward was counting out the money from his wallet, Angelica saw the young lady put a five-dollar bill on the counter and turn around with a small container holding a dark red piece of sausage on it. The young lady only briefly looked into Angelica's eyes as she went past. "Hello."

The voice was as clear as day, but Angelica could clearly see that the woman did not open her mouth. Confused by this, she simply assumed someone had said it nearby. It was strange, though: No discernable direction from which the voice came made sense. It was just there in her mind.

The Barristers met back up with the Kellys soon after that near the sidewalk. After Rosanna had swallowed a bite of her hotdog, she noticed the strange sausage that John Sr. was eating. He casually bit into the deeply crimson tube as she asked, "What kind of sausage is that?"

Seeing her husband's mouth full, "That's blood sausage. I take it you've never tried it?"

Her surprise made her voice a little louder than she anticipated. "Blood sausage!?"

Edward laughed. "Yeah, I'm surprised you've never heard of it. My grandmother used to make that stuff years ago. I never really got a taste for it."

She had reigned her voice in now that she saw others reacting, some laughing. "Oh, that sounds nasty!"

John Sr. replied, "If you've ever bitten your lip or lost a tooth, that's pretty much the taste. People used to make use of every part of the animal, blood and all."

Angelica overheard what they were saying but found her attention still looking over at the young lady in the black dress who was standing alone on the sidewalk at the corner. The woman, Sara, was looking toward the school bus where two sweat-soaked band members were staring at her. The teenagers looked positively frozen like a deer in headlights and having never seen such a "purdy" girl before. It then clicked in her head that she was getting ready to start eating her own share of blood sausage. She abandoned the toothpick previously pierced through the middle and grabbed it delicately in her hand. Sara then slowly opened her mouth and let the pork product settle onto her tongue. The eyes of the two boys were wider than the brass cymbals one of them was using in the parade moments ago. Sara paused, seeing their interest piqued. Her mannerism became more violent, however, as she dug her teeth into the casing and pierced the insides. She intentionally gnawed at it for a moment, the dark red contents inside making her bright teeth appear vicious and sharp. Still locked in her gaze with them she chewed in an also intentionally showy fashion. One of the teens seemed undeterred but the other had unknowingly grabbed his own crotch in some sort of empathy with the sausage. She then rolled her eyes and turned her nose up at them before turning away from them entirely.

Everyone's attention, however, was soon turned to the town hall as a middle-aged woman, Roberta Stevenson, approached the microphone at the small podium on the entranceway to the Town Hall. She spoke plainly and clearly.

"Hello, everyone! It's great to see you all made it to the annual Bounty and Recompense parade. Now, without further ado, I present our beloved Mayor Pinkerton."

They clapped as the mayor and the two nuns emerged in a ceremonious fashion. The crowd had gone deathly quiet as the old man wearing a stereotypical sash bearing the word "Mayor" smiled and began to speak.

"Good citizens of Miller's Run: It is my duty to inform you that this year is…," he paused, letting a little anticipation build before finishing, "a season of bounty! The harvest will be great this year!"

A quiet clap broke out among the people as he continued.

"Thank you all for coming out and I'll be counting on your votes come November."

He then stepped down from the front entryway and began to mingle with the townspeople. The nuns, however, stood stoically at the front doors and didn't say a word.

The Barristers were confused by this whole event, but wanted to simply file it away under strange traditions that had lost their meaning over time.

Twenty

It was around noon when Father Anderson's Ford Focus turned onto Holly Bush Road and made its way toward the turnaround. He was stopping by, at Rosanna's request, to bless the house and property. Edward and Angelica were uneasy about the situation, hoping it wouldn't escalate anything. The latter wasn't quite so sure why she was uneasy, but the former had images of horror films he'd seen over the years flash in his mind. He felt a little silly thinking there would be someone spitting up pea soup or hissing serpents retaliating against the priest's holy onslaught. The dread inside, deep down in the cockles of his gut, gripped him like an icy vice. Rosanna, on the other hand, felt a warm comfort knowing that the priest would sort everything out. She *believed* he would, anyway.

Rosanna stepped forward toward Father Anderson first as he exited his car. She shook his hand and lowered her head briefly before saying, "Thank you, Father, for coming out today. I know the heat is oppressive right now, but we simply felt we shouldn't wait any longer than necessary."

Smiling, "Oh, it's no trouble at all, Mrs. Barrister. It is my job, after all." He shook Edward's hand and exchanged pleasantries before he looked down at Angelica. He kneeled and extended his hand. "Well, hello there. It's nice to meet you young lady. What's your name?"

She replied confidently, "Angelica Eva Barrister."

Edward chuckled as Father Anderson replied, "Well, it's nice to meet you, Angelica Eva Barrister. I'm Father Anderson."

Still confident, "I know."

Rosanna scowled slightly as she looked down at her daughter. "Angelica! You show him the respect he's due! You don't talk to adults that way!"

Father Anderson, however, quickly pacified her. "Oh, it's all right, Mrs. Barrister. She has what folks around here might call 'grit.'"

Her head tilted in confusion. "What's that mean?"

Edward replied, smiling, "It means you're confident."

Father Anderson gently patted her on the head before saying, "Well, Mr. and Mrs. Barrister, if you're ready to start, so am I."

Edward and Rosanna were pleased with Father Anderson's acts. He maintained an air of professionalism and control while performing the cleansing and blessing ritual on their plot of land. His salt-and-pepper hair and impeccable grooming made it clear that he'd done this many times before and was always prepared to do his job and look sharp doing it.

After they had followed Father Anderson on his long trek to bless the perimeter, Edward found himself reflecting as they approached the turnaround once more. No hissing dragons, no recoiling serpents, no baying hellhounds, just the ritual. He did, however, find himself strangely craving a warm bowl of pea soup. He always did like that.

The temporary levity of the day was slowly waning, however, with each step toward the "bad" barn. It was there waiting for them like a dead and bloated skunk baking on the road in the summer heat. Subtly, Angelica and Edward could sense not only the emanations from the barn, but also a drop in Father Anderson's confidence. This seemed to be completely overlooked by Rosanna, as her mood was as stalwart as it had been since the conception of the ritual.

The four stepped up to the barn door. Rosanna opened both doors which seemed to now moan extra loudly, possibly because something knew it would add a drop of uncertainty into the quickly accumulating puddle of dread. Father Anderson continued swinging the censor back and forth as the incense smoke wafted into the environs. Despite continuing to say the prayer he suddenly found his feet stopping their journey forward. It was as if his entire body had received a halt message and his mind was out to lunch. He soon looked, however, and saw that the barn simply looked disused and disheveled. His thoughts and senses, especially the sixth one, were suddenly aware of the negative lump sum of pain, sorrow, and sinister suffering. He cleared his throat before mustering the courage to step forward and continue.

Rosanna then stepped in and failed to notice that her husband and daughter were not going past the threshold. Father Anderson then turned to where his left side was visible to the two who dared not step in. It was then that they saw something remarkable and very deliberate (the source of which was unknown at this point). The censor, previously swinging side to side, was suddenly knocked back toward Father Anderson's leg. The metal clanked loudly before it thudded against his leg and rattled out burning ashes onto his pants legs. The four looked on in acute horror as the cloth near his shoes ignited. For a moment it looked almost as if he'd been trudging through ankle-deep gasoline before starting the conflagration. Angelica shrieked briefly as Father Anderson fell to the ground and tried to put out the fire with his bare hands. Rosanna feverishly threw dirt onto his burning slacks as Edward ran toward him. It wasn't until Father Anderson grabbed his bottle of holy water from his front pocket and doused this impromptu bonfire before it went out. Thankfully he always kept one extra bottle on him, just in case of emergencies. This was the worst one, by far, that he'd encountered.

Father Anderson limped away from the whole incident with only minor first- and second-degree burns on his ankles and shins. They did seem to take a long time to heal, but he simply chalked it up to being advanced in age. The Barristers felt an obvious amount of debt toward Father Anderson. After all, things did calm down after the blessing had finished. The party, however, was just getting started.

Twenty-one

For Angelica, the next three years would go by at the normal slow-motion pace in the way children perceive. It was toward the end of the summer and she would be starting the third grade that fall. As with the end of each summer, she was sad to resume her school schedule which would involve spending less and less time with her best friend, Abby. The two of them had developed a strong bond over the years despite attending different schools. The weekends during the school year, and the majority of the summer nights, would find Angelica staying over at the Kelly house. All things considered, the routine and relationships had become more normal and quiet at the Barrister home, but Angelica still preferred to spend the least amount of time required there. The tumultuous events of their first weeks there wouldn't be forgotten, but tension between Rosanna and her daughter had lessened dramatically. Rosanna was also getting along with Edward once again, and a happy, normal lifestyle had fallen into place for the three of them.

Edward had acquired most of the equipment he needed to maintain his property, mainly through neighbors and occasionally from one of the farm supply stores in the county. It was a hassle mowing such a large acreage regularly, but he found the time alone on the tractor to be soothing most of the time. He wouldn't worry about the work that needed to be done for the architecture firm, nor any disputes that may have arisen between Angelica and Rosanna.

With some help from John Sr. and Jr., he was able to put up a sturdy fence around what would become the enclosure, topped with a roof attached to the barn, for their three goats. He and his daughter had become quite efficient at taking care of their animals, and anyone that didn't know otherwise would swear they had grown up on a farm themselves.

One important thing on his to-do list was not forgotten: He taught his daughter to swim. She took to it surprisingly well. Both he and Rosanna were concerned that it might cause some sort of flashback, or at least overdrawn anxiety, given their experience on their first day there. Quite the opposite had actually happened. Their daughter would quickly become an excellent swimmer. The acquisition of the skill had actually made her stronger. Perhaps Angelica had even learned at her early age, that whatever doesn't kill can make you stronger, if you allow it to happen. Many people may have given in to the fear and avoided open water for the rest of their days. This simply wasn't the case with Angelica. Facing her fears and learning from her experiences would guide her habitually. This bravery impressed both of her parents.

Her academic performance in school also left little to be desired. "A's for Angelica" became a standard saying in the household. If her teachers had anything to complain about, it was only that Angelica tended to be a loner. She wasn't unpleasant or unfriendly, she simply preferred to be by herself. She found most of her classmates to be relatively immature and was in no hurry to surround herself with them. Out of all of Angelica's accomplishments, however, Rosanna was most impressed with her daughter's choice to receive her first communion. Rosanna had maintained constant, but gentle, pressure on her daughter to do so. Perhaps the answers to why weren't as clear in Angelica's mind, but her mother felt that she had simply made the best choice. It was, to Rosanna, perhaps the most important decision in her life thus far.

Perceiving her daughter to be on the straight and narrow, she would occasionally turn her attention to Edward and his indecisiveness on the same issue. Sure, he was attending weekly services fairly regularly, but she and he both knew that he still wasn't one-hundred percent on board. In many ways he felt content with where he was at that point, and he didn't see any obvious motivation in moving to a new level of commitment. Edward had learned about the inherent urgency in needing to get his soul and spirit affairs in order before passing away, but for reasons he wasn't even sure of, he balked at the proverbial pitcher's mound.

As they welcomed the peace that was temporarily disturbed earlier, they made the most of their new life. Sometimes the water recedes, sometimes it swells. Other times, the hand of fate seems to pull away, perceived as welcome mercy, only to be winding up for the next punch to the face. After all, the water always pulls far away from the shore before the tsunami. In the end, the balance is always settled.

Twenty-two

Early August

Angelica had woken up early that morning after a relatively sound night of sleep. The rash of nightmares during her first weeks there had ceased for the most part. Only stock and standard dreams came to her. She had a strange dream that caused her to wake early that morning. The only thing she recalled from the scene, however, was her three goats standing around in her room and eating the cables and cords attached to her computer. Upon waking, she only attributed it to her regular early-morning chore: feeding and tending her pets.

Not long after returning from her chores, she quickly finished up her breakfast. Tossing her fork aside, she headed straight for the basement door. Opening it, she took the small basket hanging from the nail in the upper panel.

Seeing this, Rosanna asked, "You going to pick berries?"

"Yep!"

Smiling, "Bring me a bunch of blackberries and I'll make a pie for you two later. Sound good?"

"Okay!"

She darted past Edward's chair at the table and out the door. Outside, she quickly made tracks past the two barns. The barn on the left still gave her and Edward the creeps sometimes, but she'd become accustomed to just trying to ignore it.

It took her a couple of minutes running at a moderate pace to reach the destination: the mass of blackberry and raspberry bushes just beyond the bridge. Barely paying attention to her sharp breathing, she began picking the sweet, dark purple fruit. Angelica soon developed a rhythm, "One for the basket," *pluck,* "and one for my belly," *pluck.* She repeated this pattern over and over, stuffing herself near capacity having just recently eaten breakfast: the taste being too good to ignore.

The basket she brought was filling up rather quickly as she dexterously picked away. The rays of morning sun were shining more brightly now through the thicket and into her eyes. A beam caught her eyes at just the right angle, momentarily causing her to turn away. She struggled to blink away the flash that flooded her eyes with blinding luminescence. Upon regaining her vision, Angelica let out a sharp yelp, backing away from the figure that was now partially visible through the thorny growth around the berry bushes. Her fear was heightened even further as the figure of a pleasant looking older woman walked through the vegetation completely unobstructed by the punishing foliage. None of the plants having moved an inch, the figure stopped just at the edge of the shorter grass in front.

A warm smile stretched across the face of the elderly figure. "Don't be scared, dear. I won't hurt you."

Angelica stopped backing up and was unable to look away from the female adorned in plain clothes from more than a century ago. A straight and plain blue dress, adorned in front by a white apron, and topped with a modest brown bonnet. Angelica had sensed things, oddities in the environment, and even the shadowy mass in the "bad barn." This was the first time she'd seen a spirit fully formed, and it was standing only feet from her. In the back of her mind, she'd hoped the blessing put on the property by Father Anderson would have put an end to all of this. Proof that it hadn't was now staring lovingly at her with pale blue eyes and a wrinkled smile.

Angelica was surprised that she managed to get the words out. "Wh... who are you?"

"My name is Caroline, dear. What's yours?"

She was overcome with hesitation. I guess the early years of "stranger danger" speeches were really paying off now. Nonetheless, the word flowed out. "Angelica."

The uneasiness was obvious, but Caroline continued. "You got some blackberries there? They're wonderful this time of year, aren't they?"

Almost forgetting what she was doing, she glanced back down at the basket. "Yeah.... What are you?"

Caroline giggled. "I'm a person, dear! What are you?"

This sort of response insulted Angelica's intelligence, causing her to raise an eyebrow. "Then how did you walk through the plants there?"

Still grinning, "My, you're a smart one, aren't you?"

The uneasiness had caused her to override her usual manners. Cutting her off, "And why are you dressed like that?"

Caroline wagged her finger in front of Angelica before gently saying, "It's rude to interrupt adults." Seeing a brief look of shame come to the eight-year-old's face, she continued. "I used to live near here many years ago. Now as others come and go, I stay here and watch over the place. Ever hear of guardian angels?"

Angelica, still anxious, nodded her head.

"Well, good! You could say I'm the guardian angel of this property."

Angelica grabbed the crucifix around her neck. "You're an angel? You don't look like an angel."

Caroline started laughing, which didn't help ease the young girl's tension. She replied, "I'm a spirit, little one, and spirits don't always appear in the same way you'd imagine. I decided to stay here years ago. You know, that priest who came and blessed the property really helped more than you know. There are all sorts of bad spirits roaming around out there." Caroline then looked down at Angelica's clasped hand. "What's that you have there, dear?"

"It's a rosary...."

One corner of her mouth, barely perceptible, raised slightly higher than the other. "Isn't that... *cute.*"

Not able to understand her response, "Cute? What do you mean?"

Still beaming a smile, "I mean, it's too big for you, that's all."

Her eyes still locked on Caroline's visage. "I'll grow into it one day."

Seeming to be satisfied with Angelica's answer, "I'm sure you will." Seeing the apprehension still with her solo audience, "You don't need to fear me, dear. You have a special gift. Most people can't see me, but you can."

The answer caused her to tilt her head to one side. This gift wasn't something she remembered asking for at any point. "Why?"

"Well, why are any of us here? Life doesn't always make a whole lot of sense."

"I guess you're right."

The tension had dissolved some after this agreement. "There's a good girl. Now, someone on this property may ask you for help. If you're able, try to talk to him."

Now Angelica was really confused. "What do you mean? Who needs my help?"

Caroline quietly chuckled before replying, "You'll see. He'll come to *you*."

Still unclear, "What do I do to help him?"

"I'm sure you'll figure it out."

The answer was not as illuminating as she'd hoped. Any other inquiries, however, were thrown aside as Edward then called out his daughter's name, walking toward her down the path. Angelica looked in his direction and waved, then back to the thick bushes. Caroline was now nowhere to be seen. She looked all around, even peering to a shallow depth into the thick growth.

Edward approached her. "Did you lose something?"

Concern had crept to her face. "Someone was here just a second ago... but now she's gone."

Curiously, "Oh? Who was here? A neighbor?"

She glanced back at the bushes once more, then rejoined her father. "She said she was a spirit. She said she lived near here a long time ago."

"Really? Did she tell you her name?"

"She said it was Caroline."

"Was she a nice spirit?"

Still a little uncertain, "She *seemed* nice."

The conversation was certainly hitting home with him again. "Well, that's good. Did you get a good look at her?"

"Yeah, she was in pioneer clothes."

He put his arm around her. "Sometimes you'll see nice ones. If they're good to you, you shouldn't worry about them. I was pretty scared too the first time I saw one."

"How do they just show up and disappear like that?"

"I'm not sure how they do that, sweetie. What did she have to say?"

"She told me she was like a guardian angel for the land."

He hadn't felt any overwhelming negativity himself, and was relieved. Smiling, "Well, that's a good thing, right?"

Angelica nodded as he continued.

"We could all use an extra guardian angel."

The tension had melted away from his daughter.

He continued. "All right, then! Let's see if we can fill this basket up for Mommy."

Twenty-three

Later that afternoon, Angelica was lying on her bed staring blankly at the ceiling. She was waiting for Mr. Kelly and Abby to swing by their place and pick her up. There was pleasant anticipation at the thought of being with her friend, but it was heavily overshadowed by something Caroline had said earlier. Who was *he*? The one who supposedly needed help. What sort of help could she possibly have to offer? And this so-called *gift*... even though Edward never called it this, Angelica knew they shared this wonder of fortune. She couldn't yet see how it could help anyone. After all, when most people in your circle of friends and family, and even society in general, scoff at the idea, who do you turn to? Edward was certainly experienced in its effects, but he'd sought to block it out from earlier in his life and seemed to offer no explanation on how to actually use it for anything.

She was snapped from her personal reflections by her mother calling from the kitchen, "Angelica! Abby's here!"

Without hesitation, Angelica rolled off and rose from her bed, grabbing the nearby sleeping bag and bee-lining it for the kitchen post haste. At the back door she gave a brief goodbye to her parents before dashing to the waiting Kelly truck. Tonight they would be camping in the small patch of woods on the edge of John Sr.'s property. There was also another level of excitement, as she and Abby would be staying there with only John Jr. to watch over them. This detail may have been left out in the description given to Rosanna, but the new sense of autonomy was too much to pass up.

Not more than fifteen minutes later, they arrived at the Kelly farm. Once inside the side door, they greeted Mrs. Kelly, who at least shared the same hair and eye color with her daughter. Most of Abby's features, however, could be traced back to Mr. Kelly and more directly to his mother. She turned from the sink full of dishes being washed and waved to her daughter's friend.

"Hey, Angelica! You guys ready to go camping tonight?"

"Yes, ma'am!"

John Jr. entered the room from the adjoining hallway and greeted them as well.

Mrs. Kelly continued. "Good! Now Jonathon, you make sure to be nice to your sister and behave yourself!"

John Jr. hadn't really been a total jerk to his sister, but sibling rivalry was there, no doubt. He grinned at his mother. "I know, I know. I'll make sure they're asleep by eight o'clock, too."

Angelica playfully growled before yelling, "John! Don't be a punk!"

John Sr. had walked through the side doorway just then and couldn't help but laugh at the conversation he was dropping into. "Careful, Junior! They don't call her Angie-bear for nothing!" The nickname Abby had for her friend, "Angie-bear," was more a play on the sound of her last name, Barrister. But like many nicknames, it had started to take on a life of its own. Sr. continued. "Go on and get your camping stuff ready. And help them carry their stuff, too."

John Jr. disappeared down the hallway toward his own room as Abby said, "Hey, Ange, you want to see the new .22 Dad bought me?"

Angelica agreed and the two raced off toward Abby's room.

Sr. called out, "You two be careful!"

In unison, "We will!"

Mrs. Kelly asked over her shoulder, "You didn't give her any of the ammo for it, did you?"

He kissed his wife on the cheek. "Of course not."

Inside her bedroom, Abby took the small rifle from her bed. Holding the pink-stocked matte-gray bolt-action rifle in front of her with both hands, she proudly said, "Here it is! Isn't it cool?"

Angelica was overcome with a bit of awe at the weapon. It was something she'd never really been exposed to up until this point. Edward kept a pistol locked away in his safe, and had only taken it out once to warn Angelica about its danger. Even though the rifle before her was far less intimidating, she dared not touch it, only eyeing it up and down.

"Wow...," she whispered in disbelief. "It's yours?"

Even though she'd spent many a night there, John Sr. had kept the firearms and use of them away from Angelica. He had now, however, grown to like Ed and Rose Barrister and even call them friends. Now that he considered his daughter old enough to start shooting herself, he was comfortable letting Angelica learn as well. This was only, of course, after a thorough safety speech and shooting lessons. Today would be the first.

Seeing her uneasy about handling it, Abby said, "Go ahead. It's not loaded. Dad checked a dozen times."

She took the rifle in hand carefully and pulled it up to her shoulder, pointing it away from her friend and toward an outside wall. Angelica was not a fan of pink, but withheld her disapproval. "Have you shot it yet?"

Abby was saving this surprise, having restrained herself from trying it out for seemed like an eternity, but was only about thirty-six hours. "No, but *we're* going to test it out here in a minute."

The statement took a second to process. "Wait... *we're* going to? I get to shoot it, too?"

Giggling at the joy being given to her friend, "Of course! I wouldn't want you to miss out. It'll be fun!"

Her mouth dropped open momentarily in disbelief. "Ah... cool!"

John Jr. now stopped at Abby's open door, wearing a large backpack. "You two ready?" They turned and answered affirmatively as he continued. "Go ahead and put that in the case, Ab."

"I know; I am." She picked up a small carrying case from the floor nearby and closed the rifle in it before they all gathered their camping supplies and headed out for the woods.

Twenty-four

John Sr. had driven them up to the stretch of woods at the edge of his property. It was within walking distance, but he didn't want to make them haul their gear over multiple trips. There he helped his passengers find a nice place to set up their tents. They also had a pile of chopped wood nearby for the campfire they'd be making that night. John Jr. had already gone to the trouble of clearing out a space on the ground and surrounding it with stones from nearby. With two logs set up facing the fire pit, it would prove to be a relatively comfortable adventure.

After their site had been squared away, John Sr. took the three kids to the field nearby and lectured them on the ins and outs of firearm safety. All of his students passed his surprise quiz at the end as well. With the help of his son, he taught Abby and Angelica how to fire the small rifle. Abby was already trained a small amount, but she was still upstaged by Angelica, who seemed to grasp the fundamentals quickly and the regular plinks on the spinner target set up attested to that. She even gave John Jr. a run for his money on the bullseye paper target placed fifty yards away.

As the friendly marksmanship contest had finished, John Sr. pulled his son aside out of earshot of the girls. He said in a lowered tone, "Now Junior, you make sure and stay on watch. Keep that shotgun with you at all times. If anyone you don't know or didn't invite shows up, you make sure they know you have that and you're not afraid to use it. You know things can get crazy this time of year."

His tone was gravely serious despite his normal mischievous one. "I know, Dad. I won't take my eyes off them."

He patted him on the shoulder before saying, "That's my boy. Now you three start getting ready for tonight."

Later that afternoon, as the sun was well into its daily decent toward the hilly horizon, John Sr. was already back at home. John Jr. had managed to get a healthy fire going in the pit at the campsite. He also had his loaded double-barreled 12-gage shotgun propped up against a nearby tree.

Angelica noticed it and asked, "Hey, John, what's that for?"

He replied, "Just in case any wild animals bother us. Well, in case *anything* tries to hurt us."

She could tell that he was intentionally leaving the last part vague. She'd heard rumors on the playground at school that it was dangerous to be alone as a kid in Miller's Run. Angelica, however, attributed that to just gossip and a repeat of the "don't leave your kids alone" rhetoric she'd heard pertaining to all children, no matter which city or town they lived in.

He then started digging around in the large red Igloo cooler as Angelica and Abby sat on the logs and shared a quiet conversation. One by one he took several ingredients in premeasured amounts from Ziploc bags. Carrots, celery, peppers, and other vegetables were tossed into the black cooking pot set up next to the fire. After adding the chopped meat from the final bag, he hung the pot over the fire via a large metal tripod overarching the blaze. He stirred the ingredients before putting the metal lid on top of the vessel. He then checked his watch and passed out the preferred cola drinks.

After cracking the seal on his can, he took a drink. "You two having fun?"

The two girls nodded and he continued.

"So what do you two want to do?"

The two shrugged at each other before Angelica asked, "Do you know any good stories?"

John Jr. thought for a moment and answered, "You want to hear the story of that twenty-pound catfish I caught at the lake?"

Unimpressed, Abby said, "We've heard that one a million times. And the fish gets bigger every time you tell it."

Angelica giggled as John replied, "Oh, okay. You want to hear *ghost* stories?"

The smile quickly dropped from Angelica's face and John saw it. John had no idea how personal that subject was for her and would be left in the dark still. Abby herself wouldn't be adverse to it, but she'd noticed the change in mood also.

John turned to his sister now, trying to maintain levity. "You're not scared, are you, Abby?"

Trying to keep her dignity against her picking brother, "I'm not scared, John. The only thing I'm scared of is how much you stink!" She wasn't going to draw blood with that insult, but it was the best she could come up with on short notice. John was thirteen at this point, so of course his odor might have gotten the better of him some days.

Laughing, he retaliated. "Whatever, Ab! You still pick your nose!"

For that, she rose to her feet and walked over, smacking him on the arm. Hardly hurting at all, John continued his laughing fit.

During this time, however, Angelica had a strong impulse come to mind. Afraid to speak, but unable to hold back the words, "What happened at my house?"

The laughing stopped, but he was still smiling. He'd wondered if she'd said what she just said and wanted more clarity. "What do you mean?"

Looking him straight in the eyes, "I mean, what happened at my house before we moved in? No one talks about it, but I know something happened."

He had turned his gaze down after she said this. The orange glow of the fire made his face look darker than usual. His brown eyes were now burning with the reflection of the fire.

Without looking up, "You really wanna know?"

Angelica nodded.

"Okay, I'll tell you what I know. Both of you have to promise not to tell Dad."

They nodded.

"Cross your heart?"

They each made the gesture and followed up with, "Hope to die and stick a needle in our eye."

He thought to himself a moment before continuing. "Now, this is what I've heard. I don't know which parts are true, but this is what I know. You understand?"

The two girls looked at each other briefly before nodding. The sun had become occluded by the trees at this point. A plethora of insects were sounding off from all angles, trying to find a mate or just making noise for their own personal reasons. Who am I to pry? In any event, darkness and firelight were going to make this a story they'd never forget.

John Jr. sighed and began. "Here goes....

"Back in the forties, a man named Amos Harris, the man who owned the property before your family moved in, started his own farm on the plot of land which used to be part of a bigger stretch of property. What happened to Amos before that was pretty tragic. On his eighteenth birthday, he went to sign up to fight in World War II. That same day his father died while working on the Sifters Dam at the edge of town. He didn't have long to mourn because he was sent to boot camp shortly after. His younger brother and sister helped their mom out as best they could until he got back in '45.

"When he got home, his sister had just turned eighteen and his younger brother sixteen. Amos stayed and helped them for a couple of years, but eventually got married and bought the land you guys live on now. He and his brother built the house and barns that are still there today.

"Soon his wife had a baby and he was runnin' his own farm. He grew wheat and corn, had a milk cow, a few hogs, chickens, and a mule if I remember correctly. Things went really well for him for a couple of years. He had everything he could've wanted.

"Then later, for seemingly no reason, everything went to hell on him. He started drinkin' a lot. And when I say a lot, I mean *a lot*! He was stinkin' drunk almost every day! Amos even started hittin' his wife and kids for no reason. The slightest thing would set 'im off and boom! Some said it was because of the war, others because of money problems he ran into with the farm. Even though the economy was good, he had trouble payin' the bills."

He paused to take a drink from his soda can.

Abby took the opportunity and said, "I bet he was having trouble with money because he bought beer all the time."

Angelica quietly looked on at Jr., mesmerized by the story and the hypnotic flickering of the flames.

Jr. continued. "I'm sure it didn't help. Anyway, he stayed that way for a while. By the time Amos' son was eight, things were lookin' bad for the whole family. The prices he was gettin' for corn and wheat started to go down. The animals he had started gettin' sick and actin' crazy. The mule supposedly just ran off one night and never came back. The cows stopped makin' milk and weren't good for much at all. Now, if that weren't bad enough, his son ended up dying on the property. Word was he wondered off on his own one day and got lost in a cave. They never found him."

He was cut off by Angelica. "He died in a cave on our land!? I didn't even know we had a cave... not that'd I'd want to go into it now."

John continued. "That's just what I've heard, so that may not be true. Either way, his son died. Anyway, the death of son drove him completely over the edge. Somehow he managed to stay drunk every single day of the week. He drank like a fish.

"Things kept getting worse for him after that. Not three months later his wife died of a heart attack. Doctors said it was the damndest thing at her age. She was just twenty-four."

Abby interjected. "I thought she died in a car wreck."

John answered, "I've heard that before, but mostly I've heard heart attack. Now let me get through the story, Ab."

She looked down and apologized, her brother continuing.

"All right. After his wife's funeral, he rarely, if ever, left his property. After folks in town noticed they hadn't seen Amos in about a month, they sent a couple of guys out to check on him. When they got there, they couldn't believe what they found. Amos had shot himself in the head! They knew he'd been there at least a week. He was all bloated up and covered in flies and maggots like a dead opossum on the side of the road."

Abby cried out, "Gross, John! You didn't have to say that!"

John responded, "Well, that's what I heard!"

Angelica seemed to finally snap out of her trance. "What happened after that?"

John replied, "After that, I think his brother tried to work the land for a couple of years, but moved out before he went and started his family. Since then a couple families moved in and out, but never stayed more than a month or so. They say the place is cursed, but I don't know about all that. That's just what I heard." He then looked down at the pot of stew over the fire and stirred it a couple of times. An idea suddenly struck him and he looked down at the empty backpack lying on the ground. He fumbled through it quickly and said, "Dangit! I forgot the bowls and spoons. Abby, keep stirring the stew while I go to the house and get 'em."

Abby rolled her eyes, but stood up and took the wooden spoon. "Hurry up, John, we're getting hungry."

He hardly looked back as he jogged away. "I will, just keep stirring the pot!"

Once John was out of earshot, Angelica asked glumly, "Was he telling the truth?"

"I've heard the same stuff but who knows if it's true."

Angelica, with some despair in her voice, "But I have to *live* there!"

Abby looked over at her, a little surprised at the gravity in her concern. "Abby, I need to ask you something."

The wooden spoon in her hand wasn't stirring anymore. "What?"

"Do you believe in spirits?"

She looked to the darkened forest and back. The shotgun propped up against the tree caught her eye. Its power as a defensive tool, however, lost its power when talking about spirits. The volume of her voice dropped, perhaps in an attempt to hide it from anything incorporeal listening in on their conversation.

"You mean ghosts?"

"Yeah. People who've died but stick around."

Abby was still reluctant to admit it, perhaps thinking one may spring on them in response. "I don't know… I guess. Sometimes I hear stuff at night, but Dad says it's just the house settling or animals pokin' around." She returned to stirring the stew.

Angelica stepped closer and placed her hand on Abby's shoulder. "Can you keep a secret?"

She nodded.

Angelica then whispered in her ear, "I've seen spirits at my house before!"

Shocked, "For real!?"

Alarmed, she looked around briefly, then responded scornfully, "Shh! Don't tell anyone! People will think I'm crazy!"

"When did you see them?"

"Today, but it's happened a few times before when I first moved in."

"Wow... why didn't you say anything before now?"

"I didn't see any for a while, so I thought maybe they'd left or something. And like I said, I didn't want to tell *anyone*. My mom doesn't believe in ghosts and gets mad if I say anything about it."

"I'd be scared if I saw ghosts!"

"Usually I wish I couldn't, but I don't think it works that way."

An idea suddenly sent chills over Abby's body. "Are there any here now?"

Angelica could sense something nearby, but decided not to worry her friend. "I don't *see* any right now. I try and ignore it when I can... if I can." Angelica then stared at the ground as a small frown broke through.

Abby put her arm around her. "I'm sorry, Angie-bear. I wish you didn't have to see them."

"Thanks. I wish I didn't have to see them either."

Abby looked around once more. Seeing no one, she said secretively, "They say there's a woman that lives on the edge of town. They say she's psychic and can read minds. That's just what I've heard, though."

Genuinely surprised, "Really? What's her name?"

"Sara Goodwin. She lives in the big old house on Parris Road."

Angelica's eyes widened. "I've seen that house from the road. Well, I've seen part of it. It's hard to see through the trees."

"You can see it from the river. I've been fishing on our boat before and saw it. It's really scary looking." Abby looked up and saw her brother in the distance, then said quietly, "I've heard other stuff, but I don't know if it's worth telling."

They both turned to face Junior, halting all conversation. It was an obvious sign to him. "Uh-oh. You guys talkin' about me?"

Abby replied with sibling ire, "We have better stuff to talk about, John."

He snickered. "Yeah, right! Hey, why'd you stop stirring the stew? It'll burn!"

Twenty-five

Late that night, Angelica had a vivid and lucid dream:

A blast of wind pushed Angelica toward a bridge nearly identical to the one on her father's property. There was a storm moving in, the distant thunder and lightning heralding its arrival. The water of the stream was already swelling and threatening to overtake its usual flood-banks. Eddies were forming and dissolving in the muddy brown water as white crests appeared frequently in the torrent. Seeing the bridge and flood before her, she turned and looked behind her. As far as her eyes could see there was nothing but a sea of thorn bushes seven feet tall. The blade-like barbs jutted out in all directions covering the plants from earth to sky.

She turned back around and saw that across the bridge a path continued through a similar forest of thorny plants. The difference being that these thorn greeneries were adorned with blood-red roses. Angelica took three steps to the edge of the wooden structure and was shocked to see that the flora across the gap was dripping crimson ichor, despite the clear raindrops.

She hesitated for a moment before starting the way across. With her first steps the timbers of the bridge began to creak and moan loudly. Instinctively she rushed to the side and grabbed the wooden rail boards.

When only a quarter of the way across a bright flash of lightning nearly hit the bridge, causing her to fall backward and become temporarily blinded. Fully soaked by the rain now she crawled back to the edge of the warping

conduit. As her vision returned, she saw the figure of Caroline standing be-
fore her in the middle of the wide oak cross-ties. The water didn't seem to
affect this elderly apparition. Her clothes and skin remained perfectly dry.
With an emotionless expression she said, "Listen to me, little girl. Do not
believe the lies the people around you say. They cannot see what you see and
do not understand what you know. Your father chose to throw his gift away,
but you still have a chance." Seeing Angelica slowly sliding her way back-
ward, "You have to learn to trust me. Other spirits of the world will try and
harm you. They will not be as kind as I am." Angelica then pulled her way
to her feet, not saying a word. She stared mutely at Caroline for what seemed
like an hour, but of course dreams have a way of distorting these things. The
elderly spirit then said, "And do not think that witch on the edge of town
can help you. She'll corrupt your soul with lies and trickery."

Another flash of lightning and the form of Caroline was gone. The
bridge then began to groan even more loudly as it lengthened in size by six-
fold. Angelica tried to make her way across but was helpless as the opposite
bank moved farther and farther away.

Angelica snapped awake on the inside of the tent. From the light beginning to shine through the vinyl Coleman, she could tell it was early morning.
She looked to her left and saw Abby still fast asleep. Unable to quiet her
mind, she lay awake staring off into the distance.

Twenty-six

Angelica was brought home the next day around noon. Her thoughts were consumed with the sighting of Caroline the previous day and the strange dream she'd had the night before. Edward and Rosanna noticed that she was more distant than usual, but didn't worry about it too much. After all, she tended to brood from time to time and it never seemed to last. Edward had kept the encounter Angelica had from Rosanna, seeing no obvious reason for concern. The dream from the night before, however, made Angelica nervous given the change in tone from friendly old woman to an entity of whom she'd been unable to ascertain the motives. The image of Caroline's face stayed burned in her mind. She didn't even have to close her eyes to see the gaze of the spirit. One peculiar thing about Caroline's image was quirky: Her ears looked like oyster shells. Age is rarely kind to anyone and the form stuck in her mind was no different.

There was also, however, something else that intrigued Angelica. When she sought to recall the other details of the apparition, the details were hazy at best. Sure, Caroline had been seen in the same modest attire that covered her head to toe, but there was something more to it. Something elusive.

Angelica spent most of the day inside. The heat of the midday had dissolved away as gray clouds and deep bluish purple thunderheads were filling the sky. At least the hours of computer games and web browsing were enough to keep her mind off of her now nagging insight. The image of Caroline was persistent along with a growing sense of curiosity about the story she'd been told. Her intuition was telling her that there was an obvious connection. Angelica still couldn't think of how she was supposed to help anyone. Was it the man who used to live here? His son, perhaps? The encounter she had early on with Fetch was also not forefront. She thought of asking her father for advice, but there was a growing resistance in her mind to do so. He hadn't offered any advice on what to do when she'd started seeing and sensing things before (at least that she could recall). And a thorn that was stuck in her mind was another thing Caroline had said, how he'd chosen to throw this *gift* away. She supposed she was going to have to figure this out herself.

It was around 10:30 P.M. when Rosanna entered her daughter's room. "Ange, start getting ready for bed, okay?"

The thunder in the background was much closer now as the rain steadily sheeted outside. "Okay, just a few more minutes, please. I need to get to a save point on this game."

"All right, sweetie, don't forget to brush your teeth." She walked away and pulled the door closed.

Minutes later she shut down her computer and got ready for bed. As she finished, Edward came in to tuck her in. Angelica jumped into the bed and pulled the covers up to her neck. Her father kissed her on the forehead.

"All right, Ange, sleep tight."

She returned the sentiment, but he noticed the feeling of uneasiness that was hiding behind her face.

"You okay, baby girl?"

Even though she knew he could sense something was amiss, she stuck with her best poker-face. "I'm fine."

"Is the storm bothering you?" He had a feeling it was more than that, but it seemed like the correct parental response.

In a matter-of-fact tone, "I'm not scared of storms."

He believed her. "That's my brave little girl! Goodnight."

Sleep came quickly and quietly.

Twenty-seven

Later that night...

The storm has increased to a wild barrage of rain and lightning outside. Angelica suddenly sat up from her bed at a loud crash of thunder. The lightning only momentarily illuminated the room. The normal nightlight on the nearby wall was nowhere to be seen. A strange yellow light, its source unperceivable to Angelica, drew her attention down the hall outside of her room. She was seized by momentary fear, but found the pull of the light to be too much to resist. Slowly she crept from the bed, unable to see the floor beneath her feet. Another flash of lightning showed her that nothing else in her room was different, so she walked toward the light in the hallway.

Once at threshold of her room, she looked to her left and saw the source of the light. A small yellow orb, like some sort of constantly burning firefly, darted toward the kitchen. Unable to resist its pull, she slowly walked down the hallway. She was, however, unable to see any features around her clearly and was forced to grope along the walls to guide her to the kitchen.

The fight-or-flight response was already activated in her mind now, but the glow of the light, now just outside their back door, was illuminating the back porch area. The orange glow of the overhead lights at the front of the barns was barely visible, but enough to give some sense of perspective.

Angelica took a couple of steps forward but quickly stopped as something began to take shape on the opposite side of the door's window no longer covered by a curtain. She strained her eyes and was soon able to make out a humanoid shape blocking out the light. From what she could sense, it seemed to be a man. Oddly, however, his head looked to be lying limp on his right shoulder. His neck seemed to have lost its living rigidity. Her mouth dropped agape, her throat unable to make a noise.

The humanoid shape suddenly lunged at the window. He caught himself with his forearms on the outside, his lopsided face pressing close to the glass. A raspy sound, perhaps human speech in the loosest sense, penetrated through the windowpane. Angelica was frozen in fear, wanting to run. The darkness around her, however, seemed to imprison her. The faded tone coming from the man grew a little louder. Barely able to summon the strength, he uttered, "No... you can't... help...."

She stood silently shivering with fear for a few seconds before a large blast of lightning outside was followed by an echoing crack of thunder. In an instant, the figure of the man was seemingly deliberately ripped away from her vision. Angelica then, for reasons that seemed to override her fear, walked toward the door. Once there she stood on her tiptoes to look out the door's window. Unable to see anything, she darted to the windows lining the back porch. In the distance she saw a series of three lightning strikes hit the ground far away. From what she could tell they struck in the patch of forest at the edge of their property, the hill running parallel to the back porch obstructing her view.

Barely a moment passed before she started to hear liquid dripping in the kitchen. At first it seemed to be coming from the sink, but she quickly realized that the drops were increasing in frequency and their sounds were coming from all around. The fluorescent light beneath the cabinets next to the sink began to flicker on and off at random. It was enough for her see that the liquid dripping inside the kitchen was not rain, but a thick viscous substance that seemed vaguely familiar. Instinctively she was repulsed by it and started to back down the hallway. Once there she could now make out the sounds of the dripping again, only this time coming from her bedroom. The nightlight in her room was blinking on and off regularly, giving her enough reference to make it to the door. A pattern of three short flickers, three long flickers, and three short flickers again repeated itself over and over.

Standing at the doorway, she was terrified at the sight of the black substance seeping in from all over the ceiling of her room and falling to cover everything inside.

She darted back into the hallway and toward her parents' bedroom. Instead of finding the normal wooden door left half open every night, she saw a solid black steel door void of any openings.

Seeing no other way out Angelica ran for the stairs at the end of the hallway opposite the kitchen. She raced to the top and was struck by the sight of the black liquid now coming from every room's ceiling upstairs relentlessly. Suddenly a few drops of the substance fell on her skin. She cried out in pain as it burned the flesh on her forearms and the top of her head. As she then ran back down the stairs, she tried to frantically swipe the searing liquid from her body, but was unable.

Once back down in the hallway she ran to the steel door blocking her parents' bedroom. Angelica slammed her fists and forearms repeatedly against the cold metal again and again, but got no response. All at once, the house was briefly lit up by a flash of lightning, followed by a deafening crash of thunder. She saw the black bile all around her on the floor bubbling and churning....

Angelica shot awake in her bed, screaming bloody murder at the top of her lungs. Once subsided, she breathed sharply as the sound of Edward and Rosanna getting out of bed brought her back to the here and now.

Her father flicked the main light in the room on as he approached her bed. "You okay, Ange?"

As Rosanna looked about the room in concern, Angelica said breathlessly, "I had a nightmare! The house was flooded with something... and I saw a man on the porch... and...."

Edward hugged her. "It's okay, baby girl. It was just a dream. You're safe now."

Rosanna placed her hand on her daughter's back and looked at the alarm clock next to the bed which read 3:10 A.M. In her most soothing motherly voice, "You're okay, Angela. Do you want to sleep in our bed tonight?"

Her daughter nodded.

"Okay, let's go and get some sleep."

Twenty-eight

The next morning when Edward awoke, he was not surprised to see the bed vacant of Angelica. He had seen her get up at around 4:30 A.M. and disappear into the living room. As usual, Rosanna would not be disturbed from her slumber.

As he made his way to the kitchen, he waved at his daughter who was flipping through the channels in the living room. He whispered "good morning" to her and she said the same. Once on the linoleum floor, however, he noticed Angelica had quietly snuck behind him and quickly dashed past him to the dish rack next to the sink. She took a coffee mug from the other dishes and held it out in front of her. She wiggled the cup and Edward chuckled.

"Rough night?"

Angelica nodded.

He winked at her and replied in a hushed tone, "Okay, just don't tell you-know-who." He took the cup from her as she went back to the living room.

He made the coffee a little less potent that morning, not wanting to wind his daughter up too much. They shared a quiet cup together watching early morning television. He asked her if she wanted to talk about her nightmare, but she decided to just let it be.

After finishing their morning revival, he took the cups to the kitchen.

Following close behind, Angelica said, "I'm going to go and check out the woods today. Is that okay?"

He finished rinsing the cups out. "That's fine, just watch out for poison ivy."

"I will. Can I take the machete?"

Edward thought for a moment, hesitating a bit to give her the go-ahead. He was struck, however, by how much of an adult his little girl was becoming, even at just eight. Like most parents agree, they grow up too quickly. Despite the potential for a tongue-lashing from Rosanna, he relented. "All right, but be careful with it. Remember what I showed you."

"I will." Angelica disappeared down the hallway and into her room to change clothes.

A couple of minutes later, she emerged again in her bibbed overalls, now a staple garment for rural life, and a t-shirt.

Edward met her at the back door and patted her on the top of the head on the way out. "Be careful, sweetie. Be back in time for lunch."

Her walk turned to a quick jog once she stepped onto the grass. "I will!"

Once at the barn on her right, she went inside and quickly found the machete and a flashlight. Today she was going to be exploring, but she had no idea what she was going to find. John Jr. had mentioned a cave in his story, and she couldn't recall seeing one or hearing about it before that. The curiosity and sense of adventure pulled on her like a steel cable. She couldn't resist.

She had fed the goats really early that morning, but stopped by to check on them again. All three were quite familiar with people in general and enjoyed the affection she would dote on them, even if their rude "goat manners" didn't always suggest such.

Satisfied that her animal friends were secure she made her way up the then muddy path leading to the bridge. The heat of the day was already starting its stranglehold on the thermometer, making it clear that they were still in the kingdom of summer. She had found a way to secure the machete, in its sheath, around her shoulder and onto her back. The powerful Maglite was protruding from the top of the deep pockets on the side of her pants. Angelica was ready to conquer the woods and maybe the world.

As the trail neared the bridge, she stopped in her tracks. About fifty yards away, partially obscured by the berry bushes, she saw a humanoid shape manifest that she suddenly remembered seeing. Her mind was immediately hit by a word from the ether: *"Fetch? Fetch what?"* Still not understand the meaning of the word or its significance, she watched as the silhouette ebbed and grew erratically. It seemed confused about whether or not it even existed. Consciousness only partially manifested. Like the first time she saw him, it made her uncomfortable as she unconsciously made a connection with "it." Confusion and pain. She then seemed to spontaneously learn how to pull herself away from it mentally, a skill she would need from then on.

Suddenly, not far from the shambling essence of Fetch Price, in the grass next to the path, she briefly saw the form of Caroline come into view and just as quickly disappear. Still trying to locate the elusive figure, she was startled by a squawking bird that nearly hit her in the side of the head before disappearing into the mass of leaves in a short solitary maple tree nearby.

Her attention was now fully on the tree. Hearing the bird continuing to cry out in a shrill tone, Angelica then saw a clump of dried grass just over three feet off the ground. As the bird suddenly emerged again and zinged past her face, she got the hint from the protective parent: "Stay away from my nest."

As she headed back to the path, her attention was again pulled away by the sight of Caroline walking through the briars and toward the woods in the distance. Angelica then crossed the bridge over the high level of silt-laden water rushing underneath.

Soon enough she was at the edge of the woods but quickly came to the realization that she has no idea of where to start looking or what she may even be looking for. The patch of forest was large enough to easily hide something like a cave entrance, if such a thing were even there to be found. Then, as if on cue, she saw the shape of Caroline again farther down the dirt trail through the trees.

Angelica made her way a few hundred yards into the forest, the trail getting more and more choked as she went. One final spotting of Caroline's form seemed to lead her eyes to a hill of limestone hiding deep behind a thick overgrowth of vines and weeds. She couldn't make out any details from her vantage point, but saw what may have been a very slight walking trail, essentially overgrown, leading to the natural wall. She and her father had always assumed it to be just a hill of rock. Her intuition was now telling her, however, that there was something more there. She walked up and down the dirt path parallel to the embankment, but couldn't find any details beyond. Angelica then knew she was going to have to hack her way through to get closer and investigate.

Already sweating from the heat, she thought to herself, *I should've brought water.* She briefly considered going back for a bottle of such, but the drive to find out what was potentially beyond pushed her forward. She quickly found what seemed to be the path of least resistance toward the wall and swung the drawn machete for the first slash of many through the thick leafy resistance.

Nearly thirty minutes later she finally reached the limestone barricade. Thankfully the pines growing just around the perimeter had shed enough needles over the years to quash out any other plants from growing nearby. This offered a nice buffer zone in which she was able to walk around unobstructed, her head swimming from fatigue and the thick foliar aromas. Now drenched in sweat a brief summer breeze offered her a welcomed breath of fresh air. Her arms were a little tired from all of the hacking, but she didn't let it stop her. Each of the large sections of rock had their own personality. Some looked sullen and tired, covered in moss and dark with moisture. Others were more protruding and seemed to be headed skyward. One even hung out over a relatively clear area in the forest floor offering temporary shelter to any passersby. Angelica only mused on this for a short while, however, as the drive (which had then started upgrading its priority to *need*) to find a cave stuck with her.

Angelica searched up and down the face of the rocks for several minutes before seeing a small valley between two large rocks leading at nearly a ninety-degree angle into an area unable to be seen from the trail at all. Now she was hitting pay-dirt. Quickly she darted around the bend but stopped dead in her tracks. In front of her was a large wooden door, painted grayish white to blend in with the surrounding stone, stopping any further progress. To accommodate the natural entrance, it was pitched at a forty-five-degree angle. It was obvious from the attention to detail that whoever built this had placed it to last. There was cement patched all around to fill in any gaps on the edges, and the latch on the side was sealed shut by a rusty Masterlock.

Angelica looked more closely at the cement, however, and noticed small cracks here and there. Without hesitation she sheathed her machete and threw it on the ground nearby. She then quickly walked back through her makeshift path and ran back toward the family home.

A couple of minutes passed before she slowed from her jog and walked into the "normal" open barn, the other seemingly hurrying her to move along. She was relieved to not see her parents around, as they might ask why she needed the tool she was looking for: a sledgehammer. Being very familiar with the layout of the structure, she quickly found the two-handed utensil. Despite being lopsided in weight and cumbersome, she gripped it in her right hand and took off back toward the forest.

Upon reaching the path she'd made to get to the cave entrance she was overcome with the need to stop and catch her breath. The weight of the hammer and the run back had taken its toll on her body, but her mind wouldn't stop racing with the anticipation of discovering the unknown beyond the door. She took only a few deep breaths before trudging along her path and reaching the wooden barricade. Angelica then looked over the edges of the door where the patched cement was weakened with age. Finding a satisfactory spot, she took the hammer in her hands, raised it overhead, and slammed down on the target. Relatively large pieces of cement fell off underneath the nearby hinge, but the door itself was still attached strongly via the other two hinges and opposite latch. She raised the hammer overhead again and struck at the next hinge plate down. This one, however, was firmly embedded in the rock below with heavy screws and didn't budge. Undeterred, she continually struck the hinge again and again, but to no avail.

Angelica paused for a moment, heavily winded and momentarily dissuaded. The thought of stopping now seemed ridiculous and quickly give way to a frenzied series of searches for potential ways to get in. Propping herself up partially on the handle upon which her hand was resting, she leaned in to get a closer look at the latch itself. Even though the lock looked like a sufficient deterrent, the sight of the more heavily rusted latch seemed to present itself as the solution. With new vigor, ignoring the pleading of her heart and lungs to slow down, she smashed away on the fastener. The metal loop through which the lock was secured began to bend and warp with each strike. Soon enough it broke apart and fell to the ground along with the lock itself. Upon seeing this Angelica paused. What she'd been tearing away at had finally given way, but deep inside a current of apprehension desperately tried to get a last warning through. She thought to herself, *I need to catch my breath first.* The subsequent deep breaths she took were hardly sufficient, the thoughts in her mind always returning to heading inside.

One final deep breath, partially from being out of breath and also to try and sate any apprehension in her mind, before she reached down and grabbed the edge of the door. Angelica had yet to explore a cave and the blast of cold air coming from inside surprised her as she threw the door open. The chilled air offered a well-needed break from the summer heat outside, and she quickly took the Maglite from her pocket. A quick click and the area just inside the doorway was illuminated. She saw a path inside the small entryway sharply turn to her right and disappear in the direction of the hill beyond. Angelica poked her head in through the doorway, looking around the antechamber several times before realizing how much she was stalling. It was as if there was a battle for control in her mind. On one side was the insatiable thirst of curiosity and on the other an increasing amount of anxiety. She tried to reassure herself that it was simply the darkness and alien environment that was causing this. It was just enough to push herself through across the threshold. Inside she looked over the gray-and-brown walls of the cave and was somewhat disappointed by their lack of strange shapes, stalactites, stalagmites and crystalline shapes she'd seen in copies of *National Geographic* in the school library. The path leading deeper into the cave then beckoned strongly and she followed.

After giving the room a onceover, she walked toward the gap in the stone and around a corner. This became a narrow crevice and continued down a passage sure to weed out any claustrophobic adults, but wide enough for her frame to walk down without issue. As she shined the flashlight up and down the ceiling, she was delighted to see several small stalactites hanging overhead. Angelica mused on them for a few seconds before her eyes were pulled away by a slight and fast movement farther inside. It was as if something darker than the pitch-black void had been in sight only a split second and disappeared. Her eyes were then darting back and forth along with her flashlight, trying to see something. Only the thick emptiness beyond was there.

Seeing nothing further, Angelica continued on the path which slowly wound down at a very gradual gradient. Her Maglite caught something new then: the vastness of an open room much larger than the entrance room by far. As her interest piqued, she quickly stepped into the opening and was awestruck by the vast rock formations hanging from the ceiling and rising from the floor. Here was something of much greater interest. It was one of Mother Earth's hidden prizes for those willing to crawl inside. Angelica's mouth shaped to form the word "Whoa" but produced no sound. The discovery of this room alone would've been more than enough to satisfy her curiosity on most days, but the allure of what was beyond was still tugging away at her. The deafening silence caused a momentary ringing in her ears, almost drowning out the faint echoes of drops of water coming from the ceiling and plunking on the floor. Once again, however, her fascination of the room was interrupted by the darker-than-night shape darting into the distance at the far edge of the cathedral-like room. This little game of "hide and go seek" was getting stranger and more uncomfortable every minute. Despite this, her curiosity pulled her again to follow it.

She approached the roughly ovular opening and noticed a striking bit of artwork on the wall in a relatively flat spot. Standing about three feet away she shined her light up and down the scene and was reminded of images she'd seen of early prehistoric cave art at school. This one was different, however, in that it didn't show people hunting animals or the like. Strange humanoid figures, mostly human, but in the center of this pagan congregation were "men and women" with elongated snouts and pointy ears coming from the tops of their heads. In the center was a massive representation of what looked like a totem or statue of a dog-headed focus of worship. The artist, from centuries before, was able to show the frenzy and vigor of the event with the limited tools at hand: charcoal and basic clay colors.

For several moments she looked up and down scene, unsure of what to make of it. Inexplicably, she could hear the sounds of the drums being pounded around the circle of devotees, their frenzied calls and cries. What stood out most, however, was the strange howls, barks, and bays that came along with them. The line between canine and human seemed extremely blurry at best with the ruckus.

She didn't notice that she'd started leaning toward the wall. She also didn't seem completely in control of her hand as it reached out toward the images. As her digits got within inches of the surface of the rock, it was stung all over by what seemed to be an aura of icy air that left the positive numbers of thermometers far behind.

"Ow!" she quietly cried out, pulling back her hand rubbing it with the other.

The momentary shifting of the flashlight in her hand made the room almost completely void of light for a few seconds. The pain in her hand quickly seemed to dissipate, however, as she heard a distant growl followed by a sharp bark. She froze. Her eyes were nearly bugging out of her head she scanned the direction from which the sound came. Only the sound of her breathing was heard as she desperately tried to figure out why she was still wanting to go farther despite being scared out of her mind.

Moments passed as she tried to pull herself away, but to no avail. She glanced back at the artwork which now stationary and silent, then started walking deeper into the cave. Again, another passage turned a corner and journeyed on and restricted in size to a new opening. This new portal was a cramped fit, although not as much as the previous passageway, and she cautiously made her way down farther. With each step she could hear the distant sound of trickling water getting louder and louder. As her flashlight shined down the long corridor of naturally carved limestone, Angelica saw another room beyond, opening up. Yet again, she saw a shadow dart across the opening. This time, however, she was able to see more detail. It looked to be in the shape of a younger person, maybe three feet tall. Most people may have run and never looked back at the sight of this, but still, the desire to know more wasn't letting go.

Several steps later and she entered a large opening in a room round in shape. The air seemed thicker here, colder, and stifling. Her mind became cloudy, making concentration difficult. Angelica shivered, partially from the sweat still on her skin cooling her down too quickly now, and partially from a sliver of heavy metallic fear running up her back. This room was different in most every sense of the word. It was the unseen that seemed to be stronger in presence and more aware. She took the Maglite and tried to find a continuation of a trail, but only saw openings here and there along the upper part of the walls and ceiling. With her attention drawn above, she didn't notice the humanoid shape manifest before her. As Angelica's flashlight beam dropped back down, however, she screamed sharply and fell backward. The echo of the sound reverberated as she tried to make out the shadowy figure before her. Sure enough it looked like a younger boy more and more as its form became more defined with each second. With her own eyes bugging out of her head she saw that the eyes of the boy in front of her are as the last things to come into focus. Angelica's mouth quivered uncontrollably as a slight and mischievous grin crooked his lips. His subsequent giggle created no echo, making Angelica even more disoriented. Then, as if in a sign of aid, he extended his right hand toward her. She didn't move, not daring to present her own hand in return. The boy's head then cocked to one side, then the other, as if perplexed.

Angelica continued to stare mutely at the boy for what seemed like an eternity. He appeared to be wearing a recognizable garment: dark bibbed overalls and a long-sleeved shirt. His skin was glowing white, his dark hair covering the sides of his face. His expression didn't change from the precocious smile as the room suddenly got darker and much colder. Her flashlight was now catching what seemed to be shadowy smoke coming in from the openings up high. The dark substance slowly filled the room, causing her to drop the Maglite. Before she could retrieve it, however, an icy sensation spread across her skin. At first it seemed to be all over but quickly coalesced into a forming shape. Her skin was burned in what felt like a large band of frost constricting around her legs, torso, and finishing around her neck. Angelica strained to breathe and grabbed her throat in futility. She tried to rise from her knees, but could only fall and save herself from crashing face first by a split second. The ethereal frost squeezed tighter and tighter, the pain from which was the only sensation she was able to perceive as her conscious world slowly slipped from her grasp, drop by drop. A small and desperate surge of adrenaline only roused her momentarily before she fell to the floor quietly.

The gleaming pale skin of the boy's face and his glowing yellow eyes were the only thing Angelica could clearly see. The breath coming from between his sneering lips felt as cold as any freezer she'd ever encountered. Suddenly a frigid and burning pressure pressed her lips closed: his finger. He snickered, then whispered, "Shh shh... don't struggle. They like it when you fear. They like it when you fight. Just accept...." Her mind writhed fiercely, causing the perception of her body to do the same. The boy's laughter became louder, he rearing his back and impishly cackling. Regaining his composure, he pressed his finger harder, burning its form into her lips. "Shh... just accept it... let them feed on your light...."

Twenty-nine

Angelica's eyes fluttered, allowing in a small amount of light. All she could make out, however, were two large glowing yellow orbs above her. The sudden sensation of pain now was all too real. It felt as if it were all over her body, burning like fire. She could feel her body thrashing and resisting against an unseen force. The searing sensation now became more focused, grating more and more against the inside of her throat and into her chest. Here came another shot of adrenaline from her body, its instincts in full blown fight mode. Her eyes then finally opened and she could make out a familiar image: Abby's face.

"Angie-bear!? Angie-bear!"

Just as suddenly, however, her face disappeared. Now Angelica's senses were coming back online completely, and there was something indeed lodged deep inside her mouth and down her throat. With this completely foreign object refusing to budge, she grabbed the plastic tube taped to the side of her mouth, gagging and squirming. Her hands, however, were quickly wrested away and pulled to her side and held against the metal railing of the hospital bed.

She looked up and to her side, seeing an unknown face. It spoke to her.

"Angelica, lie still. We're going to have to remove the breathing tube." Her tone was direct, but compassionate. The words got through, were heard and understood, but the will to fight and live simply overrode the instructions.

Only a couple of seconds later, she felt a warm sensation flow up her arm and could feel her struggle lessen. The meds were fast-acting and halted much of her struggle without her consent. They were, however, necessary if the breathing aid was going to be removed without damaging her internally. The feeling of discomfort from the tube being lodged inside was now changed into the equally unpleasant sensation of it being removed.

The negative pressure upon its released caused her to cough and gag fiercely as a familiar voice, "Ange! Baby girl, you're awake!"

That was Dad's face all right, bursting through the wall of nurses and doctors. Such an intrusion into their workspace wasn't welcome and he was quickly pushed away from her vision again. Even though she was starting to piece together where she might be, she was still far from an answer on what happened. The spit tub provided by one of the nurses was nice enough as Angelica continued to hack and cough, spitting up sputum with the occasional speck of blood.

Several minutes passed, the urge to cough lessened and waned, but never quite left. A penlight shined in her eyes a few times here and there, people in scrubs looking at clipboards and writing things down. She was able to look up and see the clock on the wall: 3:30. And from the blackness apparent through the tops of the curtains, A.M.

As the pain in her throat and chest calmed, she felt a strong burning sensation coming from all along her body, feet to throat. Angelica put her hand up to her neck and felt the taped gauze.

A nurse then said gently, "Don't pull at that, sweetie."

As she gritted her teeth in pain, her lip contorted, making her aware of another acute location: the burn on her lips running from right beneath her nose to her chin. She groaned and tried to make herself more comfortable in bed. The mess of tubes taped to her right arm caused her momentary discomfort, but her attention was drawn to her left as they allowed her mother and father to enter the room. They were slow to enter through the lake of scrubs, but a smaller person was able to race around to the other side of the bed. Abby was there.

The nurse she nearly ran over looked down at her and laughed. "Be careful!"

"Angie-bear! I knew you'd make it!"

Her friend's optimism and spirit caused Angelica to smile. Before she tried to speak, she fought off a surge of dizziness, likely from the "cocktail" of meds they had given her. It hurt to speak, but she forced the air through her raspy vocal cords.

"Hey, Abby...." She struggled and pushed herself up in bed to see her friend better. Smiling warmly, "Glad you could...," a hard gulp later, "be here."

Their conversation was interrupted by Edward, who had now managed to make it to her bedside. He kissed her on the cheek and cupped his hands around the back of her head. "Thank God you're okay!" He eagerly hugged her, a little too tightly.

She gasped. "Easy, Dad!"

He quickly apologized as Rosanna, standing beside him, took her hand and squeezed it tightly in hers. "My goodness, you're freezing!"

Angelica replied, "I know...."

After asking for the ubiquitous "more blankets," her face of relief dissolved into one of parental concern with touch of displeasure.

"Angelica, what were you doing in that cave? What happened to you?"

As a small frown came across Angelica's face, Edward said in distaste, "Rosy! The inquisition can wait."

She squeezed the bridge of her nose between her fingers, trying to quell the urge to question her or show reproach to Edward. Rosanna felt he'd chosen the word "inquisition" very deliberately, perhaps mocking her faith. This was what she *thought*, anyway. This, however, wasn't the time or place to start a holy war.

She sighed. "You're right... I was just worried."

Abby spoke up again in her usual cheery tone. "Nothing can stop Angie-bear!"

Angelica chuckled, but was interrupted by a fleeting coughing spurt.

Rosanna, having abandoned her scorn, responded in levity, "I don't think all the security guards here could pry her away from you! She hasn't left for a second since you got here!"

As Abby stared at her friend and smiled, a tear streamed down her face. Trying to keep her composure, "That's it! You can't go anywhere from now on without me! Got it?"

Angelica was surprised that a couple of tears were slipping past her normal guard as well. "Okay... I guess I'm stuck with you then." She squeezed her hand tightly but was suddenly struck with a realization: time loss. Looking over at her parents, "How long have I been here?"

Rosanna replied, "Almost two days now."

As Angelica attempted to put the pieces in place, a doctor, complete with standard issue lab coat and suit, entered the room. Given the care and attention to his wardrobe and grooming, the head physician. His gray hair made it obvious that he'd been doing this for quite some time, and the plastic puppy-dog tag attached to his stethoscope was a dead giveaway for pediatrics. His caring blue eyes behind his glasses lit up as he saw his patient quite awake and aware. Cheerfully, "Well, it's good to see you awake, Angelica! You had everyone quite worried!"

Her dry response was something he wasn't ready for. "*You* were scared? How do you think I felt?"

Her tone with an adult wasn't to her mother's liking. "Angelica!"

The doctor's candor broke the tension immediately. "I bet you were! By the way, I'm Doctor Stevenson. I've been looking after you since you got here." He took the stethoscope from around his neck and warmed it on the sleeve of his coat. "Let me just listen to your lungs." He instructed her through a few breaths, listening in front and behind before saying, "Well, everything sounds great, all things considered." He stopped to write a couple of things on her chart before continuing. "Now, Angelica, how much do you remember? What exactly happened?"

She decided to leave out the part about the apparition of the "boy" she'd seen and kept it as secular as possible. "I really don't remember much. I was in the cave and I passed out."

Nodding his head for a moment, he continued. "What about these burns on your skin? Any idea how they got there?"

Angelica thought for a second, and even with the full explanation, it still wouldn't make much sense to anyone. "I saw some sort of black mist. I remember feeling the burning, but I don't know what caused it."

The doctor's face was showing some perplexity, despite his attempts to hide it. "Black mist, huh? That's a tough one. The burns don't look like chemical burns. Here, let me check your neck." He gingerly removed the edge of the bandage on her neck and looked over the wound. "We didn't find any residue, so we weren't sure how they got there. I'm sure you know, but they're all over you, from your feet to your neck." He looked closely at the rod-shaped burn on her lips. "And this one on your mouth is strange, indeed." The doctor folded his arms and sighed.

Edward spoke up. "We found her in the cave like that. She went there by herself, so we have no clue what they are."

Doctor Stevenson continued. "Yes, I have that on my chart. I can't say I've seen anything quite like this." He made a clicking sound in his mouth briefly, then said, "Well, I'll let you all get back to visiting. I'll be back in to check on you later, okay, Angelica?"

She responded "okay" as he left, her parents thanking him on the way out.

As he closed the door, Angelica looked over toward the sink. "Can I get some water, please?"

Edward went to get up, but Abby beat him to the punch and grabbed a cup on the table, filling it quickly. Taking the cup from her friend's hand, "Thanks, Ab." She quickly gulped down the water and placed the cup on the table tray bedside.

"Need any more?"

Smiling at her doting friend, "No, thanks."

The four of them relaxed for moment but before they were able to return to private conversation, a middle-aged woman dressed in a "power suit" complete with drab beige skirt and top entered through the door. Her tone was very business-like, and her demeanor the same. "Hello, I'm Doctor Penelope Jackson." She didn't seem too concerned with the visitation she'd interrupted. "Mr. and Mrs. Barrister, I'd like to speak with Angelica alone for a few minutes, if that's okay." She hardly looked away from her clipboard, making it clear she really didn't care if they approved or not.

The two of them knew what she was trying to imply without her even saying a word. The woman's stern face and securely pulled brown hair gave the image of someone tightly wound and "on a mission." They knew she was going to ask Angelica if *they* had inflicted the wounds. Edward and Rosanna were not pleased at all, for one instant, at her unspoken accusations. Somehow, Angelica could sense this as well. Her parents, along with Abby, reluctantly stood and left the room, knowing that any protest would be "duly noted." She pushed the door closed even though Edward was pulling it shut from the outside.

Starting again rather abruptly, "Now, Angelica, as I said, I'm Doctor Penelope Jackson."

Despite the doctor's take charge tone, Angelica interrupted. "What kind of doctor are you?"

The interruption felt rude enough, but she didn't mind explaining her credentials. "I'm a Doctor of Psychiatrics. Now, I just need to ask you a few questions." She looked down at Angelica momentarily before looking at her clipboard again. "How did you get these burns, Angelica?"

The air and attitude of the psychiatrist was enough to annoy her alone, much less the unspoken direction of the questioning. She showed only some of her agitation as she replied, "I already told the other doctor what happened. I was walking around in the cave before I saw a black mist start pouring in. I felt the burning, then I passed out."

Nary a breath could slide in the gap before the doctor continued. "Now, Angelica, I want you to know that you can tell me anything. You can trust me." The woman's tone and bedside manner were anything but trust inducing. She finally looked into Angelica's eyes as she asked, "Who did this to you? Was it your parents?"

Even this hard-nosed stalwart was not prepared for the withering glare that came to Angelica's face. This was one of the worst glares that had ever crossed her face. The corner of her lip raised, baring a few teeth. The voice that came out sounded more adult and sure than any the psychiatrist had ever heard.

Without hesitation, "No! My parents did *not* do this!"

Still taken aback, she tried to regain control of the conversation. "Uh... Angelica, I'm not saying your parents are bad people, I just...."

Cutting her off as sharply as any razor dared, "I *know* what you are trying to say. I told you everything I know!"

Still back-peddling from the crisp and direct tone, "Okay, Angelica. Look, I'm sure you've been through a lot and it's really late. I'll go ahead and let you get some sleep, okay, honey?"

Honey!? Her attempt at endearment at this point was pathetic and not taken seriously at all. Angelica's eyes were wild with fire. "Right... leave me and my family alone!"

Dr. Penelope Jackson wasn't able to shake Angelica's scornful gaze for an instant as she backed out of the room and closed the door behind her.

Thirty

It was about 7:30 A.M. when Dr. Jackson's Ford Focus pulled onto Holly Bush Road. She was there to perform a routine inspection of the Barrister property as a follow up to her line of questioning not long before. Of course, Rosanna and Edward were offended by the very thought of being neglectful parents, but they knew that going along with the demands of child protective services was the only way to go. Edward wanted to be there with Rosanna that morning, but Rosanna insisted on meeting Dr. Jackson there by herself. She had more confidence in her own unflinching attitude and so decided to take the matter into her own hands. In a half-joking tone, Rosanna whispered to Edward, "I can take her." Rosanna, of course, had no intention of actually slugging it out with the uppity shrink, but the proverbial mustard was more than strong enough to defend the family's honor.

Rosanna stood focused on the driver as the car came to a stop. Both women were there for business and so the handshake was all formal and to the point.

"I thank you for meeting me this morning so early, Mrs. Barrister. I don't want to cause your family any more trouble than you've already been through. Know that I'm not here with the intent of taking your child away, nor am I implying that you're bad parents. I wouldn't be doing my job if I didn't perform a standard visit. Do you understand where I'm coming from, Mrs. Barrister? We want nothing but the best for your daughter."

Stone-faced, "I understand. I have no qualms about showing you our home."

"Glad to hear that. First, if you don't mind, I'd like to take a look inside your home."

Motioning toward the back door with her hand, "Very well. Right this way."

Soon she stepped into the kitchen through the door which Rosanna held open for her. "Thank you, Mrs. Barrister." She wrote a couple of words down on her clipboard before continuing. "You have a nice kitchen here. The one in my own apartment is very drab." She glanced over at Rosanna, who was standing with her arms folded, clearly in no mood for idle pleasantries. "Well, everything in here looks fine. Would you mind showing me to your daughter's bedroom?"

Motioning toward the hallway with her hand, "Not at all. This way."

Once at the open door to Angelica's room, "Well, this is a nice room. Better than the one I had growing up. Being a little girl, though, I figured there would be more pink things."

Not returning the small smile she was allowing to step out into the open, "She doesn't like the color pink. Hates it, to be honest."

Dr. Jackson wrote down another note before continuing. "Well, from what I've seen, she certainly seems headstrong."

Rosanna allowed a small ray of pride beam from her face. "Just like her mother."

Somehow reassured by her words, "The world needs more headstrong and sure women these days. The days of being chained to the stove are over!"

Tilting her head to the side ever so slightly, "I actually enjoy cooking. My family finds it invaluable."

Dr. Jackson was not sure how to react. The statement didn't fit her narrative at all, nor was that answer expected.

Still staring her directly in the eyes, "Do you not know how to cook food?"

Small hints of discomfort were leaking out. "Well, I honestly eat out most of the time. Can't say I have much time to do so. I can't imagine having to cook for two other people *and* myself."

"It's not difficult. It's simply a responsibility that many people have neglected nowadays."

A short and uncomfortable silence ensued as Rosanna savored her small victory. Dr. Jackson, however, was the first to rejoin the conversation.

"Well, Mrs. Barrister, would you mind showing me to the cave where the incident happened?"

"No problem at all. This way."

A few minutes later and they were at the entrance to the cave. As the two approached, they were quick to see Edward's modifications to the door. He had reinforced the original door with pressure-treated lumber and had installed new hinges, two new latches, and fresh concrete. To make sure that would not be the only improvement, he had also replaced the old Masterlock with two new ones, one securing each new latch. There were also thick chains now running parallel to the horizontal boards that were chained below to the limestone entrance. It would take a very deliberate and concentrated effort to get into the cave if someone were so inclined.

Satisfied that no one would be getting back inside there anytime soon, the two headed back toward the house. Once next to the bad barn, however, Dr. Jackson and Rosanna were greeted with a strong waft of death's foul breath.

Rosanna coughed as Dr. Jackson pinched her nose and said, "Oh, wow! Smells like something's rotting in there! I didn't smell that on the way out just now!"

Snarling her nose and glancing in one of the side windows, "I didn't smell it either. Let me get the keys and see what it is."

She went into the house and quickly returned with a keyring. Upon opening the door, the smell had graduated to a full cloud as Dr. Jackson peeked inside. As Rosanna pulled the doors open completely, however, Penelope Jackson let out a shrill scream. Rosanna stepped back instinctively, but was quick to regain her composure. Looking inside, she couldn't see what was terrifying Penelope so.

Her hand still covering her mouth, "Oh, my god! What happened here!? Who is that!?"

Rosanna didn't hide the blatant look of "Are you crazy?" from her face. She looked toward the rafters of the barn where the doctor's eyes were fixated and bulging nearly out of her head. She looked one last time back and forth before saying, "What in the world are you talking about?"

Dr. Jackson saw the form of a hanged man swinging from the rafters. His motionless corpse was bloated with rot and wearing bibbed overalls and a t-shirt. She clearly saw his swollen tongue pushing between his lips. The unnatural blue, purple, and green pigments were prominent and squelched any other skin tone that was there before. His abdomen was inflated and set to pop at any moment.

Dr. Penelope Jackson's hand jerked and twitched as she pointed at the carcass on display. She looked into Rosanna's eyes. "There's no way you can't see that! Call the police!"

Mrs. Barrister looked at her guest with genuine confusion before looking back toward the rafters of the barn. "What are you talking about!? There's nothing there!"

"You can't be serious!"

She then looked back toward the inside of the barn and was even more surprised at what she saw next. The rafters were the only thing looking back. Sure, they were festooned with cobwebs and desiccated insect remains, but no hanging man. Not a single bone or even a rope was there for the viewing. She blinked a few times in disbelief. "No! That can't be! It was right there!" She pointed feebly at the apex of the ceiling. "There! It was right there!" Seeing the obvious confusion on Rosanna's face, "I know what I saw!"

She then watched as the doctor scribbled a few things on her clipboard before saying, "Um, Dr. Jackson, I still don't know what you're talking about."

Looking back up once more to see the emptiness staring back at her, "Look... look, everything here seems fine. I'm sorry to have bothered you. Not a word of this to anyone!"

Watching her walk toward her car quickly, "Dr. Jackson, where are you going? Are we done?"

Fumbling with the door handle on her car, "We're done! Keep a better eye on Angelica from now on!"

Rosanna watched her pull away. She was believing that Dr. Jackson had seen something horrible in the barn. From this mother's own experience, however, she could with one-hundred percent honesty say that she'd seen nothing of the sort for herself.

Thirty-one

Angelica strained to adjust her eyes to the semi bright sky overhead. It was covered with blue and purple clouds swiftly drifting by. She looked down at her hands propping herself up in a grassy clearing. All around the bare spot, however, was a seemingly endless sea of spiky thorn bushes. Walking to the edge of the circle, she tried to see through for a way out. Unbeknownst to her, Caroline appeared on the opposite side of the circle behind her. As she turned, she was momentarily startled, but soon regained her composure. Caroline's face showed a slight frown with notes of disappointment. "I see you met Timothy Harris. He can be a nasty little cuss, but I suppose you found that out the hard way."

The pain of her injuries, the burn marks running from neck to feet, were all still very real and being felt. Despite the compulsion to remain polite from years of practice, she became agitated. "Why did you make me go to the cave!?"

Caroline appeared shocked for a moment, but then amused. "What do mean? I didn't make you go anywhere, dear. You were the one determined to find that cave."

Even though Caroline was technically correct, Angelica's experience left a strong feeling of resentment. "That doesn't matter! You shouldn't have led me there!"

Caroline's face looked almost angry for the first time to Angelica. "Watch your mouth, child! What would your mother say about your tone?" At the mention of Rosanna, she instinctively brought her disrespectful anger *down as much as she could. Before Angelica could mouth an apology, however, Caroline's demeanor became more commanding. "Do not interrupt me again, young lady. There were lessons for you to learn at that cave. Some things are just better left undisturbed. No one made you take a hammer to that door and bash it open. What possessed you to do such a thing?"*

Angelica, perhaps from seeing one too many horror movies she wasn't supposed to be watching, wasn't comfortable with Caroline's use of the word "possessed," even though it was just a turn of phrase. She reluctantly conceded, "I don't know." She thought to herself for a moment, certain that she, in fact, had no idea why she was so determined to get in there. Curiosity was one thing, but this pull was nearly undeniable.

Caroline then knelt down on one knee, bringing her face close to Angelica's. Her tone was stern, but the tiny sneer at the edge of her lips suggested more. "Don't you know that curiosity killed the cat?" Angelica had heard the expression plenty of times, but Caroline's delivery of it left her unsettled. "Now, little girl, wake up and remember what I've taught you." As Angelica's face distorted with confusion, Caroline raised her hand and flicked the girl's forehead with her finger.

Angelica felt the sharp ping on her forehead as she woke up. After blinking a few times she saw the source of the blow: a tiny silver crucifix, recently placed over Angelica's bed during her hiatus by Rosanna, had fallen and bounced off of her head and onto the bed next to her. She picked it up and looked it over, it easily fitting in the palm of her hand as she rubbed her forehead with the other. As the pain of the burns she'd received only a few days before jolted across her body, a familiar voice called out.

Knocking on the door a couple of times before entering, Rosanna smiled at her and said in a compassionate tone, "Hey there, sweetie! I can't remember the last time I woke up before you."

Angelica pushed herself up in bed carefully, groaning.

Seeing the small red dot on Angelica's forehead and the cross in her hand, "Oh, did that fall on you?" She looked up at the tiny nail she'd hammered in the wall, only it was bent downward. "Oh... I'll have to fix that. Tiny nail, big hammer."

Angelica, still rubbing the sleep from her eyes, squinted at the light coming in from around the edges of her window. "What time is it?"

Rosanna glanced over at the clock as Edward walked in the room. "It's after 8."

Edward followed up, "And the Kellys said they were bringing over lunch today. They've been worried about you, too!"

Angelica perked up at this idea, knowing that Mrs. Kelly's fried chicken and macaroni and cheese were easily the best she'd ever eaten.

Edward kissed her on the forehead and smiled. "Glad to see you got some sleep, baby girl."

Angelica pushed the covers aside, but was slow to get up. "I still feel really tired."

Rosanna responded, "Probably the medication they were giving you at the hospital." Even though the situation had been deemed a more than necessary reason to sedate her, Rosanna wasn't sold on the idea of using so much. Perhaps she didn't really understand the amount of physical and mental pain that Angelica was still harboring because of the recent incident. Since they had moved to Holly Bush Road, Angelica had skirted death twice and lived to talk about it.

Edward moved the shoulder of Angelica's shirt aside to look at the bandages on her neck. He shook his head, then said reluctantly, "I hate that we have to do this, Ange, but we need to change your bandages every day. Doctor's orders."

Rosanna rejoined, "They gave us a burn cream to use. He said it would help ease the pain."

Soon, her mother and father changed her bandages. Angelica saw for the first time why she was in so much pain. What looked to be burns, the worst reaching second-degree status here and there, resembled wild lashings of ruddy pink. Starting around her throat, down across her chest and back, then finally around both her legs, tentacle-like shapes dominated. In an area on her right leg, a shape that resembled a child's hand seemed to have left its mark. Edward was particularly disturbed by that. Rosanna, still hanging by mere threads to any logical explanation anyone could come up with, refused to believe the evidence in front of her. There was no way someone's hand could leave such a burn, right? Denial can be a tricky thing like that.

She and Edward had racked their brains trying to figure out what could've caused such injuries, but nothing made sense. Even going back and trying to reconstruct the situation offered no answers. All Ed and Rose could remember was noticing that their daughter hadn't returned at the usual 1-o'clock lunchtime. Concerned, they went looking for her and eventually found the machete near the mouth of the cave. Once inside they were able to locate her due to the one good ounce of fortune: The Maglite was still shining. None of the black mist or smoke that Angelica had claimed to see was there. Edward had even called one of his friends, a geologist, back in Johnston City to see if he could make any sense of it. The only thing he could postulate was some sort of steam vent or blast of boiling water from below. Given where they lived and there being no such steam or vent when they entered, they quickly shot down the idea and tried moving on to other explanations. Edward knew inside that it was something malicious that committed the act, but he wasn't going to even suggest such an idea to Rosanna. And the thought of something paranormal, spirit or otherwise, having this much power was frightening. He had experienced an occasional negative entity growing up, but nothing like this. This was way out of his league.

Thirty-two

Later on that day, the Kelly family arrived at lunchtime with a meal Mrs. Kelly had spent all day making. Since 5 A.M. she had been up preparing the sides and main course, making sure to include what she knew were Angelica's favorites. Angelica wouldn't dare tell her mother that Mrs. Kelly's cooking was superior in most ways when it came to local traditional food that no self-respecting person would be caught without.

John Jr. found himself particularly concerned with Angelica's condition. He had stayed home during most of the trips the Kelly family had taken to the hospital to keep up the farm chores. The one time he did make it over to see her, she was still unconscious and on the breathing machine. Maybe it shocked him into realizing the frailty of life. Seeing her up and about alleviated much of his worrying, but he still felt a sense to duty to watch out for her like he did his little sister.

That afternoon, the meal having lasted an hour and a half and everyone stuffed, Angelica and Abby found themselves walking the dirt trail leading away. Abby agreed to watch over her, at Rosanna's behest, and promised not to let her out of her sight for one second.

Alone and well out of earshot of the others, Abby quietly picked up a small pebble from next to the road and sidearm chucked into the knee-high grass dancing in the sweet summer breeze. "I'm glad you're okay, Angie-bear. I've been worried sick about you."

Smiling warmly at her, she replied, "Thanks, Ab."

Keeping their pace, "Does it hurt a lot? It looks like it does."

Squinting as the sun peeked from behind the clouds, "Yeah, it hurts, all right. Changing the bandages is the worst part."

Feeling the sincerity and sympathizing, "I bet. Do you know what caused it?"

A part of Angelica wanted to fully disclose what she had experienced, but it seemed like too much to blurt out so soon. Hesitating a moment before, she said, "I'm not exactly sure what happened. We'll talk about it more some other time. I don't like thinking about it."

"That's okay, I understand. We don't have to talk about it." Seeing Angelica relieved at the idea, Abby's tone became more positive. "Hey, you want to go and see if there are any crawdads in the creek?"

That did sound like a wonderfully fun and simple pleasure to indulge in. "Yeah!" A quick thought interrupted her flight to the idea. "Wait, I'd better go and make sure it's okay with M Mom. Dad said I'm on a short leash right now."

Undeterred, "Okay, let's go see...."

She was cut off as the territorial bird Angelica had encountered days ago now squawked and tried to dive-bomb their friendly conversation.

Swatting her hand in vain at the empty air left behind, "Whoa! Must be a momma bird." She quickly looked over at the short maple tree nearby in which the bird had disappeared. Pointing, "And I guess that's where her nest is."

Their attention was quickly drawn nearby as a higher-pitched chirp began to permeate through the surrounding cloud of bug noises and other distant birds singing away. On the ground at the base of the tree was a small chick, still covered in fluff and missing any semblance of feathers. It was clear from its flopping that only one of its early stage wings was working. Whether from the fall or a defect, the chick was lame and helpless by all definitions. The mother bird suddenly emerged from the leaves and buzzed them once again, darting into a flight path above and circling around the tree.

Angelica said with concern, "Aww! Should we put it back in the nest?"

Abby was reluctant to tell her the life lesson she had already been taught, but knew it was necessary. "Dad says that when one of the chicks is lame the mother will kick it out of the nest."

Angelica was growing up on a farm, sure. The family wasn't really engaging in much agriculture, however, other than the garden Rosanna had planted nearby and the three pet goats Angelica and Edward were looking after.

"She'll just leave the chick to die?"

A small dimple appeared on Abby's cheek as she frowned. "There's no point in feeding it if it can never grow up to be an adult. That's just the way nature is."

Angelica knelt down slowly, gritting her teeth briefly to fight back the pain. She carefully took the chick in her hands. "I don't want to just leave it here to die."

Seeing a critical error that Abby had been taught by her father, "No! Now the mother definitely won't take it back."

Confused, "Why?"

"Dad says that once you have human scent on them the mother will never take it." Instinctively she placed the chick back on the ground, but mostly as a reflex to Abby's warning. Before she could say anything, however, the form of Caroline appeared just feet in front of her next to the tree. Angelica stared forward in silence as Caroline looked down at her. Abby was clearly not seeing her and continued. "Dad says it's best to put it out of its misery."

Still looking ahead at Caroline, Angelica responded to Abby, "You mean just kill it? Now?"

Abby replied, "Yeah, it'll starve to death otherwise. It could lay there all day and night just waiting to die." Her tone had become more distant. It was a lesson she'd learned, but one she hadn't gotten used to yet 100 percent.

Angelica looked back at Abby, who was still looking down at the chick, it being clear that she wasn't seeing Caroline. The voice of the spirit spoke to Angelica's mind directly, clear enough that her own ears could hear it despite the apparition's lips not moving. *"Do what has to be done, little girl. You have to grow up sometime."*

Abby, meanwhile, had stepped aside and picked up a relatively heavy rock. She handed it to Angelica and said, "Here. One hit should do it."

Angelica was not really sure why she was handing her the rock, but she took it anyway. She had heard from her parents and even Mr. Kelly that one day the day would come when she'd have to do something like this. Living on a farm had its ups and downs and here was something she wasn't looking forward to. She held the rock in her hands at chest level, straining to push forward with the deed.

Caroline's voice came through. *"Do it, Angelica. There's no other choice. Do you want it to starve to death?"*

She swallowed the lump in her throat and took the rock overhead. Still, again, she stopped.

Seeing her hesitation, *"What are you waiting for? It's helpless and dying!"*

Angelica closed her eyes for a second, then opened them again. The loud chirps for aid went unheard as it squirmed and attempted to flop away in vain.

"Do it, Angelica! Now!"

Instantly another distorted voice screamed into her ear, *"KILL THE FUCKING THING!"* This voice was nothing like Caroline's. Something between human and animal. No, it was those two combined with so much hatred and rage that it snapped her out of her train of thought and actions. Momentarily, a surge of the negative emotions crashed over Angelica, lingering a few seconds and receding. Angelica looked up at Caroline, whose face was now looking confused.

No more words from Caroline and no more words from whatever that other voice was. Abby looked up at Angelica, just now noticing that she was staring off into the distance at something she couldn't see. "What is it?"

Still not answering and staring at Caroline's mute form, Angelica's face donned the scowl that most mortals would shrink from. Without thinking she reflexively threw the rock in the direction of Caroline. It passed through the spirit without harm. But just as suddenly as Caroline had appeared, she disappeared without a sound.

She took a couple of breaths and regained her composure. "No, we have to give it a chance." Angelica cupped the chick gently in her hands before replacing it in the nest.

She would have trouble explaining the event to Abby and why she did what she did. Angelica didn't even understand the situation herself, but felt she had made the better choice. The decisions she had made, no matter how small they may have seemed at the time, would haunt her for the rest of her natural life.

Later that evening, not long after the Kelly family had left, Angelica found herself searching and searching on the internet. Despite her best efforts, she found nothing directly explaining what had occurred to her. Even vague searches for things such as "paranormal" yielded nothing close to what she had in mind.

She searched for what seemed like an eternity until she searched for a word her mother in no way approved of: "psychic." It seemed serendipitous when it suddenly came across the screen, but she knew, in the back of her mind, that this might just help. Things she had been taught at church and certainly Rosanna's opinions had influenced her to have very mixed, but mostly uneasy, feelings about the topic. What made the notion very tempting, however, was that a more detailed search revealed a psychic in Miller's Run. Not only that, but she had received five-star ratings from all of her customers, as the messages on the forum were all positive. Of course, everyone that had posted a review on the site used ridiculous account names to keep their identity private. One user name stuck out to her: "GertieMomma." The older woman she had met at the 4-H competition her first few days in the town was the most obvious candidate: Ethyl, with the horse named Gertie. So despite the bad reputation the people in town may have given her, enough of them were seeing this psychic on a regular basis to warrant glowing reviews online. After all, when she saw the title the woman listed on her profile, "Spiritual Advisor," it took much of the sting out of the other words she heard describe her. The lady herself, despite the attempts of her customers to conceal their identity, just used her name: Sara Goodwin. The profile picture was also the only true-to-life. The genuine warm smile of the woman put dwindling doubts to rest. Angelica knew she had to get in touch with her. Doubts of her being a money-hungry charlatan (again from the reputation all of the people in town seemed to share about "their kind") came and went, but she felt the risk was necessary. Sara's email address was right there on the screen and without any further hesitation, Angelica sent her a message. Its contents were simple: "I've seen spirits at our house since we moved in three years ago. I don't know where to go for help. Please reply because they have tried to hurt me. A. Barrister."

After Angelica hovered her mouse pointer over the send button for a minute she decided to go through with it and send the call for aid. Now the only question was: Would she believe her?

Angelica sat at her computer desk most of the evening, eagerly awaiting a response, but didn't receive one. The quiet and uneventful dinner left her nerves a little frayed with the suspicion that her parents, more acutely Rosanna, would find out what she was up to. Despite not knowing the exact term, she reasoned to herself that conspirator's paranoia was getting the best of her. (Rosanna didn't go through her emails that she knew of and Edward respected her privacy too much.) Then another obvious question lingered in her mind: how to get to Sara's place of business. She knew the idea of an eight-year-old driving the family Subaru across town would probably not sit well with her parents. This problem would only add to the complexity of the scheme, but she knew that if she applied her focus to it, she could think of a way around that.

Time passed and finally at 11:00 P.M., she reluctantly shut down her computer and readied for bed. That night, oddly enough, she had no nightmares.

Thirty-three

The next morning, Angelica roused from sleep at around the same time as her parents. Before breakfast she checked her email again, but found no reply. The smell and sizzle of bacon and eggs on the stove being cooked drew her away from her computer, however, despite the desperation to receive a reply.

Heading toward the kitchen, Angelica stopped at the living room as a strange and unusual commercial played. Two men, one dressed in a foam worm costume and another in a fish outfit, dance around a larger, heavyset man in the middle. The budget for the commercial was painfully low and acting level lower, but it caught her eye. The man in the middle, wearing a camouflaged shirt and blue jeans, donned a huge grin on his face and began to speak. "Do you wanna catch bigger fish? Well, then, you'll need bigger worms! At Slippery Sam's Bait Shop, we have the biggest worms you'll find anywhere! That's Slippery Sam's Bait Shop! Don't let the big one get away!" He ends the commercial by tipping his fishing cap, the other two showing their "jazz hands".... (Really? Yeah, that happened.)

Rolling her eyes, Angelica made her way into the kitchen and sat down for the morning's bounty.

After devouring the plate of food she ran out to the goat pin and fed her three friends. As soon she rushed through the chore she headed back to her room to check her inbox. Much to her delight, there was a waiting message, and it was from none other than Sara Goodwin. It read: "I'm sorry to hear about your problems at home. If you would like, we can set up a visit. It will be, of course, complimentary. Just let me know when would be a good time for you. I look forward to hearing from you. S. Goodwin."

The situation was different now. Angelica started to feel even more like an adult. Setting up a meeting to discuss real-life problems: It was intriguing and appealing to her. Now the question was: when to set an appointment and how to get there. She thought on it for a moment and: eureka! The commercial did its job, all right. Edward had promised to teach her how to fish years ago when they first moved in and now she was going to take him up on that offer. Angelica reflected for a minute before preparing a response to the email. Saturday seemed like a good enough day. No other plans were made and Edward would jump at the chance to spend some time with her. She just had to make sure Rosanna didn't want to go.

Convinced her idea would work, she responded, "Thanks for replying. I think Saturday would be a good day. Is 11:00 A.M. okay?" Send.

Sara's response was quick. "Saturday at 11:00 A.M. works for me. My home is at 100 Parris Road. I'm the only house there. Just follow the driveway and ring the doorbell out front. I look forward to meeting you! S. Goodwin."

After looking up the address on a map site, she wrote down the directions to get there. They were relatively simple given the few roads in town.

Angelica then headed back toward the kitchen, where her mother and father were talking over coffee.

Edward saw her stop and look straight at him. He smiled and said, "Hey, Ange. What's up?"

She replied, "Remember when you said you would teach me how to fish? I want you to take me fishing."

Taken aback by the immediacy of her request, "Right now? I have work to do today."

"No, not today. Saturday. And we should leave at around 10:30."

The precision of her request wasn't the most tactfully worded, but he went along with it. "Okay, we'll go fishing Saturday. And we'll even leave at 10:30 that morning. Do you know where you want to go?"

Angelica said immediately, "The old dry dock on Route 682."

Both of her parents were still impressed by her exactness.

Rosanna replied, "I guess you already scouted this place out, huh? Why 10:30 exactly?"

Well, this was a response she didn't prepare an answer for. She scrambled a second and came up with a suitable reply. "I want to make sure I have time to do my chores and watch cartoons before we go."

She was eight years old, after all, but Rosanna replied in a light tone, "Really? I didn't think you watched cartoons on Saturday morning." She had Angelica there. (Rosanna had only seen her watch them a few times here and there, but was still mainly just amused at her to-the-point tone.)

The playful tone didn't dissuade Angelica's mind from thinking her story was starting to unravel. The apprehension of being caught was already starting to get to her, despite the chances of her mother actually knowing her intentions were slim to none. An answer came quickly. "Abby said there will be a funny one coming on that morning. I want to see if I like it or not."

The reason seemed to convince them enough that nothing too strange was going on, even though their parental instincts may have suggested otherwise.

Edward chuckled and said, "Okay, baby girl, we'll go fishing Saturday. You coming along, Rosy?"

Yet another shot of adrenaline caused Angelica to become uneasy. Why in the world was he asking if she wanted to come along? He knew she didn't like that sort of thing. Much to Angelica's relief, however, Rosanna replied, "No, you two go and catch us dinner. Just make sure you clean the guts out before you bring 'em in for me to cook. Deal?"

Edward agreed to the deal and Angelica breathed a sigh of relief inside. Content that her plans were ready to be executed, she said, "Okay!" before running to her room and shutting down her computer.

She changed her clothes into suitable outdoor gear and headed toward the back door. In the kitchen she was stopped by Rosanna.

"Hey, young lady. Where do you think you're going?"

"I have to go check on the goats. Then I thought I'd pick some blackberries. I promise I won't go past the bridge."

Rosanna agreed to let her go, but stopped her as she opened the door. "Wait a second!" Angelica stepped back through the door and looked up at her.

"Don't forget your basket."

"Oh, right." She took the basket from the nail on the basement door and headed back outside.

Rosanna watched her walk down the dirt path, still uncertain about letting her out of her sight for more than five minutes.

After Angelica checked the goats, she walked down the trail toward her original intended destination: the lone maple tree with the bird's nest. On this trip, however, something was different. No squawking mother bird trying to dive-bomb her. No chicks chirping their shrill noises to get her attention. The only thing she could hear, once close, was the steady buzz of flies. She hesitated at the proximity of the tree, unsettled by the change in atmosphere. The basket fell from her hand and onto the dirt road as she looked around with uncertainty. One step at a time she approached the tree and, at first, couldn't comprehend what she saw. One of the baby birds was held against the tree. Keeping it in place was a splinter of wood shoved through the right side of its head and into the tree itself. Flies buzzed all around, landing and taking off again all over the limp carcass. She stared at it silently, not seeing the full display in front of her. Dread, sorrow, helplessness, and anxiety permeated her mind. Mute, she extended her hand toward the dead bird but quickly withdrew it as more of the scene came into view. To the left was another baby bird, only this one was crudely hanging by its neck. The device by which it was hanged appeared to be a small supple twig deliberately cinched in a loop.

To the right of the first chick she'd noticed was the third. One of its legs was stuck between two branches. Its tiny head appeared to have been crushed and from what she could see, blood was streaming down the vulgarly exploded eye sockets. And making its appearance all the worse, the body from head to toe was charred nearly black and crusted over.

Reeling, she stepped back and covered her mouth with her hand. A thought managed to slither in through her shock: She felt responsible for this. She challenged this with a logical question: Why? If anything, Angelica tried to save the bird's life. Why did this have to happen? So senseless and so needless. She looked around and saw no one. Neither her parents nor Caroline were there to offer any explanation. This was to become another "message" from something, but for the life of her, she couldn't understand what. Unable to stare any longer she turned and ran back toward their house to find her father.

Angelica eventually returned with him. Edward was shocked at the scene and just as flabbergasted. When he tried to explain it naturally, nothing remotely feasible could connect the dots. Upon thinking of a person doing such a malicious act, neither of them could fathom someone sneaking onto their property at night just to do this. The third conclusion was simply to base it on the unknown. He didn't use the word "paranormal," but the thought was shared by him and his daughter. This, and Angelica's injuries, left both him and her with a nasty snarling pit in their stomach. The two of them also came to the uneasy decision to keep Rosanna in the dark about this, unless it was absolutely necessary to do otherwise.

Thirty-four

Saturday eventually came. Angelica had risen early to make sure her chores were finished with plenty of time to spare. She also had to make sure her father wasn't lagging behind for their appointment that he was still not aware of. She even feigned watching a Saturday morning cartoon for several minutes before turning off the television and making an intentionally noticeable statement of, "I guess Abby was wrong," within earshot of her parents. Everything was going swimmingly well and according to plan except one part: when and how to convince Edward to agree to go. She wouldn't have much time to make her case. They were only about twenty minutes from 100 Parris Road, and from there it was just five minutes down the same road to the dry dock and Slippery Sam's Bait Shop. It was also a place where a large swell in the small river was at its widest. Prime fishing territory and a great boat launch.

Ten-twenty-five A.M. and Angelica was pulling on her dad's wrist to urge him to the car faster. Rosanna laughed and waved goodbye to them as they started down the driveway toward the road. Angelica looked back in the side-view mirror just to alleviate her paranoia. Her mother, of course, was already heading back into the house. She waited until he stopped at the intersection with the road and looked to turn out to begin her sales pitch.

As the Subaru with the three fishing poles in the backseat turned out, she started directly, "Dad, we need to stop somewhere before we get to the docks."

"Don't worry, we'll get worms at the bait shop. It's right there next to the river."

"No, there's another stop we have to make before that."

He glanced over at her. "Where's that, baby girl?"

"100 Parris Road."

Genuinely unfamiliar with the address, "100 Parris Road? Where's that?"

Her eyes still looking forward, "It's on the way. I need to see Sara Goodwin."

He may have heard the name mentioned once or twice, but really didn't know who she was. "Sara Goodwin? Why do you need to see her?"

"She's a spiritual advisor."

He was familiar with the term. "Wait. Why do you need a spiritual advisor?" He knew the answer as he mouthed the words, but wouldn't be doing due diligence without asking.

Finally looking at him, "I want to know why this happened to me and what happened to the baby birds."

Flustered for a moment before answering, "Ange, we can't just show up at someone's house like that unannounced…."

He was cut off. "But I already made an appointment! I emailed her and she said to come by at 11:00 A.M. today!"

Now Edward felt a tinge of being manipulated. Part of him wanted to be upset with her for it, but it dissolved quickly. After all, she was already displaying what some call "command presence" and knew she had the cheat codes to hack into and shut down his resistances. He sighed, then said, "Ange… baby girl, you know you shouldn't try and deceive your parents like that. What if your mother found out about this?"

Still assertive, "That's why I didn't say anything about it around her!"

He struggled to find sound words. "How much is this person charging? If she starts asking for a lot of money, we're leaving." Growing up he'd been financially burned when he was looking for answers in such places. Edward believed that psychic phenomenon was possible, but wasn't gullible enough to think all people claiming to be psychic were telling the truth. Far from it.

Here was a question she could easily defend against. "She said the visit is free. I told her I was having problems with spirits and she said she'd help if she could."

Edward ran his hand down his cheek and scratched his beard, one of his "tells" for anxiety. "You know, we can't tell anyone about this. If Rosy finds out about it she'll blow a gasket!"

Angelica was aware of her mother's religious beliefs and attitude toward this subject in general. This was concerning, obviously, to Edward. Perhaps more concerning was the knowledge that his wife could be jealous from time to time and wouldn't like the idea of him driving up to the house of a female stranger.

Angelica responded, "I know, Mom would kill us both."

The statement sounded a little funny to Edward, maybe because he knew how badly things would get if there visitation was noticed by anyone from town. "If she finds out, I'm blaming it all on you. And from now on, don't go making plans like this without telling me. Is that clear?"

Angelica obviously wasn't intending to injure her father and genuinely responded, "I'm sorry. I'll ask next time."

Several minutes later they slowed down at the road sign bearing the name "Parris Road." Sure enough, there was only one house at the end of a long gravel driveway leading through a well-kempt yard and around the back of a large Victorian-style home. The yard was dotted by large majestic oaks branching out and offering ample shade from the summer heat. The façade was covered with off white bricks from foundation to roof. A set of three large rectangular windows on the left side of the home, topped with an arch of stained glass, glinted in the sun briefly as the clouds overhead parted for a moment. This led over to a tower to the right, two stories tall, topped by a conical roof colored dark green (matching the rest of the trim of the outside of the house). The four windows, two at each floor, in the tower too were also made of stained glass. To the right of this the home gave way to a set of front doors. The large mahogany doors were flanked finally by a covered porch that wrapped around the front of the home and faced the river. The second story was more rectangular and its windows were curtained inside rather than the stained glass used regularly on the first floor. The roof finally angled overhead with attic space resulting. Edward and Angelica looked on in amazement at the structure, uttering phrases like "It's beautiful!" and "Wow!"

The family car pulled to a stop in a parking area just around the bend of the house, out of sight from the road. No other cars were parked there, but a nearby closed garage left the impression that someone may be home. He glanced down at the clock reading "10:52 A.M." before looking up at the back door.

Her father looking back and forth, Angelica said, "She said to go to the front door."

They exited the car and headed toward the porch leading to the front of the house. An ironic thought quickly crossed Angelica's mind. The house she and her father were going to would certainly seem to be the quintessential "haunted house" from movies and ghost stories. She, however, was going there for help with *her* ghost matters at her own home.

Edward knocked at the front door before looking up and around the woodwork of the porch. "Isn't this place amazing? And it's so well built!"

One of the large mahogany doors was pulled open, a woman in her late twenties, holding the handle. Her modern yet old-style dark green dress was a throwback to a time matching the home she was in, but clearly made for modern-day comfort. Her brown hair was tied back in a neat French braid, her face smiling warmly. She extended her hand to Edward and looked at him with her gentle, yet striking green eyes. He shook her hand as she said, "Hello, I'm Sara. Nice to meet you."

Smiling, "Hi there, I'm Ed Barrister. This is my daughter, Angelica."

Sara leaned down to shake Angelica's waiting hand. "You must be the one who sent me the message."

Angelica smiled as she was immediately put at ease by Sara's presence. "Hi, nice to meet you."

Edward chuckled nervously and said, "Yeah, and I just found out twenty minutes ago that we were even coming here."

Sara slyly smiled at Angelica. "Uh-oh! Precocious, are we?"

Angelica hadn't heard this word before. "What's that mean?"

Edward placed his hand on top of her head, messing up her hair. "She means you're a handful to deal with!"

Angelica tried to straighten her hair up as he and Sara laughed.

Stepping back from the door, "Well, come in! It's really hot out there."

She shut the door behind them as they looked around in amazement. The parlor room in the front of the house was decorated with various antique items from the late 1800s and early 1900s. Three dark wooden sofas with mauve upholstery line the walls. The walls themselves were painted off white with decorative mahogany wood panels covering the lower half of the walls that stopped at molding bordering the similarly shaded hardwood floors. The slats of the shutters were opened to allow some light in, but an overhead electrical light did most of the illuminating. At the far side of the room, next to the fireplace, sat four elegant chairs matching the sofas. They were set up in a regular interval around the circular table in the middle. On the table was a small rectangular box made of stained oak.

As they took in the view, Edward said, "If you don't mind me saying, this house is beautiful!"

She thanked him for the compliment and he continued.

"Oh, I'm an architect. I love older homes like this. What year was it built?"

Sara replied, "It was finished in 1853. It took around two years to complete."

Angelica said, "It's very pretty!"

Sara smiled warmly. "Well, thank you! Would either of you like something to drink?"

Edward politely turned her down, but Angelica said, "Can I have some water, please?"

Sara acknowledged her and looked at Edward again. "All right, and are you sure you don't need anything, Mr. Barrister?"

"No thanks, I'm fine."

She turned and left the room, her throwback style shoes making a distinct knocking with each step.

Edward saw her braid, held together by a small black bow, bouncing on her back as she walked away. Without thinking his eyes started to look down her back. Her dress may have been old fashioned in appearance, but it wasn't hiding her figure. He suddenly thought to himself, *Damnit, Ed, stop staring at her! You're married! Rosy would tear out your eyes if she saw that!* She was attractive, no doubt, and that made things a bit too uncomfortable for him more still.

He then looked toward Angelica, who was staring at his face with her eyebrow raised. She glanced back over her shoulder, then leaned in close to him. For a moment he was petrified that his daughter just caught him with his wandering eyes. A small amount of relief washed over him, however, as she asked in a low whisper, "Why is she dressed like that?"

Edward could hear the tapping of Sara's shoes approaching from the kitchen again. He put his finger to his mouth and shushed her quietly.

Sara entered and handed a small plastic bottle of water to Angelica. "Please, go ahead and sit down," directing them to the table. She sat down with them and said, "Now, as I told your daughter in my email, today's visit is complimentary." Maybe she was already picking up some anxiety about this from him. "Don't worry, Mr. Barrister, I don't even have a credit card reader." She then picked up the small oak box and set it aside. A deck of larger rectangular cards was underneath. Sara began to shuffle them.

Before they could say anything else, Angelica and Edward were startled as three previously unseen occupants entered the room. Three large black dogs, looking more wolf than dog, approached the table. Much to their relief, the three seemed friendly and docile.

Angelica said in awe, "Wow, those are big dogs! Can I pet them?"

Sara smiled and said, "Sure you can. Trust me, they know a nice person when they see one."

Edward looked over the solid black canines, their eyes yellowish orange, and asked, "What breed are they?"

Sara replied, "They're wolfdogs. But don't worry, they are about six generations removed from that."

Angelica scratched one of the dog's head as Sara continued to shuffle the deck. She then asked, "What's a wolfdog?"

Sara answered, "It's a dog that's part wolf."

"Wow!" Angelica was stopped from any more words and giggled instead as another one of the dogs licked her face.

The three looked nearly identical, but Sara knew their individuality well enough. She pointed to each in turn. "That's Clotho, that's Lachesis, and that's Atropos."

Edward suddenly remembered a classics class from college. "Oh, the Moirai?"

Seeing Angelica confused at the words, Sara said, "The Three Fates." Her answer sufficient to sate her curiosity, she finished shuffling the cards and placed the deck on the table. "Okay, Angelica, take half of the deck and place it on the table next to the other half."

Angelica did so.

Sara then dexterously slid the halves together again. "Now, I want you to think about the question you want answered today. Make sure it isn't a yes/no question and don't say anything out loud. From now until I finish the reading, don't say a word. Okay?"

Her audience listened as she snapped her finger. The two were astonished to see the three dogs all obediently sit around the table as if protecting it. All three humans seated at the table then closed their eyes and concentrated, Angelica following their lead. Sara took a few deep breaths, then began to lay out the cards in front of her one at a time. Angelica sat up in her chair, trying to see each card as clearly as she could. Although she had no clue how to interpret them, some of the images managed to stick in her mind. One card depicted three men holding swords and brandishing them at each other in anger. Another was of a man hanging from a tree. The last one that troubled her the most was that of a winged part-goat creature with a star on its chest. Sara quietly studied the entire layout, the previous smile on her face having since disappeared. Angelica and Edward waited on baited breath for words. A slight frown, which she did her best to hide, crossed her face. This wasn't a typical light-hearted reading that she was used to giving.

The gravity was faint in her voice. "I see something very powerful creating chaos in your life. It's very old and has broken many lives in the past. You are going to need a lot of help to overcome this." Sara, feeling a sudden pain in her forehead, gripped the bridge of her nose with her fingers and briefly groaned. "This entity does not want to be seen... now it's laughing at me."

Suddenly Angelica and Edward realized that the three dogs were standing and growling, the hair on their neck standing upright. The three dogs then barked a couple of times each before Sara opened her eyes, the pain gone. "It has left." She shook her head back and forth before saying, "I have to stop the reading here."

The dogs returned to their normal state and walked toward their owner, looking up at her.

Edward, seeing her distressed, "Are you okay?"

Placing her hand on the small cameo below her neck, she said, "Yes, I'm okay now." Sara then rose from her seat and said, "Mr. Barrister, can I speak to you in the other room for a moment?"

Edward rose as well and nodded his head. He looked down at Angelica. "Just wait here a minute. Okay, sweetie?"

She agreed, still trying to figure out exactly what just happened.

The two adults disappeared behind a closed door leading to a study down the hall. They soon began speaking in hushed tones, but she couldn't make out any words. Curious, she stood up from the chair and looked over the card spread, trying to make out their meaning. No luck. She was then struck by the realization that the three dogs had resumed being seated around the table and were watching her silently. Angelica didn't feel threatened. Quite the opposite. She felt protected.

A minute later the door in the hallway opened again and the two adults rejoined Angelica. Sara then had two things, one in each hand.

"Now, Miss Barrister, I have a couple of gifts for you. First, this pendant." Sara took a silver linked chain that threaded through a small ornament clasping a nearly clear piece of quartz. Placing it over her head and around her neck, "Wear it at all times for protection, okay?" Angelica nodded as Sara handed her the second gift: a large white cylindrical candle. "And if you feel threatened at home, light this... safely, of course."

Now Angelica was certainly feeling left out of the loop. She asked, "What did the cards tell you?"

Sara, still wanting to avoid troubling Angelica even more, said, "I talked with your father about that. Just remember to wear that necklace at all times and light that candle if you feel like you're in trouble. If you have any other questions just send me an email, okay?"

Despite the feeling of obviously being held from vital information, she accepted the gifts, took her instructions to heart, and left with her father. Maybe he would let her in on more of this later.

They went on to have a productive day on the river. They brought home two smallmouth bass and ate them, Rosanna ducking out of trying them for herself. The day ended with relative harmony, Angelica even getting some sleep that night void of nightmares. The problem was, someone saw their car leaving that house on Parris Road.

Thirty-five

The next morning, Angelica awoke at sunrise. She realized that she had fallen asleep with the silver chained quartz pendant, given to her the previous day by Sara, in her hand. The silver was polished and shining, coming to a lace-like clasp that gripped the teardrop-shaped piece of quartz. She didn't understand exactly why, but she felt a greater level of comfort and peace with it around. She also decided to keep the candle Sara had given her stashed away in her closet. Either of those would certainly warrant a question from her curious mother. And even though she did feel remorse when she had told lies, Angelica found the strong will to avoid immediate trouble more likeable. She was confident she could think of a way to keep what happened hidden, whether fate agreed or not.

Angelica then changed into her chore clothes and decided to keep the pendant with her, but stashed in her pocket rather than wearing it around her neck. She headed out into the hall and nearly ran into her father as he opened the bedroom door. Inside it was obvious that Rosanna was still asleep, so Edward quietly shut the door behind him. He made a shushing gesture with his finger as Angelica did the same and smiled.

"Good morning," he whispered, she returning the sentiment.

She then made her way through the kitchen and out the back door as her father stayed behind to start the coffee.

A few minutes later, Angelica was making the rounds tending to her goats. While filling up a feeding trough, barely able to hold back the hungry animals in the process, Edward stepped out from the back door and walked toward the barn. Still in slippers, his long flannel bottoms, and a t-shirt, he met Angelica at the door leading to the goat pen.

Closing the door behind her, "Hey, Dad."

"Hey, baby girl. Listen, I was thinking, it's probably best if we say I gave you the candle and the necklace. Does that sound good?"

Angelica felt that the situation had changed now that her father was speaking openly to her about a conspiracy of sorts. It caused a tinge of discomfort to push forward as she said, "But Dad, Sara gave them to me. I don't want to lie if I don't have to."

He sighed and smiled. "I'm glad you feel that way. You want to do the right thing and I'm proud of that. The problem is, if your mother finds out about where we were yesterday...."

Angelica cut him off. "I know, I know. Mom will kill us both."

The statement, despite verbalizing the peril, caused him to chuckle again. "Yes, and I don't want anything to come between the three of us. Do you understand?"

She reluctantly nodded her head as he continued.

"Good. Do you have the necklace now?"

Angelica looked back up at the house, paranoid that the ever-present Rosanna might be watching. Convinced of their safety, she took the pendant from her pocket and held it in her hand.

Edward continued. "Okay, then. Now give it to me." He took it and gripped it in his hand. "Now, this is *mine*, do you understand?"

Angelica looked puzzled.

He said reassuringly, "Just trust me."

Still not completely getting his train of thought, "Okay... why do you want it?"

He felt a little uneasy with his plan, but went on. "Now that it's *mine*, I choose to give it to *you*."

The idea was making sense to his daughter now, even if it felt as sketchy as a five-dollar cellphone.

"When anyone asks where you got this, you can say that I gave it to you, and it's true. Does that make sense?"

She raised her eyebrow a moment before saying, "I guess it makes sense. It still feels like a lie, though."

Now he was feeling an added pressure of teaching his daughter how to technically tell the truth without technically lying. "I know it may seem strange, but there are certain things that not everyone needs to know about. Remember, we're doing this to help us all."

He then held the pendant in his hands, placing the necklace over her head and around her neck.

Angelica said reluctantly, "All right. Thank you for the present, Dad."

Edward bent down and kissed her on the top of her head.

As he rose back up, she said, "What did Sara say to you when you left the room? You didn't talk about it all yesterday."

Edward checked over his shoulder, making sure the coast was still clear. He and she had their own conspiracy circle now and trust was to be paramount to its success. He replied, "Well, baby girl, she basically said that this 'thing,' whatever it is, will try and take away things you love."

She glanced off to the side, thinking to herself about the vagueness of the statement. "What do you mean?"

"Well, it may mean something like causing problems for our family. The three of us want to stick together, right?"

She nodded her head as he continued.

"So the three of us have to be strong and stay together as a team. We can't let the problems we have break us apart."

Angelica still felt like she was getting a padded version of the truth. Nonetheless, she understood the message. "Why would something want to break the family apart?"

His tone was more subdued and almost distant. "I don't know, sweetie. I wish I had an answer for that. Some people just want to see other people suffer. In all my years on Earth, I still can't figure them out."

Now a little forlorn herself, "That's sad. They should be taken away… somewhere."

Sighing again, "I wish it were that simple." He changed his tone to a more upbeat one. "But hey, we just need to stay focused on keeping the family together. We'll be fine if we stick to that. Deal?"

She shook his extended hand before he walked her back to the house for his morning cup of coffee.

Once inside the house, Angelica headed back to her bedroom and shut the door behind her. She turned on her computer and sat down at the keyboard. A nagging notion had been in her mind since she retired for bed the night before and still remained: Check your email. Perhaps the idea of her receiving an email didn't make much sense in her mind, seeing as how Abby almost always called instead. Nonetheless, she decided to pursue the "clear-seeing" hint. Sure enough, there was a message waiting for her from Sara Goodwin. She looked up at the door for a moment, listening to hear if her mother was awake. Only barely hearing her father down the hall quietly sipping his coffee and watching the morning news, she opened the email. It read:

"Hello again, Angelica, it's Sara. I know I didn't explain a lot to you at the reading, but I needed time to look into the situation more, from the standpoint of a clairvoyant. I know you have certain 'abilities,' as they are generally called. I also picked up that your father was the one who passed them along to you. This is one of the reasons why you have been experiencing what you've been experiencing. I will attach a document to this email going over breathing exercises and meditation techniques that will help you manage your skills better.

"Secondly, there is something external that you need to be aware of. As I told your father, it will go after the things you cherish most in life. Keeping your family together and intact should be the focus of everyone involved. I've had considerable trouble trying to understand what this entity is, as I've been attacked every time I look into it. If I were you, I would avoid dwelling on and thinking about it as much as possible. I know this is considerably easier said than done, but put all of your effort into it. Fear only feeds it.

"Should you have any questions about the document I provided or general inquiries, just send me a message. And despite my financial hobbies, I will not charge you for anything.

"As always I remain,

"Sara Goodwin

"P.S.: For your safety, trust none of the spirits you encounter on your property."

Angelica stared mutely at the message, reading it two and three times. She then finally felt something she wasn't even sure she knew she wanted: confirmation. It seemed as if someone else was getting a clearer picture of the inarticulate thoughts and intuition that she so desperately wanted to understand. The email did bring a reassurance of her self-perceived sanity, but mixed it into a bittersweet cocktail. Reassured by confirmation but dreading the reality: Her instincts were telling her the truth all along.

Thirty-six

Later that evening, Rosanna and Edward were alone at the Barrister farm. Angelica was staying over at Abby's house, it being the fleeting last days of their summer break from school. Having just finished their meal, Rosanna was washing up the last couple of dishes as Edward swooped in behind her put his arms around his wife's waist.

He kissed her on the neck before whispering in her ear, "We've got the house to ourselves. Let's have some fun."

As he nibbled on her ear, she said, "Ugh, but I'm dirty! I've been working in the garden all day."

He kissed her on the cheek. "That's okay, I don't mind."

She giggled, but said assuredly, "Look, I need to take a shower." Rosanna turned and embraced him, then kissed him on the lips. She then pressed her finger to his mouth. "You can wait, sweet stuff. I won't take long."

As she turned and walked away, he playfully smacked her on the behind. "Let me know if you need any help in there."

Rosanna turned and smiled, sticking her tongue out briefly in a funny way before heading to shower.

After getting her bed clothes from the closet in their room, she went into the bathroom and closed the door behind her. She stopped at the mirror and looked herself over before undoing the ponytail in her hair. The thoughts of the upcoming event made her a little more paranoid about the miniscule signs of aging in her face, imagined and real. As she rubbed her fingers under her eyes and studied the nearly invisible lines beneath them, she was overcome with a sudden and strong sensation of sleepiness. Rosanna struggled to fight back a strong yawn, but lost. After this, she muttered to herself, "Must be more tired than I...." She was cut off by another insistent yawn. *I need to get moving,* she thought to herself before disrobing and stepping into the shower.

Once inside the tub, she was only able to just drench herself before the drowsiness was starting to feel like drunkenness. Rosanna strained to focus on the bottle of body wash sitting only two feet from her hand. *I didn't... even... have a drink today...,* stammered in her mind, taking up valuable resources from basic coordination. She blinked her eyes a few times, then took the bottle in hand. Her eyes blurred in and out of focus again, as if going to sleep. The subsequent near fall, however, caused her grab one of the chrome handles along the shower wall and catch herself. The adrenaline coursing through her veins then gave her momentary clarity, but it was fleeting. Rosanna shook her head from side to side quickly, trying to wake herself up. The effort only brought her enough energy to try and brace for the inevitable fall.

Edward, in the bedroom across the hall, heard the clattering thud that resulted. He ran to the door and said with concern, "Rosy, honey, are you okay!?"

Immediately he heard a response behind the door. "I'm fine. I just slipped."

Having heard the fall very clearly, he wasn't completely convinced. "That sounded rough. Are you sure you're okay?"

The tone of the answer he heard was a little annoyed. "Yes, I'm fine. Just go lie down."

Edward still wasn't completely buying it, but he decided not to press her about it. The problem was, Rosanna hadn't said a word since her fall.

Twenty minutes passed and Edward was becoming worried. He could only hear the sound of the shower flowing and nothing else. Rosanna was always punctual with her bathing. "Ten minutes or less" was her motto for the shower and she never went over this far.

He stood up from the bed and walked across the hall. Knocking on the door, "Hey, Rosy, are you okay?"

He didn't get a response.

"Rose, honey, can you hear me?"

Still, nothing.

Wanting to leave nothing to chance, he opened the door halfway. "Rosy, you okay?" Hearing nothing he opened the door completely and was shocked to see his wife's arm hanging limp over the edge of the tub. He pulled back the shower curtain and found Rosanna unconscious and snoring quietly. Her torso was now pinkish red, discolored from the steady stream of hot water from the shower.

Frantic, "Rosy!? Wake up, honey, wake up!"

He gently smacked her on the cheek, trying to rouse her for a moment before reaching to turn the shower off.

Edward then took his wife's head in his hands. "Rose, honey, wake up! Please wake up!"

Much to his relief, she groaned and mumbled, "Hmm? What's wrong, honey?"

He kissed her on the forehead. "Thank goodness, babe. What happened?"

Although still stricken heavily with overwhelming fatigue, the here and now of the situation managed to peek through in her mind. She could feel the pain all over her body from the fall. She stirred uncomfortably. "I feel so tired. I remember... being tired when I got in. I don't remember anything else."

Edward saw his wife trying to fight off the glassy-eyed fog, but for what he knew would only be a brief time. "Let's get you dried off and in bed. Does that sound good?"

She nodded and strained to help him pick herself up from the tub.

"Do you want me to call the doctor?"

She yawned heavily before replying, "No, no... I just really need to sleep. I'm very tired."

A few minutes passed and Rosanna, with the help of Edward, had managed to dry off and change into her pajamas and climb into bed. He asked her again if she was sure she was okay, and she insisted that she just needed to sleep. He watched his wife doze off again quickly and tried to relax himself. Edward then had trouble getting comfortable as there was a certain amount of sexual drive that had been building up inside of him.

He and Rosanna hadn't been intimate in the last six weeks and needless to say, he was antsy. They had tried to bring Angelica a brother or sister in the past few months, but for whatever reason Rosanna was simply not getting pregnant. Neither of them could understand why, but at the same time were reluctant to bring it up to their doctor. That's not the easiest subject to speak about and neither of them being unable to do their role in the act brought an anxiety that kept them not wanting to know, but to keep trying.

Edward lay awake in bed for an additional several minutes, trying to quiet his mind. He was concerned that something else might have made Rosanna fall in the shower, something beyond just a failed attempt to overcome exhaustion. He then decided to try a technique that he'd grown up hearing about and occasionally tried with success: a glass of warm milk. To make sure he would get to sleep, he also took a couple of over-the-counter sleeping pills: diphenhydramine.

The remedy eventually did its job and Edward was fast asleep.

Thirty-seven

Edward, wearing only his flannel pajama bottoms, came to standing at the foot of the king-size bed on which he and Rosanna slept every night. He placed his hand briefly on one of the four posters at the foot end, smiling warmly and slyly at the sight before him. Rosy was lying on her back and supporting her head with the hand of her bent left arm. The smile on her face left nothing to the imagination of her intentions. Naked underneath the lone sheet covering her body up to her chest, she raised her eyebrows and motioned for him to come to her with her finger. As he climbed onto the bed and atop his wife, she placed her hand on the back of his neck. Rosanna then pulled the sheet aside, exposing her bare flesh and sending a shiver down Edward's back in the process. He leaned in and they begin kissing heavily. He pressed his chest against hers, feeling the soft skin of her breasts against the hair and skin on his own torso. Each kiss seemed longer and more passionate than the last. If there was a reward for his patience, he was feeling it then with accumulated interest.

The heavy, deep kissing lasted for a couple of minutes before Rosanna pressed her hands against Edward's chest, motioning for him to stand up. He complied, his wife rising to her feet as well. Once on their feet, they embraced each other tightly, staying locked in a perpetual kissing session. Rosanna then ran her hands down his back and grabbed his behind. Shortly after she pulled her face away just long enough to start to lower herself to her knees. Along the way she ran her tongue down his sternum, then his abdomen, before quickly yanking his flannel bottoms to the ground. He was surprised that Rosanna was performing this oral act, seeing as how she was always against it in the past. At some point in her early years, she acquired the belief that such a thing was immoral, and she had no intention of going against that belief for anyone. Nonetheless, he simply allowed himself to indulge in the passion and sensations of the moment. He then closed his eyes as his wife pressed him to sit on the bed, then relaxing prostrate completely. Even more surprising to him was just how skilled his wife was at this act, considering her utter unfamiliarity with it. His eyes stayed closed, he trying to control the pleasurable sensations to the best of his ability. Making it last was the only thing on his mind.

As if on cue, when he couldn't seem to hold back anymore, she stopped and climbed on top of him. His eyes stayed shut as he engaged in a long and wonderful kiss. Edward was then overcome with the intense and distinct pleasure of penetration. Scarcely able to hold off the debilitating urge to finish immediately, he groaned loudly and was answered with a similar moan and giggle. There was something different about that small laugh, however, which broke his submission to the pleasure. He opened his eyes and was shaken to see what was before him. The black curly hair and nearly black eyes of his wife were instead the face and body of Sara. The long brown hair he'd only seen a couple of days before was completely unbraided and unbridled, cascading down the pale skin of her shoulders and chest. Sara's bold green eyes were staring into his own with an otherworldly intensity. Before he could react, she leaned down onto his chest, pressing her firm breasts against him. She pinned his hands against the mattress with her own. In his mind and body, he attempted to resist, but was kept down by not only Sara's seemingly inhuman strength, but also the debilitating and euphoric pleasure. She grinded her hips against his, groaning erotically while saying, "Don't worry, Mr. Barrister, no one has to know."

Sara's sly smile grew as Edward struggled.

"I can't...."

She tightened her hips and buttocks as he growled.

"Oh, God! I can't...."

She leaned in and licked the side of his neck and face. He struggled, with futility, as a third voice from across the room, at the door, called out, "Relax, Mr. Barrister. I won't let anyone in here. No one has to know." Edward then directed his eyes to the closed portal leading out of the room. He was shocked to see an older woman, whose ears looked like oyster shells, dressed in old-fashioned, straight and plain blue dress with a white apron, topped with a brown bonnet. Even though he didn't recall seeing this woman before, there was an uncanny familiarity about her. Edward looked at the older woman in disbelief for a moment before his attention was yanked back to Sara as she grabbed the back of his head and pulled him upright. She then wrapped her arms around him, holding him in place as she rode his lap aggressively. Control of his body slipped away as both he and Sara begin to approach climax. As they both did, she dug her nails into his back, drawing blood as they sliced the skin across his shoulder blades. He closed his eyes for a few seconds, taken away by the rapture of the orgasm. Suddenly he opened his eyes, however, and was appalled by the sight before him. The warm and supple form of Sara was replaced by the cold and clammy form of Caroline. Her stark naked frame, though appearing to be that of a frail old woman, gripped him even more fiercely than ever. He then felt an overwhelming amount of pain coming from his groin as Caroline smiled. She opened her mouth to speak, but before any words escaped, several flies buzzed from between her lips and zipped around his face. A powerful waft of decay, far stronger than any semblance of such he'd experienced in his life, invaded his nostrils and nearly caused him to vomit immediately. A crooked and tormenting smile contorted her face as she said, "Oh, Mr. Barrister, you've been saving that for a long time, haven't you?" She began to laugh as he struggled in vain to free himself. The pain from his crotch was borderline crippling now as she ground her hips against his. She then ran her rot-soaked tongue up the side of his face. What would normally be saliva was, instead, a viscous black liquid running down his cheek. He cried out in pain and attempted to struggle as she hissed, "Don't worry, Mr. Barrister. No one has to know."

Edward awoke violently from sleep. He cried out in pain, feeling a distinct burning sensation across his back. He then felt moisture on his crotch beneath his flannel bottoms. He grabbed it in pain as Rosanna awoke beside him.

Edward grit his teeth and groaned loudly as his wife asked, "Honey, what's wrong!?"

He looked at the hand covering his recent erection and was horrified to see noticeable blood splotches.

Almost as shocked as he was, "Ed, what happened!?"

He quickly looked under his cotton pants. The blood was puddling up, making it difficult to see any details other than a rough outline. As he gingerly stood up from the bed, "I had a nightmare…. Ow, God!"

As Rosanna followed him across the hall to the bedroom, she could see the blood coming from his back through his shirt. "A *nightmare*!?"

She grabbed a hand towel from nearby shelf and handed it to him. He removed his flannel pants and wrapped it around the wounded area. Edward hunched over in pain as she lifted up the back of his shirt.

"Ed, you're all scratched up back here, too! What happened!?"

She took another towel and started to dab up the blood trickling down his back.

Gritting his teeth again, he stammered, "I don't know! I had a nightmare and just woke up like this!"

Rosanna shifted her attention now to the injury in front. She knelt on the floor and gingerly took the towel he'd been holding in her hand. She removed the plush cotton just long enough to see three scratches running the length of his penis. Trying to make sense of it all, "You must've grabbed it when you were asleep."

He winced as she resumed pressure on the area. "What about my back?"

Thinking he was missing the priority of the problem in hand, "What about it?"

"I mean, how did I get the scratches on my back then?"

She fumbled for an answer. "I don't know… we'll worry about that later. Let's just get you cleaned up."

Several minutes and bandages later, they managed to stop the bleeding. They had both decided to forgo a trip to the hospital, primarily from embarrassment that they would receive from the assumed cause of the injuries: rough sex. Edward was sitting on the living room couch with a towel underneath his groin and an ice bag on top to try and numb the excruciating pain. He had managed to close his eyes and calm himself for the most part, Rosanna sitting in a chair facing him.

She asked quietly, "Do you need anything else?"

He exhaled through a surge of pain before answering, "I think I'm about as good as I can get."

Still very confused about the whole situation, but keeping his condition in mind, she carefully asked, "Do you want to talk about it? Maybe we can figure out what happened."

The dream, every stinging detail, was burned into his mind. He wasn't going to forget this one anytime soon. He hesitated before speaking, opting to give the "abridged" version of what happened. Starting slowly, "Well, I was dreaming about you, believe it or not. We were going to have sex. We started off normal, everything was fine. Then, as we were nearing the end, you suddenly turned into this old woman. But it wasn't you, if that makes sense. It was a different person entirely. I've never seen that person before in my life! There were flies coming out of her mouth, she wreaked of death… she was horrible! She grabbed me and wouldn't let go! I tried to get free, but she grabbed my back and I started feeling the pain in my crotch!" He stopped, looking down and staring at the floor as he said, "Then I woke up like this…."

Even though he had went out of his way to articulate that Rosanna had morphed into a completely different person (in this version of the dream, anyway), the words got twisted somehow inside her head. She took away an imagined, or planted, thought that he may simply have been thinking that Rosanna was getting old. The known struggle of fighting the biological clock in her mind was relentless. Even though she was still just in her thirties, she was getting paranoid about age.

Nonetheless, she made sure he'd finished telling his tale before saying, "That sounds like a horrible dream. Maybe you grabbed yourself when things went wrong and… you know."

Sure, that idea had passed through his mind as well, but it only partially offered a shoddy explanation for some of the phenomenon. "How did I get the scratches on my back, then?"

She tried to, in her usual ham-fisted way, inject humor into the situation. "Maybe I knew you were having dirty dreams and tried to make you stop."

He thought to himself, *Jesus, that was awkward,* and showed his discontent with the attempt. He rolled his eyes before saying, "Rosy... this isn't the time."

Strangely, even for her, she snapped back, "Fine, Ed, I was just trying to lighten the mood!"

As she stood and stormed out of the room, "Rose... hon...," but was unable to get her attention before she went to the bedroom and slammed the door behind her. He gritted his teeth in pain as another wave came over him. "I'm the one bleeding and *I* need to apologize?"

Edward briefly attempted to get up, but the discomfort was too much. The deception and contents of the illicit dream also made him feel guilty, and perhaps, he wasn't able to forgive himself just yet. Thankfully a quilt was always on the back of the couch and seemed particularly useful at this time.

Thirty-eight

Later, the next morning, the familiar ringtone on Edward's phone was sounding on the charger sitting on the small table next to their bed. Seeing as how Rosanna was the only one in the bed, she ignored the first three rings.

Without opening her eyes, she groaned, "Ed, get the phone...."

No response, and the phone continued to ring.

Rosanna opened her eyes and pulled herself across the bed, plucking the phone from the charger. She squinted and made out "John Kelly" on the screen. Still heavy with sleep, she answered, "Hello...."

Angelica's voice came through. "Hey, Mom. Are you guys going pick me up? You said you would be here at 10:30."

She looked at the clock next to the charger which read 10:50 A.M. Suddenly realizing she had grossly overslept. "Ah, crap. I'm sorry, babe. I'll head over there right now. Okay?" She wrapped up the brief conversation with her daughter before getting up and dressed in haste.

Once dressed she headed to the living room and saw Edward starting to stir as well. She said in a curt tone, "We overslept. I have to go and pick up Angelica."

Through a yawn, "Ugh... what time is it?"

"Almost 11:00. I'll be right back."

Not much later, Angelica and her mother were returning home from the Kelly house. Angelica had barely said a word so far, instead, staring out the window at the patches of dark clouds overhead. The discomfort from her caving injuries was still causing her noticeable pain all over. She put her finger briefly on the red spot covering her lips, annoyed by the lingering sensations.

Seeing her disengaged, Rosanna tried to raise her spirits. "It'll get better soon, honey, I promise."

Not looking at her mother, she sighed. "I know."

"Hopefully they'll be healed up by the time school starts."

Her tone still distant. "I'll get picked on, I know it."

Rosanna knew she was right about that. The less-than-kind kids always find a way to drive others of their kind crazy with such imperfections. She decided to change the subject. "I'm sorry we didn't come to pick you up on time. Daddy had a rough night and we overslept."

Finally engaging her mother with attention, "What do you mean? What happened?"

Her mother had been thinking the whole trip over how to deliver this peculiar set of events. She could only try and omit as many details as possible: "Daddy had a really bad nightmare." She slowed the car to make the turn into their driveway. "He somehow got scratched all over his back. We don't know how that happened."

The gravel on the road leading up to their house was creaking and popping away outside. Angelica was taken aback not only by the illogical structure of events presented to her, but also the calmness with which they were delivered. A small scowl crept across her eyebrows. "How did he get scratched from a nightmare? That doesn't make any sense."

Rosanna figured she wouldn't buy the story at face value, but still didn't understand the situation herself. "We don't know. We can't seem to figure out what happened."

The car came to a stop and Angelica, not happy with the summary given to her, rushed into the house and quickly found Edward sitting on the living room couch. He was flipping through the channels and still holding an icepack on his lap.

She ran toward him and stopped at his knee. "Dad! Mom told me you got scratched. What happened?"

He extended his hand in a comforting gesture. "Hey, baby girl. Daddy's okay. I'm just a little scratched up."

Rosanna interjected. "I have to go to the store for groceries, you two. Ed, remember…." She then dragged her thumb and forefinger across her lips, a clear sign to not go into detail about what happened.

He nodded his head and she left through the kitchen door.

Angelica carefully sat on the couch to his right, trying especially hard to avoid causing him pain. "How did you get scratches from a nightmare?"

Edward was also at an uncomfortable loss for an explanation. "I wish we knew. I just woke up all cut up."

"Where did you get scratched?"

He replied, "On my back and…," motioning toward the icepack, "down there."

She winced sympathetically. "What was the nightmare about?"

Angelica was certainly going to be getting the heavily edited and abridged version. "Well, an old woman attacked me. She raked her nails across my back when she grabbed me."

"Ugh. What did she look like?"

He started to answer. "Well, she…." An idea suddenly came to mind. The reason the old hag in the dream seemed familiar was directly related to the person next to him. "Ange, that old woman that you saw, what did you say she looked like? What was her name, Caroline?"

Spoken of and mystically on cue, the form of Caroline appeared in the distance out toward the back of the house, near the barns.

Angelica stared off at her as she replied, "An old woman… oyster ears… blue dress, white apron… brown bonnet."

He immediately made the uncanny connection, and looked in the direction his daughter was staring. "What's wrong? Do you see her?"

Nodding her head, "Yeah, right there." She pointed for a moment before looking back at him and asking, "*She* did this to you?"

He knew something was there, but he couldn't see Caroline with his eyes. "It sounds like the same person. Maybe we were wrong about her."

She looked over the injured state of her father and felt a deep pit forming in her stomach. Discomfort soon gave way to anger. "She…." Angelica couldn't even finish the sentence as the anger boiled over into rage. "It" had hurt her and even tried to kill her. Now that it was injuring her beloved father, an irrefutable line had been crossed. It had now become her enemy without question.

Angelica then flew into fury and marched toward the back door. Edward tried with futilely to call her back. After closing the door behind her, the form of Caroline had vanished. Nonetheless, Angelica, fists clinched at her side, walked to the turnaround between the barns.

The intensity and volume of her voice at their pinnacle, she growled and snapped, "Caroline!? Where are you!? Leave my family alone! Never touch my dad again!"

Edward had managed to stumble to the door now, still holding the icepack.

Angelica jumped up and down, stamping her feet and swinging her arms. "I hate you! I hate you! I hate you... you bitch!"

Edward made his way to her, thankful that Rosanna hadn't heard her daughter, of all critical things, say a cuss word. "Easy, Ange. She probably wants you to be angry."

Good advice, but it didn't make any sense to Angelica in her current state or age. Her face flush red, she turned to Edward. "But I do hate her! She hurt me and you! First the bridge, the cave, then the birds. It's all her fault!"

Edward embraced her with his free arm. "I know, I know. We'll figure out what to do, but getting upset and yelling at her won't fix it."

Angelica began to settle, but was still somehow under the impression that her actions would somehow help. The helplessness of a situation could lead anyone to irrational answers. They don't call it "blind rage" for nothing.

Later that afternoon, Rosanna had since returned from the trip to the store in town and was putting away groceries in the kitchen. Edward tried to help as best he could, but the injuries sustained from the night before limited his involvement. Rosanna has been even icier in her disposition since her return. Edward could tell that something was obviously bothering her, but he didn't know what and knew that she would make sure he knew when the time was to her advantage.

As they started to finish unloading the bags, Angelica went to her room. Leaving the door cracked, she went to her desk and turned on her computer. As it booted up, she could hear a quiet conversation coming from the kitchen. Only murmuring initially, however, and nothing out of the ordinary. She was soon checking her email and composing a message to Sara explaining the recent situation with her father.

Meanwhile, in the kitchen, Edward was trying to get to the bottom of what was troubling his wife so much. "Rose, honey, what's bothering you? You've been standoffish all day."

Rosanna's pause at the question caused him much apprehension. He knew nothing good was getting ready to show. "I was talking with a friend of mine in the store today...."

The second intentional pause sent a chill through him. Did she know? How did she find out? He proceeded with caution toward the proverbial minefield. "And?"

With a new rock-solid gaze, "Apparently she saw 'me,'" making sure to use air quotes, "coming from someone's house on the outside of town."

It was a small community and the revelation being produced was no doubt the product of notorious gossip. He knew that the jig was up, but he stuck to playing dumb as long as possible. "What do you mean?"

With this response, Rosanna shot a debilitating face that said without words, *"You're still going with denial at this point?"* She then verbalized. "You know what I mean. Who the hell is Sara!?" Angelica had just sent the email to Sara, and the increase in the volume of the conversation down the hall now caught her interest.

You're screwed, Ed, was all he thought as he gripped the bridge of his nose between his thumb and finger. He sighed and said, "Honey, it's not what you're thinking...."

He was then cut off. "Really, Ed!? What was it, then!? You liked her 'architecture'!?"

He knew that Angelica was with him, but the thought of what actually happened would be just as damning to his wife. Her beliefs absolutely forbade the practices of such people. He tried to go with the lesser of two evils, at least to him.

"Honey, Angelica just wanted some advice. She set up an appointment with a psychic online. Ange was there the whole time with me and nothing else happened."

"What!? Don't you dare try and blame this on our daughter! You mean to tell me that she set this whole thing up and you two hid it from me? You both know I won't allow that sort of 'soothsaying' malarkey in our house! It's sinful!"

Neither noticed that Angelica has been looking out the crack in her doorway since the yelling started. Edward had to catch himself from laughing at her antiquated term of "soothsaying," not to mention her desperate attempt to avoid cursing by using the word "malarkey." No time for jokes. He was about to be burned at the stake.

"Rose, she set it up online but didn't tell me about it until we were in the car going fishing."

"Oh, oh, all right. And I guess you couldn't say no!? Do you have trouble saying 'no' to *any* female, Ed!? Someone like Sara!?"

Sweet and rosy Rosanna was really going full-tilt. He retained his relative composure. "Nothing happened, Rose! Angelica was with me the whole time! She just did a tarot card reading."

Neither noticed Angelica was standing next to them.

Rosanna continued. "*Just* a tarot card reading!? That's how it all starts! Next thing you know you'll be going over there every week for some sort of *reading*!"

The tone of her voice was now starting to tell Edward that this matter was not only religious, but also something very personal. Even with a subtext of suspected infidelity, the issue was larger than that.

"You know, I might think *you'd* do something like this, but taking our daughter, too...."

Angelica interrupted. "Stop it, Mom! Dad's telling the truth! She just wanted to help us!"

Edward doubled over briefly as a surge of pain ran through his crotch.

Ignoring it, Rosanna said, "Angelica! Don't use that tone with me!"

She paused again, hoping to back her daughter down with such. It didn't work as Angelica's confrontational posture remained the same.

"And what could this *witch* help you with that your parents can't!?"

As Edward regained his composure, he was struck by the image of his eight-year-old daughter standing toe to toe with someone much taller than herself.

His daughter snapped back. "What about the cave!? What about Caroline!?"

Rosanna returned, "Angelica, no one should be nosing around caves by themselves anyway! And who's Caroline!? Another floozy, Ed!?"

He tried to answer, but was cut off by his daughter.

"Caroline is a spirit that lives on our land! She's evil! Dad and I didn't say anything because we knew you wouldn't believe us!"

Rosanna grabbed her own head and groaned in frustration. She quickly fired back, "All right, I've had enough of this from you two! There's no such thing as ghosts! Stop trying to blame everything on an imaginary boogeyman!"

Edward tried to speak again. "Rose, honey, listen...."

She barked back, "No! I'm not listening to any more of this nonsense! Young lady, the next time you leave this place it'll be for school! Is that clear!? And you, Ed, I hope the couch was comfortable, because you get to sleep there until I say otherwise!"

Later that night, Edward decided to search out his wife, who'd been upstairs searching through a spare bedroom for a particular box. Still slowed from the pain in his groin, he barely reached the staircase in the hall as Rosanna stepped onto the top stair holding a large box in her arms. He recognized it immediately as a box he privately referred to in his own mind as "The Ark," as it was the box Rosanna had packed full of religious artifacts from her previous home. She had agreed to tone it down a bit on the iconography, but the recent events caused a complete backlash. In Rosanna's mind, it was needed now more than ever.

She walked past him toward the kitchen, barely giving him a glance as she passed by him. As he turned to face her, she placed the box on the kitchen table and said, "Ed, come and help me unpack this box." Her tone was direct and short.

He didn't resist. One by one they unpacked each crucifix, Bible, portrait of St. Mary, portrait of Jesus, the whole shebang. As they got toward the last pieces in the box, Rosanna went and took a hammer and nails from a drawer in the kitchen.

She then stopped and said, "Ed, you may be undecided in your faith, but I won't have our daughter grow up a heathen." She then took two crucifixes from the box.

As she walked by and down the hall, he said, "Ouch! That wasn't necessary."

No attention was paid to his remark and Rosanna soon reached her daughter's bedroom door. Without a knock or warning she pushed the door open with enough force to cause it to bang against the doorstop on the wall. The intrusion caused Angelica to suddenly close her email page (she still waiting on a response from Sara), and look up at her mother in confusion. Angelica then said mildly, "Hey, I thought we had to knock before coming in."

Her mother replied curtly, "My house, my rules. I don't need permission to go anywhere here."

Edward had managed to get to the doorway as Rosanna turned and began to hammer a nail into the far wall. With each blow, Angelica felt more and more that her personal space was being violated in some way. But there was something else, some other feeling of displeasure. Something, what thing she couldn't articulate, was oozing anger and resentment. This wave of emotion seemed to be coming from the house itself all around. She hung one foot-long crucifix on the wall and headed to the adjoining wall. As the hammering continued, Angelica could sense the surrounding resentment becoming slightly stronger. There wasn't really anything to say. Her mother didn't believe in ghosts, so she sure as hell wouldn't understand this inarticulate sensation. If Edward knew, he was keeping silent. Perhaps he was just going along with the leader of a small-scale inquisition in his own home to avoid total meltdown.

As she finished hanging the second wooden crucifix, complete with the attached body of Jesus, she looked at her daughter and said sternly, "There. Now when you need help, that's who you turn to. Understand?" She didn't wait for a response from Angelica and left the room.

As the door shut behind her mother, Angelica reached over to make sure her quartz amulet had remained hidden in a desk drawer. She was going to have to be clever with it from now on.

Thirty-nine

Angelica awoke in her bed. From the clear sky outside, she could tell it was late morning. Oddly, the window glass was missing, the frame alone remaining. She could hear the birds chirping merrily, insects buzzing about, and a gentle summer breeze washing through the trees in the distance. The familiar smells of the season wafted in over the sill. Suddenly, a man appeared from the left side of the window. She instinctively lurched away from the opening as he pressed his hands against the window frame on the outside. Angelica stared at the man and vaguely recognized him. His short, brown, oil-slicked hair was disheveled, matching the state of his clothing. He was dressed in worn overalls and a once kempt shirt that was now covered in dirt and sweat, no doubt from years of toil. Most disturbing, however, was the way his head lay limply on his left shoulder. She recognized this same feature and assumed him to be the man she'd seen in her dream once before at the backdoor. His blue eyes, looking a little crazed, focused in on hers. He then spoke in a heavily rasped and throaty voice. "Please, little girl, don't be scared. I know I look scary, but I won't hurt you." Angelica, either frozen in fear or wanting to hear him out, remained stationary. A sharp breath, sounding like he was trying to breathe through a straw, followed. He continued. "You're the only one who can see us... please, you have to help us...."

Her own eyes wide with fear, she hesitated before asking, "How... how am I supposed to help you?"

He strained before saying, "Sara...." Before he could finish his sentence, he was suddenly and violently ripped away by an unseen force that seemed to pull at his neck. Angelica was stunned for a moment, but quickly ran back toward the window and looked outside to her right, the direction in which he was pulled. To her horror, she could see the man being steadily pulled along the ground. The source of said action appeared to be emanating from the older woman sitting atop the near side of the fence of the goat pen next to the barn. Caroline, smiling a crooked smile, was holding her right hand above her head, pulling at the struggling man's body as if on an invisible string. The fear and astonishment Angelica was feeling suddenly changed to rage at the sight of this monstrosity toying with her prey. She quickly climbed out her window and walked along the back side of her house before stopping at the turnaround in front of the barns.

As the body of the man went limp and crumbled before Caroline, Angelica pointed at her and yelled, "Stop it! Stop it now!"

Amused at the little girl seething in front of her, "Well, well! This one has a temper, doesn't she?" As she laughed, the sound reverberated throughout the entire property. Sneering, "What's the matter? Is baby Ange going to throw a tantrum?" Again her laughed echo all around.

Still fuming, "Shut up, you old hag!"

Positively amused, she laughed again. "Do you really think getting angry and calling me names is going to help? You're pathetic! All of you meat-puppets are the same! Let's ask my other guest...." She raised her left hand in the air as the form a young boy materialized from what appeared to be a spring of blood bubbling from the ground. The clothes, the hair, the face: It was Timothy, the boy from the cave. His body hung limp, upright, as if suspended from above. "You already know Timothy here." She laughed again as the pain from the injuries in the cave singed and burned like the day they were first inflicted. Angelica dropped to her knees, gritting her teeth helplessly in pain. Caroline giggled before saying, "I bet that hurts, doesn't it?"

Starting to recover from the pain, Angelica growled, "I... hate... you...."

Caroline replied, "Tsk, tsk! That's no way to behave in front of company! Here, Timothy, wave to Angelica." She then motioned with her left hand as Timothy's left hand awkwardly rose and waved robotically back *and forth. "And here we have 'Old Man Harris,' I don't think you two have been properly introduced. Wave hello, Amos!" She then motioned with her right hand, Amos' hand also waving mechanically. Angelica had managed to get to her feet again as Caroline continued. "And I can even make them dance—watch!" Caroline then pulled a violin from behind her back and started to fiddle away. The tune was rhythmical, but the notes were off-key and painfully loud to Angelica's ears. Savoring her work, she watched as the bodies of Amos and Timothy twisted and jerked strangely to a dance of pandemonium.*

Caroline soon brought the improvised song to an end, causing the last note to resonate on the strings. As the note ended, so did the animation of the bodies of Timothy and Amos. Angelica then screamed, "Stop it!"

The old woman laughed again. "But look, I can even make them talk!" At this, Caroline snapped her fingers and looked toward Timothy, who then stood up. He was clearly reluctant to obey her unspoken command, causing Caroline to shout, "Now, boy!"

He slowly climbed upon the fence and sat next to Caroline. Her left arm suddenly disappeared behind his back and was then shoved forward. His body responded in motions that indicated the old lady's arm being rammed up through his torso from behind and below. As his eyes begin to glow yellow his mouth opened. In a normal speaking voice, "Hello, Angelica. My name is Timothy Harris and I'm a little shit."

Caroline then demanded that Amos also sit on the fence. With her right arm, she repeated the actions done to Timothy and began to make Amos speak in the same manner. "My name is Amos Harris. I gave up on life, killed myself, and now I rot in hell."

Seeing this, Angelica instinctively reached for a necklace around her neck, but neither the crucifix nor the quartz pendant were there. Caroline then laughed again and said, "Are you looking for your trinkets? They won't help you."

Still speaking in a calm tone, the body of Timothy said, "Yes, Angelica. Don't fight us or you'll only feel more pain."

The body of Amos said in a similar tone, his head moving about like a bobble-head toy, "Yes, young lady. Respect your elders."

The two bodies then began dancing up and down in rhythm, together chanting, "We dance... we dance... we dance the dance macabre!" Both bodies dropped to the ground at the end of each repetition, rising again afterward. The chant grew louder and louder, causing Angelica to cover her ears. "WE DANCE... WE DANCE... WE DANCE THE DANCE MACABRE!"

As the voices mercifully stopped, Angelica looked up at Caroline. The old woman then slung the two bodies free from her hands and onto the ground next to her. They crumpled over and started to ooze blood from their mouths. She descended from the fence and walked toward Angelica, smiling. Caroline's left eye was now different, however, as it alone glowed yellow and twitched erratically. Standing just feet in front of Angelica, the hag said, "You see what I want you to see. You think you're clever, but you're not."

As angry as ever, "Shut up, you old bitch!"

Caroline then stepped closer, her hater unwilling to move. "That temper of yours might just get you in trouble someday." In an amused tone, "Blind with rage, blind with rage." She then extended her hand toward Angelica's face and opened her palm. "Blind with rage... blind with rage... ." Caroline's hand only briefly and partially obscured the young girl's vision, but a stark change occurred. Angelica's vision was then tinted crimson red as if a colored lens had been placed over her eyes. The old woman watched and laughed as Angelica tried to rub her eyes clear. She then walked back toward the pen next to the barn as the three goats, Agnes, Coffee, and Pop Tart curiously emerged from their enclosure. "Oh, look! Your little friends are here to play, too!"

Seeing the old lady dressed in pioneer clothes approach the pen caused an immediate reaction. She knew Caroline would only offer more pain at this point. Angelica ran toward the pen as fast as she could, but was suddenly flung into the air by a violent surge of blood coming from the ground beneath her like a geyser. She soon landed on the ground several feet away and was overcome by the paralyzing pain of the fall. Unable to move, she groaned, "Don't touch them!"

As Angelica was staring up at the dark red sky, only a slightly different hue from the other elements around her, she saw Caroline's face suddenly appear over her. The old woman's left eye still twitching and glowing, she *said threateningly, "Red sky of morning, little bitch take warning!" Angelica closed her eyes and screamed furiously....*

Angelica jerked awake, her heart pounding away and her teeth clamped shut hard. She quickly looked back and forth around her room. The window pane was still in place. Despite the many horrid images she'd seen in her dream, she couldn't shake the suspicion that she needed to check on her goats first and foremost. She glanced over at her clock, 5:45 A.M., before slipping on her shoes and running down the hall and out the backdoor. As the screen door slapped against the frame behind her, she started to see the aftermath of an indulgence in manic and senseless slaughter. "NO!" she cried, slowing at the fence to the goat pen. Angelica then yelled out first in shock, but it soon gave way to a rage she'd quickly become accustomed to when dealing with Caroline.

Rosanna and Edward jolted awake at this. Edward, still on the couch in the living room, wanted to dash straight outside to his daughter, but the pain brought him to the floor. His wife saw him on her way to the kitchen, but paid little attention before running out the backdoor. She quickly made it to the turnaround and saw Angelica seething and kicking the fence. Nearly speechless, "Oh, my...," she made the sign of the cross, however, before finishing. Angelica then ran over to a spot in the fence where the head of Agnes was pushed through one of the small rectangular holes in the fencing. Normally these holes were far too small for the head of such an animal to fit through, but it seemed to have found its way through one, nonetheless. Despite the head of the goat staring forward and upright, the body was twisted completely upside down at the neck. The morning sun caught the golden iris of the animal, defining its rectangular pupil, as it fixated on nothingness. The tongue hung limp from the mouth and off to the side, frozen in its last bleat of terror. Angelica tried desperately to free the head, but was unable.

Edward had emerged from the back of house by now and limped his way over to Rosanna. "What happened?" he asked her with a dumbfounded tone.

His wife had no answer as she now saw another fixation of the gore show: The head of the goat Coffee was detached from the body and stuck to the wall of the barn. Ten feet up in the air, pinned by some violent force to the wood by a large rusty pitchfork, the rough and ripped neck beneath steadily dripped blood below. Beneath, as if propped up, the body of the slain animal sat unnaturally on its haunches, the forelegs drooping to their sides. Bits of vertebrae, muscle, and the trachea of the beast sprouted haggardly where the head used to be attached. Nearly throwing up on her husband, Rosanna turned away and dry heaved on her knees. Edward tried to comfort her, but she was too distraught for any of it.

Angelica, with tears streaming down her cheeks, climbed over the fence of the enclosure and now saw the inarticulate remains of Pop Tart. The head was lying face up, smoldering and charred. Tiny wisps of gray smoke rose and twirled in the breeze as she was only able to discern various parts of the animal here and there. A hoof, a slab of fur and flesh, and blood-soaked bones, were all strewn upon the ground at random. Angelica briefly looked up at the door leading inside which was, as she always left it, shut and locked. Still boiling inside, she kicked the side of the barn repeatedly in anger. As her foot inside her shoes begins to beg for mercy from the pain, she dropped to her knees and felt the hopelessness setting in. The swirl of curses and damnations in her head was too heady and she instead simply began to weep.

Recovering from her vomiting and wanting to also get away from the carnage, Rosanna said, "I'll go call the police."

As she disappeared into the house, Edward stepped forward to the fence. He managed to convince her to get out of the pen.

Once over the fence, she walked toward him and embraced him as he carefully went down on one knee. Sniffling, "I had a dream about Caroline again last night. She did this! I know she did!"

Edward, not really sure what to do, replied, "We'll figure this out. We'll have the police check it out and see if they...."

With noticeable agitation in her voice, she interrupted. "I know Caroline did it! Don't tell me you don't believe me, too!"

He put his forehead to hers. "I believe you, sweetie." He paused, then noticing something odd about his daughter's eyes, "Ange, what happened to your eyes?"

Angelica had yet to look in a mirror since the dream the night before. The whites of her eyes were now heavily stained red.

Looking over both of her eyes closely, "It looks like some blood vessels burst in your eyes. Can you see okay?"

Confused, and a little scared, "Yeah, I can see. What do you mean blood vessels burst in my eyes?"

Keeping composed, "It's nothing to worry about, I don't think. We'll go and see the doctor as soon as we can. You let me know if you have any trouble seeing, okay?"

Rosanna now reappeared on the back porch and made her way toward her family. As Angelica nodded at her father's question, her mother then saw the damage caused to her eyes. "Oh, my goodness! Angelica, are you okay?" She went through the same rigorous inspection that Edward just performed.

He said reassuringly, "I think she just blew a few blood vessels in her cornea. I had the same thing happen to me once in high school. She can see fine."

Rosanna showed concern on her face. "Oh, honey." She hugged Angelica briefly before saying, "The sheriff said he would be right over."

Angelica was tempted to reassert that Caroline was responsible for the whole thing, but argument from the night before kept this idea in check.

Forty

Several minutes later, the sheriff of Miller's Run was seen pulling his car onto their driveway and heading up the long gravel scar. The brown Crown Victoria soon came to a stop near the turnaround. Out stepped a somewhat portly, middle-aged man with aviator glasses. His khaki brown uniform was super starched and crisp along with a matching cowboy-style hat faced with a shining gold star. He adjusted his holster laden belt, mostly from years of habit using this gesture as a way to indirectly remind everyone that he was carrying a gun. He extended his chubby hand (or as he would put it, "strong") and shook that of Edward's. His mannerisms and tone seemed to indicate an annoyance with being woken up so early for a call.

"What seems to be the problem here?"

Before anyone could verbalize an answer, Edward pointed to the kill site at the barn.

The sheriff looked up and found his mouth agape for a second without his consent. He stepped closer to the fence and said, "What on Earth happened here?"

Angelica, having been told to wait inside the house, peered unnoticed out one of the windows in the kitchen.

Rosanna then said to the sheriff, "We don't know. Our daughter came out to feed them earlier and this is how she found them."

The rotund sheriff walked up and down the fence line, examining the mess. Seeing the intestines strewn about, he said, "They could've been visited by a pack of coyotes last night."

Edward spoke up, pointing at the head of Coffee the goat affixed to the wall of the barn. "I don't think coyotes did that."

The sheriff thought to himself for a moment, then replied, "Very well could've been vandals. It's hard to say. Do you know anyone that's out to get you or anything like that?"

Rosanna replied, "No, nothing like this."

Edward added, "The door was closed and locked when we got out here. Our daughter always brings the goats in at night and locks the door."

The sheriff replied, "Well, she may have forgotten to do that last night."

Rosanna said with disbelief, "Why would someone do this and then go to the trouble of locking the door behind them? That's assuming that she didn't lock them in the barn last night, which I know she did. And if it were locked, who would go to the trouble of unlocking the door, letting them out, killing them and then locking the door back behind them?"

Edward quickly added, "And there's only one key to that door and it's inside on the key holder next to the back door."

As the sheriff paused a moment, he remembered back, several years ago, when the police were called out to investigate animal slaughters like this before. He wasn't in law enforcement at that time, but he looked into it once he was elected sheriff. He poured over the case notes, but couldn't figure anything out beyond what his predecessors had done. Now he was being called out here for the same thing and it troubled him. No explanation now, and from the evidence he was seeing in front of him, he wasn't making any progress. Plus, there was just something about the case and property that kept him wanting to stay away from the place. Even with his trained mind and experience it caused a discomfort in his gut when he was dispatched to their home. Holly Bush Road was a place most people in town knew about and none, including law enforcement, wanted to go.

He snapped out of his brief reflections and said, "All right, let's double check and make sure the door's locked."

Rosanna stepped forward and said, "Right this way."

She then led him to the barn where, sure enough, the door was still shut and locked. She folded her arms and looked at the sheriff for any train of logic he could devise. Nothing.

As Edward limped to the open doorway, the sheriff said, "Well, at this point I'll file a report, take a statement from you all and take a few photos. I don't know if we'll find out who did this, but we'll give it our due diligence."

Rosanna, noticeably agitated at his lack of immediate results, said, "And that's it?"

Equally annoyed from her disrespectful tone, "Yes, ma'am, that's about all we can do right now. I don't see any footprints or much else evidence to single anyone out. Sometimes things like this happen and there ain't a whole lot to be done. That is, of course, unless they hit somebody else, too."

The sheriff did his work and finished in relatively quick time. This partially was due to the years of experience and ceaseless drive to leave as soon as possible. When he thought about it on the ride back to the station, it seemed silly, but he had learned to trust his gut, albeit a copious one, over the years.

Seeing the sheriff starting to pull away, Angelica rushed back to her room and shut the door behind her. Once there she sat down at her computer to check her email. A familiar situation played out: a new message from Sara Goodwin. Despite her normal proclivity for words, the message only read: "I had a terrible dream last night. What happened? S. G."

Angelica, surprised at her punctuality and directness, replied with a message detailing the events in her own dream and the bloody spectacle outside.

Forty-one

Sheriff Beasley took a sip of hot coffee from the cup which displayed the words "Hot Stuff," a moniker he in no way resembled. The file he had removed from the nearby cabinet contained many pieces of paper. Since he had been elected sheriff five years before he'd only been up there a handful of times himself. The house on Holly Bush Road was far enough away that if no one was living at the house, it would be easy for trespassers to do what they willed. The times he did go up there were mainly to chase off teenagers who'd heard the local rumors of the place and were curious to see it for themselves. He knew they would be there either by a teacher from school calling him and telling him what they'd overheard, or a passerby seeing lights on the property when they knew no one lived there at the time.

He took another sip and hesitated, staring reluctantly at the bundle of call reports. He kept a tab in the file to show where he'd taken over as sheriff. It was only about a quarter of the reports, but it was enough to concern anyone that knew the statistics. He recalled the first time he'd headed out there for a trespassing dispatch. Five teenagers, all but one from Miller's Run High School, were snooping around the house before he arrived and were starting to head toward the cave. They were far enough away from the house that they didn't hear him approaching via the driveway. Like a chubby cat he got out and followed the human mice until he saw them stopping and looking around for the mouth of the cave. When finally got close enough to shine his flashlight on them and yell for them to freeze, he was surprised that they didn't run for it. Two of them were dressed in standard "Goth" attire, all black clothing and make up. The others were just along for the ride. When he asked what they were doing, the Goth boy said, "We're serving the will of Manos, sir!" He couldn't help but crack up along with the rest of his friends.

The Goth girl then responded with a smile, "Just devil stuff, Officer. You know, blood sacrifices and all."

One of the other boys behind her yelled, "Satan! We're here to worship Satan!"

Needless to say he wasn't very polite in return. Perhaps overstepping protocol he drew his service pistol and forced them all to leave. They pissed and moaned at first but were soon on the way off the property.

Other incidents like that happened, sometimes they would break into the house. Other times they were trying to find the cave. It was usually different kids and always at least one local.

After placing the recent report at the back, he closed the file and picked up the phone on his desk. He dialed the number for St. Mary's School for Girls in Cedar Hill. Once connected, he asked for Sister Francis and was soon speaking with her.

"Hello, Sister Francis."

In her usual direct tone, "Hello, Sheriff. Is something the matter?"

"Funny you should ask." (She seemed to know, somehow, often). "I just got back from a very strange call."

She could tell he was leading her along. "Okay, and?"

"Well, it was out on Holly Bush Road. Seems like things may be kicking off again."

She paused a second before responding. "What exactly do you mean?"

"Something went and mutilated three goats that the Barristers have on their farm. It was a rather... disturbing scene."

"And?"

"Well, the goats weren't just killed. There were parts of them scattered all over the place. Doesn't look like any coyote or cougar kill that I've ever seen."

She paused again, exhaling deeply before saying, "It has been a few years. I suppose it's due."

He too sighed. "I was afraid you'd say that."

Forty-two

Later that evening after dinner, Angelica had gone off to her room. Rosanna and Edward were sitting at the table in kitchen. The two of them were having a glass of wine. Rosanna mostly abstained from drinking alcohol, but the stress of the events made the treat seem more desirable than usual.

Edward, in a hushed tone, said, "So, Rose, what do you think happened last night?"

Finishing a sip from her glass, "I don't know. I don't see why someone would sneak onto our property and do something like that. It doesn't make any sense."

Ed stared off at the wall on the opposite side of the room. He replied, "What else should we do about it?"

She too was looking off into the distance, blank on any good ideas. "What else can we do?"

He replied, "We have to look at all the crazy stuff that's been happening recently. Ange's trip in the cave, my injuries, and now the goats."

Rosanna took a familiar tone. "Ed, really? How could these things possibly be connected?"

He knew it wouldn't be easy trying to provide an explanation, or a correlation at best, but he tried. "I just think it's a hell of a lot of bad luck to just suddenly pop up. Don't you?"

Still unwilling to budge, "I will admit that it is a strange amount of bad luck, but everyone has days like that. Sometimes weeks."

"Angelica had a dream last night about that old woman that attacked me in my dream: Caroline. We've had the same person appear to both of us now."

Obviously annoyed, "Ed, I thought we decided that we weren't going to blame our problems on the boogeyman! Stop it with it ghost crap already!"

Still maintaining his composure, "Well, if you're convinced that ghosts don't exist, do you believe that the devil exists?"

Not appreciating his tactics of finding a soft spot in her iron-clad defense, "Of course I do, Ed. You know that. But I don't think we should...."

In a maneuver he only rarely used, he cut her off. "Then you must believe in demons, right?"

Still stalwart, "You know I do, Ed, but this isn't a movie. Okay? This is real life, not *The Exorcist*. We can't blame all of our problems on demons either."

"Rosy, I'm not blaming all of our problems on demons. I'm blaming them for the past several days. Look at me! How did I end up with these scratches all over me!?"

Still baffled by it, but unable to relinquish her position, "Ed, I don't know. I really don't know. What are we supposed to do? Go to Father Anderson and tell him we have demons running around?"

"Why not?"

Rosanna laughed sarcastically before replying in the same tone, "Ed, we would run out of the community! Father Anderson would think we were crazy if we told him that!"

Still dumbfounded by her stubbornness, "What will it take to convince you that something very bad is trying to make us miserable, to make us break!?"

She decided to close the open floor of negotiations. "A lot more than this, Ed! A *lot* more."

As she stormed out of the room, Edward gripped the bridge of his nose with his forefinger and thumb.

Meanwhile, Angelica was in her room reading an email from Sara. It was a reply to her description of the slaughter. It read:

"You have my deepest sympathies and I hope that you'll contact me if you need any help with grief. Whether or not you can see it now, you will recover. It's a terrible loss, but you're strong: I can tell.

"Now as far as spiritual protection is concerned, there are things you can do now to help stack the balance more in your favor. A technique I've used in the past many times may work for you. You'll need to get a fairly large amount of salt. I'd suggest getting your parents to help with that. Once you have the salt, take it and pour out a line of it, clockwise, around the outside of your house. If you feel you need more protection (and it sounds like you need all you can get), you can also put salt in the four corners of your room.

"Furthermore, there are stronger techniques to use, but I'll need a bit of time to get them together. I will go ahead and acquire the materials just in case.

"Finally, remember to keep that pendant close and burn the candle I gave you when safe and possible. Obviously, have your parents help you with that. Practice the meditation techniques I sent you earlier, but first and foremost, put up the salt barrier.

"Wishing you light and love, as always I remain,

"Sara Goodwin"

As Angelica finished reading the email, she looked over and saw the picture she kept on her desk next to her computer. In it she was smiling and standing next to Edward and her three late goats. Malaise and sadness formed a murky miasma in her mind. The anger she had been feeling quite steadily all day had worn her out. Three animals she'd loved and cared for were now dead. And of course it wasn't just their deaths that bothered her, but the way they died troubled her most. Her mind briefly connected, in a sort of sympathy, with the terror and pain they felt. She quickly, however, withdrew from such thinking, as it made her loss even more punishing. The terror was similar to the day she had almost drowned herself.

The sadness caused her to dwell for a few moments, but the advice from Sara was at least something to try. She got up from her chair and made her way into the kitchen. There Edward was sitting by himself at the table still sipping on a glass of wine.

Seeing her, "Hey, baby girl."

"Hey, Dad." Angelica lowered her voice. "Dad, I need salt."

A little confused, but replying in a hushed tone as well, "We have salt. Why are you whispering?"

She knew the name she was about to mention was a hot-word in the house at the moment, so she whispered in his ear, "Sara said to pour it around the house. She said it would protect against spirits."

That technique was something he'd heard about years ago, but only now recalled. He wished he'd thought of it sooner, and replied softly, "You know, I completely forgot about that. It might just work." He looked outside at the setting sun giving its last rays of the day. "If we hurry, we can finish before dark."

He then led her out the door and toward the "normal" barn. In it, Edward had three bags of rock salt he'd stashed away for the coming winter handy. Quietly, the two of them then headed back outside and encircled the house in a barrier of salt. Much to their delight, Rosanna does not discover them.

Afterward, as Edward made his way to the couch to sleep for the night, Angelica went to her room and closed the door behind her. She looked up at one of the crucifixes and grabbed the rosary around her neck. By rote, she said three Hail Marys and offered a simple request: "Please protect me."

Forty-three

The next morning, Angelica awoke at her usual at-dawn time. Strangely, and to her unsettling, she didn't dream the night before. Completely by habit, she changed into her chore clothes and headed out toward the barn. Of course, there were no animals there to take care of any longer.

Only after she stood at the turnaround in front of the barn did it fully sink in. Her three goats were dead and there was no bringing them back. It's odd how the mind works sometimes. Often, it's not until the usual routines of life leave the most obvious reminders of the loss that one starts to feel the long and straining sadness. It hit her hard then as she looked up at the blood stains Edward tried his hardest to clean off, but was unable. Tears silently fell down her cheeks, but she didn't allow it to hijack the anger. The anger, just steady embers in the morning sun, was causing her to look around. She was looking for someone specific, obviously: Caroline. Caroline, however, was nowhere to be seen. Of course, she wouldn't show on Angelica's terms. She was far too clever and cruel to allow such conveniences. Angelica then walked into the barn and looked around at the various tools therein. She saw the feed scoop she'd always used hanging on the wall. It offered a stinging reminder of the emotional wound. The latched feed container, the goat's milking station—all of it fueled the resentment that was continually growing. A murky mess of detestation was clouding her thoughts. In an impulsive attempt to vent her anger, she clamped her teeth together, took a nearby ax, and whacked it into a wooden stud in the wall.

It was a haphazard way of venting the fire, but it helped some. She then sat quietly and stared a hundred yards away through the solid wall of the door. Forlorn and withdrawn, she wrapped her arms around her knees and sobbed quietly. She didn't notice Edward has limped to the doorway of the barn. He consoled her as best he could.

Later that day, around noon, Edward was up on a ladder applying a primer coat to the stained panels of the barn's outer wall. Angelica, sitting on the top of the fence, was the first to see a blue pickup truck turn onto their driveway.

Rosanna, who was holding the base of the ladder for Edward, said, "I wonder who that could be?" Straining to see the driver, "I think it's Ethyl."

Edward stopped painting and climbed down as the Silverado pulled in closer and came to a stop. The kindly old woman inside waved at them. A small black fur ball inside jumped into her arms before she stepped out of the truck and shut the door.

Embracing the solid black puppy in her arms, Ethyl said warmly, "Hey, Barristers! How are you?"

Angelica, finally interested in something that brought a subtle smile to her face, walked over and got a closer look at the puppy. Solid black fur covered his body, which looked more wolf than dog. Its eyes were a strong orange color which stood out greatly against the fur. Rosanna said, "Hey, Ethyl. Whatcha got there?"

The older woman replied, "Well, I heard about your livestock getting attacked and I figured you could use a guard dog."

Angelica felt a surge of warmth course over her, quite eager to accept the dog.

Rosanna replied, "You heard about that already? That was just yesterday."

Ethyl smiled and said, "Well, I know CPR and a few other things, so I keep a walkie-talkie in the house in case I'm needed on an emergency call. I heard the sheriff called out and knew it couldn't be good."

Angelica was petting the happy puppy, its red collar bearing a gold nametag that glinted brightly in the sunlight.

Edward smiled and said, "Well, thanks, Ethyl! That's really kind of you."

Rosanna, of course, spoke up. "Wait, wait. Are you two going to take care of it?"

Angelica was bouncing up and down giddily as Edward said, "Of course we will!"

Ethyl then handed the puppy to Angelica, who accepted it without hesitation. As the dog licked Angelica's face, "See there? He's your best friend already!"

Angelica then read the name on the tag: "Cerberus." She looked up at Ethyl. "Did you name him already?"

Ethyl replied, "I didn't name him, no, but the owner did. She's a good friend of mine. A dog that belongs to her recently gave birth and she has more than enough. If you want to name him something different, I'm sure it would be okay. After all, he's yours now!"

Angelica replied, "I won't change his name. I like it. Cerberus...."

Edward, knowing the source of the name, "Cerberus. Yeah, that's a nice name."

Rosanna, thinking she'd heard that name before, tried to remember the source but could not. She smiled and said, "Well, thank you, Ethyl. We really appreciate it."

Edward and his daughter stepped into the shade of the barn and doted over their new playmate.

Ethyl leaned close to Rosanna and said, "I know from experience that the best way to get a kid to take their mind off of their lost pets is to give 'em a new one." She suddenly groped for a piece of paper in her front pocket. "Oh, I almost forgot! Here's a little cheat sheet for how much to feed him and which shots he'll need."

Rosanna took the list and immediately felt like her family just got another money sink in place of the goats. Looking and seeing her daughter and husband smiling again, however, made her change her mind and accept the new vigilant friend.

Forty-four

Later that night…

Rosanna was dressed up and ready for an elegant meal at a restaurant Ed had chosen ahead of time: On Point. The name was fitting, as it was perched on a hilltop overlooking the river that ran through Johnston City. It was also named as such for having the reputation of being "on point" with quality. Rosanna quickly remembered the setting and attire, as it was the night he proposed to her. Happily remembering that day, she prepared for what should be a very pleasant dream. They sat at the same table. It was the best seat in the place, as it gazed out upon the river from the adjoining corner windows. As they were presented their menus, Rosanna was almost too giddy to concentrate on ordering. After taking their wine request, he walked away.

The waiter soon returned and served the wine. After this, she ordered her dish: rack of lamb. She remembered the dish he ordered years ago: a strip steak. When the waiter asked what he would have, however, he said, "I'll have the Goodwin Ham… raw, of course."

As if taking an everyday order, the waiter replied, "Of course, sir. Excellent choice."

Once the waiter had left, she said to Edward, "I thought you liked steak."

Nonchalantly, "Everyone gets tired of the same old meat after a while. I need to try something new."

The name of the dish was certainly odd, and the request for "raw" was unheard of. She continued, however, with the conversation. Gazing out at the stars shining in the sky, "A beautiful night, isn't it?"

Not really feeling the good vibe she was trying to put out, "Yeah, it's okay, I guess."

This was certainly different now from the night she remembered. Ed was terribly nervous but trying to hide it with a bit of chatter. He seemed detached now. Concerned, "Ed, are you okay? You don't seem like you want to be here."

Clearly bored, "Yeah, you know how it is. If you've been here once, you've been here a million times."

"I thought you loved eating here."

"I did, but I'm tired of it." He looked around impatiently for a few seconds before turning his gaze toward the kitchen. Seeing something catch his eye, "Finally!" The waiter, dressed in his pristine uniform, was walking in front of a shapely woman, in her twenties who was wearing a form-fitting and stylish black dress.

Once at the table, the waiter took the dish from the tray in his hand and dropped it loudly on the table in front of Rosanna. "Your rack of lamb, ma'am."

The brown-haired woman with green eyes now stepped toward Edward. She bent down and rested her hands on the table as she looked closely at Rosanna. She smiled and said nothing. All at once, Edward slapped the woman's behind. Clenching her buttock still, Edward said, "Now that's more like it! I could bounce a quarter off of that!"

Rosanna, outraged, said, "Ed! What the hell are you doing!?"

A coy smile crossed the woman's lips as she replied, "You heard him, didn't you? He's tired of that droopy meat you're carrying around." Suddenly, the younger woman turned and raked her arm across the table, clearing the dishes off which crashed loudly on the floor. She then climbed on the table and got on her hands and knees, facing Edward and letting out a flirtatious growl.

Clearly interested, Edward stood and began kissing her. Rosanna watched in horror. "Ed, stop it!" She stood up and attempted to pull the *young lady away from him. The waiter, however, yanked Rosanna away and threw her to the ground nearby. Before she could recover, the waiter took Rosanna's hair in hand and dragged her toward the restroom across the dining area. The diners, more perplexed by the struggling Rosanna, paid no attention to the scene unfolding at the table in the corner. Just before being thrown effortlessly into the ladies' room, she saw Edward preparing to mount the young lady on the table.*

Once inside the marble tiled bathroom, the waiter said in a level tone, "Ms. Caroline, this woman did not like her meal. What shall I do with her?"

As Rosanna struggled, the waiter's hand still clasping her hair tightly, the older woman in antiquated clothing said in a mocking tone, "Aw, did someone not like the Goodwin Ham? Too bad you're all wrinkled up and worn out. That Sara Goodwin will rock Edward's world!"

The waiter was somehow able to keep Rosanna from getting away, the white cloth draped over his level left arm not budging. Yanking her back to submission with his hand, "Shall I dispose of this one, madam?"

Before Caroline could answer, Rosanna said with rage, "I'm going to fucking kill you!"

Feigning shock, "Oh, my, Rosy! What a dirty mouth you have! Remember what they told you in school all those years ago? Cussing makes Jesus cry! Waiter, punish her!"

He calmly replied, "Yes, ma'am," before violently slamming Rosanna's forehead against the stone sink top.

Rosanna awoke, only this time in a clearing amidst a large field of thorns and briars growing to nine feet tall. She looked around but couldn't make out where she was at or how she got there. The color of the sky also was also unsettling: vibrant red. Seeing dark black clouds flying past overhead, she went to the edge of the clearing. She tried to push aside some of the plants, but was unable to get far at all. Then, from behind her, she heard a familiar voice call out, "Mommy, come here! I'm over here!"

Rosanna quickly turned and saw her daughter standing in a clearing connected to a previously blocked path. As she stepped closer, however, her daughter's eyes began to glow golden yellow. Hesitating, "Angelica... is that you?"

Smiling, "Of course it's me, Mommy! Let's go play with Caroline!"

Now noticeably apprehensive, "No. No, you stay away from her, Angelica—she's nothing but trouble!"

The signature scowl came to Angelica's face. Her voice now was much lower and grave. "Mommy, I'm not asking you! We're going to play with Caroline now!" Her daughter then made a beckoning gesture with her right hand before walking toward the briars. Strangely, they seemed to not affect her. Rosanna was suddenly jerked forward and slid along the ground by an unperceived cord. The thorns did, however, affect Rosanna and she was dragged through the bushes. The sharp nettles tore dozens and dozens of slashes across her body, from her face to her feet and everything in between. The branches of the bush crackled and swished as a crooked path was formed behind her. She cried out in agony the entire time, demanding that her daughter stop, but to no avail.

Angelica reached a new clearing and stopped once her mother was inside it. Rosanna struggled to get to her feet, the pain nearly unbearable as blood covered her entire face and body. With her mother on her hands and knees, Angelica leaned in and said with a low and pleased tone, "Aw, you're all bloody now! That's okay. Sara's going to be my new mommy. Daddy says you're all used up!"

Blood from her lips was starting to creep into Rosanna's mouth. She spit some to the ground before replying angrily, "That little slut will not break up our family! Do you hear me!?"

Shaking her head in disappointment, "Mommy, Mommy... if you weren't such a bitch, maybe I'd love you more."

Rosanna tried to stand, but was suddenly struck from behind. Her face smacked the dirt and she felt a hand grab the hair on the back of her head. Yanking on it and pulling her face up, she then saw Caroline's visage in front of her. The old lady then said strongly, "Your husband and your daughter no longer love you! Not even your own god loves you! You're worthless!" Rosanna struggled in vain to rise again, but was kept down on the ground. Caroline continued. "Worship me, and maybe I'll make your suffering short lived! Worship me!"

Struggling and gritting her teeth, "Go to hell!"

Caroline then laughed loudly and sharply, the sound echoing all around. "Too late! We're already here!" The old lady then pulled Rosanna's head back uncomfortably hard, causing her mouth to open. Caroline then leaned in and placed her open mouth over Rosanna's. She choked and gagged as she felt the old woman's gnarled and twisted tongue push in and down her throat. Feeling the invasion fully, her eyes closed....

Moments later, she could not see her surroundings clearly as her eyes tried to focus. Seeing few distinct markers in the environment, blue-green tile and a tiny bed in the middle of a large square room. The cold fluorescent lightning overhead gave the immediate impression that she was somewhere sterile, cold, and clinical: the hospital. She looked around groggily as the haze was lifted from her eyes. She immediately knew that something was drawing her attention to the middle of that unremarkable room: the tiny bed. The nametag on the foot of the bed bore the name "Eva Leone," scrawled in what she thought was the reddest crayon she'd ever seen. It was crude at best, highly indicative of the care level given. She slowly stepped forward, knowing good and well that nothing pleasant lay beyond. Past the point of no return, she noticed that the plastic sides of the tiny bed were previously obscuring another container inside: a stainless-steel bedpan. The lights overhead shined down as the silver surface reflected back distorted echoes. Before she could clearly see the contents of the waste container, she was overwhelmed with a powerful and staggering smell of decaying flesh. She hesitated to move further for a moment, covering her mouth with one hand and her other on her abdomen trying to convince her stomach not to evacuate its contents everywhere.

It took a few moments to convince herself to move forward, but she soon was compelled by an unseen will to keep going. A couple of steps forward and she was finally able to see into the bedpan. What was there was horrifying, but strangely not unexpected to her. The unopened eyes of a rotting fetus, only about three months old, stared toward the ceiling. Tears of disgust and pain came to her eyes as they took in the image of the bloated carcass, its skin deeply bruised in shades of purple, green, and everything in between. Small trickles of black blood dripped from each corner of the mouth of the not-to-be child. "Tears" of black fluid dripped from the corners of its eyes and onto the pan below, making a soft *plink* sound with each drop. As the same black fluid then started to drip from the anus and genitals, she back away in absolute terror. She covered her mouth to try and not scream. She couldn't, however, contain it.

As she continued to stagger backward, she suddenly stopped by what she thought was a wall or pillar in the room. It was, however, Caroline. Her head was partially lowered, giving her eyes a predatory quality as she looked into Rosanna's. "Tsk, tsk, Rosy. Too brutal a job to do on your own? Had to get the doctor to do it for you? At least I had the common fucking courtesy to do it with my own hands with my little 'problems.' They really do eat too much, you know?"

Shock, mixed with a tinge of anger, "How could you!? How did you know about that!? I only told two people!"

Now advancing closer and shoving her shoulder with her hand, "Oh, I can read you like a book, Rosy. You know who else can read? Angelica."

Being shoved on the other shoulder and driven backward blindly, "Oh, God, I hate you!"

Rosanna now bumping into the bed, Caroline smirked and hissed, "Oh, He saw it, too, Rosy. He saw the whole thing! The way you were so confused and conflicted about another man shoving it home. It was so cold, wasn't it? Sent a shiver up your spine! Why, I would dare to say you enjoyed it a bit. It was exciting having another man rooting around in there, wasn't it?"

Rosanna was stunned and was ready to smack the face of Caroline clean off, but a sound from behind jolted her from the act. Crying... gurgling, bubbling at first, then deeper and more guttural. The sounds maintained their baby-like sound, however, as the mother-not-to-be looked down at the clumsily twitching mass. "Oh, God...," she stammered, stunned motionless by the sight before her.

Caroline was then somehow in front of her across the bed, looking down at the misshapen head that started jerking side to side. As she placed her open palm over the body, Rosanna could see a faint yellow glow coming through the thin eyelids. They then slowly lifted, revealing the revolting orbs beneath. Staring directly into Rosanna's eyes were completely black spheres, save the hotly glowing yellow irises in the center. They *strangely resembled an eclipse, only the ring of the sun being visible around the opaque moon.*

Rosanna, her hand trying to cover her mouth, strained to get out the words. "No... no! It was dead! There's no way it could... NO!"

Raising only her left eyebrow, she smirked. "Well, then. Looks like the doc didn't earn his paycheck that day. Seems he didn't quite finish the job."

Rosanna's hands then covered her ears as the screams from the twitching fetus became even more shrill and forceful. Each burst of sound coming from the crusty black lips of the body was preceded by a thick goopy black liquid that splattered all over its face and chest. She then found herself burning inside with a white-hot flame that seared all rationality. She wanted to make the crying stop, at any cost. "Shut up! SHUT UP, YOU LITTLE BITCH!"

Her head still partially lowered, her eyes wild with a fevered zeal. "Do it! End its suffering! You started it, now finish it!"

She closed her eyes briefly and let out a primal scream of frustration and hatred. Her own eyes now wide with fury, she stepped forward toward the bed. As she looked down at the writhing mass in the bedpan, it glared back and quickly sent a projectile of the black bile toward her face. Only pausing a moment to hurriedly wipe a speck of it away, she quickly reached down and grabbed the wiggling legs of the once-fetus. She jerked it out of the bedpan quickly and ran at the nearby wall. The head and torso of the vile thing smashed and distorted in shape as it struck the tiles on the walls. It left splatters of the sickening fluid all over as it fell to the floor. The decaying flesh had sloughed off in Rosanna's hands, leaving only the tibia and fibula protruding from each knee. The cries, however, only lessened somewhat as it writhed and twitched violently on the floor. Determined to make the cries stop she reached down and grabbed the bones and flesh at the knees and one blow at a time smashing the slowly relenting hunk of flesh, bone, and bile quieted, and eventually stopped. The only sounds Rosanna could then hear were the hurried pace of her own breathing and her heart pounding away in her ears.

She didn't hear the other spectator enter the room either: "MOM!? WHAT DID YOU DO!? THAT WAS MY SISTER!" Rosanna turned around sharply as a chunk of blackened flesh coasted down the tiles behind her on the charcoal-colored blood. Unlike before, at the other level of hell in the dream, Angelica appeared frightened and confused. She issued a pleading command: "Stay away from me! You're crazy!"

The angry mother growled, "You know too much, Angelica! Why can't you mind your own damn business!?" Her hands extended in front of her, she lunged at her daughter. The spry child, however, was much faster and made it through a set of doors that were previously not there. As Rosanna tried to run through them as her daughter did, however, they became as rigid as stone. She wasn't going to be following her out that way.

"Well, Rosy, it looks like little Angie has been a bad girl. You remember what happens to bad girls, don't you? What happened to you, you little bad girl?"

Rosanna's rage seemed to hastily melt to fear. She knew what was coming. She knew who was going to appear from behind the doors on the other side of room, some ten feet tall. She backed away hastily as a stern and fanatical creature pushed through them: Dearest Mother Leone, her own disciplinarian. This facsimile, however, was over eight feet tall, a good two and three-quarters feet taller than she remembered. She was wearing the garment she usually wore: a plain black dress, garnished only by a white collar at the neck. Her hair was fastened back tightly in a bun. The whole getup seemed desperately old fashioned, out of place and time, and rigidly restricting. That was, however, the entire point. And now this relic from the past was walking toward her daughter, who was speechless and petrified with fear. Mother always had that "Medusa" effect on her. She suddenly thundered, "So, Rosanna Leone, it seems I was right about you all along! Not only did you commit adultery with some guy you barely knew, but you went and murdered the baby as well! God has a special place in hell for the likes of you, you disgraceful harlot! It's time for your lesson, Rosanna! It's for a lesson in repentance!" Rosanna knew what was coming, but dared not move. Mother's loving hand reared back completely and followed through with a massive slap to her daughter's cheek. The blow was easily enough to knock her to the ground and even slide a couple of feet along the tile floor. "Now Rosanna: Turn the other cheek!" She dutifully struggled to her feet, stood as erect as she could and waited for what was coming next. The second blow knocked her to the ground again. Blood flew freely from within and spattered across the wall, its color clearly contrasting the blue-green tiles and black blood from the still fetus. Right, left, right, left, right left…. The blows seemed to last an eternity, as these flurries always did.

After over a dozen slaps to each side of the face, the eight-foot mother looked down on her daughter and sneered. She could see Rosanna wasn't getting up, and so kicked her abdomen from the side with her Victorian-era pointed black shoes. Rosanna reacted to the blow, groaning loudly as her diaphragm struggled to operate her lungs. Satisfied, at least for the time being, Mother Leone bent down at her daughter's head. Talking over her gasping breaths of her offspring, "Life is pain, Rosanna Leonne. I suggest you teach that little cunt daughter of yours a thing or two about it. She's overdue for a stern hand."

The tile was sharply cold against Rosanna's cheek as she continued to gasp for air and groan painfully. The cold light of the room slowly faded, mercifully, to black.

3:00 A.M.

Rosanna awoke in bed feeling the pain of every injury suffered in the dream. The sheets were covered in her own blood and stuck to her as she turned to get up. Strangely, however, Rosanna herself did not seem to be in control of her own body. It was if she were playing spectator and someone else was at the wheel. She rose slowly and quietly and headed to the hall. Edward, who was fast asleep on the couch, did not hear her enter the living room. For several minutes she stood there, watching him sleep as blood steadily trickled down her skin. The dream was still heavy in her mind and charging her emotions. Rosanna became more and more angry, but did nothing as her body was still beyond her control. She wasn't even sure if she was still dreaming or not at this point.

Her body soon started to turn away from its vigil of her husband and walked down the hall toward Angelica's room. As she placed her hand on the doorknob she could hear her daughter's new puppy start to bark. Opening the door, she saw Cerberus standing in a threatening posture and continuing to yap. The noise had woken Angelica and she looked up at her mom's silhouette in the doorway. As Rosanna then stepped into the light of her daughter's nightlight the wounds covering her and the resulting crimson ichor became clear.

Obviously fearful, Angelica uttered, "Mom? Mom, what happened?"

Cerberus continued to bark as Rosanna stood silently looking at Angelica with a blank stare.

Moments later, Rosanna stepped forward and said, "Shut that mutt up!" The voice that came out, however, was not her own. The voice was far deeper than her normal voice and growling, somewhat animalistic and demonic. Rosanna then suddenly raised her right hand and quickly backhanded the puppy from the foot of Angelica's bed.

As Cerberus thudded against the wall and yelped out, Angelica said angrily, "Stop it! What's wrong with you!?"

Edward by now had heard the commotion and got up off of the couch in the living room. As he headed down the hall, Rosanna was pinning her daughter to the bed by her shoulders. Angelica struggled as her mother started gripping her neck tightly.

Rosanna growled, "You have been a very bad girl, Angelica! You need to die!"

Edward, now in the room, ran and grabbed his wife and pulled her away from the bed and onto the ground. "Rose! What the hell are you doing!?"

Rosanna, still watching her body react without any control of her own, managed to push him away and back at the door. She hissed, "You always were weak, Ed! Too damn weak for this world!"

As Angelica coughed, Edward had a sudden impulse. He grabbed the nearby crucifix on the wall and shoved it into Rosanna's face. He shouted, "This is Rosanna's god! She worships Him! You have no control over that!"

Rosanna then let out a ghastly scream and clutched her head.

Seeing that he was making impact, he shouted, "Get away from my wife! You're weak before the cross!" Edward wasn't even sure what he was saying or why he was saying it, but the effectiveness drove away doubt.

Rosanna suddenly dropped to her hands and knees and convulsed. As Angelica scooped up Cerberus and placed him back on her bed, Rosanna began vomiting up thick black fluid onto the floor.

Starting to recover from her puking, she muttered, "Ed... Ed...."

He turned on the overhead light and saw the extent of her external injuries. Both he and Angelica were taken back by her being covered in her own blood and the countless scratches all over her body.

Edward saw the injuries were all organized in clear groups of three. Taking his wife into his arms, he looked up at Angelica and asked, "Ange, are you okay!?"

She nodded and clutched Cerberus tightly as he whimpered.

Then looking at his wife, who had tears in her eyes, "Rose, what were you doing!?"

Now regaining full control over her body, she wept and said, "Ed, it was horrible! I couldn't stop myself from doing that! I know you won't believe me, but I didn't have any control over my body! I couldn't stop, I swear!"

Angelica quickly and sharply asked, "Now do you believe us!?"

Edward felt an impulse to chastise his daughter's question, but he himself wanted to know the answer. Rosanna only looked up at Angelia briefly before continuing to cry, unwilling to answer the question with an obvious answer.

Forty-five

Obviously still traumatized from the encounter with Rosanna, Angelica was unable to go back to sleep. She tried catch a nap on the sofa in the living room but couldn't as her parents were in the bathroom trying to clean up Rosanna's countless scratches.

After nearly forty-five minutes Angelica headed down the hall to her bedroom. Walking past the bathroom door, which was left cracked partially open, she shot only a quick glance from the corner of her eyes. Close behind her, Cerberus followed.

Angelica, locking her bedroom door behind her, coughed uncomfortably as she turned on her computer. In a hazy half-asleep and half-awake state, she waited for the startup screen to fade to desktop. She yawned uncontrollably as the background image, a picture of her and her father showing off their small stringer of fish, came into focus. As she reached to position her keyboard she found her left hand trembling. It was her first encounter with a nervous tic of her own. She clinched her fist closed and open several times to try and get rid of it, but it was only partially subdued.

Soon she was online and going to her email account. Without thinking she composed a message to send to Sara detailing the new level of insanity the family was experiencing. In a postscript she also asked if Sara sent her the puppy, as it bared an obvious and striking resemblance to her three dogs. Given the very late timing of the email, she hit send and hardly expected a response until the next morning. Angelica then turned off her monitor, but left the computer running. Cerberus looked on attentively from the foot of her bed as she was overcome with an impulse. She decided to act on it. She headed toward the dresser on the opposing wall and slid it in front of the door. It seemed like overkill at first glance, but she wasn't taking any chances.

For over an hour she reclined in her bed, unable to sleep and occasionally petting Cerberus. who was fading in and out of a series of naps. Her body wanted desperately to sleep but the images of her mother and what she had just tried to do were always there to jolt her back awake. She then found herself staring at what seemed at first to be an inconsequential spot on her ceiling. For whatever reason she couldn't seem to take her eyes off of it. Then, from seemingly nowhere, a small drop of thick black fluid began to coagulate and form over the white plaster overhead. As the drop became larger, Cerberus suddenly awakened and turned his gaze toward it. The weight and size of the globule then overpowered its hold on the ceiling and it quickly fell to the beige carpeting on her floor. They both got up to investigate the new tiny puddle. Cerberus stepped ahead of Angelica and sniffed it briefly before suddenly backing away with a barely audible whimper. All at once the drop seemed to take on a life of its own and hastily glided across the floor and toward an adjoining wall. It disappeared under Angelica's bed before reappearing on the wall over the headboard. They watched it then go directly toward the crucifix above. The cross then popped off the wall and landed directly where Angelica's head normally rested on her pillow. In a flash the drop of fluid raced straight across the wall, over the corner, and proceeded to pop the other crucifix, recently placed by Rosanna, onto the floor. Cerberus yapped with his puppy bark as the droplet then disappeared into the plaster of the ceiling overhead. At this she realized that whatever that just was certainly didn't like the cross. Instinctively she then decided to grab her rosary, close her eyes, and repeat Hail Marys until she felt more at ease. The entire time, the quartz pendant also remained in her grasp.

At around 7:00 A.M., Angelica jolted awake from what couldn't have been more than a ten-minute nap. Seeing the sun well into the sky through her curtains, she rose from her bed and walked to her computer. Despite doubts in her mind to be hopeful, she couldn't help but check her email. Surprisingly, to Angelica, Sara had responded to her email. It read:

"First and foremost, I'm sorry you had to experience what you did. I STRONGLY advise you to contact Father Anderson immediately! I will enclose a link to his email if you don't already have it. Make sure the message you send indicates the severity and urgency of the situation. If you want, I will also send him an email detailing what you have told me.

"Also, I would like to have your parents get in contact with me, either by phone or email. We will have to discuss an urgent plan of action.

"As always, I remain,

"Sara Goodwin.

"P.S.: And yes, Cerberus is from the lineage of my own dogs."

Angelica knew the situation was severe at this point and was thankful that someone was being honest and open with her about it. As she looked up at the dresser pinned against the door, however, she was hesitant to move it. Suddenly a deep thud came from the back of the chest of drawers. Angelica jumped in her seat, but was quickly relieved to hear the voice of her father on the other side.

"Ange? You okay in there? It's just me."

Still uncertain, knowing her mother was also on the other side of the door in the house, she said, "Okay, just a second." She stood up and walked toward the door, pushing the dresser aside.

Edward, seeing the dresser askew, was troubled by his daughter's attempt at barricading her room. "Baby girl, you don't have to do that. If you're afraid, just lock it."

Looking over his shoulder, then back at him, she whispered into his ear, "Where's Mom?"

In a hushed tone, "She's lying down in our bed. Don't worry, she's okay now."

A small frown came to her face as she said, "*She's* okay? She tried to choke me! Why did she do that!?"

Sighing first, he replied, "I don't know, Ange. From what she told me, I think she saw Caroline in a dream last night."

It was now obvious to Angelica that they were all sharing a source of pain. This didn't make the situation any better, however, as they weren't sure how to solve the problem. Lowering her voice back to a whisper, "I told Sara about what happened. She said we need to contact Father Anderson right now. She also said you and Mom should call her and that she'd help."

Edward knew that getting in touch with Sara, at this point, would be sending him straight into a proverbial minefield. "Look, I think we'll just stick with contacting Father Anderson. I'll give him a call today."

She was reluctant to just leave it at that, but found herself too fatigued to complain. "Okay, Dad."

Reassuringly, "Don't worry, sweetie, we'll get this figured out." Even though he was certain they would try, he couldn't guarantee to his daughter, or himself, a positive outcome. The word *possession* was swimming through his mind, but he didn't dare say it aloud around his daughter. "Now, let's go to the kitchen and I'll make you some scrambled eggs. Does that sound good?"

Angelica agreed and followed her father to the kitchen.

Behind the closed bedroom door, Rosanna sat awake in bed, staring off into space. With her rosary in hand she mutely recited her own Hail Mary marathon unable to fully accept what she knew may be true. The idea of her actions coming from her own will, or that of another, shook her to the core with equal ferocity.

Later that evening, Father Anderson had already agreed to come and pay them a visit and was pulling up their driveway. It took a bit of convincing, but Edward managed to persuade his wife into having the meeting. Rosanna was wearing a long-sleeved shirt, despite the heat of summer, to cover up the small lacerations all over her skin. Father Anderson was soon at the door and was greeted by Edward. After Angelica, Rosanna finally greeted him but kept her head lowered as if ashamed.

The priest then said warmly, "Rosanna, I'm glad to see you up and around. Edward told me all about what happened."

Still embarrassed by the marks on her face, "I'm sorry I look like a mess, Father."

In a comforting tone, "Now Rosanna, don't worry about that for a second. I'm your priest, not pageant judge."

Edward then said, "Oh, please, have a seat. Would you like a cup of coffee?"

Edward motioned at the ready pot on the counter nearby as the priest replied, "I'd love one, thank you. Just a little bit of cream in there if it's not too much trouble."

He poured the older man a cup and handed him a container of cream from the fridge. As all four of them sat at the dining room table, he continued.

"If it's okay with you all, let's get right down to business." Seeing them all ready and willing to speak, "Now Rosanna, tell me exactly what happened last night."

As her husband reassuringly squeezed her hand she quietly began. "Well, Father, I remember having a really bad dream last night. I remember being dragged through a patch of thorns and getting scratched up all over. Then an old woman was mocking me and trying to get me to bow to her... or something like that." Shen then sniffled loudly, her face flushing heavily. "The next thing I know I came to with my hands around my daughter's neck!" Tears were then flowing from her eyes. "I could see what I was doing but I wasn't in control! I couldn't stop!" She wiped her cheeks with a tissue before continuing. "The next thing I remember is waking up on the floor."

As Father Anderson looked at her with concern, Edward said, "We've all dreamed about the same person. Her name is Caroline. Whenever we see her, bad things start happening."

Trying to get a better understanding, the priest asked, "Have you only seen her in dreams or have you seen her when you're awake?"

Angelica jumped in. "I've seen her in my dreams but I've also seen her on our property."

Rosanna stared at the table in front of her as Edward said, "Yeah, Angelica is the only one that's seen her during the day walking around. She's seen others before, though."

Father Anderson then asked, "So Angelica, do you have any imaginary friends?"

She felt his tone was condescending, but she only showed a slight frown. "No, I've never had an imaginary friend. I've been seeing spirits for a while now and I know the difference."

The priest chuckled at her. "I understand. I didn't mean to imply that you're making this up. I apologize, Angelica."

Normally Rosanna would've been quick to chastise her for such perceived disrespect. She then, however, only continued to stare blankly at the table. Even Edward was surprised by her lack of motivation to take control of the conversation.

He continued. "So has anything else occurred that I need to know about?"

The three of them, mostly Edward and Angelica, though, went into detail about the many strange and fear-inducing events that they had been through. They shared everything about their first few days there: Angelica nearly drowning, Rosanna's experience with the tapping and the drab barn... all of it. Every strange event that they could recall up to the present day was discussed.

An hour and a half passed before they started to wind up their conversation.

Father Anderson said, "Well, I see you all have had quite a lot of strange things happen here. The next step for me to take will be contacting the local paranormal investigations crew to come in and investigate your home. Based on what they find I'll have to submit any evidence to The Church and go from there."

Concerned, Edward asked, "How long will that take? We're having major problems right now!"

The priest responded, "I'll let the Miller's Run Paranormal Investigations team know that it's urgent and they'll arrive as quickly as possible. After that it may take a couple of weeks to...."

He was cut short, however, as the rustic branched light fixture overhead creaked loudly. The four of them watched as one screw seemed to loosen itself and fall to the table with a metallic plunk. As another did the same, the bulbs and fixture broke loose and crashed down on the table in front of them. They all lurched away from the table as a loud crunching crash traveled through the house.

Each checked for injuries on themselves as Father Anderson crossed himself before saying, "Right, I'll make sure that the M.R.P.I. gets here urgently! In the meantime, I brought three blessed medallions for each of you to wear. Keep them on you at all times."

Rosanna, breaking her previous silence, said, "Don't you have enough evidence now!?" Her tone was certainly not the usual one she showed for members of the clergy. Desperation, however, was in control.

Father Anderson replied, "I can see things are dire here, Rosanna, but the proper procedure must be observed. When The Church gets the report I send them I don't think we'll encounter any problems. But again, sufficient evidence must be presented before we can find a solution. In the meantime, I'll bless you with this consecrated oil to help keep you safe."

He then removed a small bottle of oil from his pocket and made the sign of the cross on each of their foreheads. "There we are. In the meantime, I'll pray for all of you. Should you feel threatened again, recite The Lord's Prayer and Hail Marys. You must stay strong as a family and as individuals during this time of peril. May God be with all of you."

They soon escorted him to the door and reluctantly waved goodbye. That night they would all be sleeping in the living room, not wanting to face the night alone. Edward on the couch, Angelica on the sofa, and by her own choice, Rosanna slept on the floor in a sleeping bag. It was her small way of trying to reestablish a relationship with her daughter. Still quite stricken with guilt, it would take a long time before these small acts of personal penance would stop. Needless to say, Cerberus was quickly becoming very protective of his new friend Angelica.

Forty-six

The next morning at around 7:00 A.M., Edward awoke to the sound of his phone ringing. As he reached for it, he noticed Angelica was gone and Rosanna was still asleep. Rubbing his eyes, "Hello?"

"Hello, Mr. Barrister? Hi, this is Roberta Stevenson from the Miller's Run Paranormal Investigations team. How are you this morning?"

He yawned before saying groggily, "Ah, good morning. We're doing okay, I suppose, given the circumstances."

Paying heed to his tone, "I'm sorry to call so early in the morning, but Father Anderson told us about your situation there. He said it was a very urgent matter. As luck would have it the entire team can be there as soon as today if you're available."

Now perking up a bit, "Yes, today would be great! We're going to be here all day. Come by whenever you like!"

"That sounds great. How about we plan on showing up at around 1:00 P.M.? That will give us time to set up our equipment, do a couple of interviews, and decide on our course of action. I'll have three others coming along with me to help, if that's okay with you." Roberta didn't disclose the names of the others coming. She didn't know that one key member of the team would cause friction immediately upon arrival.

"Yeah, that's fine. That'll give us time to straighten things up a bit." Edward looked down at Rosanna and smiled as she started to stir from sleep. He continued. "And again, thanks for coming on such short notice. We're on Holly Bush Road. Do you know where that is?" He knew pretty much everyone in Miller's Run knew the location of Holly Bush Road, but the question was standard fare.

"Yes, we know how to get there. We'll see you at 1:00 P.M. then."

Edward then quickly said, "Oh, wait, how much is this going to cost?"

Roberta said merrily, "Oh, we don't charge for this, Mr. Barrister. It's our hobby outside of work, so we get paid with evidence. Actually, you could offer some sort of payment as a goodwill gesture."

"How much are we talking?"

"Not money, Mr. Barrister, just two votes in the next town council election. Fair?"

Chuckling, "Yeah, that sounds reasonable."

They wrapped up the phone conversation.

Edward put the phone down as he said to Rosanna, "Great news, hon! The paranormal investigations team is coming today at 1:00."

Clearly relieved, Rosanna said, "Thank goodness."

A black BMW, followed by a black van, drove steadily down the road toward the Barrister home. The driver of the BMW was Sara Goodwin. She had been plagued by increasing nausea as they came closer to the turnoff at Holly Bush Road. The occasional dizziness seemed only minor and in brief flashes. Nonetheless, she persisted.

As soon as the house came into view, she looked to the side for a moment to take in the sight. It suddenly dawned on her that she had been seemingly avoiding the place subconsciously. It had been at least a year since she drove this way.

Suddenly, as her gaze turned back toward the road, she saw the shape of a shaded figure, sans an articulated head, standing directly on the midline of the asphalt. A shrill voice, one she would come to know soon enough, cried out in her ear: "FETCH!" Sara violently jerked the car to one side of the road, barely missing the drainage ditch next to it. Once past the apparition, she yanked the car back onto the road and continued to slam on the brakes. The van behind her also came to an abrupt stop.

The occupants of the van got out as soon as it came to a stop. With the smell of burnt brake pads lingering, Sara opened her door and began going through a series of painful dry heaves. The little stomach acid that came up left a nasty acrid taste in her mouth.

Roberta cried out in concern, "Sara, honey, are you all right!?"

Struggling to speak between the strong contractions in her abdomen, "Yeah... yes, I'm fine."

Placing her hand on Sara's back. "What happened? Why did you swerve like that?"

"I saw someone in the road. It was a spirit, but my reflexes took over. Are you all okay?"

"We're fine...."

Before she could finish, Sara jerked her sternly into the car by her arm. No one in the van, and certainly not Roberta, saw the car that came tearing ass down the road around the nearby oxbow in the road. The resulting breeze nearly pulled the door shut behind her.

Ron narrowly dodged the Dodge Viper that continued to blaze on down the road. He yelled, "You could've kill someone, you asshole!"

Of course, the driver of the Viper was long out of earshot.

Roberta, regaining her footing outside of the car, said, "Thank you, Sara! I'd be dead if it weren't for you!"

Sara raised her hand in acknowledgement, but doubled over in pain.

"Are you still sure you want to do this?"

After taking a gulp from her bottle of water, "Yes. I have to."

Later, Sara would be able to pinpoint the source of the voice that resounded so forcefully in her mind.

The vehicles soon came to a stop in the turnaround in front of the barns. As Roberta and Ron stepped out of the van and headed toward the house, Sara gripped the pendant around her neck and lowered her head. The silent words she spoke were hers and hers alone. The two investigators from the van walked on to the door, aware of Sara's preparation ritual. They knocked on the door and Edward soon opened it. Still inside, he didn't see Sara step out of her car.

Roberta then said, "Hello, Mr. Barrister. I'm Roberta. We spoke on the phone earlier."

He smiled and shook her hand. "Hello! Please, come in."

He was stunned speechless as he then saw Sara step into view. She smiled and waved at him as he tried to swallow the lump in his throat.

The three team members entered the kitchen and stood with the three Barristers.

As they shook hands, Roberta started, "Nice to meet you all! I'm Roberta, this is Ron." Edward shook his hand and she continued.

"And you've already met Sara."

Edward wanted to run from the room at this point, but his basic manners wouldn't allow it. He smiled nervously. "Nice to see you again, Sara."

Rosanna now recognized the younger woman in the black dress. It wasn't the same dress she was wearing in her dream, but it was close enough. Unlike the one she was wearing the day of the meeting with Angelica and Edward, this one was more modern. Rosanna could scarcely control the glare coming from her face. Sara noticed it, as did everyone else.

Nonetheless, Sara extended her hand. "Hello, Mrs. Barrister. It's nice to meet you."

In a curt tone, Rosanna replied, "Yeah, it's nice to meet you, too." After briefly shaking her hand (more akin to presenting her hand in the lowest shade of politeness), Rosanna looked over at her husband and said, "Ed, can I speak to you in the other room, please?"

Edward knew he was doomed now. He even thought that the spirits they'd been plagued with would show him more mercy in comparison. They excused themselves and disappeared into their bedroom, shutting the door behind them.

Once inside, he did his best to keep his voice down. He whispered, "Rosy, hon, I had no idea she would be here! Roberta didn't mention a word about it!"

The walls could scarcely contain the growing muffled words that were exchanged back and forth.

Meanwhile, in the kitchen, Sara was crouched down and talking to Angelica. "I hope you're doing okay."

Starting to feel exhausted from all of the accumulated turmoil, Angelica said, "I'm okay, I guess. I'm really tired."

Roberta then said, "Well, honey, we're going to try and see if we can help you all out. If we work together, we'll get through this."

Angelica looked at Sara's smiling face and was overcome with an impulse. She quickly embraced Sara's neck and said quietly, "Please help us! I'm scared!" For Angelica, this was rare. She, for unknown reasons so far, didn't feel she could show this type of vulnerability to her mother.

Sara, taken by the gesture, said endearingly, "Oh! It's okay, Ange. Can I call you Ange?" She nodded her head as Sara continued.

"We're going to do everything in our power to help. And do you want to know a secret?" Angelica nodded again as Sara said, "It's perfectly normal to be afraid, even for adults like you." The words did well to disarm, even if only slightly, some of the tension for Angelica. She was willing to take any small remedy she could at this point.

Rosanna and Edward rejoined the room. Much to Rosanna's chagrin, she saw the comforting gesture from Sara. She shot Sara a subtle glare before looking at her daughter. "Angelica, don't bother her like that."

Smiling, Sara replied, "It's okay, Mrs. Barrister, I don't mind."

Roberta then said, "Oh, there are four on our team. Tony is doing research at the library and town records office. He'll be here later on."

Edward replied, "That's fine. Hey, let's all go have a seat in the living room."

Once in the living room, the others, besides Sara, sat.

Before they began speaking, Sara said, "If you all don't mind, I don't want to know any more about what's going on here. I need to keep my mind clear during my walk. Do you mind if I start outside on the property?"

Rosanna was happy to see her leaving the house as Edward said, "No problem at all."

Angelica then asked eagerly, "Can I come with you, Sara? Please."

Rosanna quickly answered, "Stop bothering her, Angelica!"

Still smiling, "I don't mind if she comes along, Mrs. Barrister."

Rosanna reluctantly agreed and the two of them made their way outside onto the back porch.

As they neared the turnaround, Angelica asked, "Where do you want to start walking?"

Sara replied with a smile, "I'll need to concentrate for a minute. When I feel something pull me in a certain direction, I'll let you know. In the meantime, make sure don't say anything. It might disrupt my train of thought."

Apologetically, "Oh, I'm sorry. I'll be quiet."

"I didn't mean to sound rude. I just need to concentrate. Just stay close and try to pay attention to your own instincts. Are you ready?"

Angelica nodded as Sara continued.

"Good. Now, just give me a moment and...."

Sara closed her eyes and started to purge distractions from her mind. Angelica looked up attentively and soon emulated her new teacher. They stood in the turnaround briefly before Sara got a heavy feeling of dread from the drab barn on her left. The emotional stains from decades ago, and even farther back, were palpable and stifling. She opened her eyes and looked over at the other, kempt, barn.

"Let's look at that one first." Sara stood silently in front of the open doors, staring at the ground. Seconds later she said, "Okay, many, many animals have died here. I know your goats were killed here recently, but there were hundreds killed before this." Trying to focus, she continued. "And I'm getting that they weren't killed to be eaten either. There's something more to it than...." A surge of pain stabbed suddenly into her mind. She gripped her head with her hands and said, "Something is really trying to keep me from seeing things here." An image quickly popped into her mind: that of an older woman. Trying to open her eyes, "I saw you!" She said this in tone of momentary triumph, but quickly regained her composure.

Sara then heard a voice internally say, *"You'll see what I want you to see, witch!"*

Seeing her in distress, Angelica asked, "Are you okay?"

Rubbing her eyes with her fingers, "I'm okay. Just let me concentrate." She stepped up to the barn then and placed her hand on one of the doors. Quietly she said, "You had something to do with it... but what?"

She tried to focus in on the answers she'd been seeking, but her mind was obscured from anything further. A thick black fog was all around, blotting out any hope of sight.

Her attention was then quickly pulled back in the direction of the house, but somewhat farther away in the open grass. Angelica turned her attention that way as well and gasped quietly before placing her hand over her mouth.

Sara, seeing the same thing as she, said, "You see him, right?"

Angelica nodded and said in a hushed tone, "Yes. I've seen him walking around before."

Sara, keeping her calm demeanor, replied, "He doesn't mean any harm. He's lost… very confused. I saw him in the road as we were getting ready to pull in. He's stuck in his death state."

Angelica's eyes widened. "What's that mean?"

Her eyes still on the shadowy apparition with the nearly missing head. "It means he's stuck in the way in which he died. I don't think he even knows he's dead. Someone, or something, is keeping him confused and trapping him here."

Still noticeably uneasy, "I don't like thinking about him…."

"He won't harm us, not intentionally."

The two then watched as the spirit walked away and seemed to dissipate into the air and vanish from sight.

"We'll have to try and help him. But for now, I need to see more."

"For some reason, the word 'fetch' keeps popping in my head…."

Before Angelica could continue, Sara recalled what happened moments before their arrival. "I heard someone say that in my mind, too, right as we were getting ready to pull into your driveway. I don't know what it means, though."

"If it helps, I think I saw him when we first moved in here three years ago."

Perplexed, "Maybe we'll get more information later. For now, I'll continue my walk."

The two of them then stepped out toward the drab barn. Sara sighed and focused in on the building. Suddenly the image of an older man flashed before her eyes. His head rested limply on his shoulder. She heard a name come to mind and said it aloud, "Amos…." No more information was perceived, however, as what seemed to be a psychic veil of darkness fell over the structure as well.

Struggling for a moment, "I don't think I'm supposed to see this yet. There's another clue somewhere on the property, farther away."

Meanwhile, back at the house, Roberta and Ron were explaining the upcoming investigation to Rosanna and Edward. Roberta, having just returned with a modest plastic case, placed it on the table and opened it. Inside it was custom-fitted foam cut out to the shape of the audio recorders inside.

Taking one and showing it to the Barristers, she said, "We'll be using these devices to gather any audio evidence we can. We try to keep a thorough record of each investigation, but it's also for trying to catch EVPs."

Rosanna asked, "What are EVPs?"

Ron answered, "Electronic Voice Phenomena. Sometimes we get answers to questions that we don't hear with our own ears at the time."

Rosanna was still skeptical about the procedures. "So you can hear dead people talking on the recorder?"

Roberta, picking up on her subtle disbelief, "Yes, you'd be surprised at the answers you can get when you review the recording. We've had quite a few over the years."

As Roberta handed Ron a recorder, he said, "If it's okay with you, we'd like to go ahead and start asking some questions. If something answers, we may know where to set up later on for better results."

They agreed to the search and stepped aside as he and Roberta each turned on their respective recorders.

Ron then asked, "Are there any spirits here with us now?"

Rosanna was still holding on to slivers of skepticism, despite the current events. She watched and listened as no answer was verbalized.

Ron continued. "What is your name?" He paused and waited.

No audible response.

"How many spirits are here with us now?"

He waited and again, no verbalized response. The recorder in his hand, however, suddenly became very warm. As the heat quickly increased, he cried out and dropped the recorder on the floor. He cried out, "Shit!" while shaking the hand that held the recorder.

Concerned, Roberta asked, "Ron, are you okay!? What happened!?"

He answered, "The recorder! It's burning hot for some reason!"

Not convinced by the theatrics, Rosanna reached down and tried to pick it up. She too felt the pain and dropped it quickly. "What the...? It *is* hot!"

Edward took her hand and looked at it. "Careful, honey!"

The pain fleeted away as Rosanna asked, "Has that ever happened before?"

Roberta replied, "That's the first time we've ever had anything like that happen."

Ron, using a handkerchief he took from his pocket, gingerly picked up the recorder and quickly placed it on the nearby coffee table. He blew over the recorder a couple of times before saying, "If that thing isn't fried already, I'd bet the farm there's something on there!"

They all looked at the device in astonishment, waiting for it to cool down.

Meanwhile, Sara paused after walking onto the bridge spanning the large stream bisecting the property. She closed her eyes a few moments before saying, "Something happened to you on this bridge, didn't it?" Without seeing Angelica nod, she continued. "Something here has had it in for you since the day you got here."

Amazed at her clarity, "Yeah! I was sitting on this bridge three years ago and someone pushed me in! My parents didn't believe me, but I felt someone push me!"

She continued off the bridge and down the path. "I'd say you're lucky to be alive. Let's keep going. There's still something farther away."

Still in wonderment, "How did you know all that? I never told you about that day!"

Sara quickly motioned with her hand for silence. Angelica quietly apologized as the stroll continued.

Several yards down the path, Sara said, "The one who's tormenting you... she keeps going back this way down the path. She travels this trail often, almost every day. But why?" The medium was staring at the ground, searching images unseen to Angelica. "She's been going there since way before your family moved in. I think she's been here since the 1800s. Something is drawing her back to the spot... farther in." She looked down at Angelica. "Let's keep going. I should find something here soon."

Back at the house, the four were standing around the coffee table in the living room. The now cooled recorder was plugged into a laptop that Roberta recently brought in.

Ron was accessing the recording on the screen. "I think it might just be intact. Let's see here...." He managed to find the file and opened in. The sound of the questions played back. The first question was unanswered, as was the second. After the third question, "How many spirits are here with us now?" an answer came through.

A distorted chorus of voices answered, "MANY!" The tone was strained but powerful, leaving a permanent place in everyone's mind. The recording then continued on without further words, only finishing when the recorder was stopped upon cooling.

They looked at each other, dumbstruck, before Roberta said, "That's the first time I've heard that answer!"

A little annoyed that Roberta sounded like a kid getting a new result on a science project for school, Rosanna said, "That's it?"

Ron answered, "That's all that's on the recording, Mrs. Barrister. Now we at least have something to go on. We'll go ahead and start unloading the rest of our gear and get to setting up, if that's okay."

Edward replied, "Certainly."

Angelica and Sara drew close to the cave, but not close enough to see the path Angelica had cut several days ago.

Sara stopped on the trail and said, "Okay, there's something very powerful near here. It's beneath us, way underground... a cave. The cave where you met... *a puppet*? That's the word I keep hearing: 'puppet.' The old woman you mentioned in your email, Caroline... this is where she goes. But why?"

As she attempted to dig further with her mind, she suddenly saw multiple humanoid figures appear all around. Angelica, now terrified, saw them, too. The various creatures, all around eight feet tall or more, showed themselves as solid black silhouettes, some standing on the ground, some in the trees, and others on the rocks protruding from the hill.

Speechless at first, she then looked down at Angelica and said, "They... they know we can see them! They've been here the whole time but I didn't know! We have to go back; they're very powerful!"

As they steadily headed back toward the bridge they noticed the shadow figures now lining the path and standing at varying distances from it. Sara made sure to retain her composure, helping Angelica do the same. The horde, however, did not follow. They only watched.

Once at the bridge, they stopped momentarily to look back. Sara and Angelica gazed helplessly as the shadowy shapes revealed their eyes. They were all identical in color, each orb resembling some sort of sinister sun overhead at noon.

Trying unsuccessfully to reign in her fear, Sara gasped, "What the hell!? How did I not see them!? They've always been here!"

Even more concerned than her, Angelica said, "They've been here since we moved in!?"

Reluctantly, she shared the newfound truth. "They've been here for centuries!" In the blink of an eye, however, they all disappeared from view. "We only see what they want us to see...."

Roberta, outside with Ron unloading gear from the back of the van, saw Sara and Angelica walking away from the bridge quickly. Roberta asked as they came within earshot, "Sara, are you two okay?"

Sara replied in a grave tone, "There are dozens of powerful entities on this property. Angelica and I both saw them."

Ron responded, "Really? Do you know what they are?"

Sara, still flustered, "I'm not sure just yet. I need a break."

Angelica then asked Sara, "Do you want something to drink?"

She replied, "Yes, that would be nice." As Angelica ran to the kitchen inside, Sara said to her team members, "Whatever they are, there are a lot of them. All I know is they've been torturing the living *and* the dead here for centuries!"

Around twenty minutes later, Sara was seated in a wooden chair on the back porch with Angelica alone next to her. Finishing up a bottle of water, she said, "Thanks again for the water. Now, I think I'm ready to see that other barn."

Eagerly, "I'll get the keys!"

It wasn't until a few seconds later, when she returned with the keys, that the eagerness melted to dread at the thought of where they were going. Angelica showed her the correct key to open the padlock on the barn door and they walked toward it.

As they got to the door and Sara put the key into the padlock, Angelica said, "We don't.... Oops, I'm sorry. I shouldn't tell you anything."

Sara smiled at her and winked, then turned the key, opening the way inside. Before she could open the door completely, however, a wave of lightheadedness overcame her. She recoiled slightly but took a deep breath and pressed forward. Stepping inside, she quickly said, "Okay, I may have been a little off before. Even though many animals died in the other barn, many more have had their lives taken here. It goes so far back it's difficult to say when it all started." She walked around the structure, her head lowered in reflection, as Angelica barely crossed the threshold. Sara continued. "The air is thick with death here. It's taken on a life of its own. So much bloodshed...."

Angelica now sniffed the air as her nose sensed something new.

Sara, without looking back, motioned her hand at her. "You smell it, too, don't you? The blood...."

Angelica nodded silently as Sara continued to look about.

Suddenly her attention was drawn to the loft above. She stared at it, at first saying nothing as Angelica's gaze turned there also. The two of them then saw a vivid image jump into their psyche: a man hanging lifelessly, by the neck, from the rafters above.

Angelica was jolted by it, but Sara, maintaining her composure, said, "Amos... this is where you took your life, isn't it?" She heard a confirmation in her mind. Still gazing at the rafters, she said, "They tortured you. They took everything from you. You lost all hope. And now, even in death, they hold you here." Sara then turned and looked at Angelica with a clear look of pity on her face. Sara's gaze, however, was suddenly pulled away. She continued. "Wait... there's something in here you want me to find, isn't there?"

Seeing her looking all around the structure, Angelica asked, "What are you looking for?"

Sara made a gentle shushing sound with her hands before saying, "I'm not sure... just look around for anything out of the ordinary."

They searched the area for only a short time before finding something strange. In the back stall in one of the far corners of the barn, a large steel lid was covering what appeared to be an old well. The lid was securely fastened by another heavy duty lock.

Sara looked down at the crudely etched cross, now rusted with age, which scarred the center of the metal. "Did you know this was here?"

Angelica, confused as well, shook her head.

"I wonder if any of these work...." Sara tried the other keys on the keyring, but none fit. She paused a moment, then placed her hand on the center of the lid. She mumbled, "This has something to do with it... but it's not clear. There's something more." Sara then stood up and said, "The answer is somewhere else. Let's check up there."

The two of them then met at the ladder leading up to the second floor. Sara then looked down at Angelica before grabbing hold of the wooden rungs and climbing up. After stepping onto the landing she turned and helped her young tagalong reach the top safely. With a smaller area to search now, Sara quickly saw something only faintly conspicuous. She walked over to what looked like a small container wedged into a purpose-built slot in between two ceiling rafters. Once she pulled it free, the heavily rusted child's lunchbox showed only an etched name: Tim. Sara then kneeled down on the floor. Angelica was looking on as she placed the box on the wooden boards. She then popped open the latch, revealing a folded sheet of murky paper stained from the occasional drop of water containing rust. After unfolding the sheet of paper she unknowingly grabbed the previously hidden necklace from around her neck and gripped the silver Celtic knot in her hand. She silently read the words on the paper, Angelica leaning in to see them as well. The following was written, somewhat sloppily, in ink:

"If you find this, consider this my last warning. I have lost everything. My wife, my son, and all of the crops and animals I used to own, are all gone. Do not be tricked by what lives here. It only wants to hurt you. No matter how much blood, no matter how much sacrifice, it will never be enough. I tried to appease it, but I failed. The more I gave up, the more it demanded. Once I had nothing else to give it required one final sacrifice. I do this so that my son might be spared. At this point I'm not sure if this will work, but it's the only chance I have to free my son's soul from the devil's hand.

"Take my words to heart and leave now! No one and nothing should live here!

"May God have mercy on my soul.

"Amos Harris."

Sara couldn't stop the small tears that briefly trickled down the sides of her face. She sniffled and wiped them away with her hand. "There's so much pain attached to this. So much suffering...." Sara then cleared her throat and said, "Okay, I know what happened here now. Let's head back to the house."

Forty-seven

About an hour passed and Sara was now seated quietly on the edge of Angelica's bed. Having just finished walking throughout the house and getting her impressions thereof, she jotted down notes in her small notebook with a pen. As she finished a thought her attention was brought up to the door where Angelica had quietly opened it. Smiling at her curious friend, Sara said, "It's okay to come in now. I'm nearly finished with this."

The eight-year-old entered her room with Cerberus following closely behind. Angelica asked, "Do you need anything?"

Sara reached down to pet the panting puppy and said, "No, thank you, I'm fine." She then looked up and around at the furniture and said, "I really like the color scheme you have going here!"

Smiling, "Thank you! My favorite colors are black and white... and red, too."

"Hmm, don't you like pink?"

Repulsed by the idea, "Ugh, no! I've never liked the color pink!"

Chuckling, "Well, that's something we have in common! I've never liked it much myself."

Angelica then approached her and said, "What kind of braid is that you have in your hair? I noticed it on the day we came over. It's really pretty."

Sara smiled warmly and placed her small notebook to the side. "Aw, thank you! It's just a variation of a French braid. I can show you how to tie it if you'd like."

Angelica nodded her head and quickly found an elastic band nearby.

Now taking the implement in her hand, Sara explained, "Okay, it's actually really simple. Do you know how to tie a standard braid?"

Angelica nodded and Sara continued.

"Okay, it's pretty much the same technique. Just start here...." She then proceeded to tie the braid and explained how to do it.

As Sara neared the end of her demonstration, she paused and looked toward the upper part of Angelica's bedroom window which was covered by a curtain. After feeling Sara's hands release the finished braid, she turned and faced her.

Seeing the distraction in her face, Angelica asked, "What's wrong? Do you see something?"

The psychic stood and nodded, then walked to the window and parted the curtains. No more than ten yards away stood the form of Caroline. The old woman's face bared a sadistic smirk.

Sara then quietly said, "I can see her now. She wants me to see her. I'm getting bits and pieces about her life, but not much."

Angelica now stood on a small stool she'd taken from nearby. Quickly seeing the elderly woman's form, "That's her, all right...."

Still staring forward, "I get the impression that when she was alive, she was well known in the community. She was somewhat of an outcast. I'm sensing that she spent the last years of her life mostly alone. She had children... more than one. She lived near here, but I'm getting that this house wasn't here at the time." Sara's vision of the past was abruptly cut short. "And... that's all I'm seeing. She's not letting me see anything else." Sara quietly reflected for a few moments before suddenly revealing, "Caroline doesn't like your family because you're Catholic." The psychic tried to see more, but was unable.

Angelica asked, "Why doesn't she like Catholics?"

Still mentally searching in vain, "I don't know why. All I know is that she doesn't like any of you because of that." Sara sighed and continued. "There's something more to it, though. I know it's there but I'm just not connecting the dots yet. There has to be more to it than that." At a psychic impasse, Sara said, "Maybe Tony will find out more with his research." She then secured her pen to the small notebook with an elastic band. "Do you want to see what kind of we gear we use to investigate?"

Angelica smiled and nodded, then made her way to the living room with Sara.

Several minutes later, Roberta was standing next to the van parked outside and waving to the man, Tony, pulling up the driveway. Nearby, Sara was standing next to the opened passenger door of her BMW. In the seat was an opened plastic case that held a large concave instrument attached to a speaker headset.

Sara took the dish by the black handle and placed it in Angelica's hand. "Okay, this is called a 'parabolic dish microphone.' It amplifies sounds from very far away." Sara then pointed to a small bird that was perched atop the distant bridge spanning the stream. "Now, put the headphones on and point the antenna at the bird. You should be able to hear it clearly from here."

The practically inaudible bird now came through clearly as Angelica looked up in disbelief. "Wow! It's like it's right in front me!"

Sara smiled and said, "Sometimes this can help us hear spirits more clearly. Roberta and Tony both swear by it."

The man in his early forties, Tony, now approached Angelica and shook her hand. He said jovially, "Hi, you must be Angelica! Sara has told me all about you. My name is Tony."

She replied, "Nice to meet you, Tony."

Looking her in the eye, he said sincerely, "Sara tells me you're one brave little girl! Trust me when I say that our team will do everything we can to help you all take care of this problem. You have my word on it!"

The afternoon sun highlighted his salt-and-pepper hair and diluted tan. Most importantly of all, Angelica could tell he meant every word he said.

Later, as the sun descended toward the horizon, Tony was speaking with the Barristers as the rest of the team was busy finalizing the positions of the cameras and recorders throughout the house. He took a drink from his water bottle, then said, "Now, the way we typically do these investigations is pretty straightforward. I've spent the past several hours researching the property, old land deeds, newspaper articles, etc. I still have a few things to search for, but I should be finished with that in the next couple of days. After we finish our investigation here tonight, we'll put all of our information together and present our findings to your family and Father Anderson. After all of that is said and done, Father Anderson will make the decision on what to do next."

Edward looked over at Rosanna, then back at Tony. "So have you been able to find out anything about the house so far?"

Nodding, "Yes, I have found out a lot of information so far. I'm going to meet with the librarian and the town historian later on tomorrow. Once I have that information verified, I'll share it with you all. I always double and triple check my sources before I present it as facts."

Rosanna squeezed her husband's hand briefly. "We really appreciate you all helping us. It means the world to us. Sincerely, thank you."

The investigation would certainly bring them answers, some wanted, some not. They would find, however, that more answers so often only breeds more questions. If anyone in the group of living souls on the property had their doubts about belief in the paranormal, or at least a willingness to abandon a long-held label of "impossible" placed thereon, they would be crumbled to the ground that night.

Forty-eight

Edward decided to take his cup of coffee outside. With the others busy inside, he took a few minutes for himself. Sipping on the hot beverage inside the ceramic vessel, he walked lazily down the dirt trail and toward the bridge. The golden disk in the sky was melting the colors of the horizon into a pool of gold, red, orange, and purple.

As he stepped onto the wooden planks he placed his cup of coffee onto the flat wooden rail and reflected on the recent set of oddities in his life. How could it be that something most people wouldn't take seriously, a visit to a claimed psychic medium, could now be causing absolute havoc in his life? What sort of web of confluences could bring that same psychic to his doorstep and into his home? And never mind that this psychic happened to be a woman he secretly lusted for, even if for just a few moments. *"I'm only human,"* he would repeat to himself, over and over. Of course, telling that to Rosanna would bring no mercy or compassion. Even if her religion, her savior, taught her since she could remember that forgiveness is the only way to play, she wasn't willing to let these circumstances fly by.

The circular path of attempting self-forgiveness, and trying to think of a way to convince Rosy to do the same, left him grabbing the bridge his nose in pain. Perhaps in an attempt to accept the scrambled mess of fate on his doorstep, he mused, *"If this is some sort of higher plan, God must have a sick sense of humor."* Thankfully his wife had not a psychic bone in her body, as far as he knew. If she had read that thought, he'd be even farther up shit creek and barely hanging onto the last plank of wood, the flimsy paddle lost miles back.

His eyes still locked on the sunset in the distance, he suddenly snapped to and nearly knocked the coffee cup into the stream. The phone in his shirt pocket was ringing. Relieved that the brief adrenaline-induced rise in his pulse and blood pressure were all for naught, he took it in hand. "Hello?"

A familiar and comforting voice answered, "Hello, Ed, it's Mom."

Strangely, thoughts of his mother had popped into and out of his head all day, but he wasn't expecting her to call. Maybe he should've expected it, knowing full well that his mother was the one who'd shared her "abilities" with him. His father sure as hell didn't believe in that sort of thing. He would always chalk up his wife Gena's so-called perception to just an odd quirk she had. Sure, she could supposedly tell when bad things were going to happen, things she couldn't otherwise know about, but he just reasoned that if you worry about everything, sooner or later you'll be right to. Arthur Barrister would tell his wife, "If I had fifty thousand monkeys at their own typewriter, one of them would eventually type up Shakespeare. And I damn sure wouldn't kiss its ass to write another one."

"Hey, Mom. How are you?" He took a sip from his cup.

"Well, Ed, I just felt like I needed to call you. Is everything all right there?"

He thought for a moment, tempted to just go the route of pleasant conversation and leave out the events unfolding. Knowing she would see through it, he gave an edited version of matters at hand. "Well, things have been better, let's put it that way." Ed looked down at his cup, futilely hoping it won't need further explanation.

Concerned, "What do you mean? Is something wrong with Angie? You know I worry about her."

He sighed. "Well, the three of us have been 'experiencing things,' if you know what I mean."

The worried mother in her dominated her tone. "I thought you had the place blessed by a priest. What's happening now?"

"Well, since Ange had her run-in with that spirit in the cave, things have been going tits-up around here. Something killed her goats and then Rosy...."

Edward then stared ahead, his mouth hanging open, jaw muscles unresponsive. He didn't hear the voice of his mother repeatedly saying his name as his eyes gazed upon a new scene in the distance toward the small forest. Humanoid shapes, dozens upon dozens, stood silently all around him. They inhabited seemingly every nook and cranny of the foliage. The same entities that had shown themselves to Sara and Angelica earlier were now staring at him. Well over a hundred tiny suns were unwavering in the eye sockets of the solid black shapes scattered about.

Only barely aware of his phone now, he muttered, "Mom... I have to... go...."

A sharp and intense wash of panic engulfed him all at once from head to toe. The phone trembled in his hand as it slowly parted from his ear. He was suddenly taken back to a scene that he'd successfully forgotten for most of his life. Only seven years old, he was lying in his bed with his eyes fixated on the doorway facing his bed across the room. There in the frame, as with every night, a tall shadow man stood hulking in the doorway. Every night he would lock onto the yellow eyes of the creature before him, paralyzed. On some nights, he wouldn't sleep at all. Even hiding under his blanket wouldn't make the bad man go away. Most nights the seven-foot giant (to him it would seem more than ten feet tall) would just watch, attempting to slowly dismantle his sanity and nerve. In some respects, it worked, as Edward would go out of his way to try and forget this, to try and block it out. Years of mental sleight-of-hand had left him blind, or so he hoped, to the spirit world. But like a manic mail carrier feverishly banging on his door every day of his existence, life was waiting with tons of spiritual parcels to sort through. The seven-foot giant wasn't at his door now, no. There was now a multitude of shadowy invaders on his property, right next to his home, reminding him of the truth. If he had worked all his life to keep his proverbial third eye (the "spirit eye," as some call it) closed, something was now tearing it back open like the skin off of ripened orange.

He didn't notice the phone fall from his hand and into the stream with a loud plunk. Almost stuttering, he quietly muttered to himself, "If I c-c-close my eyes, they'll go away." His voice sounded almost exactly the same as he did when he was seven and tried to placate himself in the same way.

His eyelids clamped as tightly as possible, he said, "Go away! You can't hurt me! Go away!"

Ed stood silently, a dry lump in the back of his throat barely swallowed as the sound of a distant crow in the forest cawed hectically before taking flight. The strain of his heightened breathing was then starting to become noticeable. He tried to embrace the thought that all would be right in the world when he opened his eyes. Even if he didn't really believe his own rationalizations, he would attempt to use them once he opened his eyes and nothing would be there.

Finally he did open them, and what he saw was not what he'd hoped. Although all of the shadowy figures in the distance had disappeared, one and one alone now remained. Even though its shape was mostly humanoid, the edges of the apparition seemed to ebb and flow like a slowly flickering flame. In that instant, despite the figure not moving, a large baseball-sized rock flew toward him. He flinched and brought his hands up to his face but the rock splashed harmlessly in the stream directly in front of him. As the water from the plunking rock covered his shirt and face, he staggered backward and fell onto the ground. Hardly able to acknowledge the relief of not seeing another figure in front of him, he scrambled to his feet and bate a hard line back to the farmhouse.

Forty-nine

Meanwhile, Angelica and Sara were standing on the back porch having a conversation. Angelica, despite only having a handful of online conversations with Sara, was immensely enjoying their time together. Angelica felt that Sara spoke to her more as an adult, or at least that's what it felt like compared to her parents. She didn't have any major problems with the way her parents and teachers normally spoke to her, but this was refreshing to her in every way.

Inside the kitchen, unbeknownst to them, Rosanna was pouring herself a cup of coffee. She walked over to the nearby window and looked through the small divide in the curtains without disturbing them. It was then that she saw something different about her daughter's hair: the French-style braid that Sara had recently shown her and also wore in her own hair. *"That bitch!"* The thought surprised even her with its tone. She abandoned this feeling of momentary shock and let new feelings of possessiveness flare into existence. A caricature of parental protectiveness whooshed through her mind.

"Your daughter looks like a little whore now!"

The voice she heard was disturbingly familiar, but distorted. How could she be hearing the voice of her mother so clearly? Her mother was still alive, clinging to life in a euphemistically named nursing facility: *Sunny Acres Adult Care Facility*. And even if she were dead, Rosanna still strangely didn't believe she would be able to hear her voice. Deep down she knew that even if she had believed in her mother's spirit coming back to haunt her, she wouldn't want to experience that in any form. Even though she revered and respected her mother, and perhaps out of obligation, loved her, the relationship was always cold. Never mind that her relationship with her mother often reflected through to her parenting style with Angelica.

Regardless, the voice of her mother was crystal clear. It was as if she were standing right next to her, muttering in her ear.

The sound caused her to turn around and scan the kitchen. All she saw was Tony walking to the living room and sitting down on the couch, checking a series of cable connections hooked to his laptop computer on the coffee table. Not wanting to draw any attention to something she might be labeled "crazy" for later, she turned and looked back out the crack in the curtains. Her eyes fixated again on the braid in her daughter's hair.

"Are you just going to stand there and let that witch turn your daughter into a little whore!? A damnable street-walking, soul-stealing whore!?"

Regardless of the source of this voice, she blindly heeded its words and stepped toward the door. Suddenly thrusting it open, she startled both of them before she looked down at her daughter and said, "Angelica! I told you to stop bothering her! Now go to your room!"

Looking back toward her mother with reproach, "But Mom, we were just talking! I didn't do anything wrong!"

Sara started, "Really, Mrs. Barrister, I don't...."

Rosanna cut her off, however, still looking down at Angelica. "I told you to go to your room!"

Angelica showed no attempt to hide her scowl. She did, however, storm past her mother and to her room. Rosanna, not saying a word, glared hotly at Sara, gritting her teeth and letting out short, sharp breaths through her nose. The slash marks from recent dream looked more threatening as her pale skin went pink with flush blood in her cheeks.

They stood for a few moments as Sara's face, normally gentle and smiling, took on a more solid and serious expression. The woman known as Mrs. Barrister was now staring at her only two feet away. Sara knew. Sara could see something foreign heavily influencing her. And even though she couldn't clearly make out a definite shape or even a vague one, the strength and level of control it exerted frightened her. Perhaps even worse, she sensed that whatever this was manipulating Rosanna was also aware that it is being perceived. This force was so brazen, so confident, that it merely scoffed at this notion. *I want you to see me. And I want you to know that I don't care because you can't do a damn thing about it!* The entity wasn't Caroline, but something far worse.

Sara backed down and took a couple of steps toward the lip of the porch. She managed to catch herself, however, as she nearly stumbled over the edge. Rosanna then turned back around and reentered the house, the screen door slapping loudly against the doorframe behind her.

As she disappeared into the house, Sara now turned and headed toward her car parked in the turnaround. She then saw Edward walking toward her. What struck them both immediately was that they were both clearly distraught, perhaps by different, or similar, things. Seeing the concern on Sara's face made him temporarily forget about his own encounter. "Sara... you okay? What's wrong?"

"I'm all right. I think your wife is really upset with me."

This was certainly no surprise to Edward. He *knew* his wife hated her, despite only knowing about her existence for a few short days. And to think Sara wouldn't be able to pick up on that would be sheepish. "Uh-oh. What happened?"

Fifty

Later that evening, as the sun had set, the investigators and the Barrister family all stood in the farmhouse living room ready to begin. Despite the brief encounter that Edward and Sara had had, Rosanna had continued to silently feed the fire of suspicion and increasing anger. She looked between the curtains and saw Edward put his hand briefly on Sara's shoulder to comfort her as they approached the house. And even though this was the raunchiest of highlights from that brief moment, it was enough to cause the proverbial steam in her boiler to creep dangerously higher and higher.

The investigators were now primed with their equipment in hand. Tony was seated looking at the screen of his laptop as Ron and Roberta each held a digital voice recorder in their respective hands. Sara was standing on the far side of the room away from Rosanna. Sara could sense the obvious tension that had been growing in a crescendo since her arrival. Her arms folded, she quietly nibbled on her pinky nail and tried to steal the occasional glance at Rosanna, hoping to not be noticed. A glance at Angelica, who was behind and between her parents and in the hallway next to the room, brought her momentary solace before the sharp eyes of Rosanna caused her to glance away immediately.

Tony looked up at Roberta and Ron and said, "Okay, guys, the cameras are up and running and everything looks set. You can start recording when you're ready."

Roberta then said, "From this point on, let's keep conversation to a minimum. Try and not whisper if you can, as the recorders will pick it up and we don't want to confuse that with spirit voice. Ron, do you want to start?"

He nodded and he and Roberta synchronized their record buttons. Ron then asked, "Are there any spirits here with us now?"

They waited in silence a moment before Rosanna interrupted, annoyed, "Didn't you already do this earlier today?"

The flare of anger caused Sara to briefly look at Rosanna, the emotional fire almost visible to the naked eye.

Roberta, still composed, responded, "Mrs. Barrister, we're just reestablishing connection. We start off all investigations the same way."

Edward tried to put his arm around Rosy to calm her, but she jerked her shoulder away and made a barely audible sound of aggravation: "Hmph."

Ron, now keenly aware of the negative energy radiating from the lady of the house, continued. "If there are any spirits here, how many?" He waited a few moments, then asked, "Can you hear us speaking to you?" Another wait. "Can you understand what we're saying?"

After they paused for another answer, Roberta asked, "What is your name?"

At this question, the puppy Cerberus, who had been sitting diligently by Angelica's feet, whimpered. Sara, who was also feeling the atmosphere changing in a subtle way, looked at him helplessly for a moment before returning to stare at the floor once again. Angelica reached down and tried to sooth the worried canine with a gentle scratch on his head. Both she and Edward were also sensing this sinking, darkening, proverbial vapor slowly infiltrating the room unseen.

Roberta then asked, "What is it that you want from the Barrister family?"

They waited for an unheard answer for a few moments.

The seasoned investigator then said, "Okay, Ron, let's check and see if we got anything."

Suddenly a change in the light in the distance caught Edward's eye. He looked through the kitchen and toward the turnaround. "Huh, that's weird. The light above the barn just went out."

As Ron and Roberta rewound their respective recorders, Sara looked around uneasily, wanting to speak, but almost afraid to. Barely audible to the group, she said reluctantly, "They're drawing strength... not that they need to."

Ed looked at Sara with concern.

Rosanna then said in a heavily skeptical and sarcastic tone, "Really?"

Sara only glanced up before lowering her head again.

Trying to keep the investigation on track, Roberta said, "Okay, let's see if we got anything on the recorders."

She pressed the play button. Immediately Ron's voice played back. "Are there any spirits here with us now?"

Following the question, they all look wide-eyed in amazement as a series of taps, in clear groups of three, sounded off from seemingly all around the room.

Roberta, shocked, stopped the recorder and rewound it. "What in the world was that?"

Angelica replied in a detached, yet grim, tone. "It's them...."

Sara looked at her briefly with sadness, well aware that her friend was sensing the same things she was.

Roberta played the sound bit again, but no one was able to make out clearly, at least from the raw audio itself, what was making the noises.

The recorder continued to play, reaching Rosanna's disbelieving protest. At the end of Roberta's explanation and after the grunt of displeasure from Rosanna, a small giggle could be heard in the background. Roberta stopped the tape and rewound it a short bit.

Ron looked up with interest. "You all heard that, right? The giggle?"

They all nodded in agreement.

Rosanna then turned quickly to look down at Angelica. She said scornfully, "Angelica! I thought they told you to be quiet! Why did you giggle!?"

Sara finally looked up. "Mrs. Barrister, she was quiet the whole time. I know it wasn't her."

Rosanna rebutted, "I didn't ask you, *Sara*!" She looked back down at her daughter, whose face had shifted to its signature scowl. "And you, be quiet!" The angry mother sighed, as if trying to relieve the pressure. She then said in a negligibly softer tone, "Keep going. I'm fine."

Angelica looked up at her mother from behind with an expression of pure disbelief at the bald lie she just told. Angelica then folded her arms as Roberta played the recorder through the last section and through the giggle.

Now, on the recorder, after Ron's voice asked how many spirits are there, the response was chorus of taps, in sets of three, which came from all around the room. As the organized, yet chaotic, tapping sounds seemed to suddenly fade, a loud drawn-out beam of feedback blared through the small speaker.

Not pausing the recorder, Roberta said, "There has got to be something wrong with the recorder!"

Sara suddenly insisted in a more confident tone, "There's nothing wrong with the recorder. They're communicating!"

Rosanna quietly glared at her before looking back over at Roberta. The recording continued. As Ron's voice asked if the spirits can hear them, the recorder only played feedback. In the same instant the television was turned on, seemingly of its own volition. At first, only static was shown on the screen and heard through the speakers. All at once, the television began to flicker quickly between channels. There appeared to be no obvious pattern until it cycled through the four same channels over and again. One word from each channel was heard in succession: "I... can... see... you. I... can... see... you...."

Roberta tapped the recorder on its side, trying, and hoping, she could make it stop. The TV cycled over and over as the recording continued. When Ron's voice asked if they understood, the cycling of the television changed. It then settled on five different channels in its pattern.

The speakers on the LG flat-screen responded, "We... can... understand... you...," followed by a canned laugh track. "We... can... understand... you... hahaha!" As this played over and over, the volume slowly increased. "WE... CAN... UNDERSTAND... YOU... HAHAHA!"

The volume soon caused everyone to cover their ears as Edward tried first with the remote, then manual buttons on the side, to lower the volume. Unable to bear the sound anymore, he quickly jerked the power cable from the wall. Mercifully, the repeated phrase stopped and the television fell silent.

Ron, finally able to speak over the ringing in his ears, "Is everyone okay?"

They all nodded, except Angelica. She looked down at her feet and didn't see her companion, Cerberus. She disappeared down the hallway toward her bedroom and found the dog dazed and whimpering, the sounds and energy being overwhelming.

Undeterred, Rosanna said, "Keep going."

Roberta pressed play on the recorder once again, picking right back up at where the next question was audible. As Ron's voice asked the name of the spirit, a blaring, disembodied forest of moans and cries, more animalistic than human, blasted through. Angelica heard the sound playing and poked her head out of her doorway. The choir of seemingly hell-chained sounds was capped off by yet another loud beam of feedback and static. Even the investigators were absolutely stunned by how much volume the small recorder was putting out. Roberta immediately pressed stop.

Edward looked at her with obvious worry. "I'm guessing that's a first, too?"

Roberta silently nodded her head.

Tony, looking very interested in his laptop screen, said, "Mr. Barrister, does the upstairs guest bedroom have a leaky roof?"

They all stepped toward the screen and look at the camera feedback. Angelica also took a step into the hallway, looking silently up the stairway. On the screen, displayed in the green and black tones of a night-vision lens, they saw small drops of what looked like thick black fluid pecking and plopping on the top of the lens casing and sliding in front of the lens itself.

Edward replied quickly, "It shouldn't be leaking. I put that roof on myself two years ago!"

Roberta then said, "And it hasn't rained in days!"

Angelica suddenly called out from the hallway, "It isn't water!" She knew all too well about the black crud that seemed to announce that miasmic presence.

Tony suddenly said from the living room, "Ron, go and see what that is. We can't have it dripping on the camera like that."

As Ron headed for the stairs, Angelica said fretfully, "Don't touch it! It's poison!"

Looking at the screen on the laptop still, he watched a display box go blank. "Ah, crap! Roberta, the camera in the master bedroom just went out. Will you check on it?"

She agreed and hurried down the hall toward the room.

Rosanna, meanwhile, looked over her shoulder and said, "Angelica, I hope you aren't messing around back there! Don't touch their cameras!"

The accusations were getting automatic at this point and Angelica knew it. She replied in frustration, "I didn't touch anything!"

Sara, trying to defuse the anger, replied, "Mrs. Barrister, she didn't go in your bedroom. I've been able to see her this entire time."

As she said this, she felt tinges of regret before finishing the sentences. Rosanna was almost at her boiling point.

Rosanna's face was flush red with anger. "I didn't...."

Before she could finish her sentence, however, a large spark fired from the back of the television set, causing everyone to back away and stare dumbly. The screen then flared to life. They all first looked at the power cord, which was still lying on the floor unplugged.

All at once, music began to play through the speakers as a strange ripple of static flashed wildly on the screen. At first they only heard the regular electronic drumbeat of the opening. As it went on, the image quickly adjusted to a familiar one. Sara's eyes widened as she saw a distortion of light glide through the room. Angelica, in the hall, tried to adjust her eyes to make out the strange and subtle bending of the visible spectrum. All she knew for sure is that it was bad. Very bad. Edward looked surprised and confused as he also saw something out of the corner of his eye, but nothing more. Honestly, he truly didn't want to see anymore and the blinders his mind were accustomed to placing over his sight were only partially working at this point.

Suddenly, much to their surprise, the image displayed on the disconnected television turned to that of seemingly someone walking through the house with a video camera. The image on the screen included everyone in real time and glided slowly and deliberately toward the hallway. Sara looked back and forth between the displayed image and the blurred entity moving about.

POP! ZAP!

Roberta and Ron both looked on in dismay as each camera appeared to short out in front of them. The four in the living room watched on the big screen as the nefarious mass made its way into the master bedroom. Roberta backed away suddenly, apparently seeing the distortion of light for herself. The big screen also then showed her falling back and nearly hitting her head against the wall.

The video feed then quickly cut to an image that at first was hazy and dim, but quickly came into focus. On screen was the master bedroom, only now in a different time. From the speakers, "You let me violate you...."

No one there recognized the song but Sara. This immediately became a moot point, however, as the image became a familiar scene to one of the members of the family: Edward. Unable to comprehend that everyone was watching this, he painfully recalled the details of the erotic dream he'd had not long ago. Only in this version, the role of his wife was replaced by Sara entirely.

As if now caught in some masturbatory act, he dashed at the TV and began violently pressing the on/off switch. It didn't stop. He growled, "Stupid piece of shit!"

Sara blushed fiercely and turned away ashamed, despite knowing she never partook in the scene.

The screen then showed the dream sequence with every detail. One might even call it master camera work, but Rosanna was not impressed. No, Rosanna's face was bubbling up from red to purple. The rage was so thick, so pure, that she could only snarl out several inhuman sounds before screaming, "I KNEW IT!"

All eyes immediately turned to her.

As Ron ran down the stairs, he saw Rosanna clench her fists then charge and kick over the television set onto the ground.

Edward, stumbling backward from the flat screen being knocked over, heard an unsettling rendition of his mother's voice in his ears: *"Your wife is going to kill that girl, you know, but you're too weak to do anything about it! Go on! Start crying like a little bitch! You always were a disappointment to me!"* It certainly sounded like his mother, but obviously wasn't. She'd never said anything like that to him, especially not in that tone. The words, however, did manage to force their way in and muck with his emotions like a heavy foot repeatedly stomping a mud puddle. Now came the emotions he'd just felt again for the first time earlier that day. He felt like the little seven-year-old boy again, helpless to stop the invasion in his home. In fact, he briefly and sporadically felt the presence of the "bad man" that used to stand at his doorway, watching.

In the same instant, Rosanna also heard the voice of her mother coming through loud and clear in her own ears. *"That little bitch is here to ruin your family! She's worked her magic on your weak little husband and wants your daughter for herself! Kill her now or they'll mock your weakness forever in hellfire!"*

Sara turned just in time to see Rosanna violently kick the television set from its table and onto the floor. It continued playing, "You let me desecrate you…." The volume began to climb again, filling the room and hallway with the cries of ecstasy coming from the speakers. "You let me penetrate you…."

Meanwhile, Angelica was dashing from her room to see what the commotion was. Upon seeing her mother knocking down the LG and brandishing her fist at Sara, she heard a voice in her own mind. It was Caroline. *"Your mother is going to kill that girl! And when she's dead you'll have no one else to help you with your little 'talent'!"*

Angelica unknowingly verbalized the words. "Shut up!"

As Rosanna pointed her finger directly at Sara, Caroline's voice broke through again. *"Don't be stupid, child! Look there! She's going to kill her!"*

Despite the reflex to ignore the warning, she was overcome with a sinking realization: Caroline was right. Rosanna has nothing but lethal intentions in her eyes and emanating from her frame like carcinogenic radiation.

In a fit of anger, Angelica screamed out, "NO!"

The television continued the song. "You let me complicate you…."

Sara's full attention was on Rosanna, who was walking toward her steadily. She hardly noticed Cerberus running down the hall and barking wildly at the deranged mother in front of her. She also didn't see Angelica in a dead sprint coming down the hallway behind her mother. The eight-year-old then let out a primal scream, a war cry, before leaping madly onto her mother's back and grabbing her face tightly. Angelica's small, but sharp, nails scratched fiercely and wildly at Rosanna's eye sockets from behind. She cried out through gnashing teeth as Angelica's left fingernails dug mercilessly into her left eye. Her right eye was also clawed, but only scratched superficially.

Edward scarcely believed his eyes initially and stood there stupidly trying to comprehend the scene. Rosanna, however, bellowed out an otherworldly howl and grabbed her daughter's right hand before biting it without relief. Like a wild dog (or, perhaps, figurative bitch), she clamped down as if trying to ground a struggling gazelle.

Sara, too shocked to react, watched helplessly as Angelica cried out in pain before falling from her mother's back and onto the floor. As Rosanna attempted to recover, Edward leaped into the fray and pulled Angelica into his arms, shielding her as he enveloped her.

Ron, meanwhile, had run down the stairs and was now on the ground floor witnessing the melee struggle.

Roberta, seeing the situation as well, called out to her teammate, "Tony! Grab the holy water!"

Then she and Ron make their very best effort to restrain Rosanna, both having to use their entire weight to barely contain the snarling lady of the house.

Before Tony could get to the large plastic case sitting on the kitchen table, however, the container was flung by an unseen force toward the sink. The lid, unsecured previously, flopped open, spilling the contents all over the floor. A couple of voice recorders, a spare camcorder, and many feet of wires, crumpled on the linoleum. He scrambled to find the contents in the dark kitchen, the only light coming from the lamp in the living room.

Ron then called out, "Bring the crucifix, too!"

Frantically Tony searched the ground, but was unable to find the implements being requested. Meanwhile the television continued to play the video, essentially unexplainably, of Edward's dream. The song, "Closer," by Nine Inch Nails, went on its merry way. Only Sara had ever heard it before, and it reminded her of something in the recent past. She couldn't quite place it at the time, but the familiarity rang true.

All at once, however, everyone, save Cerberus who continued to bark feverishly, went relatively silent at the scene playing out before them. Rosanna's snarls and growls continued as Ron and Roberta turned her around and saw an unsettling image. Before them, drifting down the hall, was a crucifix from Angelica's room. Only Angelica and Sara could see Timmy's ethereal form hoisting it in his hands in front of his face. Behind him, at the opposite end of the hall, Caroline stood and watched, hardly hiding the pleasure on her face. What could be seen by everyone, however, was the thick black fluid that seemed to be dripping spontaneously from the silver cross and onto the floor.

Angelica cried out, "STOP IT, TIMMY!"

He paid her no mind.

A final line played out from the television speakers as the video dream came to a close: "You get me closer to God!"

The crucifix, still being held by Timothy Harris, was shoved long end first into Rosanna's partially opened mouth. Along the way it managed to chip four of her front teeth: two on the bottom and two on the top. As it was crammed in all the way to the perpendicular sides, it caused Rosanna to gag fiercely.

Heard only by Angelica, Sara, and Edward, Caroline cried out maniacally while laughing, *"Partake of the body of Christ, idolater!"*

Seeing her mother choking on the silver icon, Angelica was struck with an overwhelming need to suddenly help her. The desperation and anger she seemed to have toward her mother vanished almost as quickly as it had come on. As Ron and Roberta continued to try and restrain her flailing arms, Angelica walked up to her, grabbed hold of the perpendicular branches, and rather harshly placed her right foot on her mother's forehead. She grunted and groaned, pulling against the relic with all her strength against the wretched force that held it fast. Soon, however, the crucifix was dislodged, Angelica falling backward and onto her bottom. In a twisted way, one could almost liken it to a crude ceremony reenacting Arthur pulling the proverbial sword from the stone. Her mother, meanwhile, got loose in the restraining arms of Ron and Roberta.

As his wife choked and coughed heavily on the ground, Edward was quick to check on her, but also mindful to keep himself between his wife and his daughter.

Soon enough, Rosanna seemed to be regaining her composure. Her first glance up, however, was directed at her daughter. The mother's eyes still seemed to burn with residual anger as a steady trickle of blood from each orb's socket ran down her cheeks. Edward was quick to turn and place himself between them.

Unaware of her own actions, Angelica's eyes were wild with fear. The adrenaline in her system wasn't letting her relax for a second. She had even taken up a posture in which she held the moderately sized silver crucifix cocked to the side, ready to defend herself if necessary.

Then, only Rosanna seemed to see Angelica's left eye wink. Despite the overwhelming urge to take this as a mocking gesture, the sight of her daughter poised to strike her with a cross caused her to drop back down on the floor. Even as she wept bitterly, Angelica was hesitant to lower her guard.

Fifty-one

At this point, it didn't take an ordained priest to figure out that Rosanna was possessed. I'm sure the vast majority of psychiatrists would disagree, and only a few might even consent that, "She believed she was possessed," but that's it. The paranormal team would still have to come back to the house and do a more conclusive investigation, this time with an accompanying priest, and maybe even absent of Rosanna and Angelica. If they were to be there, they would have to be under close supervision. Neither Rosanna, Angelica, nor Edward would argue with that.

It was Edward's quick thinking, and the consensus of everyone there, that all should leave the property immediately. Time there would have to be limited if their own safety and sanity were to be spared. It was also Edward's idea to send Angelica to her friend's house, Abby Kelly, to spend the night. The problem was, how to get her there. Sara reluctantly volunteered to take Angelica there, regretting it only because she knew it would upset Rosanna, possessed or not. But given the circumstances, it seemed like the best option. Splitting the two up immediately was vital for their safety.

The rest of the paranormal team accompanied Rosanna and Edward to a hotel out of town where the couple would spend the night.

Fifty-two

Angelica's hand ached under the bandages hastily, but adeptly applied by Tony. There had been a little bleeding, but the wound, reddened indentations of Rosanna's teeth, was mostly unsightly and sore. Her fingertips, however, found the leather upholstery of Sara's BMW pleasant to the touch.

They were just down the driveway, Holly Bush Road, when Angelica said, "I really like your car."

It amused Sara that Angelica was somewhat detached and not really fretting over the incident that they had all witnessed. Smiling, "Well, thank you. I think it's worth the money."

A pause ensued as Angelica watched her parents and the other investigators turn onto the road and away from the house.

As Sara stopped and looked both ways at the intersection, she said, "How are you holding up? I know we had to leave in a hurry, but we want everyone to be safe."

She pulled onto the road and headed the opposite direction of the investigation team's van. In that van, Edward was embracing his still crying wife and reassuring her that Angelica was safe. Of course, he didn't yet mention where she was going.

As the car left the gravels for tarmac, Angelica checked her backpack on the floor of the car, trying to remember which things were hastily tossed in. She had the essentials for an overnight stay with Abby, but she wasn't going there under the best of circumstances as they were accustomed to.

The cylinders under the hood gently growled with increasing speed and she said, "I'm tired."

Sara placed her hand comfortingly on her shoulder, but only for a moment. She then said, "How far away is your friend's house? What did you say her name was?"

Small talk, something she knew adults did to try and ease tension. She didn't mind. "Abby. She lives about fifteen minutes from here."

Feeling more and more comfortable as Holly Bush Road was nearly out of her rearview mirror, she replied, "Do you two go to school together?"

She let the disappointment show in her voice, being in comfortable company, "No, I go to St. Mary's and she goes to the public school in town."

In a sympathetic tone, "Aw, that's too bad. At least you're going to a good school."

"Well, it's okay, I guess. The teachers can be mean… I mean stern, and I have to wear a uniform. Abby doesn't have to wear a school uniform. Lucky…."

Sara could definitely relate. "Believe me, I know what you mean about the nuns there. You know, I went to St. Mary's, too."

To Angelica, the similarities they shared were increasing faster than she could keep up with. "You did?"

"Yep. I didn't always get along with them either. But, that's in the past now." Sensing her friend was going to follow up with questions, she then said, "Enough about that though. How about some music?"

Angelica nodded. "Okay."

Sara's darted back and forth between her iPod and the road. She pressed play. Suddenly, through the speakers, came a since-recently familiar voice and music. The singer's voice came through the speakers solidly: "I wanna fuck you like an animal!"

Obviously startled, Sara nearly veered off the road before pressing the stop button on the device. The song ceased. Exasperated, "Dammit! Of all the songs to start on random…." The "random" shuffle function had lost the definition to both the inhabitants in the car. This was not only because of the song, being the same as the one that played on the television just recently during the dreamscape peepshow, but also because it started mid-song. That's not supposed to happen now, is it?

Detached in tone, Angelica said, "It won't leave us alone, will it...?"

Sara didn't want to concede to the idea, but knew it futile to try to deny. "Maybe not. But let's not give it more strength by dwelling on it." She handed the iPod to Angelica. "Here, why don't you pick a song? Anything you want."

Angelica scrolled through the menu and soon enough found a song. "I've heard this on TV, but Mom said I shouldn't listen to this type of music."

As the song began to play, Sara immediately recognizes the guitar intro. "You won't tell her, will you?"

Sara smiled. "No, it'll be our little secret. I promise."

The percussion soon kicked in, and the song's driving rhythm was more pronounced. It was "Enter Sandman" by Metallica. The sounds were aggressive, but it seemed soothing somehow. It was helping to ease their tension. And perhaps there was even a small amount of delight seeping in from this "forbidden" entertainment.

Hetfield called through the speakers, "Say your prayers, little one...!"

Sara laughed. "I have to say, I like your taste in music so far!"

Finally, Angelica cracked a smile and chuckled at a kindred spirit. "Thanks."

A little farther down the road and a mutual silence had taken hold. Sara could sense something in Angelica's mind wanting to come out. She said reassuringly, "You know, you can ask me any questions you want. I know it's scary when people like you and I feel like no one else understands, so fire away."

It only surprised her for a moment, but then she remembered the "gifts" they shared. "The nightmares: What do you do about them? I can't sleep sometimes for nights on end."

Sara sighed, knowing there was no easy way around them. "I would keep doing those exercises I gave you, but given where you live I'm afraid it's going to be hard until things there get straightened out. It may also help if you're away from the property."

"Now that you mention it, I don't really have many nightmares when I'm at Abby's house. Nothing like the ones I have at home anyway. And I've been doing the exercises. I'm working on visualizing things in my head, the light surrounding me and all that. A lot of times I get interrupted by something, though. Whatever it is messing with everyone on the property. It almost feels like it chokes the light around me. It's really scary sometimes."

Sympathetically, "I know it's frightening for you at times, but we're doing our best to get things straightened out there. Father Anderson should be able to help with that." She could tell Angelica knew they were trying their hardest. Sara continued. "I don't know if you've experienced this yet or not, but have you ever heard of lucid dreaming?"

Genuinely perplexed, "No, what does that mean?"

"Well, sometimes you can actually take control of your dreams. A lot of times, it feels like you're just watching a movie or that you're just not in control of anything. Sometimes, and you can get better with it if you try, you can actually take control of what's happening in the dream to an extent. It's as if you are very much aware that you are dreaming and your conscious will takes over. It's exhilarating at times when you accomplish it."

Taking control of her dreams. This definitely piqued her interest. "Really? I've never felt in control in my dreams. It's like I just 'react' to everything instead of thinking."

Delighted at her friend's understanding, "Ah, good! You're beginning to understand then. Next time you're in a dream, good or bad, try and take control." She didn't the see the large white animal darting from a field next to the road. "Don't be surprised if it doesn't...."

Now she saw the large white shape clearly on the road suddenly in front of them. Thankfully for anti-lock brakes, the car's tires screeched loudly in agony but managed to come to a complete stop just in time. After their heads jerked forward, then smacked back against the back of the seat, the solid white deer looked at them calmly as if not worried about its curtailed date with death. The albinism made its eyes pink, but a bright yellow orb reflected back due to the headlights. The eye shine only made Angelica uneasy for a moment before she realized it wasn't one of Caroline's kind. The ears on the beast twitched as it partially lowered its head. Angelica and Sara stared at it silently.

Much to their surprise, a second animal joined the scene. It would be expected that another deer would be following close behind this doe, but this wasn't the case. Before them a smaller-than-average wolf gently pitter-pattered onto the asphalt. Its lustrous black coat was well kempt and healthy. Only its paws had what one might call white socks, along with the fur of its face and a white collar-like hair line at the base of the skull were a different shade.

At this point they both expected the deer to take flight (even wondering why it hadn't kept moving in the first place), but it didn't seemed bothered by the canid. In fact, the two animals seemed more confused at the company of their human watchers rather than their friendship. Both animals then stared mutely at the car, unmoving and unflinching.

They gawked at the two for what seemed like an hour (really only less than a minute) before the animals casually gathered speed on the blacktop and leaped over the fence parallel to the road.

Angelica had heard the term "albino" before, but still wasn't one-hundred-percent sure what it was, other than a solid white animal. Despite this, Angelica obviously knew that those two animals were usually at odds with one another. She then asked, "Why didn't the wolf attack the deer?"

Sara was stumped with the other side of the question. "Why didn't the deer run away? I've never seen that before in my life! That has to mean something... some sort of omen."

There was another term Angelica had, at best, cursory knowledge of. Nonetheless, she knew the event was very significant if it made her normally calm mentor lose her focus. "What's it mean, then?"

The car still didn't move. "I don't know exactly. I've read about things like this happening, but never anything *exactly* like this! I'll need to read and reflect on it." Only now did she look over at Angelica. "Are you okay?"

Still looking out the windshield at the dark field to their left, "Yeah. You?"

"Yeah... I'm fine." Sara then slowly pressed the accelerator, heading on down the dark road.

Not long after the encounter with the deer and the wolf, Sara's car approached the driveway of the Kelly homestead. "Turn left up here, onto Mayfield Drive."

Sara had seen the gravel road plenty of times before but didn't know the occupants by name. She looked down at the clock on her car stereo. It read 10:53 P.M. "And they're expecting us, right?"

"My dad called and talked with her dad and he said it was fine."

It was shortly after this that Sara started to ask a question that made her feel uncomfortable. "Angelica, you know that what you saw on the television wasn't real, right?"

She had heard the sounds of the sex dream coming down the hall, but barely saw any of the graphic images. She knew enough, however, to know what they were doing. "I know. It was a lie."

Sara was only partially relieved, but still better than before. "Right, it was deception. The things at your property are fighting dirty, and they'll do anything they can to cause trouble." The headlights of the car reflected off of the white letters on the brown sign: "Mayfield Dr." Sara continued. "You know your father and I have never, and never would, do such a thing. Do you understand?"

The momentary "a grown-up is teaching me a stern lesson" tone surprised Angelica, but she knew Sara felt embarrassed, and even a little uncertain about it. Sometimes those funny little thoughts can get unintentionally twisted when spoken aloud and heard by others. She replied dutifully, "Yes, ma'am, I understand."

Sara immediately sensed the coy undertone, and snickered. "That's good. Now let's see... yep, looks like they left the light on for you."

Just about that time, Mr. Kelly stepped out from the side kitchen door and waved at the approaching vehicle. The car pulled to a stop at a gravel circle next to the modest farmhouse. "Now Ange, if you need anything, and I mean anything, you give me a call on my cellphone. I'll keep it by my side all night. Do you have my number?"

"Not with me...."

Sara then took out a small piece of paper and a pen from her purse and wrote down the number for her. She handed her the yellow slip of sticky-tape memo. "Day or night, you call me and I'll pick up. Okay?"

"I will. Thank you." It surprised Sara that Angelica reached up and hugged her tightly before exiting the car, but she didn't shy away.

Once her passenger was out and at the door, Sara waved a final time to both before turning around and heading down the driveway and homeward.

Mr. Kelly held the door open for Angelica. She was surprised to see both John Jr. and Abby standing and waiting for her in the kitchen. Both of the Kelly kids saw Angelica's bloodstained corneas and bandaged right hand.

Mr. Kelly was the first to speak. "Lordy, girl, what have you been into?"

Angelica was tempted to tell the truth, having always been told that truth was the best option. This situation, however, didn't seem to warrant such "unnecessary" honesty. Quite the opposite dominated her mind. It was the fear of the Kelly family finding out that made it completely "necessary" to lie through her teeth.

As Abby approached her friend, along with her concerned brother, Angelica said, "It's been a little crazy the past couple days. I'm sorry, but I don't want to talk about it."

The father replied warmly, "Ah, don't worry about it. I won't pry. You look worn out. Why don't you and Abby go ahead and get ready for bed. Now Jr., you be nice tonight."

He had not one ounce of mischievousness in mind as he replied, "I won't, sir. Not a drop of aggravation." "Not a drop of aggravation" was a new phrase he'd started using, often with some hints of mercurial tendencies, but his father could tell he was serious enough.

As his father retired to the living room to watch some of the nightly news on the television with his wife, John Jr. followed the two girls down the hall toward Abby's room. Her bedroom was right across the hall from his.

He stopped in the doorway as the two girls went into her room. He paused a moment before asking, "Hey, Ange, do you need anything? Anything to drink or eat?"

She shook her head. "No thanks, John."

He looked down at her bandaged hand and started to reach for it. "What in the world got hold of your hand?"

She obviously didn't want to discuss what she'd recently experienced with her mother and father and the paranormal team. She pulled it away quickly. "It was my puppy. He just got a little rough when we were playing."

John saw the reaction, and remembering not only what he promised to his father and seeing the exhaustion on her face, he pulled back. He also decided not to ask her about the bloody pools and branches of blood staining the white part of her eyes. "All right, I'll leave you two alone. Let me know if you need anything, Ange. Goodnight." After their replies, he left their room and made his way over to his own.

The door shut to John's room. Abby could hear him go through his usual short routine before climbing into bed. She was genuinely taken aback by how nice her brother was being to her friend. He wasn't mean by anyone's definition, but he had a minor sibling rivalry that sometimes bled through to keeping her friends at arm's length.

She only dwelled on it for a moment before saying, "You look really worn out. You can just sleep in my bed and I'll sleep on the floor. Mom just washed the sheets and pillows, so everything's clean."

Always touched by her friend's kindness, "I'm fine, Abby. I think I could lie down on the road and sleep I'm so tired."

Pretending to be stern, "Now Angie-bear, you're going to sleep on this bed and like it! Don't make me take you out to the shed!"

Angelica's quick giggle was suddenly overtaken by a yawn. Wiping an eye with her hand, she said, "I'm too tired to fight. You win." She then took her backpack from her shoulder and said, "All right, I need to go change and brush my teeth."

She then disappeared into the hallway and headed to the bathroom. Once there, she closed the door behind her and stared into the mirror. Still disturbed by the red splotches and broken vessels in her corneas, she began to feel uneasy again for the umpteenth time this evening. Quite a marathon of that going around that day. Her bandaged hand then slowly rose and stopped midair just below her chin. It was then that she also noticed faint spots of bruising here and there at the base of her neck, something she hadn't noticed until just then. What came to mind next was not a feeling of apprehension of Caroline, the property, or even her mother. It was a feeling held more commonly in eight-year-olds: "I'm going to get picked on in school so bad for this."

It wasn't until a few minutes later that Angelica reappeared in Abby's room. Abby was putting the final touches on the sleeping bag and mat she'd setup on the floor for herself. The bruising on Angelica's neck, however, immediately caught her attention.

"What happened to your neck!?" she exclaimed suddenly.

She put her finger up in a hush gesture before saying in a lowered voice, "I'd rather not talk about it...."

Her friend was temporarily stifled, but insisted, "Angie-bear, you can tell me anything. It won't leave this room, I promise."

Angelica stared at the floor for a few moments before reluctantly saying, "I told you about what happened to my goats. Now I think whatever did that is attacking my family. I get really scared sometimes when I think about it."

Abby knew that prying further would only create resentment. She conceded to comforting her friend instead. "I'm sorry you're going through this. You know, I'm always ready to listen if you need me."

A tiny amount of shaking started to show up all over Angelica's body as she raised her right hand to her mouth. She turned around as the first tears leaked out. She did her best to hide the sniffles and hiccups, but Abby knew immediately that the dam holding back the emotions was giving way. "My mom...." Even then she was reluctant to go farther.

Circling around her side to face her friend and hug her, she said, "Aww, Angie-bear... it's okay."

They embraced until the uncontrollable surge had calmed, giving Angelica more ability to speak. "My dog didn't bite me...."

Abby knew something was wrong with Angelica's previous excuse, but wasn't sure where the explanation lay. "What did it, then?"

She wanted to say, but was still uneasy. She looked back at the door to the room, which was still solidly closed. No one outside the room was making any noise. Only the faint and distant sound of the television set was coming through. Nonetheless, Angelica moved close to Abby's ear. Wiping tears off of her cheek with her bandaged hand, she whispered, "My mom...."

Abby was stunned and silent as she looked wide-eyed at her friend. Only one question popped up. She said it softly, "Why?"

Still speaking quietly, "You have to promise me you won't tell anyone. Pinky swear?"

Abby agreed, even complying with the binding gesture after.

"I think she's possessed."

Abby was again flabbergasted. She had been to every Protestant service at her own church for as long as she could remember. The subject of possession was not mentioned once that she could recall. The only familiarity she had with the matter was a movie that her brother had gotten hold of and let her watch. Of course she also had to swear to him that she'd never tell another soul about that. So far she hadn't. Now, however, the suggestion of the real thing playing out before her was almost too much to comprehend. She thought that sort of thing only happened in movies, and that it probably (and that was a big probably) never happened in real life. Angelica, however, was as close to one-hundred-percent honest with her friend as was allowed. Now, naturally, she had to take it more seriously.

Seeing her friend speechless, she said, "You think I'm crazy, don't you?"

The questions of how something, whatever it is, possessing someone else, didn't make sense. Explanations would just have to wait. "No, I don't think you're crazy. You're my best friend!"

Relieved, "Thanks, Ab. I can always count on you."

They would stay up almost an hour more, even after Mr. Kelly insisted that they go to bed, talking about what had just happened. Meanwhile, in his room, John Jr. lay silently on his bed, unintentionally overhearing the story he knew Angelica wouldn't tell him in person. He felt genuine pity and concern. He knew, however, that he couldn't simply bring up the conversation casually or burst into their room and try and comfort Angelica. His mind would simply race a good half an hour about the situation before dwindling off to sleep himself.

Fifty-three

Meanwhile, as the BMW Sara was driving was turning onto the road and driving away, Edward and Rosanna were seated in the middle seats of the van. The plain black Dodge was surely and steadily pulling away from the proximity of Holly Bush Road as Rosanna attempted to regain her composure. Edward hugged her tightly as she sobbed hysterically. Tony had managed to bandage her scratched eye before they left the house. They all appreciated, especially that time, that he was a paramedic volunteer. When he examined her closely, he came to the conclusion that the only scratching was on her eyelid itself. He urged her repeatedly to get her eye examined at the Emergency Room at the local hospital, but she refused.

With her uncovered eye, she looked back and forth in the front area of the van. Not seeing her child, she quickly turned and looked toward Tony in the seat behind her. Nearly panicking, she said apprehensively, "Where's Angelica!? Where is she!?"

Her husband answered reassuringly, "Don't worry, hon, she's on her way to Abby's house. She's going to spend the night there. I talked to her parents and they were fine with it."

Still uneasy, "You didn't tell them about what happened, did you!?" Even now she was desperately hoping to maintain a positive image amongst the members of her community.

"No, I didn't tell them what happened. I just said it was a 'family emergency' and he didn't ask another word."

She was calm for a moment, but once she realized who all was around her, she asked sharply, "Wait. How is she getting there? You didn't have John Kelly come out this late to pick her up, did you!?"

He had a bad feeling this detail would quickly come up, and it did. "Rosy, it's okay. Sara volunteered to drive her there. She's in safe hands."

The very idea of Angelica being alone with Sara overwhelmingly infuriated Rosanna at this point. "What!? You let that little bitch take my daughter away!? She'll corrupt her Ed, don't you see!? That little whore is probably twisting my daughter around her finger as we speak!"

Rosanna's outburst did not fall on deaf ears. Now everyone was staring at her. Even Roberta, while driving, was shooting glares back at her.

From the front seat, Ron spoke up in a stern "no bullshit" tone. "Mrs. Barrister, with all due respect, I've known Sara since she was a little girl. I don't know a more kind and generous person. Now you're opinion is your own and you're entitled to it, but don't talk so poorly about our friend when we're all here and listening. It's downright rude and disrespectful."

Everyone was silent for a few moments. Rosanna found the urge to react and lash out, maybe even pontificating about Sara's immoral usage of divination to smear her character. Perhaps it was the peer pressure of the group (not even Edward was defending her words at this point) or the distance from Holly Bush Road growing larger that brought her to heel. The fires of anger, it seemed, were no long being fed with the same consistency as before. It was dissipating. Her mouth went agape dumbly in disbelief.

It wasn't long before the silence became unbearable and Rosanna said with genuine remorse, "I'm sorry... I... I sincerely mean it. All of you.../" Somehow her tear ducts had found another internal source upon which to draw moisture. Although crying, her tone was not hysterical now. "Ed, Ron, Roberta, Tony: I'm sorry. I'm so sorry! I don't know what's happening to me!" She had to take in a quick gulp of air to continue. "I'm going crazy and I don't know why!" Rosanna covered her face with her arms. "You all must hate me and I don't blame you!" She then pressed her face against Edward's chest as he embraced her once more.

She then heard the voice of her mother in her head. *"Aww, little Rosy is going crazy! They're going to lock you away in a padded cell now! Look! They all know you're crazy!"*

Rosanna showed no external signs of even hearing the words, but they embedded themselves deep in her mind.

Tony, who was petting Cerberus in the backseat, put his hand reassuringly on Rosanna's shoulder. "Mrs. Barrister, we're going to get through this. One way or another, we'll get you your house and your life back."

Ron then turned and said, "That's right. Once we finish gathering and presenting our evidence to Father Anderson and The Church, we'll fight this with everything we have."

Roberta's glares had now gone back to just glances. "We won't give up on your family, Mrs. Barrister. You can count on it."

It took them around thirty minutes to arrive at the closest hotel in the direction they were driving. As the van came to a stop in the Holiday Inn parking lot, Ron looked over his shoulder and said, "Okay, Mr. and Mrs. Barrister, I'll go get you a room setup. Just wait here and I'll be right back."

Edward immediately added, "We'll be right back, Rosy, okay?"

She nodded as Ron said, "Just wait here, Mr. Barrister, I can cover it. It shouldn't take long."

A minor curtesy battle just broke out.

Ed replied, "No, no. You guys have put up with enough already, I don't expect you to pay for our room, too." At this point, neither person wanted to make a big deal about it, so they simply both went in and settled the arrangement with Ed saying, "I owe you one," in return.

As the two disappeared into the front lobby, Tony stepped out of one of the side doors in the van and took a seat next to Rosanna. She was, at the very least, comforted by the fact that almost no cars were in the parking lot.

Tony said as he sat down, "Okay, Mrs. Barrister, let me take a look at your eye again and make sure everything is all right." He slowly pulled the tape away and exposed the now clotted eyelid that was stained pink and red. He took a penlight from his pocket and had her look left to right, up and down, all while checking her pupils for proper response. Everything looked in order as he said, "Mrs. Barrister, I really wish you'd go get a doctor to check your eye."

She blankly replied, "I'll make an appointment Monday."

Tony then sighed. "All right, you're the boss. Everything looks okay for now. I'll leave some extra bandages with you. Change the dressing once every six hours or so, or sooner if it starts bleeding again. I'll also give you a tube of antibacterial gel to put on it. Can't have it getting infected."

Fifty-four

It wasn't long before Edward and Rosanna were alone in the hotel room. Tony had promised to look after Angelica's puppy until things settled down. Rosanna was seated on the foot end of one of the queen-sized beds in the room and staring quietly at the wall. Edward, meanwhile, was unpacking the few things they'd managed to toss in the bag before heading out the door. He looked up momentarily. Even he was still a little uneasy about being locked away with her, alone, after what had just happened. He said quietly, "Rosy, are you okay?"

Silence. Edward now saw that her head was slightly rocking back and forth rhythmically. She did so for what seemed like an eternity without responding. The seconds ticked by mercilessly. He half expected to see Rosanna's head spin around and spit out pea soup. That, however, was just Hollywood stuff, he reassured himself. His ears, now heightened with awareness due to the silence and tension, began to hear her gentle breaths one at a time.

He went to speak again, but was cut off by her soft-toned voice. "I'm fine, Ed."

He didn't move. He was still unwilling to lower his guard completely.

She then said with sincerity, "Ed, please...please don't lock me away somewhere. I'm not crazy. You know that, right? I'm not making this stuff up for attention."

The pleading tone broke through his guard. He then sat down beside her on the bed and put his arm around her. With as much love and reassurance as he could muster, "Babe, no. I would never do something like that to you! We all know what's happening and we're working to stop it. No one thinks you're crazy!"

"You know that's a lie, Rosanna! They're all getting ready to take you to the nut-house! You'll be locked away and have to wear a diaper every day like me! They'll have to come and scrub you clean of your own filth every single day!"

The sound of her mother's voice was accompanied by vivid images of her mother wasting away at the "Sunny Acres Nursing Home" about an hour away. Her dementia was bad and accompanied by long periods of catatonia. Even on the days she would momentarily break free from the invisible chains on her mind, she would only spout curse words and be guaranteed to assure everyone that entered her field of view, and plenty who didn't, that they were going to hell. To her, there was no way around it and she was God's burdened messenger. Apparently no one was worthy of mercy and forgiveness to her.

After a small silence, "Do you really mean that, Ed? Promise me you're not going to have me committed. Please promise me!"

He was distraught at the fear in her voice. "Yes, honey, I promise! No one here is going to put you away anywhere, not while I'm around." He hugged her close and kissed her upon the top of her head.

She hugged him in return and said, "I love you so much, Ed. I don't say it enough, but I do love you."

"I love you too, Rosy, and I always will."

The tears were making her eyes sting now. Instinctively she placed her palm over the bandage and winced. "Ow...."

"You okay, sweetie? Do you need me to change the bandage?"

"No, I'm all right."

He brushed the hair from her face. "Hey, why don't you go and get ready for bed and we'll try and get some sleep. We've all had a long day and need some rest."

"I like that idea." She kissed him on the lips before taking a soft t-shirt and pair of flannel bottoms and heading to the bathroom to change.

She shut the door behind her after flicking the lights on inside the tiled room. Now, in the unflattering light of the bulbs overhead, she was seeing herself for the first time in the mirror since the recent incident. Her eye was puffy (along with the unseen one beneath the bandage) from the recent torrent of tears. The cuts all over her body were still healing and pink which contrasted with her otherwise pale skin. The padded bandage over her eye looked bulbous and distended, even though it was just big enough to cover her eye socket. The final nail in the beauty coffin, for her, was shown when she opened her mouth and saw her damaged front teeth. Again, her eyes stung freshly from the warm tears silently dripping down.

Quivering with emotion, she then said quietly, "I can't go to church like this! I look horrible! What will people say about me!?" The whirring of the overhead fan kept Edward from hearing the words.

"Look at you, Rosanna! You're a vain little bitch and your mother hates you for it! God hates you for it!"

The words stung and hurt deeply. They also tapped into a healthy well of resentment she had long harbored for her mother. Many feelings, uncomfortably negative feelings, were bubbling, grinding and churning beneath the surface. She was too tired to stave them off. Whether she liked it or not, they were there and she was going to have to deal with them before they became too toxic to hold onto any longer. Regardless of this, she would sleep through the night relatively peacefully.

Fifty-five

12:55 A.M.

At the Goodwin house, Sara was staring silently at the champagne glass in front of her bubbling merrily. Her mood was not merry, nor was this a celebration. The visit to the house on Holly Bush Road had left its marks and taken its toll. She had done a wonderful job keeping this suffering from everyone around her, but now there was no other warm body in sight to impress. Trying to decompress still, she took a solid drink from the glass, finishing it off. Tonight was going to be a night of trying to forget things. Thankfully she'd written everything down that she'd needed to remember in her notebook... no need to worry about forgetting anything pertaining to the case. So if she could escape the pain of the invisible wounds inflicted for even just the night she would gladly take up the offer.

"Please slow down, Sara...."

The caring voice only caused her to fill up another glass and quickly finish it off. She then turned around and looked at the clock on the wall. The antique ticked away, reminding her that it was past her routine sleeping hours. She then looked back down at the bottle on the small fetching table she'd set up in the kitchen herself. Sara always thought the formal dining room too big for her meals. She was almost always alone unless a client wanted to stop by and ask if any quick money or handsome suitor was in their future. This was, however, the middle of night, and no one stopped by at this hour.

Several silent minutes passed before Sara poured the last of the champagne bottle into the glass. Knowing full well that her mind was racing far too fast to suddenly give way to sleep, she rose from the kitchen table and headed into the downstairs bathroom. The first couple of steps were a little uneasy. The alcohol was starting to do its job, all right.

Once in the bathroom she reached up and opened the mirrored door of the antique medicine cabinet hanging over the matching sink below. Not much was kept in here, but one particular bottle was all she wanted. It took her eyes a second to focus, but sure enough, it was the sleeping pills. She unscrewed the cap, removed one Lunesta, and returned the bottle to its resting place. Sara only used these in dire straits (which were coming with subtly higher frequency in the last few days).

"Break glass in case of emergency!" she mused.

Back at the kitchen table she popped the small pill into her mouth and washed it down with the rest of the champagne.

"Sara... you know, you shouldn't mix those."

She muttered in response, "I'm fine...." Knowing the alcohol had yet to take on the complete effect, and that the sleeping pill would take thirty to forty-five minutes to kick in, she headed for the cellar door nearby.

"Please, dear, watch your step. You're tipsy and it's so dark down there!"

More annoyed, "I know what I'm doing!" She flicked on the light switch next to the stairwell. Before proceeding she paused and said, "I'm sorry." Now looking over her shoulder, "It's not your fault."

Sure, no other warm bodies were there with her, but something else was. It was someone familiar that Sara could see around her most places she went. Still calm and loving, "It doesn't bother me. I know you're hurting and I know you want it stop. I wish I could make it stop."

Sara put one hand on the railing heading down into the open bricked room. As she carefully walked down the stairs she said, "I can't do anymore now. Please, I need this."

Distraught and concerned, but knowing she couldn't control her, the voice replied, "You are your own person and I can't change that."

Sara walked past a few brick columns and archways that lined the walls. Her heels were ticking away on the stones of the floor in a slightly arrhythmical fashion. The wine cellar held vintage bottles here and there all over, but they were only typically reserved for special occasions. She didn't care. The bottles only served one purpose tonight.

She took one of the dark green glass bottles in hand, only barely glancing at the label. Her speech was slightly slurred now. "You're right. You always are. Always, always, always…." Her words then tapered off as she carefully made her way back up the stairs, holding onto the railing and fighting her increasingly uncoordinated legs.

Once in the kitchen, she turned off the lights and closed the door behind her. She slammed the bottle unintentionally hard on the table, causing the glass to bounce up a millimeter or two before coming to a wobbly landing. She then took the corkscrew from the nearby counter and worked it into the cork of the bottle. Sara turned and faced her companion. "And you know what… the crazy part is… I think that Rosy Anna is a damned psycho, whether or not she's possessed! Did you see the way she looked at me!?"

POP! The cork came loose and out.

"You're right, she was possessed. The Barristers are in a great deal of trouble."

She finished filling the wine glass with the deep red beverage. "I am right! Ha! Now I'M the one who's right!" Sara had trouble focusing on her companion as she pointed at her and smiled. Her voice faded again as she said quietly, "I'm right…." She then knocked the glass back and proceeded to gulp down the entire glass in one go. A surge of dizziness overcame her as the alcohol inside was working into her system. She grabbed hold of the table and said, "Whoa! I need to sit down before I make myself look stuuuuupid!" The sound of her own voice made her laugh at this point.

"Sara, please, at least go to the living room and sit on the couch. What if they find you lying on the kitchen floor?"

Her speech still heavily slurred, "You know, that's a good idea. I'm 'a go in there." She giggled as she took the bottle in hand. She considered taking the glass, but left it on the table. "Won't be needing you anymore!" She giggled again before taking a swig from the dusty bottle in hand.

"Do be careful. Watch your step."

Once in the living room of the mansion, she sat on one of the couches and put her feet up on the coffee table directly in front of her. She then took another drink from the bottle.

"Do you know how old and expensive that table is!?"

Sara knew, but only responded in mocking mimicry. After another hearty gulp from the bottle she said, "Who cares, anyway. You can't take any of it with you, now can you?"

Sara's world slowly became more distorted with each drink and eventually dark.

Fifty-six

Angelica was suddenly aware that she was on familiar ground: the family property. The sun in the distance had fallen below the horizon, but a belt of golden light still bowed up over the disk and stretched outward in both directions. The remainder of the sky was dark and thick overcast. This stagnant twilight gave the features of the landscape strange golden glows with reliefs of deep shadows. When she first looked down, she believed her eyes to be playing tricks on her as the ground and its plants all resembled a dying light brown color. She then bent down to pick up a few blades of tall grass, only to find them actually brittle and dry with decay. It crinkled and scratched in her hands as she rubbed it between her palms, then let it fall delicately back to the earth.

Angelica then focused on her surroundings and found she was near the stream. Much to her chagrin, however, the bridge that was normally there was nowhere to be seen. Looking back over her shoulder, the forbidding walls of thorns lining the path and leading to the dark forest beyond made her want to go in the other direction.

Step by step she headed toward the stream. She could smell the coming rain. There wasn't a breeze, but she could feel the moisture in the air around the stream on her cheeks. Once at the banks of the stream, however, the water was replaced with the black fluid she'd become so accustomed to seeing. It flowed and cascaded over the rocks of the stream bed in a similar fashion to water, but slower and thicker. She couldn't see anything in this *fluid except the glowing yellow eyes of hordes of minnows (or something that she thought moved like minnows) darting back and forth, left and right, all over. As she stared at the ebony flow, a single word sounded and echoed in her mind: corruption. She knew good and well what it at least represented, but the word alone only led to more questions.*

The brief section of the stream she could see before her looked much deeper than she remembered, and she wasn't going to take any chances with the black fluid or its unsettling little "fish." Reluctantly, she turned and headed back down the path leading away from the stream.

She walked for what seemed like only a few seconds, but in the altered state of dreamland, time was strange. Distance and the passage of time are usually different than the conscious, waking world. Nevertheless, the path wound all too quickly toward the darkened forest. The briar orgy all around made sure she had no other feasible options but forward. The only way out was through.

Once at the threshold of the forest, she became acutely aware of something, or the lack thereof. The only sound she could hear was the babbling stream beyond. Even that was fading now. This was unnerving, but something shiny in the woods beyond caught her eye. It was faint and glowing yellow. It wasn't like the eyes of the things she'd become used to seeing. Its shine was more artificial. The sight of what she quickly concluded to be a flashlight was a welcome one in the otherwise foreboding foliage. Only a few steps in and she was able to wriggle it free from the scant offshoots of various wild underbrush growing beneath the barrier briars. When she turned around to shine the flashlight behind, however, the path only lead behind her ten feet or so before ending abruptly at a solid wall of thorns and brambles. Those certainly weren't there before, were they? The only way through was ever more apparent.

It took her a few seconds of indecision, mainly from fear and dread, but she pressed forward, nonetheless. The fallen leaves and decaying patches of grass along the path crunched under her bare feet. These and the occasional twig now started to register painfully on her soles with each step. "Where are my shoes?" she thought to herself. Strange how oddly we're equipped in dreams at times.

Suddenly, from in front of her, what felt like a tremor surged through the ground and past. It didn't go any farther than this single pulse and it only caused her to momentarily lose her balance. She could feel her pulse pounding away in her neck now as her heart rate took off with a fresh shot of adrenaline. Nothing like a mini-quake to make you remember you're alive. She braced her hands against the ground while on one knee, waiting for the next wave to come, but it didn't. What did follow was a sudden gust of wind that whipped instantly and fully through the surrounding foliage. The thorns and branches of the barrier plants ticked and clicked against each other. The sounds seemed to come in insanely quick groups of three, barely perceptible to anyone hearing them. The trees of the forest groaned and creaked in a disturbing tone. Angelica could tell something was amiss, but it didn't register completely right away. The groans sounded more like they were sourced from something not of the plant kingdom, but rather the animal kind.

She waited out the initial gust of wind. It didn't fully dissipate, but became more manageable after the flying thorns and other debris from the surrounding plants stopped stinging the exposed skin on her face and arms.

The trees were still faintly moaning and crackling when she stepped forward and began to shine the flashlight all around. These were most peculiar trees at first glance. Their shapes, odd shapes not typically found in plants, bulging from beneath the bark, made her uncomfortable. She focused in on one at a fork in the path before her. The path split in two directions at this point. This wasn't like the actual path she remembered on the family land. This was dream-time chicanery at work.

Angelica approached the tree cautiously as it slowly swayed back and forth in the cold breeze slicing through. The wood creaked more as her light slowly found its way to the area around the peak of the main trunk of the tree. Was there a strange burl at the top? Perhaps, but it rested neatly on top of the main support structure. The light revealed what looked like a human head, twisted to the side with branches sprouting out and off to an angle from it. She didn't believe her own mind. Surely she was just attributing human shapes to the burl on top. This seemed less likely an excuse, however, as her light now showed the shapes around the rest of the tree. Two large branches, and only two, came off perpendicular to the burl and reached for *the sky. The many tiny branches from the arms also looked like fingers with then many smaller offshoots looked like the veins and arteries of the human circulatory system. It made some sense, after all, because like veins and arteries, the branches carried and distributed nutrients throughout the system. A strange parallel in plain sight of everyone almost every day. The comparison, however, did not amuse Angelica in the least. She'd seen pictures in a human anatomy book at school, but she hadn't made the connection on her own. No, something else was revealing this to her now and she was only made more uncomfortable by it. Was it Caroline? Maybe, or something else. She didn't know.*

She stared at the tree swaying in the breeze for only a few seconds before something startled her into freezing still all over. What appeared to be the mouth of the burl emitted a foul odor before spurts of black fluid began to churn up and fall, cascading down the side of the tree and staining the bark. The gurgling sound and stench of the fluid caused her to then back away and feel a sudden and overwhelming sensation of nausea, much worse than any she'd felt while awake. Her mind could only associate the smell with rot and decay, mixed with other things she didn't know about, or want to know about.

Angelica then turned to the right fork of the path and started to run deeper into the forest. As the fear rose in her throat she could hear a loud cracking behind her, like some godawful whip of torment which flung thorns at, and occasionally into, her back. She could feel a little drop of moisture (blood) trickling down her back here and there. With each bounding step she passed angry and hostile plants that seemed to lash out in their own unique way. The air passed in and out of her increasingly dry throat. Pure flight mode was engaged. No reasoning, no understanding, just run like hell for the nearest exit. There wasn't, however, a convenient doorway with a red-lettered EXIT sign in this dream. Only the faint light of the flashlight going up and down in her swinging arm was showing the way deeper into the forest.

Suddenly a voice called out, "Angelica... stop running...." It was a familiar voice, and the snapping of the dark foliage behind her had stopped. She gradually came to a stop herself, breathing heavily and turning to see that the wall that was chasing her before was now stationary. Her chest ached from her lungs desperately trying to keep up with her fleeing body parts.

She went to turn away from the wall of thorns behind her, but had to give it one more glance with the flashlight before turning her back to it. Her feet felt like they were on fire at this point from the sticks and stones that were in no shortage on the path.

As Angelica tried to catch her breath she was jarred out of feeling minutely safe by a sudden and proximal strike of lightning. This lightning, however, was not the color she was accustomed to. It was black, blacker than any pocket of darkness in the forest around her or in the overcast sky. It struck a nearby tree. The blast had knocked her back a couple of feet, but she was not hit directly. The smell of the rain in the air suddenly filled her nose along with the smell of something else familiar. The aroma's source didn't register with her right away but it was unpleasant. She felt drops of liquid from the tree shattering splatter onto her face. Angelica then raised her flashlight and saw the rough outline of the wreckage before her.

She remained still for several seconds before the familiar voice called out again. She knew it now to be Sara's voice. "Angelica, I know you're afraid, but you have to look. You have to know…." She felt relieved to hear her voice, but didn't like the task she was being asked to perform. Still calm and confident, "I know you're hurt, but you can't stop now. Lucid…." She didn't necessarily understand the word "lucid," but she knew what Sara was getting at.

Suddenly, like a room being completely illuminated for the first time, it clicked. Angelica was aware that she was dreaming. She felt a tiny amount of her own will step in and take control. Tiny drops of rain then began to fall regularly and pepper the forest. With new steadiness she approached the struck tree and shined her light on it. Upon pointing the flashlight near the top, however, she was startled to see that this tree had a burl which bore a striking and undeniable resemblance to a man she'd seen before: Amos Harris. Although his skin was now bark, she could make out his twisted expression of agony beneath. Below the burl, black fluid was pouring out heavily and the trunk of the "tree" was oozing with dark brown and black facsimiles of intestines and other viscera. Without moving its lips, the head spoke. "We take… we take, but must give back… we must give back!"

The rain was coming then down heavily as Angelica suddenly fell backward and onto her backside. Much to her horror she suddenly realized what that other smell was mixed with the rain: blood. The blood was raining down from the heavens as if hell had torn it open. She screamed and tried to wipe fluid from her face and arms as the flashlight lens became covered, tinting its light. As the panic began to take over once again, she ran off toward the blackness of the forest, screaming in terror.

Only a few steps away and Angelica trod unknowingly on a large patch of ground that gave way. She screamed as she tumbled down the pitch black hole. She fell long enough to consciously know that she was falling. It only made the whole thing worse when she finally splashed loudly into a massive body of liquid. Thankfully, she now knew how to swim. Unfortunately, however, the fluid was not water and had a black soupy texture. She found it difficult to swim, but through hasty strokes and having to doggie paddle at one point, she managed to break the surface. The dark fluid streamed down her face as she managed to spot a small shoreline several feet away. The cavern she'd managed to fall into was faintly lit with an eerie yellow glow. She scrambled for the ground and tried to sling as much of the inky fluid from her skin, but it clung fiercely. As she cleared some of the muck from her eyes with her hands, she gained a clearer perspective of the source of the glow. The size of the cavern was also more clearly visible now and it was massive. Sheer walls ebbed and flowed for hundreds of feet into the distance. The glow… the glow being produced was from hundreds of yellow eyes all glaring down at her from the ceiling. She knew them to be the same source as Caroline's eyes and the horde of eyes that peered at her and Sara earlier that day. They stared… she screamed.

Angelica awoke breathless in Abby's bed. She was covered in sweat head to toe. Her eyes wide and wild, she looked down at Abby, who was still sound asleep on the floor in her sleeping bag. The clock near the bed read 3:30 A.M. and only faint moonlight shone in through the window nearby. The visions and emotions of the dream were still fresh in her mind. The moisture on her back caused her to remember the wall of lashing briars and thorns that chased her, along with the blood rain and black bile-like substance. Concerned, she reached around and pressed the back of her hand to her skin. She was then relieved to see that only sweat was there. Apparently the injuries didn't follow her out of the dream this time. Her intuition told her that it was due to being farther from the property. Whether the reason or not, it gave her some level of comfort.

The minutes ticked by ever so slowly. Her mind simply wouldn't allow her to go back to sleep. Although exhausted from consecutive nights of poor sleep, she found it impossible to nod back off again. She would simply have to wait until 5:00 A.M. when her friend was accustomed to getting up for farm chores. Staring off into the darkness was becoming a hobby at this point.

Fifty-seven

Meanwhile, Sara paid her own visit to the Barrister property. She found herself walking toward the house up the long driveway. Approaching her from the opposite direction was a disheveled man: Amos Harris. He walked gingerly with each step, seemingly stricken with pain from head to toe in every bone, muscle, and joint. As she calmly approached him, he said with a lowered head, "Miss Goodwin, please... will you please try and help me and my boy?" He began to weep in a contorted position, his head barely able to face her. He then dropped to his knees and placed his hands on the gravel. He groveled but kept his distance, "Please, Miss Sara... please, I'll do anything to save my boy!" He was kept at bay by respect, but also because of a protective light that seemed to emanate from her frame. Sara felt uneasy about his posture, but was intent on helping him. She extended her hand to touch his neck, but as she did the swirling clouds overhead began to rumble with thunder. A small crackle of jet-black lighting spread over the cloud like a grotesque blood vessel before disappearing and producing more thunder.

Sara then had to fight back her own small surge of fear before saying, "Amos, stand up. Stay by my side and my light will protect you."

As she extended her hand to him, he suddenly grabbed it with unanticipated speed. There was a small instance where she felt threatened, but his words soothed her worries: "Thank you, Miss Goodwin! Thank you!"

She helped him to his feet. She then saw up close the injuries that plagued his body: his spirit body. Some of these were injuries sustained in life to his physical form. Others were traumatic for emotional, spiritual, and mental reasons. The injuries looked like black stains, saturating large puffy circles all through his clothes. He'd been through a lot, but Sara couldn't hope to heal him completely in one go.

After he was standing again she looked up the driveway and saw the house as it was many years ago. The fields were covered in large brown stains of dying and unproductive soil and dead crops. The corn crop, what was left of it, was almost completely wiped out. Even the grass around the house and the small garden were not spared of this mysterious blight.

There suddenly appeared an almost exact copy of Amos Harris from the barn to their right. He was missing most of the injuries currently showing on his body. As they approached the house, the facsimile of Amos entered the back door and went into the kitchen. Knowing this was a significant part of his life, Sara asked, "What happened here, Amos? Why is this playing out?"

Sara's light extended to cover him, making it easier for him to speak. He replied, "This was the first day of the blight. We woke to everything looking like this. No warning, nothing. The entire year's crop was wiped out. We were low on money because of the prices we got the year before, so it nearly bankrupted us. My family and I didn't know if we'd have a place to live."

They then headed to the back door and looked in through the screened wooden portal. Inside, the part of Amos that played out in the scene was speaking to a petite woman, dressed in plain clothes sitting at the kitchen table. "Honey, I don't know what's happened out there! The whole farm's gone to hell on us!"

The short woman approached him and hugged him. Sara could feel the pain radiating from the scene as well from the wound it caused Amos. The woman then said, "Amos, don't worry about it. We'll get through it some-how. We survived the stock market crash that nearly wiped out the known world and we'll get through this."

The current version of Amos, his head still somewhat crooked in how it lay, said warmly with tears in his eyes, "Sweet, sweet Janet. Always there to comfort me. I knew then, and I couldn't tell her that we were going to be in for hard times... desperate times. It must have affected her more than she let on."

The scene before them dissolved away to an empty room. Sara then felt herself being pulled toward the barn. Amos stepped off the porch and began walking along with her. Even then that barn was the better of the two, not having as thick a dark aura about it.

Upon approaching the barn, the two saw the facsimile of Amos seated in a simple wooden chair at a table just inside the open doors leading to the interior. In the light of day he was reading from a ragged Bible, desperately trying to find passages of salve and comfort. He knew of a few off hand, but they only brought minor relief.

Sara was then startled by the appearance of the form of Caroline. It took her a moment, but realized that her form was just a residual memory now playing back. The black lightning overhead extended and caressed a dark gray and brown cloud momentarily before dissipating into thunder. The memory-figure of Amos was also surprised in this looping series of events. Caroline's form then spoke with calmness, but with obvious sternness: "Well, Amos Harris, are you going to sit there and cry over spilt milk or do you want me to show you how to get your farm going again?"

The form of Amos then asked, "Who are you!? Why are you dressed like that!?"

The curt old woman then snapped back at him, "My name is Caroline! Now do you want your wife and only child to starve or are you going to listen to me!?"

The image of Amos then looked off into the nearby field where his young son, Timothy, was kicking through the dried and decaying grass in the field. He was looking for grasshoppers to catch. There weren't any to be found, but he looked, nonetheless. The image of Amos then looked up at Caroline and asked, "You know what happened?"

Still short in tone, "How this happened is irrelevant. Do you want to get your livelihood back or what!? I won't offer my assistance again!"

He was a little shocked by her aggressive approach, but he hadn't any answers with which to counter. The scene then faded away before them, leaving the barn empty again. Sara, unable to connect the dots so far, asked, "What happened? What did she have you do?"

Amos then looked away. He slowly answered, "Miss Goodwin, I... you'll see."

The two of them then saw another copy of Amos leading a goat from the barn across the turnaround to the dark barn on the other side. The goat was protesting, kicking and dragging its hooves and making all sorts of panicked noises. Sara and Amos then watched as the same goat nearly wriggled free before the image of Amos was able to climb over its back and use his weight to keep it from squirming. Its freakish screams unsettled both Amos and Sara as it was towed to the back of the dark barn and over the well in a far stall.

The image of Amos suddenly looked back toward the door as the image of Caroline approached. He had managed to hold the goat over the uncovered portal as she yelled at him, "Do it, Amos Harris, or your family will starve!" Without another moment of hesitation he took the large skinning knife from a sheath on his side and slid it quickly across the goat's exposed throat. The cut was smooth and fast and the blood flowed freely from the severed veins and arteries. He held the head over the hole so that the blood spilled inside the well.

The last seconds of the animal's life seem to take an eternity. Finally the blood stopped flowing out. Caroline then said, "Now throw it in! Nothing goes to waste!" The image of Amos then proceeded to fold the animal's neck, with great resistance, so that it fit into the opening. He then pushed on it with his foot, but was unable to make it go all the way in. He then took a nearby posthole digger and drew it overhead before slamming it down fiercely against the carcass. A handful of hits later and the body dropped from view and splashed loudly far below ground.

As this scene dissipated before them, Amos said shamefully, "I grew up on a farm my entire life. I've slaughtered many animals for food or to put them out of their misery when they were sick, but I never felt contempt for the act like I did that day. It felt unnecessary, but I didn't have a choice. I actually thought she would help me. I was desperate and stupid."

They were then startled by the voice of Caroline, who said in a coy tone, "I see you, Sara Goodwin. I see you, you little harlot!"

Sara was surprised, but not terribly concerned. She was very sure of her light barrier. Amos, not so much. Sara then said, "I know you're there, Caroline. You're not going to scare me away from helping these people!"

Caroline replied, still unseen, "If you were smart, you would be afraid. If you were smart you would've never shown up in the first place!"

She responded more forcefully, "You won't win this! We're protected!"

"Do you really think your light alone is going to save you? You will be corrupted like everything else!"

Sara then decided to cease speaking with her as she felt her attention being drawn to the back porch of the house. On it played out another scene from Amos' past. The shorter woman, Amos' wife Janet, was stepping out onto the walkway leading to the dark barn. As she approached the cracked open door, the sound of a chicken squawking frantically in the back was drawing her closer. As she looked in, the sound suddenly stopped. Amos had just slit the throat of the chicken and was letting its warm blood trickle into the well. Janet then inhaled in surprise. It wasn't the site of a chicken being slaughtered that surprised her, but the fact that Amos was tossing it into the open well. She called out loudly, "Amos, what are you doing!? You'll taint the well and we need all the meat we can get right now!"

Amos barked at her, "Janet! I told you not to come in here when I have the door closed!" He then started to walk toward her with the skinning knife still in his hand. His fingers and palms were covered in fresh blood as well as splotches all over his shirt and bibbed overalls. He had slaughtered more than one animal so far that day. Amos' eyes were wild with anger and surprise as he slowly approached her without another word.

Janet felt her pulse skyrocket at this point, as well strong pain radiating down her left arm. She clinched her shirt over her heart with her right hand as she cried, "Amos!? What's... what are you...?" Her throat then started to spasm as her heart tried to keep up, unsuccessfully, with her body's demands. She then fell to the ground and started to groan fiercely, unable to articulate any more words.

Amos, then snapping out of his saturation of rage, dropped the knife on the ground and ran to her. The image of Amos then placed his fingers on her wrists and felt only erratic fluttering instead of a regular beat. Soon, even that disappeared. In a panic he cried, "What's wrong, Janet!? Talk to me, girl! What's happening to you!?" The image of Timothy Harris then ran out the door. Before he could speak, the image of Amos said, "Go and call the doctor, boy, I think your mom's having a heart attack!" Timmy's form then disappeared back into the house.

He and Sara watched as the last moments of the recollection played out. The facsimile of Amos wept loudly as he tried to get a response from his unresponsive wife. Sara then asked with compassion, "She was so young... what happened?"

He replied, "A heart attack. Only twenty-six and she died of heart attack. The doctors said it was a mystery. She'd never been sick a day in her life. To then just up and have a heart attack... it doesn't make any damn sense! And I had to watch her die without being able to do anything about it!"

As the scene slowly dissolved away Sara said, "Amos, there was nothing you could do."

He replied, "I know... believe me, I know...."

"But you blame yourself, don't you? You think you made her have that heart attack."

"Yeah... yes, ma'am, I believe I did."

"But you also know that something here on the property was the agent that killed her, not you."

"I believe that now... mostly, anyway. I know I had a part in it, even it was this land that did the most damage."

Sara felt pity for him as she replied, "I know you blame yourself, but you have to let that go. You didn't kill her: you have to believe that completely or else you'll be stuck with this moment happening again and again for as long as you allow it."

Before she could continue, however, another blurry set of images played out into many scenes before them. It was like she was seeing many television screens playing different stories all at the same time overtop one another. The scenes had a common theme that bound them all together: Amos dragging animal after animal to the dark barn and slaughtering them over the well. Chickens, goats, sheep, pigs, and even a handful of cattle were brought in and disposed of in the earthen opening. The cattle were especially difficult to get down into the well as he had to use a hacksaw to remove the limbs and cut the torso into pieces that would fit in the modest opening in the ground. Labor-intensive and messy work to be sure.

They watched the events for nearly a minute before Amos finally said, "It was her, Caroline, who told me to do that. She said I would have to make regular sacrifices at the well or the land would wither away and die. Things would occasionally get better, but it would never stay that way. She was always demanding more and more. She said the land was hungry. She said that people had always taken but never returned anything. She even said God wanted me to do these things because they used to sacrifice animals in ancient times and it enraged him that it stopped. I know I shouldn't have believed her, but I did. I was desperate and I wasn't thinking right."

Sara and Amos then walk over toward the garden next to the house where they saw a few plants here and there returning to life. As the image of Amos and Timothy were harvesting the vegetables therein, Sara said, "She was just stringing you along, wasn't she?"

"Yes, ma'am, she did string me along for quite some time."

They then saw a scene play out in the normal barn of the property. In it, Amos was milking their last milking cow as Caroline approached. The old woman called out, "Amos! I thought I told you that you to slaughter that cow! Why is it still alive!?"

His image replied, "Miss Caroline, please, it's our last milk cow! If I sacrifice this, we won't have any milk to use! We'll starve!"

Caroline's form became enraged at this. "What!? You *don't* make the decisions around here, I do! You'll lose your son if you don't do what I say!" That scene then dissolved away into emptiness.

Amos then led Sara over to the window of the house at Timmy's bedroom (which was Angelica's bedroom in the present time). Inside they watched as the image of Amos walked in and checked on his son, who was covered up and in his simple metal framed bed. The facsimile of Amos then pressed his hand on Timmy's forehead and said, "You're burning up!" He then took a thermometer and slung it up and down a few times before placing it under Timmy's tongue. "Let's see what your temperature is."

He waited about thirty seconds before removing and reading the mercury. "One hundred and six degrees! We've gotta get that fever down!" He then took the rag from the nearby bedside table and soaked it in the bowl of water next to it. He wrung out the water and said, "You just stay here and keep that rag on your forehead. I'll go and make you some chicken noodle soup."

As the scene faded, Amos looked at Sara and said, "I knew he was in trouble. A fever that high is hard to recover from. It happened so suddenly. I called the doctor and he said he would be there the next day, but by the time he showed up, it was too late."

Sara asked, "Did the fever take him?"

"Not directly, no. When I got up early the next morning to check on him, he wasn't in his bed. I looked all over the house and all over the property, but I couldn't find him."

Perplexed, "What happened then?"

As if still not believing it happened himself, "A bunch of people from the town came and helped form a search party. It wasn't until they brought in a bloodhound from the sheriff's Department that we were able to track him down. His scent led to the cave out in the woods up yonder. They then sent in a rescue group, but they didn't find him... his body, until a week later. It's awfully dangerous in those limestone caves on this property. They lead somewhere... dark."

"What exactly do you mean?"

He started to respond, "Well, Miss Goodwin, it's...." He was cut off as another small scene played out in the turnaround as a stretcher covered in a white sheet came to a stop. The two men in overalls carrying it stopped and lowered their heads and removed their hats as the image of Amos went over and lifted up the sheet. The stricken father then dropped the sheet and walked away in horror after seeing the mangled, and what could only be described as heavily decayed and digested, corpse of his son. Only his clothing and remaining hair were coherent enough to properly identify him. The features of his face were black, blue and red, puffed up and starting to slough off. The eyes were gone completely. The image of Amos then dropped to the ground and cried out in pain. He pounded his fists on the ground and yelled inarticulately. The scene then faded away as a blackened wound on his spirit form seemed to grow a tiny amount.

Sara then placed her hand on his shoulder to try and comfort the current spirit body of Amos he began to weep. She said tenderly, "You don't have to see that again. It's still eating away at you."

After regaining some of his composure, "I don't want to see that again. I don't want to live through that again. But Caroline... Caroline tricked me one last time."

One final series of images then played out before them. In it, Amos sat in a plain wooden chair in the turnaround with a nearly empty bottle of Wild Turkey. He'd only started on the full bottle of whisky that morning and was nearly finished with it around 3:00 P.M. The image of Amos only looked up briefly as the form of Caroline approached him with a fiercely scornful look on her face. She barked, "Amos, you lay about drunk, I told you this would happen! You're out here stinking drunk when this was all your fault!"

His speech was slurred as he said, "Dammit, you old hag, I have nothing left to give! Whadda you want!?"

She lashed back, "I see that so-called 'liquid courage' has made you plain stupid! Do you know where your little boy is right now!?"

He took a swig from the bottle. His face was flush with blood as the tears started to fall again. "He's dead and gone! He's buried in the town cemetery!"

Her tone then became more sly, "Oh, that's not completely true, Amos Harris." She then extended her right hand. In response to the gesture, the image of Timothy Harris' decay-ridden body appeared burst into flames. "Look there! He's burning in hell as we speak!"

The bottle of whisky fell from his hand as he stumbled out of the chair and fell to his hands and knees. He extended his rough hand before him. "But he was baptized! He never did anyone any wrong!"

Caroline smirked and replied, "You can't claim to know his every deed, Amos Harris! In his final moments he was cursing at God himself and damning him for his own stupidity! He became quite the little blasphemer in no time!"

Amos then placed his hand into the image of his son writhing in agony as the fire burned, but did not consume him. It was only an image, so his hand met nothing but air. The screams and the expression on his son's face were enough to penetrate him with sickening fear down to his very soul. This wound was one of, if not the, absolute worst injury that stayed with his spirit form.

After Amos had groveled and grabbed at the illusion long enough, Caroline said, "But Amos, fate is going to give you a second chance. I happen to know that if you give yourself up, your son Timothy will be spared of this fate. What nobler end than to give yourself up for your son. It's so appropriate since you believe God gave his only begotten son to the world. Well, don't you agree with that, or have you lost your faith, too!?"

His head was certainly not in the right place, but her words seem to ring within him. His tone was then saturated with desperation, "Of course I believe that, but why would God ask me to do this!?"

Sharply, "How can you know the will of God!? Do you think you're so righteous!?" He shook his head and continued to sob. Caroline then said, "Then do as I say! Go and say your final prayers and make it quick! I'll be waiting in the barn."

The final moments of the drama proceeded. The image of Amos slowly climbed the wooden ladder leading up to the loft of the barn. Over his shoulder was a long rope and in his right hand was Timothy's lunchbox. The rain outside was starting to sprinkle as a cool summer storm was rolling in overhead. After placing the lunchbox in the spot in the ceiling rafters he pulled a chair from behind and placed it near the edge of the loft. It was then that he took the rope in hand and looked at it blankly for a few moments. Seeing him then hesitate, Caroline asked, "Well what are you waiting for Amos? Tie the noose and get on with it!" He then turned and looked at her. She asked, "Do you even know how to tie a noose!?"

He shook his head. Caroline then hastily talked him through the process. After this he tossed the noose over a wooden beam sitting just beyond the loft's edge. Amos then climbed on top of the chair and slid the noose around his neck. Suddenly a cool breeze came through the partially opened doors. He found it strange that this caught his attention to the point of distraction. The breeze then died and the room went deathly silent. Cinching the rope more tightly, it suddenly hit him. The full force of what he was planning was on top of him. This was it. It was all over after this... or so he thought. Amos then began to hesitate on the chair, but his balance was unsteady from the hard hits of the alcohol.

He stood there for a good twenty seconds before Caroline hissed, "Quit stalling, Amos, and do it! Step off the chair and meet your maker!"

The tears once again returned as he muttered, "I... I can't... I can't do this, it's not right!" He then started to reach up and loosen the noose.

As he did this, however, the image of his son suddenly appeared and was running into the barn. "NO, DAD, STOP!"

This completely stole his attention and was all the distraction Caroline needed. The image of Caroline then kicked the chair from under his legs. Amos tried to grab the rope, but his efforts proved ultimately futile. Caroline cried out maniacally, "Jerk and squirm, you horse's ass! Dance the sweet dance of death for Aunty Caroline!" Her laughter continued on as the image of Timothy was "allowed" to watch his father's final twitches and spasms. They eventually slowed. As they did, Caroline was not content and kicked his body repeatedly.

Eventually, the body of Amos Harris would stop its death throws and only swing lifelessly in the summer breeze. They didn't find the body for several days.

Sara could scarcely watch anymore as the image of Amos' face contorted and turned purple. Mercifully the scene faded away. As she was getting ready to speak, the present form of Caroline sounded from all around the dark barn. Sarcastically, "Aw, poor Amos Harris took a bit of tumble, didn't he? That first step is a tricky one, eh, Amos?" She then laughed loudly.

Aggravated, Sara said, "You contemptable bitch! You disgust me! Don't think for one second that I'm going to let you fool anyone else!"

Caroline's voice replied, "Oh, no, the witch is getting angry! Isn't that going to 'weaken your light'? Those emotions can be a slippery slope, you know."

Sara almost lashed back in anger, but something Caroline said was true. Her emotions were getting her carried away, but there was something familiar about what she'd said. It made her stop and regain control of herself. This spirit Caroline knew too much to be just an ordinary haunt. Sara took a deep breath and led Amos away from the barn. She said quietly, "Amos, I'm going to be back for you and your son. Do you understand? Stay here and I promise I'll return."

Mockingly, Caroline said, "Oh, no! The little bitch is going to return! I bet she thinks she's figured all of this out. You think you're clever, but you're not!"

Suddenly a loud series of thuds rang through the sky in groups of four. Not three, four. A few seconds elapsed between but they were insistent. Sara was confused for a few moments, but then lowered her head and said deliberately, "Sara, wake up!"

KNOCK, KNOCK, KNOCK, KNOCK.

Saaaaara! Sara dear, are you in there?"

A stinging pain that shot from her eyes to her head greeted Sara as she woke up from being curled up on the couch all night. She pulled her head to the left and right with her hand, popping the crotchety vertebra and cartilage in her neck. She had fallen asleep in a clearly awkward position. The knocks on the front door felt like shotgun blasts going off in her ears, never mind the nausea and dizziness. Sara drank like a pirate the night before and had clearly overstepped her own limits.

The urge to answer the door was overwhelming at this point. Anything to stop the damn knocking! She steadily stepped toward the front door with one hand covering her eyes from the offending sunlight coming in through the windows. As she reached for the deadbolt and chain, she groaned loudly, "I'm coming!"

The knocker outside stopped midway through a group of four knocks. She opened the door to a familiar face.

"Hey, Roberta. Come in. Please don't make a lot of noise, I have a splitting headache."

Roberta made an apologetic noise and said, "I didn't mean to wake you, Sara. You're usually up by now."

This caused Sara to look up at the antique clock ticking on the wall. It had might as well have been whacking her on the head with a steel hammer. 10:30 A.M. "I didn't know it was so late already."

Seeing the haggard expression on Sara's face as they sat down in the living room, Roberta asked, "Rough night?"

Pinching the bridge of nose and yawning first, "You could say that. It seemed like it took me forever to get to sleep."

Roberta looked down at the empty bottle of wine, but Sara didn't notice. She then said, "I hadn't heard from you this morning and I got worried. You weren't answering your phone, so I decided to come and check on you."

Her back popped and protested as she stretched it. "Did you guys find out anything else?"

"Well, Tony was able to dig up some things at the library and public records. We've got a decent amount of information now and should have enough to present to Father Anderson after we do our second investigation tonight."

The "second night" part made her vividly remember her promise to Amos and details of her dream. Even though she dreaded returning, she knew she had no other choice but to keep her promise. "I think I learned a couple of things myself last night. I had a dream… a very vivid dream."

Sara then divulged the details of the dream to Roberta who listened attentively. She also wrote down as many details as she could remember. They were going to need all the evidence they could get to convince The Church to take action.

Fifty-eight

It was around 10:00 A.M. when Edward and Rosanna were nearing Holly Bush Road. Ron had picked them up from the hotel that morning in his Chevy pickup truck. For the duration of the drive, Rosanna had remained fairly silent. Edward kept his arm around his wife's shoulders as she lay her head on his chest. Despite reasonably comfortable accommodations at the Holiday Inn, the investigation team and the Barristers were all strung out. The second night of investigating was going to be particularly taxing to all, but it was necessary.

As the truck pulled into view of the property, the three occupants were all suddenly dumbstruck at the sight before them. "What in the world...?" Ron's words were barely audible and trailed off as the property's owners couldn't believe their eyes. Seemingly every blade of grass, every leaf of weedy flora, and all the green in the holly bushes lining the driveway had turned light brown. Sure, most of the plants on the property would turn color every year in the descent of autumn, but it was still summer. And the knowledge of seeing the plants thriving and growing well just the day before made it incredibly strange. To further drive the point home, the unsettling blight seemed to stop organically and fluidly along the edge of their property all over.

Rosanna looked on in silence as her husband, befuddled, said, "I've never seen anything like this in my life." Looking at Ron, "Have you?"

The two of them didn't seem to notice the line of six cars that had stopped on the side of the road coming from the other direction. A few of the locals had stopped and gawked for several minutes before they arrived. Rosanna, seeing the small crowd, ducked her head into her husband's chest as Ron honked the horn, hoping to move the human cattle along partially blocking the road. "Damn rubber-necks." He then looked over at Edward. "I've never seen anything like this in my life…" Ron checked behind him and all around, looking at the neighboring properties. Everyone else was experiencing the lush green bounty that a steady summer had provided.

Soon, the gawkers began to pull away from the roadshow and moved on.

Once out of sight, Edward whispered, "It's okay, hon. They're gone."

Rosanna cautiously looked up and could obviously see the despair in the property. As if sensing something quite unholy about the whole thing, she instinctively crossed herself in silence.

The truck slowly creeped up the long gravel scar leading to the house, the tiny pieces of rock popping and stirring up a larger than usual cloud of dust the entire way.

As the truck came to a stop in the turnaround, Rosanna could see the remains of her garden next to the house. A pitiful sight, to be sure.

Rosanna then stepped out and walked toward the uniformly brown plants and the mysteriously rotten vegetables on the vine. She had just watered them the day before and they were quite healthy then. Now they were covered in gnats and withering away at an unnatural pace on the dry dirt mounts that formerly supported the stalks. She called out to her husband who was approaching from behind.

She poked the almost completely black remains of a tomato with a stick and said, "Ed, I can't believe this! I just checked on these yesterday!"

He kneeled down at the now exposed body of a potato that seemed to be forced up out of the earth. It stank heavily and the sight of it combined caused him to cover his mouth. Puzzled, "Look here… this isn't natural. Potatoes don't push themselves up and rot overnight." He looked back at Ron, who was approaching the scene now. "You ever see anything rot this quickly?"

It was clear to him. "No, sir. I remember seeing the garden yesterday myself. Roberta and I were talking about it before we came in. I remember saying that the tomatoes looked especially good."

Suddenly, the phone in Edward's pocket began to ring. He immediately knew who it was. He was late in picking someone up, again. "Hello?"

His daughter was on the other end. "Hey, Dad, are you going to pick me up? Mr. Kelly said he would drop me off later if it was a problem."

"No, sweetie, I know I'm late and I'm sorry. We were just running a little behind getting here. I'm heading that way right now."

They said their goodbyes.

Edward then said, "I have to go pick up Ange, honey, I'll be right back. You okay here?" She indicated that she would be and he kissed her before he climbed into the family car and headed down the driveway.

Fifty-nine

About forty minutes later, the car returned to the proximity of the property. Seeing the blight before her, Angelica looked on with astonishment. Not paying attention to her own words, "Oh, shit!"

Surprised momentarily out of the here and now, "Whoa! Ange, who taught you how to speak like that!? Your mother would...."

He was cut off. "No, Dad! I dreamed this would happen last night." She then got lost in her own words again. "In the dream, all the plants and grass died. But there was more...."

He wasn't sure if he wanted to know more. Angelica was stone dead serious, and that was never good. "What else happened?"

Still staring off into the distance as the car crept up the driveway, "I don't want to say. You understand, right?"

"Yeah... I understand, baby girl. I used to see things in dreams that would happen the next day, too. Now, not so much. Just remember: Sometimes things you dream about don't come true."

Using a word her mentor Sara had used the night before, "You mean deception?"

Surprised at how on-point she was, "That's right." Now beaming with pride, "You know, you're handling this much better than I did when I was a kid. My brave little girl." He cupped his hand on her head gently.

Only mildly soothed, "I'm still scared, though."

Reluctantly, "So am I, baby girl, so am I."

Sixty

It was around 12:30 P.M. that same day when Edward heard his phone ring once again. Angelica and Cerberus were now walking around the property, the latter sniffing the ground diligently as the former touched the myriad of desiccated plants in disbelief. Edward and Rosanna were sharing the unpleasant work of removing the rotten plants from the dead garden.

Edward looked down at the caller ID on the screen and moaned, "Ah, crap. What does *he* want?"

Rosanna looked up at him with an inquisitive glance.

He responded, "It's Mark."

His wife then rolled her eyes in discontent.

"Ugh...." He then answered the phone with forced politeness. "Hello?"

The voice on the other end replied, "Heya, Eddie-boy! How are ya?"

Rolling his eyes but maintaining the pleasant façade, "Hey there, Mark. I'm good, and you?"

"I'm good, but that's not what I heard about you. I hear you're having some tough times up there."

Feeling that there was an ulterior motive to his call, he was really having to concentrate on being civil. There's helping, and then there's *prying*. The latter was suspected as he replied, "Well, I guess things are a little hectic up here right now. Just lots of life stuff going on."

"*Hectic? Life stuff!?* I heard it was worse than that. That's why I decided to stop by and see if you needed anything."

Definitely opposed to the idea but being courteous, "Ah, Mark, there's no need for that. We're doing fine, really."

Edward then saw the white Acura sedan coming around the bend and down the road toward their driveway. "Too late! I see you!"

As Mark abruptly hung up the phone he turned onto their driveway. Edward called his name in vain a couple of times before saying to his wife, "Dammit, he's here!"

Rosanna, still very much aware of, and ashamed of, her appearance, suddenly rose to her feet and said, "I can't be seen like this, Ed!"

He wasn't going to protest as Rosanna disappeared into the house letting the screen door slap shut behind her. Inside Ron and Roberta were hooking up there equipment again. Now Edward was going to have to put up with Mark by himself.

Angelica squinted as the sun shone in her eyes. She saw the car approaching and started walking toward the turnaround with her puppy in tow. Ed wanted to scream to her, "Dear God, Angelica, stay away from this prick! Save yourself!" but manners forbade it. He reluctantly waved to Mark as he put his car in park and stepped out.

As he opened the door, "Hey there, Mark. How are you?"

Angelica stopped next to her father as Mark said jubilantly, "Heya, Eddie-boy! How's it going?" He looked side and to side before saying facetiously, "I knew you were green at this whole farming thing but I didn't know you'd kill every last plant on your land!" He clapped his hands together once as he laughed aloud. He then adjusted the aviators on his face and looked down at Angelica. "Well, if isn't little Angie! The more you grow, the more you look like your mother."

Despite his attempt at connecting with her, she was staring daggers through him and it was obvious. She hadn't really been around him much since they moved, but that day, for some reason, she couldn't stand his presence. Perhaps she could see through his charades more quickly and wasn't in much of a position to humor him with adult placation. Not to mention that godawful wig he was wearing. Who did he think he was fooling with that rug, anyway? Maybe if he hadn't skimped on the money and either bought a better piece of human upholstery or just went for implants, he wouldn't be so obviously fake.

Edward looked down and could nearly feel the icy aura radiating from his daughter.

Mark then extended his hand rather sheepishly at Angelica and said, "Gimme five, Angie!"

Edward then watched in silence as Angelica turned and walked away from both of them without a word. She wasn't giving one or two, much less five.

They both watched in silence as she strolled away before Edward shrugged and said, "She's had a really rough time the past few weeks." He turned and faced Mark again, really wanting to follow his daughter and just walk away. He couldn't.

He rolled the sleeves of his white button-up shirt to his elbows as he said, "Kids these days... No matter." Mark then slapped Edward on the arm, an attempt at a friendly gesture, before turning and looking at the black van parked nearby. "Whatcha got here? Pest control?"

Edward certainly didn't want to divulge any more knowledge of the situation than was politely necessary. "Yeah, something like that."

Movement from the upper story of the house suddenly caught their eye. It was Rosanna quickly shutting the blinds.

Mark attempted to wave, but it was too late. Motioning at the window, "What was that about?"

"Eh, she's having a hard time, too. She might be coming down with the flu, but we're not sure."

Mark shrugged again.

Edward then decided that too much time was being wasted standing around the house. He wanted Mark to get to the point and fast. He motioned toward the path leading between the barns and toward the stream.

An uncomfortable silence followed for a few moments before they approached the bridge.

Mark then looked side to side and said, "Any idea what happened to all the plants here?"

Polite, but cool and distant, "No, none at all. We came home this morning and found it like this. Everything just died for some reason."

"How long were you gone? Maybe someone put DDT or Agent Orange on everything while you were out."

He couldn't tell if Mark was being serious. He really hoped he wasn't that stupid as he replied, "On all our acreage? Look around! Unless a squadron of crop dusters snuck in overnight and carpet-bombed us, I don't think so. Besides, we were only gone maybe ten or twelve hours."

"Where were you all at? Shopping all night at the Walmart the next county over?" He chuckled.

Edward's patience was being tested now. *Mind your own damn business!* he thought to himself. What he said was, "We were just staying at a hotel on the edge of town. We just needed a night away from the house is all."

They were then crossing the bridge as Mark said, "Uh-oh! Is your house haunted, Eddie-boy!? I know you used to be into that spooky shit!"

Would you quit babbling, you ass wipe!? Get to the point! Edward gripped the bridge of his nose with his forefinger and thumb while saying, "Nah, nothing like that, Mark." Mark laughed as Edward then said, "So to what do we owe the pleasure? I know you wouldn't waste a tank of gas just to come out here and see me for shits and giggles."

He chuckled again. "I guess you know me all too well, Eddie-boy. Truth is, I did want to come and check and see if you were okay, but I was also looking at properties in the beautiful community of Miller's Run. Nice country out here but it's definitely ripe for development. Have you seen that big Victorian mansion out near the river? That place is on prime property!"

Yep, he'd seen it, been there, and knew the owner. Edward, however, didn't even get a t-shirt for his troubles. "Yeah, I've seen it before. You looking to live life on the farm, Mark?" *Dear God, please say no….*

"Nah, hell, Eddie-boy, I just want to snatch up some land and sit on it a couple of years. I have some inside knowledge that the town might be looking to expand and develop. Not really sure what they had to work with, so I took the day off to scout. You have any local knowledge? I'd say you and I could go in fifty-fifty on something and make a sweet profit!"

There it was: money. Always grabbing for the money. At this point, Edward thought Mark pretty much knew that he had been found out long ago, so why even bother trying to hide it.

"Can't say that I do, Mark. I haven't really been looking out for that sort of thing. Tell you what, if I hear anything, I'll give you a call." *Like hell I will.*

He laughed and slapped Edward on the back. "I hope so, Eddie-boy! I might have given away too much there! Can I trust you?" He laughed again and slapped him on the back once more for good measure. "Ah, you're good people. I know I can trust ya!"

Slap my back again and you'll be carrying your nuts home in an ice pack! Edward laughed awkwardly, even letting some of it show through the politeness visage.

Mark's tone then dropped to a more serious one. "Seriously, though, Eddie-boy, I can tell something is bothering you. Problems with your Rosie there?"

You're really going to bring up my wife right now!? With suggestions of gravity, "No, what's that supposed to mean?"

He put his hands up apologetically. "Whoa, easy there, buddy! I was just asking. Look, I know it's rough being a family man and all. Been there, done that. Hell, *doing* that. But I also know that men have certain urges, certain cravings."

He looked at him more sharply. "What are you getting at?"

They were well along the path at that point, far out of earshot of any warm bodies. The woods beyond were all but completely vacant of noises from various critters.

Mark looked around nervously before saying, "Well, Eddie-boy, I'm talking about, you know...," he made a pushing motion, back and forth with his fist, "we need a little *action* on the sly."

Edward knew Mark had no problem engaging in such indiscretions here and there, but he wasn't going to tolerate the idea. "No, Mark, I don't need a little *action* on the sly."

He quickly tried to shush him, then said, "No, of course not! I wouldn't dream of it myself!" He then jokingly cleared his throat and leaned in closer. In a softer tone, "Not that you would, but if you do, you just let me know and I'll see what I can do. Let's just say I've *heard* about these college girls out of town that will rock your world!"

With reproach, "Mark, for God's sake you're forty-two! What about your wife and kid!?"

Still keeping a quiet tone, "Easy there, Eddie-boy, they're fine! I still come home to them every night! I still put food on the table! They're none the wiser and I couldn't be happier!"

You sound pretty fucking desperate to me, Marky-boy! He hid none of his displeasure as he replied, "I don't want to hear another word about it, Mark! I love my wife and daughter! I'd never do such a thing!"

He put his hands up again in an apologetic gesture. "Okay, okay, forget I said anything. It never happened." Mark then began to plunk the empty bottle of water he'd been carrying nervously on his leg as they walked.

It wasn't a few steps more when something caught Mark's eye. A dark discoloration stood out near the wood-line. "Hang on a sec there, buddy! What's that over there?"

He pointed, but Edward didn't recognize it. Thick black fluid was oozing forth from a small patch of ground surrounded by dead plants.

Mark rushed over to it eagerly as Edward trotted behind him.

"Wait, slow down!"

Edward had a bad, a *very* bad feeling, about what it was. Mark, however, only saw black gold.

He knelt down at the small oozing wound in the ground as Edward stood over him. Despite his friend's words of caution, Mark stuck his finger into the fluid and raised it up, letting it cascade onto the ground.

"I don't wanna get your hopes up, but I think you may have oil here!"

Hesitantly, "I don't think that's oil...."

"Well, it isn't cow piss." He then sniffed the fluid, then recoiled. "Oh, man! Smells like death! Ugh, but I think natural gas leaks out of the ground near oil. Tell ya what...." He then put the empty water bottle on the ground, top open, and allowed the thick black liquid to pour in. "We will just send this off to good old Gary and see what he says." After he filled the bottle halfway he replaced the cap.

Gary was their mutual friend. He was also a geologist. And even though he had helped Edward get the job at the architecture firm at which he worked, he had also vicariously introduced him to Marky-boy here.

Still feeling the negative energy surrounding the fluid, "Be careful with that, Mark. You don't know what it is."

"Exactly, Eddie-boy, that's why we're going to send this to Gary! You might be sitting on a gold mine here!"

With the smell of potential money in the air, it wasn't long before he was jumping in his car and making his way back home. Mark would almost surely expect some sort of "finder's fee" if the substance turned out to be crude oil. Edward couldn't care less at that point and was just happy to see him go.

Edward waved as Mark's Acura came closer to turning onto the road. Just before, however, Mark was startled by an unfamiliar voice that sounded loudly in his ears. *"Looks like your ship has finally come in, Marky-boy!"*

The voice was so clear that it caused him to temporarily lose his focus and nearly hit the black BMW that was approaching the driveway. The driver was laying on the horn. He didn't recognize the voice, but it was Caroline. He also didn't recognize the vehicle that was now stopped a few inches short of his still moving car. Perhaps he may have recognized the driver if he weren't so distracted. He only waved that follow up wave as a sign of saying, "I screwed up, but I don't care! Thanks for not hitting my dumb ass!" The palpitations of his heart were stifling at first, be managed to get himself under enough control to continue on down the road. It wouldn't be the last time he'd hear sweet Caroline whispering is in ear. She had a knack for that sort of thing.

Sara watched as the Acura pulled away, feeling a sense of déjà vu. The license plate, the car… where did she know that from?

As she muttered a few expletives under her breath, she was suddenly interrupted by her rogue iPod: "I wanna feel you from the inside…." It was the same song as the night before, "Closer."

Flustered, she quickly yanked the cord from her car's stereo system and the song stopped. That song, however, jogged loose a memory. That tune made her recall why that car was so familiar. Only now the car was far out of sight and there really wasn't much she would've intended to do anyway. She wasn't the kind to chase someone down and drag them out of their car.

Edward had seen her pulling into the driveway and waited on her at the turnaround.

She pulled the car to a stop and got out. Edward started to say "hello," but was cut off. "Mr. Barrister, I apologize, but can I ask you a question?"

Confused, "Uh, sure."

"This may be coming out of left field, but please hear me out. That man that just left: Was his name Mark Keller by any chance?"

Very surprised by her on-the-nose question, "Yeah, how did you know? A friend of yours?"

Disgusted and curt, "No."

"Oh, you *have* met him then. Don't worry, I'm not a fan either. I just have to work with him. He's one of the reasons I moved out here."

"I've had the unfortunate pleasure of meeting him, yes, but only briefly. I don't want to insult a colleague of yours, but... let's just say we met on some of the worst terms."

His tone was somewhat light. "Uh-oh. I've heard a million stories about that jerk."

Her tone was still very grave. "No, I really mean it. I caught him doing something that only a really lecherous bastard would do."

Edward now listened with all seriousness. "Oh, God. What happened?"

Angelica was now approaching them from several feet away and waving at Sara.

Sara returned the gesture. She said in a lowered tone, "Can we speak about it over there? I don't want her to hear about it."

Edward then said to his daughter, "Hey, hon, could you give us a second? Just grown-up talk for a minute."

Angelica was somewhat dejected, but gave them their space.

Sara called out, "Hey, Ange. Don't worry, I'll talk with you in a minute, okay?"

She replied, "Okay, Sara!"

As Sara looked back toward Edward, she was startled by a figure standing in one of the upstairs windows. It was Rosanna. She was just standing there staring at them with a blank expression on her face.

Several silent seconds passed before both of them waved to her, but got no response. Rosanna quietly stepped away from the window and shut the blinds once again. They made sure to stay in view of the window. They weren't going to leave anything to the imagination in the scene of them just talking. Besides that, Angelica was watching from a safe distance. No implications of "funny business."

Sara started quietly. "Okay, the reason I knew that was him was because the last time I saw him, I was chasing him out of my apartment while I was in college not too many years ago. I ran out after him and snapped a picture of his car with my cell phone. But, that's the end of the story.

"The way it started, I was coming back to my apartment one evening. I was a senior and my roommate was a junior. Her name was Julie. It was finals week and I needed to study. Julie was already done with her exams and she was looking to unwind. While I was upstairs in my room studying, she came in with a guy and they disappeared into her bedroom. Now I wasn't intent on disturbing anything, but the music coming from her room was suddenly turned up really loud. I couldn't concentrate. I went downstairs to ask her to turn it down. I got no response at first, so I knocked louder. When that didn't work, I had to open the door. When I did, I was horrified to see what was happening inside. There Mark was taking her shirt off, only she was out cold. I guessed she'd drank too much, but that wasn't stopping him. Seeing me, he knew he had to get out of there, as it was obvious he wasn't going to stop otherwise.

"I ended up chasing him out of the house, yelling every swear word at him that I knew. I took out my cell phone and snapped a picture of his car as he was peeling out of the parking lot. A little bit of detective work online and boom, I found the name Mark Keller. He never came back again and he's lucky he didn't."

Edward was pinching the bridge of his nose with his thumb and forefinger as he remembered bits of Mark's suggestion for "action on the sly" earlier on. He groaned, "Oh, Jesus. I knew he was an asshole, but that's disgusting!"

She lowered her head for a moment before looking up at him again. "I'm sorry to be the one to tell you, but it's hard to forget that sort of thing, much less forgive. And that song that was playing last night, the one on the television here...."

Edward nodded uncomfortably at the subject being brought up again.

She continued. "Closer... that's the song that was playing that night. I knew it had some sort of significance but only realized what that was a few minutes ago."

"Whatever is here is really screwing with our heads." Then embarrassed, "Ah, shit, bad choice of words. I'm sorry."

"Don't worry about it. Whatever is here is clearly very powerful to know all that."

It wasn't until then that Sara noticed the fall of the vegetation all over the property. The encounter with Mark's Acura completely distracted her up until this point. She and Edward then walked toward Angelica, who was approaching them with Cerberus close behind. Sara blindly reached down to pet the dog on the head as her mouth opened in awe at the decay on display.

Edward then said, "Crazy, right? This all happened last night! You were here yesterday: everything was green. You ever seen anything like this?"

Staring off in the distance at the monumental loss of plant-life everywhere, "I've never seen phenomenon this powerful! I… I don't what to say."

Angelica replied, "Even the leaves have fallen off of the trees in the forest. I think most of the needles on the evergreens have turned brown, too."

Sara then caught a whiff of the remains of the decay in the garden. It caused her to stare silently for a moment with her hand to her chin, debating a decision. The decision she made, despite potential risks, was in their best interest.

Edward inquired, "What is it?"

Seemingly out of nowhere, a large raven suddenly swept down and landed skillfully on the roof of Sara's car. It seemed to match the black color of the car perfectly. They all watched in silence, expecting the large corvid to take off immediately. It did not, however, and sat staring back at them, Sara in particular. Spellbound, they didn't seem to breathe a single collective breath, realizing the potency of the event. As Sara tilted her head to one side, perplexed, the black bird mimicked. Again to the other side. Angelica could then sense a strong aura radiating from the creature. Dark, ancient, mysterious. It wasn't evil, however, as she was coming to understand it.

Several long moments later, Sara unconsciously muttered, "Morrigan?"

At this utterance, the bird immediately took flight and soon disappeared in the distance. Edward and his daughter then looked over at Sara as she said, "Just a moment.…" She opened her car door and fished a small vial from her purse sitting in the passenger seat. Turning to face her audience again, she unscrewed the top from the glass container full of oils, seeds, and a couple of small flower petals. Looking at both of them in turn, she asked, "Okay, do you two accept this blessing? We can't afford to take any chances."

They each nodded their head as Sara took a small amount of the fluid within and made elaborate markings on their foreheads each in turn. She muttered something each time, but it was only barely audible to her recipients and not discernable. She then placed her hands in front of Edward and Angelica's faces and lowered her head, again speaking in the inaudible tone. They had instinctively followed suit and only looked up again when she was finished.

As Sara indicated that she was through, Angelica immediately asked, "What's in that bottle?"

She replied, "That's my secret formula. Maybe I'll tell you about it someday."

Sixty-one

Mark was cruising down the highway now as the radio played the "Best of the Oldies" on KIDC radio. His uneventful drive, up until this point anyway, was suddenly interrupted. The signal from the radio broke sharply as the entire audio system shut off. He tried repeatedly to turn it back on and adjust the volume, but nothing worked. Not even static came through.

Jarringly, the voice of Caroline burst into audible range. "Rohypnol... really, Marky-boy? You had to resort to that after all those years?"

Mark began to fidget with the knob on the radio again, but to no avail. He then blurted out nervously, "I'm not hearing this... I'm not crazy!"

"Oh, you're hearing me, Marky-boy, loud and clear! You kept those pills handy since your college days in case you needed to use them again!"

He then looked down at the clear bottle half-full of the black viscous substance he'd taken from the Barrister Farm. Strangely he'd kept it propped up in the passenger seat. It was as if he made an immediate connection between the two.

He still didn't want to believe. He then stammered, "You can't talk! Y... You're just a bottle of oil!"

Calmly, "Now you're the one talking to a bottle, Marky-boy. Maybe you are crazy after all. But hey, you might be able to get enough money from this find to pay for years of therapy!"

Mark then replied angrily, "Bottles can't talk! Shut up! Shut up! Shut up!"

Caroline snapped, "Up here!"

He looked up and at eye level could see two glowing yellow orbs staring back at him, but nothing more. He swerved into the other lane momentarily, causing yet another driver that day to fire a salvo of profanity and exercising his horn. He was met with the same "asshole wave" as he returned to his lane.

The radio then came back to life with a sizzle and a pop. The rest of the drive home would be silent, but Mark never stopped glancing down at the bottle of black fluid.

It was evening when Mark eventually pulled his car to a stop in the chunk of suburbia he'd called home for so many years. His wife and kid were on vacation at her parents' house an hour away. Truth be told, she and Mark had had an argument that got really ugly and the vacation excuse was just that: an excuse.

Now even though Mark was rather spooked by the bottle of fluid, he'd taken into the house with him. The past couple of hours in silence gave him the confidence to try and overcome any goosebumps that remained.

Once inside, he placed the bottle on the kitchen counter. As he was turning to make his way to the bathroom, he was startled by Caroline's voice again. "Coming home to an empty house again, eh, Marky-boy?"

He wanted to ignore her, but it was becoming futile at this point. He shouted over his shoulder, "Shut up! You're not real!"

A few more steps down the hall and he'd slammed the bathroom door behind him. He unzipped and nervously tried to proceed with urinating. Her voice, however, was coming from just inside his large bathroom now.

"Julie was all too real, wasn't she!?"

At this remark he fell to the side and onto the floor. Piss was running copiously onto the tile now. "That's a lie!" As he said this, he looked wildly around the room but couldn't see her.

"Whether or not you actually got to *score* that night or not is irrelevant! Your intent was very clear!"

The two glowing orbs he'd seen in the car previously now shone again a few feet away. This time, however, they were surrounded by a cloud of black mist that seemed to undulate and only briefly take humanoid shape before returning to ambiguity. Mark began to cry out and mutter incoherently.

Caroline then hissed mockingly, "Looking from here, it's obvious why you have to drug your women! What was the girl's name you drugged first...? Kimberly! That's it, isn't it!?"

Still fighting to control himself rather unsuccessfully, "How did... how did you know... that?"

Caroline growled inhumanly. It slowly dissolved into a laugh, however, before she said, "Because she's right here, Marky-boy! I doubt you care, but she killed herself that following spring! She found out she was pregnant after you had your way with her and she couldn't get over the melancholy! Poor dear slit her wrists in the bathtub and her parents found her the next day! Now she burns in hell! Behold your victim!"

The image of Kimberly, naked and streaming blood from her sliced open forearms, said through tears, "Why did you do that, Mark!? I thought we were friends! I thought you might be a nice guy! Was it worth it!?"

Mark feverishly called out, "Oh, God, Kimberly, I didn't know! Why did you kill yourself!?"

Caroline then hissed, "You know, she killed two people that day, Mark! She was nearly at term with her baby!"

At this he simply groveled on the ground and stuttered, "Oh... God... why!?"

The form of Caroline then became somewhat more humanoid, her face being the distinguishing feature amidst the black cloud. She leaned her head in close, her face inches from his own. She then said slyly with a guttural tone, "You know, Mark, I don't believe you've ever been penetrated before." Her face went blank for a moment before taking on a sadistic grin. "Let's see if you're partial to it!"

She then brought what now resembled a hand to his cheek and grazed the fingers across his skin. Much to his horror, however, the fingers slowly elongated into inky black tendrils. They then quickly and aggressively found the only orifice a man has down below. Caroline's eyes then went from glowing yellow suns to nebulous black holes.

A deeper and inhuman voice then came from Caroline's mouth as the tendrils scoured his lower digestive tract. "Let's see what you're hiding in there, Marky-boy!"

As they probed farther inside, he screamed at an agonizing volume. The violation, unlike his own, lasted for what seemed like an eternity. The pain reached levels he never thought imaginable.

His cries did drop a few minutes later, but only out of confusion as the tendrils seemed to withdraw. The pain, however, was only marginally better. His insides were still burning like the sun as he attempted to push himself up off the floor. With his pants around his ankles still, he was only able to make it to one knee. He then felt hot tears stream down his face as he feebly stood back up, his legs giving him more trouble than a newborn animal just out of the womb.

Caroline's voice then came through again as she then appeared in the hall in front of him. "Come on now, into the kitchen. You'll need a good, stiff drink to take the edge off."

Unable to speak, Mark stumbled into the hall and found himself obeying her commands. His mind only marginally resisted as he took each tentative step with his hands and forearms against the wall. He didn't even notice the trail of blood dripping down behind him drop by drop onto his faux-expensive wooden floors.

As he approached the kitchen counter, his eyes were fixated on the menacing plastic bottle. He stumbled toward it and picked it up into his hand.

The voice of Caroline then said, "There you go, Marky-boy, have a drink. It'll make you feel all better, I promise."

The fact that he had used almost used those exact words on Kimberly all those years ago was not lost. And perhaps he felt bad for what he had done, but he found the punishment he was now seemingly receiving was far too severe. Strangely, however, his arms followed her commands. He slowly unscrewed the cap and took the bottle up to his mouth. Despite the strong rotten smell coming from inside, he knocked it back and swallowed it all gulp by gulp. Every drop of the black fluid seemed to escape the bottle and fill his throat. The impulse to wretch was almost overbearing, but something kept the contents inside.

Mark then began to convulse, falling to the ground once again.

The fits of shakes lasted for a few minutes before he was finally able to begin a slow and painful crawl back down the hall. As his hands splattered the small drops of blood on the floor he was made very much aware that his body was no longer under his control. Something was moving and manipulating him from the inside.

Eventually he would make his way into his home office. There he proudly kept a shotgun passed down from his father, a neat and clean Remington twelve-gage. The gun was mounted on a wooden rack along with five shells. He claimed it was for home defense, but it was more for show.

He then took the gun in hand and one of the shells. After loading the single round of buckshot, he worked the pump which loaded the brass, plastic and lead combo flawlessly into the bore.

Abruptly, he then looked down at his exposed genitalia, which seemed to shock him momentarily back into control of his own body and mind. "What am I doing...?" he strained.

His head, however, was then violently thrust against the wall. He was seeing constellations in his office now as Caroline said, "Don't struggle, Marky-boy. It's so much messier when you do."

Mark's body then seemed to fall back into compliance.

In control once again, Caroline said mockingly, "Now you know what to do, Marky-boy. Just suck it like a Popsicle. That's what you told your wife, wasn't it? Weren't you surprised that she did that so well on her 'first time'?"

Caroline laughed maniacally as the pain of the words struck deep into his mind. He was always suspicious of her claiming to be a virgin the first time they had sex, but now it seemed he was right all along. Regardless, he put the muzzle of the barrel into his mouth.

The face of Caroline then leered directly into his. "Now give Aunty Caroline a kiss!"

His finger fumbled for the trigger and soon found it....

It was several days before his wife and kid returned from their vacation. They found Mark's body in his office. His pants were around his ankles. The floor was stained with blood and his own filth in copious amounts after a post-death evacuation. What was left of his head was splattered quite liberally all over the walls of the office like a demonic fireworks show in freeze-frame.

The coroner found strange things when he examined the emasculated remains of Mark Keller. A strange and corrosive agent had all but eaten away his lower intestines and anus entirely. His blood was also considerably darker (nearly black) than expected.

No traces of what he thought to be crude oil were found anywhere on the property or inside his gullet.

At least the funeral director had the decency to provide a closed-casket funeral. No one would be seeing Mark's face around again.

Sixty-two

Rosanna stared silently at the picture of herself, her husband, and daughter in the room upstairs. She remembered taking the picture as it was the last one taken at their old house in Johnston City. Emotional eddies, ranging from sentimentality to sadness, swept through her mind. She remembered being happy that day. It was the day after Christmas and Edward was wearing a red Santa hat. He hadn't started growing out his beard and mustache yet. He too looked happy. Even Angelica was smiling. She had a piece of red garland wrapped around her neck like a shimmering scarf.

And the Christmas tree in the background. She always thought Edward's decorations went a bit overboard, but seeing how much fun he and Angelica would have putting it all together made her keep her "you guys are just plain silly" comments to herself.

Her mind chased the obvious reason things were so different then: innocence. Maybe she and Edward had their share of adult things growing up, but Angelica had yet to start having the night terrors. Even though she'd occasionally seen an "imaginary person" (Rosanna's words, not Angelica's), they weren't usually threatening. All of these occasions seemed to pass through Rosanna's mind now as she questioned her own views of reality. The past three years (and especially the past few days) were enough to make anyone question their sanity or perception of life as they knew it.

The dreamy reflections were suddenly drained away as the reflection of the glass frame showed two glints of bright yellow and a face she'd seen not long ago in her dreams. It was as if Caroline were standing right behind her.

Rosanna turned around quickly but saw no one there. Her heart was already pounding away and her breath went shallow. Caroline's voice was clear in Rosanna's mind: *"I see you, but you can't see me!"* Her laughter then filled Rosanna's ears.

Rosanna replied in a sharp whisper, "I saw you, old woman!" The apprehension inside was now being converted into anger. "I don't care why you're here or what you are, you will not break this family apart! So help me, I will see you cast into hell!"

"My, my, my! Aren't we quick to condemn!"

This actually stung Rosanna a bit. Even though she'd experienced nothing but torture from this spirit, who was she to judge whether someone was hell-bound or not?

While trying reign in her fury, "God will judge you, then!" These words caused her to cross herself.

"God forsook this place ages ago! You're just more chaff for the fire!"

Rosanna, maintaining her whisper, "You won't tear this family apart! I won't let that happen!"

"That little cunt daughter of yours… she and I have a lot in common, you know. Something you would never understand. Of course, Sara knows all too well."

"You leave my daughter out of this! If you're so strong, why pick on her!? I can take any abuse you throw at me!"

Hissing, *"You'd be wise to stop running that mouth, baby killer! The damned here will tear your soul to shreds! Besides, you don't even know if I'm real! Crazy Rosanna, just like the dear old mother that shat you out!"*

Seething and raising her voice, "Here I am! Come out and fight, coward!"

She then looked around the room silently, but no one answered. At first she was confused by the absence, but soon she felt the determination building inside herself. Yes. Yes she now believed without a doubt now that nothing, not this so-called spirit "Caroline," or any other agent of darkness was going to destroy what she, her husband and daughter, had created. She was never surer of anything in her life. She was going to need that confidence.

Rosanna then said a "Hail Mary."

Her eyes then burned with certainty as she said, "Leones don't run!"

Rosanna Leone Barrister had just declared holy war.

She made her way over to the window and peeked out of the blinds. Below she saw Sara talking with Angelica and walking past the normal barn on the right. Rosanna was still uncertain about Sara, despite the twenty-something's friends' protests. She thankful that no one seemed to notice her voice being bellowed out moments before.

Only after watching them unnoticed for several minutes did Caroline's words start to make sense. Angelica's "gifts" were the only thing that came to mind. These same gifts she shared with her father and apparently with Sara. Decades of faith and indoctrination, however, still left those ideas with an unpleasant aftertaste. And even deeper, farther down, a small drop of black fluid seemed to infiltrate her mind. The thought of all of this being psychosis and/or mass hysteria lingered like a distant crow cawing away.

Sixty-three

Meanwhile, near the bridge, Angelica was walking beside Sara. The latter looked down at the dried-out plant matter. As she knelt down she could see the occasional splotch of dark discoloration in the soil. She let her hand graze the tops of the withering blades of grass, but only briefly. Sara's sense of what was lying beneath was sharp and she wasn't taking any chances. A small cloud of faint dust twirled in the breeze in front of her face, causing her to shield her eyes.

As she stood back up, Angelica asked, "Do you think *she* did all of this?"

They had both agreed moments earlier to try and minimize the mentioning of her name or dwelling on it. The two of them could only do so much to avoid it.

Sara replied, "I don't think one human spirit could do all of this. We're dealing with something much more complex."

Angelica didn't need to be reminded of the images in her dream the night before. There were an entire cave-full of shadowy beings that made their presence well known. She sighed as she looked at the many defoliated trees in the distance. "I was hoping I was wrong about that. My dream last night... I was hoping it wasn't true."

Sara didn't have to ask about any details to imagine the sort of dream Angelica had had. The effects were obvious. She responded, "I hope it helps to know that you're not taking this on by yourself. I'm here for you. The entire team, and especially your parents, are here for you, too. Father Anderson will be coming today to oversee the investigation tonight." She could see the words only had a mild effect on Angelica's mood. Sara then knelt down to eye-level with her. "Hey, *I've* got your back. You remember that. We're 'Spirit-Seeing-Sisters,' in it until the end." Sara looked her square in the eyes and extended her hands warmly. Angelica then placed her hands on top of hers. Sara then stood and kissed her on top of her head. She held her hand on the way back to the house.

Edward witnessed the scene from afar and was warmed by it. The thoughts of what Rosanna might think were still in the back of his mind.

Meanwhile, Sheriff Beasley was shutting the door to the Mayor Pinkerton's office. The mayor didn't bear his usual warm politician smile. The sheriff's face was also in a no-nonsense arrangement as he produced his smartphone and quickly found what he was looking for.

"Sir, here are the photos you asked for."

Taking the phone from his extended hand, "How bad is it?"

The sheriff replied, "It's not good. Have a look...."

Mayor Pinkerton slid his finger across the touchscreen, sighing and shaking his head. "Hell, I've never seen it this bad. Sounds like the type of blight they had back in the 30s. Didn't happen to get any shots from the mouth of cave, did you?"

He raised his left eyebrow slightly as he said with a pinch of light sarcasm, "With all due respect, Mr. Mayor, I don't get paid enough for that."

He wanted to be disappointed, but quickly understood the meaning of his words. "Eh, hell. Can't say I blame you."

"By the time I got there, there were already four cars lined up on the side of the road. You'd think they'd never seen dead grass before."

Handing the phone back, "Well, you know what his means. It's been a while, but I suppose it's due. I'll tell the others about it."

Putting the phone in his pocket, "It would be a lot easier to deal with if that family hadn't moved in up there. I'm surprised you let them stay."

"As much I would've liked to turn them away on day one, I didn't have a chance. St. Mary's sold them the place, and any lawyer or judge worth a bucket of piss wouldn't stand for those kind of shenanigans."

Sighing, "Eh, I know, I know."

He paused and looked up at the town's seal and a symbol that adorned the wall behind the mayor and his desk. Above the shield bearing a mallet and anvil in the upper left corner, and a scythe and wheat stocks in the lower right, was a singular all-seeing eye. Mayor Pinkerton enjoyed the symbol, it reminding him of the exploits of relatives of the same name.

The sheriff chuckled as looked into its gaze. "You know, with the name Pinkerton, you should've run for sheriff instead of me."

Standing up from his seat, "And leave the family office? Not a chance. My father and grandfather would turn over in their graves if I did something like that. Besides, someone needs to watch over *you*, am I right?"

Shrugging, "I'm as innocent as fresh lamb's wool."

He sighed again. "Yeah, yeah. Sure, sure." With some gravity returning to his voice, "You just stay out of trouble and I'll deliver the bad news to those who need to know."

Sixty-four

It wasn't much later when Father Anderson arrived. He did his best to maintain a smile and positive attitude despite seeing the devastation on the way up the driveway. Ron had also briefed him on the phone that morning on the events of the previous night, so he was well aware that the situation could turn worse at any point during the investigation on this night.

Before he was even out of his car, Rosanna was approaching him and waving. With everyone else out of earshot, she asked to speak to him privately, and he agreed to.

They went through the usual platitudes of greeting one another, she and he both commenting on the sudden failure of the plants on their property and theirs alone. It wasn't long before she was asking a question about what was bugging her.

"Father Anderson, I have to ask you a question. I don't mean to pry, but... how do I say this? What's your opinion of Sara Goodwin? How well do you know her?"

Father Anderson was not given the details of the dream peepshow that aired on the television set the night before. Ron simply told him that a "raunchy" video started playing on the television that had been unplugged. He didn't feel the need to go into any more than that given the audience. But thinking that Father Anderson couldn't smell old fashioned jealousy lingering in the air would be sheepish. After all, one of his job duties was to alleviate the way people felt about the often unpleasant side-effects of being human.

Sin or not, jealousy was here to stay and never go away. He didn't, however, want to voice any assumptions.

"Well, I know she's been working with the paranormal team there for the past few years. She's a charitable soul and has always been a pleasant person since the first day I met her." He paused a moment, then continued. "Let's see, that's been nearly twenty years now. That's when I moved to the area and took up my post at St. Mary's."

Rosanna wasn't expecting Father Anderson to launch into a tirade about how she was the town whore or town drunk, but maybe there was a small and dark part of her being that wanted him to say something bad. Anything, really. Maybe she was a reckless driver and always sped like a bat out of hell. Maybe she said cusswords in public. Maybe she wore too much makeup. Maybe she farted in church one day. Hell, anything but a glowing review. But was she really expecting her priest to start dumping on a woman she barely knew?

Hold the phone, though! She thought of something particularly bad right away. "I've never seen her at mass before."

Father Anderson could sense the tiny hint of giddiness in this question. Yep, good old green-eyed jealousy bubbling up. "Well, that's true. Then again, she did go to St. Mary's when she was growing up. And it's not in *my* nature to pry either, so I don't press her about it." Rosanna could tell he was inflecting that word just for her.

She was eager to try and change the tone of her inquiry. At least enough to not sound so pushy. "I just don't know about the whole psychic thing. I really have trouble believing such a thing is possible."

He smiled warmly. "Well, that's easy, Mrs. Barrister. We only need to consult the first book of Corinthians for that. There it discusses different gifts that people of faith may receive. Healing, prophecy, the working of miracles, discerning of spirits. People can be born with talents that even we don't fully understand to this day. That doesn't make them inherently evil."

Rosanna was genuinely surprised. Was the answer so plainly written in front of her face all along? "Really?" She paused for a moment. Suddenly she felt overcome with shame at the thought of this speck of disrespect. "I'm sorry, I didn't mean to imply that you don't know the Bible."

Father Anderson chuckled. "It's no problem at all, Mrs. Barrister. I know you didn't mean anything. Besides, it's quite a large book. I don't expect everyone to know every verse by heart at the drop of a hat. We're only human."

She relaxed a bit. "So what about Angelica? I think she may have a talent, but I don't know what it is exactly."

"Well, I don't know for sure, but if she shares similar talents to Miss Goodwin, I'd imagine you could ask her for advice."

The thought of approaching Sara like an adult on an even keel still stung a bit, but she had ran out of excuses. "I suppose…."

Gently, "We have to think of Angelica in this situation. None of us here want to see her grow up with any unnecessary struggle. I trust Miss Goodwin, and if she's so inclined, she could help guide your daughter through things you and I may never begin to understand."

"I suppose you're right."

Sixty-five

Not long after her conversation with Father Anderson, Rosanna had managed to find Sara, alone, at her car. She was getting a small stick of lip balm from her purse. As Sara turned to see Rosanna only a couple of feet from her face, she gasped out in surprise. Rosanna's face was stern, but not hostile.

In a matter-of-fact tone, "Sara, can I speak to you for a moment?"

Her subtle frown tried to hide her apprehension. "Sure, Mrs. Barrister."

Sara quietly followed her toward the normal barn on their right.

They stepped into the shadow of an overhang. Sara realized that everyone else was in the house. It caused her uneasiness to grow a bit more as Rosanna seemed to search for the right words in her mind. It was obvious she was struggling inside. Instinctively, Sara had folded her arms and was keeping a safe distance.

Rosanna eventually spoke. "Sara, I know we've gotten off on a bad foot." She sighed and looked off into the distance. A sprinkling of pain began to tingle in her mind as she continued. "I don't really know you that well and maybe I jumped to a few conclusions." That tingling in her head was getting stronger. "If I made you feel uncomfortable in our home, I apologize."

Sara looked on silently as the pain in Rosanna's head got worse. Sara could see that she was struggling and silently nodded. Something in Rosanna's mind was fiercely resisting her intentions of making up with Sara. The conflict, however, seemed to bring about an antagonistic response from

Rosanna. She knew at this point that a darker part of her, and some alien force, wanted her to stay angry. Furious, even.

More determined than ever to finish, "No. I *know* I made you feel unwelcome and threatened. I'm sorry. I hope you forgive me."

Rosanna could feel the sharp pain in her mind disappear, but it made a much larger hole of dread and uneasiness suddenly materialize in her stomach. Her mother's voice was clear in her mind again: *"You're going to regret that!"*

Sara tilted her head to one side, confused for a moment. A hint of disbelief still lingered in her voice. "Thank you. I accept your apology."

Looking her square in the face, "And as far as Angelica goes... as long as you respect our faith, I'm okay with you helping her with her talents." She extended her hand. "Deal?"

Rosanna didn't really ask for her to help, mind you, but Sara decided to trust in the fact that Rosanna already knew she was helping her.

Sara extended her hand and shook Rosanna's with as much certainty as she could muster. "Deal."

Sixty-six

The sun had just begun to pull its remaining rays from the horizon when the investigation team and the Barrister family set out to begin the second night of evidence hunting. The events of the night before were still fresh in everyone's mind, and no one was wanting to take any unnecessary chances. Rosanna had taken her stance next to her husband. Frustratingly for her mother, Angelica had been placed nearby between Father Anderson and Sara. It was for her own safety, but it stung like lemon-soaked hell in her mind. Angelica would occasionally look up at her mother with barely hidden apprehension. It seemed to resonate with a point that Rosanna held during her own childhood: She was afraid of her mother also. Both of her parents were strong, but her mother was more of the controlling and dominating type. She always tried to avoid crossing that line herself, as a mother, but found the boundaries more blurry and hard to see now that she was a parent herself. How much of Angelica's grandmother was now just being echoed in Rosanna in her motherhood? She prayed it wasn't too much.

The three members of the paranormal team then looked to Father Anderson for the go-ahead to begin the investigation. He nodded. Ron and Roberta then pressed the record buttons on their respective digital recorders.

The former then asked aloud, "Are there any spirits here with us now?"

Everyone waited in silence a few moments before Roberta asked, "Are you the same spirits we spoke to last night?"

Again, several seconds of quiet passed.

Ron then asked, "What it is that you want from the family who lives here?"

They waited, then stopped their recorders and played them back aloud. They were able to hear the sound of their own voices, but no responses. No taps, no knocks, nothing. Roberta looked at Ron and shrugged.

The former then said, "Let's try a few more questions. If we don't get anything in here, we'll try Angelica's bedroom."

Meanwhile, Sara was simply staring into the distance, her head slightly lowered. She was concentrating. Angelica looked up at her, also sensing something strange. More accurately, it was the lack of something that they both sensed that worried them. Sara looked down and knew her young pupil had picked up on this, too.

Ron then noticed her and said, "Is something wrong, Sara?"

Without looking up, "It... they, aren't responding. It's like there's nothing here...."

Angelica then said with glum gravity, "Deception...."

Sara's face had already gone gray as she replied, "Exactly...."

Tony then looked up from the screen of his laptop and said, "Why don't you two go ahead and ask some questions in Angelica's bedroom. That's been a hotspot for activity with her."

Ron and Roberta then looked to one another before heading down the hall.

As the two investigators disappeared into the eight-year-old's bedroom, Rosanna felt that stinging sensation return to her head. She closed her eyes and rubbed them as Edward looked down at her, concerned.

"You okay?" he whispered.

Her eyes still shut, she tried to nod it away. "Yeah, I'm fine. Just a headache."

Sara heard her and fished a couple of Excedrin from her purse nearby. As she handed them toward Rosanna, however, there was something familiar in her gaze. That not-all-there look had returned to the mother's eyes. And despite Rosanna's struggle, it had still managed to peek out and spook Sara a moment.

She paused briefly and silently stared before saying, "Thank you, Sara."

Sara nodded silently in response. Strangely, Rosanna's eyes didn't break their gaze with Sara's. The former put the two pills in her mouth and swallowed them in a quick gulp. Only after a few seconds more of uncomfortable silence did Rosanna force her gaze away and back toward the floor.

Angelica had sensed and seen that. The whole scene made her uncomfortable. Father Anderson also witnessed the act and tried his best to soothe Sara's concern with a silent nod.

Tony watched the display on his laptop as the two investigators in Angelica's bedroom then began to record audio once again.

Ron could be heard down the hall asking, "Why do you torment this family?"

Silence.

Roberta then asked, "Are you a human spirit?"

Pause.

Ron called out, "Is your name Timothy or Amos Harris?"

Angelica and Sara both knew neither Timothy nor Amos would be answering. They kept silent, however, as Ron and Roberta rewound their recorders and listened to the audio. All they heard was the sound of their own voices asking questions.

The pain in Rosanna's head had gotten worse. It had reached the point of constant distraction in her mind.

Edward looked at her with concern. "You want an icepack, hon?"

She replied with her eyes closed tightly, "Yeah... sure."

Father Anderson had put his hand comfortingly on Rosanna's shoulder as she clearly and distinctly heard the voice of Caroline say, *I bet that hurts, doesn't it?*

Rosanna then lurched away. She looked like a scared child to everyone around her as she asked, "You heard that, right?"

The onlookers seemed surprised at her question. Neither Sara, nor Angelica, had heard it.

Tony had looked up at her from his laptop screen with genuine curiosity. He'd had years of experience with this "personal experience" category into which he filed this, but he was always interested in hearing about the events first-hand. "What did you hear, Mrs. Barrister?"

With everyone looking at her, Ron and Roberta now approaching the living room once again in curiosity, Rosanna was reluctant to respond. The voice sounded clearly in her head again, *"They know you're crazy—look at them!"*

Rosanna then exclaimed, "Why can't you hear that!?"

They all looked at her in confusion, even her husband, who'd returned with an ice pack. Her breathing had become suddenly sharp. She then felt the first tears leaking from her eyes. They felt cold on her flushed cheeks.

"Please stop staring at me...."

Amazing how quickly Caroline had pressed the right buttons to make her unravel so easily. She then decided to press a few more.

As her husband embraced her, she felt a sharp series of prickling sensations in her lungs. They soon went from tickles to crackles of mini-lightning. Her lungs all at once lit up in burning pins and needles. The voice of Caroline, ragged but detached, said, *"I bet that hurts, doesn't it? You know, one of my brothers was killed by consumption when I was just five. He said it hurt like hell. He'd cough up blood... pieces of lungs, really... right there onto his shirt. It went a little something like this."*

Rosanna's brief nagging cough had quickly escalated into the deep and throaty cough of someone with pneumonia or tuberculosis. Each spasm in her chest stoked the damnable flames in her lungs. She dropped to her knees and gasped for air as she coughed up tiny flecks of blood, spraying it onto the hardwood floors like tiny water balloons at a vampire's birthday celebration.

As the sanguinary specks continued to fly, Angelica and Sara were both startled by a deep, gravely, inhuman voice that blasted their mind.

The latter looked down in shock. "Did you hear that, too?"

The voice was enough to give her momentary dizziness. She quickly recovered and replied, "Yeah...."

Father Anderson had taken to blessing Rosanna's forehead with the holy oil he was carrying in his pocket. As he made the sign of the cross, she felt her pain quickly subsiding.

Roberta then looked back at Sara and asked, "What did you hear?"

Sara replied with concern, "It said that we need to remember *who runs this show.*"

It was not even a minute later when Rosanna's sudden recovery had given way to a shot of fury. She felt one-hundred-percent again and was ready for a fight. As if completely forgetting the power just exercised over her, she called out over blood-soaked teeth, "Is that all you've got!? You're weak! It'll take more than that to stop me!"

Everyone looked on in shock as Rosanna issued clear defiance to the invisible powers all around.

Father Anderson was quick to warn her, "Never challenge these forces directly! You can't win like that!"

Rosanna replied with force, "But God will protect me! He's on our side!"

A voice then blasted the room. The bass of the sound was enough to shake the walls. The tone was hellish and seemed to be gurgling fire. Only three syllables came out, but everyone heard it all too clearly: "WE THINK NOT!"

Father Anderson crossed himself at this utterance as the tears started streaming from Rosanna's face again. This time, however, they were impeding her vision. She strained through a new red tint and could scarcely make out everyone around her staring once again. What everyone else could see was that the tears were like blood. They were blood. Rosanna tried to wipe them away but it only seemed to make it worse as the crimson ichor smeared completely across her pupils.

The situation only got worse from there, however, as steady trickles of blood began to fall from her ears and nose. The iron-laden smell was thick in her nostrils and becoming faintly noticed by everyone in the room. The smell of blood was in the air for sure. With an equal parts mixture of fear and anger, she let out a primal scream. Just as soon as she did this, however, she was overcome once again with a fierce cough even worse than before.

Angelica recoiled in fear and hid behind Sara as Father Anderson and Edward hovered over Rosanna who had now collapsed to the ground. The spasms in her chest grew to a new intensity as she then felt another unpleasant sensation creeping in through the background. Her jeans were soaking wet. No, she wasn't wetting herself in the traditional sense. What came out stained the front and rear of her jeans a deep reddish purple. She was bleeding from every orifice all at once.

Seeing this, Father Anderson began to splash holy water on her more aggressively. Making the sign of the cross repeatedly over her with the water, he shouted, "In the name of the Father, the Son, and the Holy Spirit, I rebuke you, unclean spirit! I command you to leave in the name of the Saints and the Holy Trinity!"

Sara would try and press Angelica's head against her side to shield her from the sight of her mother in such shape, but there was no way around it. Horrified, she watched as Father Anderson was repeating his condemning words and slinging the anointed water like bullets from a hand gun. They seemed to be doing the trick, to an extent, but the copious blood made it hard to tell for certain.

As Rosanna's coughing fit had started to reside she breathed in heavily and continued to spit red liquid from between her lips. This seeming ascent back to normalcy, however, was interrupted by a sharp crashing sound from just outside. Its soundwaves shot through the house like an artillery round from a Howitzer. It was the sound of lightning striking close; ridiculously close. And there wasn't light emitted from it, but darkness instead. The darkness momentarily flashed and suppressed the light before escaping again. No one saw the black lightning directly as it was the seeming consumption of light that revealed the only clue as to its source. Even if seen, being comprehended would be nigh impossible for most.

Everyone had dropped to the ground in less than a second as the house shuttered.

As the occupants of the living room attempted to regain their composure, the cameras' feed into the laptop was momentarily disrupted. Tony climbed back onto the couch as Edward asked, "Is everyone all right?"

Sara had her arm around Angelica in a shielding posture. "You okay, Ange?"

She nodded.

As Ron and Roberta checked on Rosanna and Father Anderson, Tony said in amazement, "Holy crap, guys! There's something on the walls in the other rooms!"

Confused, Roberta asked, "What do you mean?"

Tony pointed at the laptop display as Ron then looked their way also. They could see what looked like letters scrawled onto the walls violently. Unable to see them very clearly, Ron and Roberta each took their flashlights and headed down the hallway. In Rosanna and Edward's room, and Angelica's, were written a sentence. Neither of them knew what it said. A couple of the words looked vaguely familiar.

From Angelica's room, Ron called out, "Father Anderson, I think you might want to come and take a look at this!"

"Just a moment! There's something in the kitchen also!" The priest was reading the words scrawled in thick black fluid from violent beastly nails on the kitchen wall. It not only looked written, but also burned in, making slight indentations in the drywall.

The kitchen wall read: *"Potest, quod non corrumpetur. Necesse est quae possit expleri."*

Father Anderson then said, "Tony, take a photo of this. It's Latin, I know it is." He read it aloud and said, "Something about needing to be satisfied... I'll have to translate it later."

Tony then followed the priest as he made his way into the bedroom of Edward and Rosanna. Edward was trying his best to comfort his wife as Tony snapped a picture of the text on the wall of their chamber.

The flash lit up the room as Roberta said, "Is that Latin, too?"

Father Anderson replied, "Yes, let's see..." He then read the words aloud: *"Abyssus Sumus."* He pondered only for a moment: "We are the abyss?"

Finally they entered Angelica's room where the third message was also scrawled and burned into the wall. Ron was backing away from the words as Tony snapped another picture for their records.

Roberta then said as she was leaving the room, "I'm going to go and get something. I'll be right back."

Father Anderson read the line, *"Puella decernet."* He thought for a moment and said, "The girl will decide?"

Sara had now entered the room with Angelica behind her. She leaned in to look at the black "ink" that was used to write the messages. It stained as dark as the diabolical ink from the Kraken. She couldn't make much sense of the Latin, but the energy radiating from it was purely malevolent.

Suddenly a series of images flooded Sara's mind. Most of them consisted of Roberta in very different circumstances than she was in currently. One of the worst was Roberta standing over the body of her murdered husband as she desecrated and dismembered his corpse in the shed out behind the family home.

Another image of Roberta came through, this time with her feeding the parts of her murdered son's limbs into a wood-chipper out behind their family home. Yes, in these scenes, Roberta had destroyed the two people that meant the most to her in the world and she was disposing of the bodies.

Finally, the image of Roberta blasting her own skull open with a 9mm was the closer. Sara knew this was a warning. She came to from her momentary blackout with her hand around Roberta's wrist in the there and then. In Roberta's hand was a small pocketknife. She was looking to take a sample of this mysterious fluid. Sara didn't know Marky-boy had taken a small sample earlier and paid for it dearly, but this didn't cause her grip to flinch for an instant.

Sara then said strongly and surely, "No one touch that stuff! No samples, no nothing! It *will* corrupt you!"

The team and everyone else at the investigation were smart enough to listen to her words, much to their reasonable fortune.

It wasn't a second or two later that another bolt of lightning struck near the house. This time, however, it was standard-issue and briefly illuminated the windows of that side of the house. Angelica screamed as an image seared onto the window of her room was briefly brought to light. Sara had instinctively wrapped her arms around her as Father Anderson quickly entered the room and turned on the light switch next to the door. To their horror and amazement, the window glass had been stained with a disturbing set of images.

As Roberta shined the light onto the surface, Angelica only gazed upon it for a moment before turning away. The scene, in a deranged and aggressive style, showed several townspeople standing around what was obviously a bonfire with three stakes pointing upward from the middle. The townsfolk were all reveling and cheering as the flames licked the screaming bodies of the three women, each with her hands tied behind their backs on their own stake. The woman on the left was quite disheveled and crowned with straggling gray hair that cascaded over her naked, sagging and drooping body. The female in the middle appeared younger. Her naked body was nearly completely engulfed in flames as her head reared back in intense pain. Her hair was long and pitch black. To her right was the third female. Also naked, but older than the female in the middle. She two cried out in pain as the fire seared her flesh and the lining of her lungs inside. Her long brown hair poured over her shoulders, but was also being burned aggressively by the fire.

And barely visible, completely surrounding the crowd of people was an amorphous ring of jet-black, faintly humanoid shapes, all with glowing suns for both eyes, looked on in approval.

The images on the glass caused immediate revulsion to both Sara and Angelica. Father Anderson was troubled, but also shocked at how it was obviously made in a fashion meant to mock the appearance of stained-glass in a place of worship. He made the sign of the cross with splashes of holy water but they all quickly hissed and sizzled before evaporating almost immediately. At first he took this as an obvious sign of evil energy recoiling at contact with holy water, but as he stepped closer he could also feel a lingering infernal heat radiating from the glass. He then noticed that the wood all around the edges of the window had a distinct scaly char that released tiny wisps of light gray smoke into the air. The black pattern of char also made the wood appear to take on a reptilian visage. They only threatened to set the wood ablaze, but never did.

Seconds later, Sara was taking Angelica to the hallway when Tony suddenly appeared from the living room into the hall. Nearly crashing into them first, he quickly ducked to the right and turned on the lights to the Barrister's master bedroom. The image on the screen in his laptop had caused him to react so quickly that even Sara paused for a moment to see him shine his flashlight onto their window as well. Angelica also couldn't help but look and bore witness to the tainted depiction. This scene was seared into the glass in the same fashion as the room before. On this pane of hell-stained lead crystal was the image of a large heavily gnarled tree which bore the weight of several people hanging from their respective nooses. One of the people hanging was clearly an elderly man dressed in priestly garments. The two people to his right were a man and woman in their middle-aged years. The man had a brown beard and hair while the woman to his right had long black hair. They were dressed in modern clothes. The two people next to them were a disheveled man dressed in bibbed overalls covering his stained shirt and a younger male. He was dressed in a very similar fashion to the father figure next to him. And to make the scene even more disturbing were the dozens of ink-colored humanoid creatures that pulled and gnawed at their extremities. The broken necks of the hanging bodies seemed to be barely able to support the pulling in all directions clearly shown by the angle of their heads heavily exceeding the normal load capacity assigned to them.

The sounds of Rosanna still coughing in the living room became clearer as Sara tried to shuttle Angelica toward the kitchen and away from the horrors on display. Edward had managed to get a towel from the bathroom and was wiping the blood from her lips.

Seeing this, Angelica, her voice trembling, asked as she passed, "Mom, are you okay?"

Edward replied as Rosanna continued to cough heavily, "We're going to take her to the hospital. She'll be okay, I promise."

Hearing this, Rosanna looked up at her daughter. The red filter over her eyes only made the hallucination worse. Instead of seeing her daughter's face, she saw the face of Caroline. Her ears were also part of this deception as she heard the words, *"Red roses were always my favorite...."* Caroline's face then laughed in a balance of giggling and cackling.

It was then that Rosanna suddenly lunged at her daughter. She growled and snapped her teeth as Edward held her back, barely, with all his strength.

Sara then called out, "Father! Get in here, now!" She then protectively put herself between the mother and father and urged Angelica toward the kitchen.

Father Anderson was quick to respond and began another salvo of holy water blessings.

From the kitchen, however, Angelica screamed once more. Sara had turned on the light overhead and the final window in the set of three was revealed. In this tainted glass depiction was the face of Caroline. On it was the unsettling scene of her hair flying wildly in all directions from her head. Her eyes were bright yellow against her nearly gray skin. Her mouth was grotesquely wide and pulled at the corners of her cheeks to resemble a distinct and wretched grin. The area inside her mouth was completely filled with bones, blood, intestines, muscles, and complete limbs. It was a jumble of bits and pieces that would urge the question of if all these pieces could be made whole again. A more fleshly and bloody version of Humpty Dumpty.

Angelica hid her face with her hands as Sara pulled her close again.

Father Anderson had heard her scream and had managed to quell the red Rose enough to turn and see the image on the kitchen window door. He then said with haste, "Quick, get her out of here!"

Sara nodded, looked down at Angelica and said, "Come on, Ange, we have to go outside. Don't look at the door." She then quickly, but gently, took Angelica by the hand and hurried her out onto the back porch.

Father Anderson then called out to the team, "Everyone, come to the living room! We have to get Rosanna to the hospital now! It's far too dangerous to stay here!"

The paranormal team quickly complied and met up. They decided it was simply best to leave their equipment there for the rest of the night.

As Father Anderson opened the backdoor he saw Sara with her arm around Angelica. The two were next to her car and it was then that he noticed something strange. The moonlight shone on them flawlessly. There wasn't a cloud in the sky in sight. Something was obviously missing from what would be considered normal weather.

He then called out to her, "Sara. I hope it isn't an inconvenience, but will you take in Angelica for the night? We're taking Rosanna to the hospital and I don't think she needs to see her like this."

She replied, "That's fine with me if it's okay with Angelica." She looked down on her warmly as Angelica nodded in response.

Father Anderson replied, "Thank you, Miss Goodwin. And one other thing: Do you notice something strange?"

He pointed to the sky. Sara and Angelica looked up and seemed a bit puzzled.

He continued. "Not a cloud in the sky... strange considering we just went through a few lightning strikes just a minute ago."

Sara then looked at the luminous full moon overhead and said, "You're right...."

The priest then replied, "I think I've seen more than enough evidence for my report."

At this, Sara nodded as Father Anderson went back toward the house to aid the team in helping Rosanna. Sara whisked away her young friend in her BMW without hesitation.

Sixty-seven

Sara's car came to a stop in the driveway that looped around to the back of her large home. As she turned off the headlights, she could hear her three wolfdogs barking happily within the fenced-off area in the expansive back-yard. After greeting them at the gate, she let them out and they followed her to the backdoor along with Angelica. Once inside, Angelica looked on quietly and morosely. Seeming to notice this, the canines each lightly whimpered and nuzzled her gently. One even licked her face which made a brief smile show. Sara looked down and returned the expression, but knew she didn't expect Ange to just snap out of it.

Noticing this, Sara placed the back of her hand on her cheek and said reassuringly, "You're okay now. You're safe here, I promise."

Angelica looked up briefly and was only able to pull one corner of her mouth into a polite smile. It soon faded. Sara then saw a single tear glide down her cheek. Angelica's bottom lip then extended into a pouty frown. Sara knew she was fighting every hint of tears. She kneeled down in front of her and looked her in the eyes. Quietly, "It's okay to cry... you have every right to...."

Angelica had picked up the habit of fighting the tears, mainly because of the attitude of her mother toward it. In some ways it was "tough love." Angelica didn't see it that way. Maybe deep inside she knew her mother meant well, but the suppression was never easy and seemed sloppy. Crying alone wouldn't "solve" anything, as her mother would say, but it never felt right keeping it in. Angelica then looked up into Sara's eyes. For the first time since they'd met, Sara's eyes looked tired. Her pale skin made the contrasting light hues of pink on her eyelids show even more.

It wasn't long before Angelica allowed the tears to flow freely. It had the imperative in the squall of emotions she was sailing through. Angelica then reached forward and threw her arms around her. The free flowing tears offered a bitter but necessary outlet. Sara gently cooed and caressed her head in the best way motherly love can. Although Rosanna did her best to offer comfort at times to her daughter, she wasn't as liberal with the affection. The warm embrace and light perfume that Sara wore comforted her.

As the tears began to recede from clouding her vision, she noticed three empty wine bottles on the kitchen table in the distance. She knew it was quite a bit of alcohol, but Sara didn't smell of it at all. She didn't pry. She had simply forgotten to throw them away from the night before.

Feeling that her friend was past the worst of the initial tears, Sara, with her arms still around Angelica, pulled back slightly and asked, "Do you want something to drink? I have juice, soda, and water in the fridge."

Angelica nodded.

Sara then went to the fridge nearby and took out a bottle of water. "Here you go. You hungry?"

Angelica shook her head.

"Okay. Now drink up. You have to replace all the water you just lost with those tears." She winked at Angelica as she opened the bottle. Sara then noticed the wine bottles on the kitchen table nearby and proceeded to throw them away.

"I can be so messy sometimes...." This statement seemed to be more of one out of embarrassment at the implied amount of alcohol consumed. The rest of the room, and house all over, was immaculately spotless.

Angelica then wiped away the remaining tear streaks from her cheeks as one of the dogs licked her on the cheek again. She briefly smiled again. Sara still had her back turned to her and was rubbing her own eyes.

Concerned, "Sara, are you okay?"

She took in a quick breath and turned around. "Yeah, I'm okay. I just have a headache." She sighed and smiled. "Actually, if you'll excuse me a second, I need to get a couple of aspirin from the bathroom. You need anything?"

Angelica shook her head.

"Okay, sweetie, I'll be right back."

She watched her mentor disappear into the hallway. She petted the one dog that stayed, the other two having followed Sara into the hallway. It began to whimper again before licking Angelica on the cheek.

She then called out, "You're house is really beautiful, Sara. I love it here."

Sara was looking at her reflection in the mirror above the sink in the bathroom. She replied, "Thank you! I love it here, too."

She could then see the same redness and fatigue that was setting in heavily in her eyes. Those same tired and troubled eyes then beheld the image of a middle-aged woman appear behind her from thin air. Most might be frightened at this, but Sara knew this spirit well: her mother. The apparition of Cornelia Goodwin was comforting. She would always be there to remind Sara that she was never truly alone.

Sara then whispered softly, "Hello, Mother...."

She then closed her eyes and heard her mother's words in her head. *"You've been through hell today, and so has your new friend. Go and rest, you'll both need it. And don't worry, you're safe here, as always."*

Sara smiled warmly and whispered, "Thanks, Mom... I love you."

"I love you, too...."

Her image faded from sight. She was buoyed enough to don a gentle smile before returning to her friend in the kitchen.

After a few minutes had passed, Sara was escorting Angelica up the main grand staircase to the second floor. The finely stained wood molding, wainscoting, and expensively adorned wallpaper, all paid tribute to Victorian splendor in every square inch of space. Angelica looked in amazement at all the details and was simply overcome by the history and energy radiating from every wall and every corner. It was almost dizzying trying to take in all of the art and craftsmanship that surrounded her. She paused at the top of the stairs and gawked. Sara then turned and smiled as her friend looked on.

Angelica then said, "This house is *so* pretty! You're lucky to get to live here!"

Pleased, "Well, thank you. I am quite blessed with this place." She looked down at her watch which read 12:30 A.M. "I think we've both earned a good night's sleep. What do you think?"

"Yeah, I guess so. I'm not sure I'll be able to sleep too well after what happened, though."

She placed her hand soothingly on the back of Angelica's head and said, "I know, sweetie. We can stay up and talk about anything you want. How about that?"

"Okay...." Seeing Sara smiling warmly at her, "You know, Sara, I think you would make a great mom...."

She blushed at this. "Well, thank you, Ange! How about this, though: You already have a mom, so how about you just think of me as your big sister. You can be the wonderful little sister I never had growing up. How does that sound?"

"That sounds like a deal to me!"

Sara then embraced her again.

When finished with the show of affection, Sara stepped back and said, "Okay, now I'll show you to your room. Don't worry, it's right next to mine and I'll be right there if you need me."

The impromptu sleepover was enough to, if only briefly, cause Angelica to forget about the events.

As Sara switched on the antique stained-glass lamp nearby, "All right, Miss Barrister, will this suffice for the evening?"

Briefly giggling from the playful tone (mainly due to the fact that Angelica found the room breathtaking and far more beautiful than any room she'd ever stayed in), she replied, "I love it!"

"Good. Oh, and if you want, I have some old pairs of sweats in my room. Probably more comfortable than jeans and a t-shirt to sleep in. Want me to go get them for you?"

Angelica nodded and smiled.

"Okay, just wait here and I'll go find them."

Sara stepped out into the hallway as Ange looked around the room in amazement. The rich smell of the varnished wood filled the air as she glided her hand along the arm of an antique chair next to the bed. The smell of the leather lining chair was something she could see herself never getting tired of. Even the metal chandelier above the bed (perhaps a bit more plain, comparatively speaking to the rest of the home's furnishings) looked as if it belonged there along with every other piece of furniture. It was all well planned and maintained since inception. It was clear that everyone who had lived there in the past and did so currently cherished the home. On one of the walls nearby hung a framed color picture that appeared to be rather modern. It depicted a couple and their child. Given the resemblance of the woman to the child, and obviously Sara, she figured that it was her parents.

As Sara returned to the room with the clothing, she noticed Angelica curiously gazing at the photo.

The latter said, "Hey, is that you, Sara?" She pointed to the child, who appeared to be about five or six years old.

She smiled. "Yep, that's me! That's my mom and dad there with me."

"You were so cute! Your mom is really pretty, too!"

Blushing again and grinning, "Well, thank you!"

"Do your parents live around here, too?"

The smile waned. "No, they both passed away a few years ago."

Angelica's smile had also vanished. "Oh... I'm so sorry, I didn't know.... "

She gently touched Angelica's shoulder before saying genuinely, "It's okay, sweetie. I didn't expect you to know that."

As Sara placed the folded sweats on the bed nearby Angelica's gaze turned to the hallway. Her eyes widened a bit and she tilted her head to one side. Angelica had just seen the image of the woman in the photograph suddenly appear in the hallway. One second she wasn't there, and now she was just there as if present all along. The apparition smiled at her warmly as Sara noticed Angelica's facial expression of befuddlement.

"Wait... is that... her?"

A bit surprised herself, "Oh, do you see her?"

Sara then turned and looked behind her. Sure enough, she saw the spirit of her mother standing there. As soon as she had appeared, however, she disappeared from view again.

"Yes, that's my mother. Most people can't see her, but I guess you and I aren't most people, are we?"

Whereas most children her age would be positively frightened, Angelica felt only warmth and compassion coming from the spirit. "No, I guess we're not."

"She passed away when I was just ten years old. She was in a car accident. A drunk driver swerved into her lane one night as she was coming back from visiting a friend out of town."

She expressed the sincere empathy within. "I'm sorry I brought it up. That's terrible...."

"It's okay, sweetie, I know you weren't trying to pry. At least she stayed to become of my spirit guides. Motherly love doesn't go away, I suppose."

"I guess not...."

Realizing she'd brought up a touchy subject with Angelica, Sara said, "Okay, how about you change into those sweats and I'll go and get ready for bed, too. After that we'll stay up and talk if you'd like."

Smiling, "Okay!"

She started toward the door but stopped just shy. Turning back to Ange, "By the way, do you know what sage smudging is?"

Angelica shook her head no.

"Okay, I have some in my room. After we change I'll teach you how to use it. Does that sound good?"

Angelica nodded.

A few minutes later Sara returned to the guest bedroom with a wine glass and bottle, along with a large brown and white feather and a small cylindrical bundle of dried out sage held together by string at various points. Angelica was sitting on the bed in her oversized loaner sweats with her legs crossed.

Sara placed the bottle and glass on the table next to the bed and asked, "You don't mind if I have a glass of wine, do you?"

Angelica shook her head but was a little confused about the politeness Sara displayed. She replied, "That's fine, it's your house." She briefly chuckled.

Smiling, "Okay, don't worry. I'm not going to get drunk or anything."

She then poured herself a full glass and placed the cork back into the bottle. She took a small sip from the glass and returned it to the nightstand. She then produced a lighter from her pocket. Sara then handed the bundle of dried sage to Angelica, who looked it over and smelled it. It was only slightly acrid.

Sara then said, "Okay, that is dried sage. People have been using this plant to ward off negative energy in sacred spaces, homes, you name it, for millennia. Burning it slowly and allowing the smoke to fill the room will dissipate a lot of negative energy, and sometimes even entities. Now, I already smudged the entire home just yesterday, but I'll show you how to use it yourself. When you go to mass, you see the priest carrying the censor at the beginning and end and waving it back and forth in the aisles, correct?"

"Yeah...."

"Okay, well, it's a lot like that. The priest is offering the incense to God and also blessing the sanctuary itself. With sage, you can help level out any unbalanced or negative energy that might be there. It's not a cure-all, per se, but it's a powerful tool nonetheless. Would you like for me to bless you with it now?"

"Sure, that's fine."

"Great. This should help to dissipate a good deal of the negative energy you and I no doubt experienced tonight and hopefully leave us feeling more at ease and peaceful."

She then flicked on the lighter and held the flame under one end of the bundle. She carefully blew onto the small embers forming a couple of times to enhance the ignition. A steady plume of gray smoke slowly rose from the embers before eventually disappearing into the ether. As the cylinder reached a steady and controlled burn she used the feather in her other hand to direct the purifying billows. The slightly acrid smell of the smoke smelled of cleansing not only in a chemical way, but also in the energy contained within and released by it. Angelica then instinctively closed her eyes as Sara waved the feather back and forth over the sage bundle and directed the energy and smoke toward her. All the while she softly chanted, "May the blessings of light and love be with you always. May the negative and unbalanced energy within and without be banished here and now."

Around a minute later, after intense concentration and effort, Sara felt the blessing was sufficient.

Angelica opened her eyes and said in a calm tone, "I do feel different now. I'm still tired but I don't feel as nervous as I did before."

Smiling, "Great! I'm glad I could help. Now, do you want to learn to do that for yourself?"

Tools and methods. Now Angelica was finally feeling a little more confident with something, anything, to try and drive back the darkness that seemed to be permeating her existence now. "Yeah, of course!"

"Great! Okay, first...."

Sara then went into details about how to focus her concentration and energy projection by furthering the lessons she had previously sent Angelica in an email. She also told her the words to her chant, or prayer, until she learned it by heart.

Angelica would go to sleep that night and find at least a few hours of rest in this sanctuary from the darkness.

Sixty-eight

2:45 A.M.

Nearly soundless she glided down the hall. Her eyes had adjusted to the darkness in her room, but she still was unfamiliar with her surroundings. Only a small antique lamp on an equally dated table in the hallway showed the way to Sara's door.

At the door, she hesitated... her dad didn't mind being woken up for things that go bump in the night, but her mother was a different story altogether. Now she was hoping that waking another adult in the night would not be gender-specific.

Still, she hesitated....

Finally, *knock, knock, knock.*

Inside her bedroom, Sara had been battling to try and sleep herself, but she wasn't winning. She was staring off into the dark void that surrounded their beds every night. The knock was faint, but she heard it.

She called out, "Is that you, Ange?"

"Yeah, it's me. I'm sorry to bother you, but can we talk?"

Slightly amused at the maturity in her voice, Sara replied with a soft smile, "Sure thing. Come in."

Angelica turned the beautifully carved glass handle on the door. As she stepped inside Sara was turning on the lamp next to her bed. She also looked down and noticed a nightlight nearby plugged in and shining away. Maybe it was okay be afraid of the dark even when you became an adult.

Sara, in her flannel pajamas, sat up and patted her hand on the edge of her bed. "What's the matter? You having trouble sleeping?"

Angelica noticed the empty wine bottle on the floor but only out of the corner of her eye. Sara didn't seem to notice. "Yeah.... When I close my eyes I just keep seeing the windows, the writing... but worse, I keep seeing Mom. She was really trying to hurt me and I didn't even do anything to her!"

Quite a bit to have dumped on you after waking up from troubled sleep, but Sara decided to try and help. She thought for a moment, then said, "Sweetie, I know it's hard to take in. This has really escalated in the past few days. But remember: Father Anderson and I are doing everything we can to help you. It may not seem like we're making a difference now, but we have to do our due diligence to deliver the best remedy."

Only partially comforted, "But what's wrong with Mom? Is Caroline making her do that stuff?"

Sara felt obliged to use a word she hated to bring out, but it seemed the only way to express her feelings on the matter. "From what you've told me and what I've seen myself, I think it's more than Caroline. She's only part of it. There's something older and more powerful there on your property. It may require, and I hate to use the word because of the stigma attached to it, a Minor Rite of Exorcism on your property."

Her eyes widened. "So *you* believe she's possessed by the devil?"

"That's not entirely up to me to say. I can only offer my side of the story and Father Anderson and the rest of the team will have to rely on The Church to make that decision. But as far as the Minor Rite goes, that's focused on your property, not just your mother. I don't think she's completely possessed, no."

Angelica's feeling of despair was slowly phasing to anger. Even if it wasn't just Caroline, she was an integral part of it. The fire in her eyes surprised Sara as she said with clinched fists and gritting teeth, "I *hate* Caroline! I hate her guts! She's ruining our family and I hate her!" The splotches of the burst blood vessels in her eyes made the appearance of her signature scowl look almost otherworldly.

Sara placed her hands on Angelica's shoulders. "Sweetie, calm down. She *wants* you to be upset! She wants you confused and not thinking clearly—

that's how she gets inside you! Your mother gave into her rage tonight and challenged the spirit—never do that! You'll only be hurt and defenseless in the end!"

Sara's pleading managed to get through and caused even Angelica to be surprised at how quickly she flew into a rage. She let her hands go limp. They trembled. She looked around in confusion. It seemed as if a certain part of her mind, a certain behavioral filter, was bypassed and all anger flowed naturally and freely. This wasn't her... at least she hoped it wasn't. But if it wasn't her, who, or what, was it?

Her eyes now lucidly looked into Sara's. She was hearing her more clearly again. "That's it, Ange, deep breaths. Control your breathing, control your body and mind."

A few calming breaths later, "I don't know why I got so mad. I mean, I know I should be mad but it was so strong."

Sara caressed Angelica's cheek in a soothing gesture. "I think that place is having an effect on you. It's having an effect on all of us."

She could see the troubled look on her face. "Are you okay, Sara? Is it hurting you, too?"

Realizing her perceptive friend was reading her emotions well, "I'll be okay. When you encounter things this negative, they always leave scars."

Angelica could tell she had touched on something deeper inside of Sara. Unspoken words of the damage she had been taking to her mind and spirit were shared. She was suddenly overcome by a sense of gratitude, knowing that Sara was enduring pain for her and her family without so much a word of complaint.

Angelica then asked curiously, "Do the scars stay with you forever?"

Wishing she could deliver better news, "In some ways, yes. That doesn't mean you can't heal, it just means you won't forget about them anytime soon. Does that make sense?"

Angelica looked down at the floor for a moment before answering, "Yeah, it makes sense."

She kept her eyes down and hesitated to speak further.

Sara noticed and said, "I can tell you're holding something back. What is it, sweetie? You can ask me anything."

She looked side to side before looking up at Sara. "Is that why people drink alcohol? I mean, does it make the pain go away?"

At this point Sara knew her friend was watching her sharply at all times. She hesitated. "Well... um, that's a tricky subject."

Feeling she'd overstepped polite boundaries, "I'm sorry, Sara. I didn't mean to say... I mean, I don't think you're a bad person or anything for it. Mom drinks wine, sometimes Dad has a beer, but... I guess I just don't get it. I've smelled it before and it stinks." She nervously looked up and around. She continued. "You're not mad at me, are you?"

A small smile crept onto Sara's face. She placed her hand on the back of Angelica's head and caused her to raise it. "I'm not mad. Like I said, you can ask me anything. As far as the wine goes... I sometimes drink it when I'm having dinner, but I also go a little overboard and drink it in excess." She searched for the right words before continuing. "It's only a very temporary escape from the feelings that *sensitives* like you and I experience on a regular basis. But know this: It's very easy to let it get out of control. Many people become addicted to it and it takes over their life."

"What's *addicted* mean?"

"It's something people can experience when they develop a seemingly unquenchable need for something. People who battle addiction often end up hurting themselves and others around them. Let's see, how do I put it? Imagine it's a hot summer day and you've been outside running and playing for hours. You're going to be thirsty, right?"

Angelica nodded.

Sara continued, "Imagine if you kept being thirsty and no matter how much water you drank you kept wanting more and more. Addiction is like that, in that you'd never be able to completely quench that thirst, twenty-four seven."

"You're not addicted, are you?"

"To alcohol? No. Honestly if you ever have a hangover from drinking too much you may quit after the first time. But remember: moderation. Of course, until you are twenty-one, no wine at all. Are we clear?"

"Yeah, I don't think I'd like it just from the smell alone." A thought suddenly crossed her mind. "Wait, what about communion wine?"

Reassuringly, "Wine at communion is perfectly fine. It's only a small amount and obviously very important to the Catholic faith."

Quickly following up, "What's the word you used to describe us? Sensitive?"

"Yes, people use different words to describe our 'talents' or 'gifts.' Psychic, empaths, sensitives, amongst other things. There are more specific definitions with those words, but the average person doesn't really know the difference. Either way, it's all a matter of time before we come to understand our gifts. You will too someday."

Angelica paused and stared at her folded hands in her lap. She then broke the silence. "Do you know anyone else in Miller's Run that's psychic? I mean, are you and I rare?"

She thought for a moment before replying, "You know, I think you and I may be the only ones in this town. I mean, your father passed your gifts to you, but I think he decided long ago to close himself off as best he could."

"Does it get any easier? I mean, dealing with the dreams and all."

"The more you practice and the stronger you get, the things we go through won't be as bad as they are now. It's like any skill, really. Similar to, let's say, math. You're learning the basics now, but by the time you graduate high school, these lessons you're learning now will be automatic and easy. But you have to do your part and study. At least you're fortunate enough to have me there to teach as much as I know. Feeling all alone in the world when you're born with abilities can be demoralizing and make you prone to despair." A small silence ensued, but Sara spoke up. "Just remember that sensitives like us can often pick up the emotions around us. Sometimes from living people and sometimes from the dead. Even the residual energy in a place can change the way you feel and think. You'll get better as you go, but always try and remember that just because an emotion suddenly overtakes you does not mean that it's yours. You may just be channeling the energy of something else. You'll know the difference more clearly one day, I promise."

"I really appreciate you helping me, Sara. Thank you."

Sara gently kissed her on top of her head before looking down at the clock on her nightstand. "Oh, wow, it's really late. We should both be asleep by now. Tell you what: When I was a kid and couldn't sleep my mom gave me Benadryl. It's not the best-tasting stuff, but you need your sleep. Want to give that a try?"

"Sure. Do you have any orange juice to take the taste away after?"

"I actually do have some in the fridge. How about you go ahead and get into bed and I'll bring those right up. And if you're already tucked in when I get back I'll tell you a story."

Angelica was quick to reply and get under the covers. Soon enough, Sara was at the guest bedroom door with a glass of orange juice and a bottle of Benadryl. Angelica took down the small dose of syrup with a grimace, but it soon disappeared with a few glugs from the juice glass.

Angelica pulled the covers up to her chin and listened as Sara spoke. "Okay, I'm going to tell you about the first spirit that I saw. I was just five years old and had only been going to St. Mary's for about a month. One day when we were out at recess I saw a nun walking around that I didn't recognize. I didn't think anything of it at first because I only knew a handful of people there. The reason I knew she was a spirit was because I saw her walk through some of the thick hedges without disturbing them. She then walked through the short brick wall that lines the sidewalk heading to the gymnasium. You know which area I'm talking about, right?"

Angelica nodded.

Sara continued. "Well, I think she could tell that I was the only person who saw her because she approached me the next day when I was bending down to tie my shoe. One second she wasn't there and the next she was three feet in front of me. She had a very kind face and the thing that stood out the most about her were her eyes. They were very light blue, nearly gray. So much kindness and compassion in her eyes. I looked up at her and she smiled. She placed her hand on top of my head. I felt the pressure and weight of her hand, but only three seconds later she disappeared."

"Were you scared?"

"No, not all. I knew something was different about her, but I never felt any fear. In fact, for the rest of my time at the school I would see her here and there in many different places. It was as if she would pop in every now and then to check on me.

"Sadly, after I graduated, I never saw her again. Of course, I only saw her at the school, so that may be where she prefers to stay."

Angelica yawned deeply. "Do you think she's still there?"

"I'm not sure. I haven't any reason to go back to the school, so I can't say. I don't see why she wouldn't be."

Angelica picked up on the inflections used in her sentence. "It sounds like you didn't like it there."

She chuckled a moment, then said, "Well, I had my problems there, but that's a different discussion altogether."

"Did you get bad grades?"

"Oh, nothing like that. I was a straight-A student. But like I said, my problems there can wait for another night."

Even though she was tired, a small portion of Angelica wanted to keep going. She was learning so much about her mentor and was able to speak freely. Reluctantly, she knew she was at the portion of the evening where bedtime trumped everything else.

"Would you like for me to leave this lamp on?"

Angelica nodded.

"Okay then. And I'll call first thing in the morning to see how your mom is doing. Let me know if you need anything else."

Angelica yielded to another yawn before replying, "I will. Thank you, Sara."

"Sleep tight!"

The door nearly closed, Angelica quickly called out, "Sara, wait. Just one more question."

She peeked her head back in. "Sure."

Her eyes heavy with sleep, "Who's Morrigan?"

Her face hiding the momentary surprise, she replied, "Morrigan?"

"Yeah, Morrigan. You said that name earlier today when we were outside at the car."

She chuckled. "You're right, I did. Tell you what: When things settle down I'll tell you. Deal?"

She sighed, but her need to sleep was winning against her curiosity. "Okay." She looked down briefly before returning eye contact. "What if things don't settle down?"

Looking at her confidently, "They will, sweetie, I promise."

They said their "goodnights" and were finally able to rest in the coming hours.

Sixty-nine

Angelica felt the subtle urge to open her eyes and complied. She couldn't tell what time it was but guessed it couldn't have been long after she fell asleep because the windows were still dark through the delicate curtains.

She felt the need to rub her eyes and did so. Suddenly, to her right side, she saw a human figure appear. She may have been startled otherwise by the being, but she quickly surmised it to be Sara's mother. Cornelia Goodwin's gently smiling face looked down at Angelica and communicated without moving her lips. "Don't be alarmed, Angelica. We just wanted to warn you about the things that want to destroy you and your family."

Certainly this message seemed to carry immediate worry given the situation, but she calmly thought the words, "What do you mean? Caroline?"

Suddenly a male voice came from the other side of the bed. "Sara is correct. She knows that there is much more going on here than even she's letting on."

Angelica recoiled slightly at the man, dressed in clearly nineteenth-century attire, who seemed to materialize out of nowhere. The chain of pocket watch gleamed brightly in the room as it disappeared into his silk vest. Angelica's eyes widened as Sara's mother's spirit said reassuringly, "Don't be frightened, dear. That's just my great-grandfather, Cornelius. And yes, he's my namesake."

Angelica hadn't sensed any negativity from him. She was only startled by his sudden appearance. His face was gaunt, but kind, and topped with a receding hairline that bore thinning white hair. He smiled and said, "I didn't mean to startle you, Angelica. I must insist, however, that you follow us to the window over there. There's something of grave importance that we must show you."

Angelica paused a moment and looked back toward Cornelia. The image of Sara's mother smiled and said, "You need to see this. It won't be easy, but life rarely is. Come to the window."

Cornelia smiled and motioned with her hand toward the window of the guest bedroom. As Angelica climbed off the bed and started approaching, she could see a faint glow coming from the exterior. They approached the paned glass and each of the spirits flanking her pulled back on their respective curtains. Looking below she could only see, at first anyway, a series of faint lights scrambling back and forth within the border of what appeared to be the stone fence next to the road. Slowly, however, the images came into focus. What looked like dozens of glowing canines, more akin to wolves in shape and size, were pacing back and forth along the barrier. The fence itself seemed to emit a golden glowing light that stretched toward the heavens. Each animal was just as opaque as any embodied creature she'd seen in her physical form.

What troubled her, however, was the stark blackness that lay on the other side of the barrier surrounding the property. She could easily see a human figure walking up and down the length of the road. The spirit quickly locked eyes with Angelica. Sure enough, it was the glowing yellow orbs and antiquated clothing that gave her identity away. It was Caroline. And from the looks of it, her face expressed the truest sense of anger and frustration.

Cornelius' voice then came through. "You see there, that woman is completely corrupted. She only wishes to bring harm upon you and Sara."

Caroline stopped pacing and stood squarely with her hands hanging at her side. She stared contemptuously at Angelica as Sara's mother spoke. "She can't cross onto this property, but you can't stay here forever. You will need all the help you can get to survive out there."

Angelica then said, "But I don't want to see Sara get hurt."

Cornelia responded, "Neither do I, sweetie, but she's tougher than you may think. She's strong and knows what she's doing."

Angelica felt a tinge of comfort cross her mind at these words, but that feeling was soon dashed as Caroline found a direct line to Angelica's ears.

"You can't hide in that house forever, you little cunt!" The glowing golden wolves guarding the premises growled and snarled as the oyster-eared spirit spoke again. "Auntie Caroline will be waiting for you. And remember, you will have to make the decision...."

Caroline didn't leave the road's edge and instead simply continued to stare daggers at Angelica. The latter turned away and looked at Cornelia again. "Don't listen to her. She will mix truth with lies. She can't be trusted!"

Whatever sort of barrier had been erected around the property was holding Caroline back, but Angelica knew that the spirits of Sara's family were correct. She would have to return home at some point and there wasn't a protective aura around that place, not by a longshot.

Cornelius, in a gentle voice, said, "It's time to wake up, Angelica. Don't worry, Sara will keep you safe as best she can."

Sara's mother added, "And we'll help you too in any way that we can."

Angelica's attention was then drawn back to the window. She could see Caroline raising her arms straight over her head. She then gestured with both limbs in a manner that looked as if she were throwing something at the wall. Suddenly, from behind Caroline, a wall of black liquid welled up like breakers on a beach. The viscous fluid flowed around Caroline and crashed onto the wall. Despite the force of the muck it only caused flashes and flickering gold light to appear the length of the wall. The barrier held.

Seeing the lack of damage inflicted, Caroline simply dissipated into the liquid not to be seen again.

Seventy

Knock, knock.

Sara only partially cracked the door as she said, "Good morning, Angelica. Are you awake yet?"

"Yeah, come in." The morning sun beaming in between the curtains from outside caused her to squint and rub her eyes.

Sara was already dressed for the day and smiled as she entered the room. "I let you sleep in a little. Do you feel any better?"

"I feel a little better. I had a weird dream last night."

"Oh, do you want to talk about it?"

"Sure. I was in this room and your mother and her great-grandfather, Cornelius, had a message for me...."

Angelica relayed the dream's details to Sara.

As she finished, the latter said, "I'm glad that you got a chance to speak with them. I have a painting of him in my library on this floor, if you'd like to see it."

Sara led her young friend to the painting and sure enough, it was the same man from her dream.

Moments later, after the brief conversation about the fact that Sara had been visited by this same relative over the years, she said, "Now, I just got off the phone with your dad a few minutes ago and he said that your mother is doing fine. They want to see you. I told them I'd take you home to change clothes and then head directly over to the hospital. Does that sound good?"

There was a part of Angelica that wanted to just spend the day with Sara and her alone. But even though she hated Caroline, she was right: She couldn't stay there forever. She agreed to in a noticeably neutral tone.

Sensing this, "I understand if you're hesitant, but your dad said there would be a surprise waiting for you there."

She cocked her head to the side in confusion. It wasn't her birthday or Christmas, so what was the occasion? It didn't really matter, the kid side of her was instantly giddy with anticipation. "What is it!?"

"Don't be silly, I can't tell you that!" Sara laughed.

Angelica smiled. "Not even a hint?"

"No, not even a hint. But if you eat breakfast and hurry when you get to your house you'll find out sooner!"

It wasn't long before Angelica finished the plate of scrambled eggs and the two of them were off to Holly Bush Road to get a change of clothes.

The black BMW turned onto the driveway as the yellowish brown decay and blight still clung tightly to the property. A gentle summer breeze was blowing and made the grass and plant remains look like the scant hairs of the scalp of an elder whip exhaustedly back and forth. No words were shared, however, as both looked at the devastation with the still lingering sense of disbelief.

Sara pulled the car to a stop in the turnaround and put the gear shifter in park. The two exited the car but stopped in their tracks as they noticed something very different and wrong with the house. Sara placed her hand on Angelica's shoulder as they looked on the backside of the house. The three windows that were converted into hellish stained glass from the night before were no longer there. They weren't broken and they hadn't been reverted back to their original state. There was simply an opening at the three portholes.

Seeing this, Sara went back to her car and fished out a weapon she'd always carried on the floorboard of the driver's seat. It was easily concealed and easy to reach. She took the extendable baton in her hand and with a flick of her wrist extended it all the way out. With her eyes glued to the side of the house she fumbled with her hand in her purse and found her cellphone.

Sara then said, "Angelica, get back in the car while I call 911."

She followed the instructions but paused before getting in. "Did someone break in?"

Sara had already pressed the numbers and was waiting on the dispatcher to pick up. "I don't know, sweetie, but I don't want you getting hurt. Just wait...."

Angelica shut the door.

A calm voice came over the phone. "911, what is your emergency?"

"Yes, this is Sara Goodwin. I'm over at the Barrister residence on Holly Bush Road and I think someone may have broken into the house."

"Are you currently in the house?"

"No, I just pulled in and three windows are missing...."

Sara relayed the story and the dispatcher assured her that the police were on their way.

With the baton still firmly in her hand, she gave a forced smile to Angelica, who was at least mildly comforted by it. She then quickly looked down at her phone and called someone else.

A familiar voice answered. "Hey, this is Ed."

Sara replied somewhat exasperatedly, "Mr. Barrister, it's Sara. Angelica and I are over at your home and it looks like someone may have broken in. Three windows are missing."

Confused, "Missing? Broken?"

"No, I mean missing entirely. The three windows from last night, *those* three, are not there now. No glass, nothing."

"Are you two okay?"

"Yeah, we're fine. Ange is in the car and I'm getting ready to get in myself. The police are on their way."

"Okay, you two just stay safe and I'll be there as fast as I can."

Seventy-one

It wasn't long before the sheriff had pulled into the driveway to see Sara and Angelica locked inside the BMW with the engine running. He quickly drew his service pistol and performed a thorough search of the house and immediate premises. He found nothing out of the ordinary at first, until he saw the blood stains from Rosanna's injuries from the previous night. Of course, he didn't know whose blood it was or why it was there. When Edward pulled onto the driveway, the sheriff had already deemed the clear of criminals, but highly suspicious. All three were standing near the sheriff's car when Angelica noticed a second face in the passenger's seat. Concern was across his face as he saw the fetid plants all over the ground. As soon as he looked up and saw Angelica, however, the corners of his mouth pushed up the outer edge of his mostly white, but still peppery mustache. He waved.

Even before the Subaru had come to a stop, Angelica was running to the passenger door. The older man became exited and was quick to bend down and snatch up the eight-year-old. Her smile was the largest she'd experienced in weeks.

"Grandpa Leone!"

He kissed her on the cheek. "How's my favorite *nipotina*?"

She giggled. "I'm your only granddaughter!"

"That's true, but you're still my favorite!"

Sara approached them with a smile. "That's the surprise I was telling you about, Ange!"

The sheriff approached Edward and pulled him aside. "Mr. Barrister, I'd like to ask you a few questions inside. It will just take a second."

The three others at the car looked at him concerned, but responded diligently, "Sure thing." Looking back, "Just wait here, guys."

Once they were within sight of the blood on the living room floor, Beasley asked, "Do you happen to know whose blood this is, Mr. Barrister?"

He sighed, "Yeah, that's my wife's blood. Things took a turn for the worse last night during the paranormal investigation." Edward looked over his shoulder to make sure no one was in earshot, then said in a lowered tone, "This will sound crazy, but Father Anderson believes there is a genuine case of demonic possession here. She started bleeding last night out of nowhere. The doctors and nurses at the hospital were all stumped when we told them what happened."

His right eyebrow alone firmly raised with unabashed suspicion. "Demonic possession? Mr. Barrister, you and your family are free to practice any religion you want, but I'm sure you know that my job is facts-based."

Partially putting both hands up to his chest in an unconscious move of self-defense, "I know, it sounds crazy. There were several witnesses here last night and it was all recorded on film." Pointing a few feet away, "There, that camera recorded everything."

The sheriff walked over to the camcorder and paused as he put his hand on it. "Okay, Mr. Barrister, you understand that I'll have to take this as evidence. It's not I like I can just write it off as 'demonic possession' in my report and be done with it."

"I understand completely. That's the paranormal team's camera and I'm sure they're fine with turning it over."

Looking back toward Edward, "I'll make a note of your cooperation in my report." His gaze suddenly turned to the doorway. Seeing the spectators outside now clumping up in the kitchen, "No one come into the living room; it's a crime scene. I'm going to have to take samples of this blood to make sure this all checks out."

Sara spoke up. "Sheriff, I saw what happened last night and so did Angelica."

"Well, Miss Goodwin, I'll have to get a statement from you and Mr. Barrister."

She replied, "That's fine."

The sheriff continued. "I appreciate that. Now, Mr. Barrister, I need you to go and check to see if anything was stolen. It looks like some vandals were here, broke your windows, and spray-painted some graffiti on the walls."

Sara was going to answer, but Edward started, "Those words were written on the walls while we were still here."

Confused, "Wait, *you* wrote that stuff on your walls?"

"No, the writing just appeared there after the power went out."

Sara added, "We think it was the...," she searched for the right word, "*entities*, that are causing the problems. They did this."

His tone still dry, "So Roberta and Ron really have you guys believing this hook, line, and sinker."

Clearly offended, Sara replied sharply, "Sheriff, you know we have nothing to gain by doing this! We don't get paid for it! We're trying to help them!"

Edward motioned in a calming manner at Sara before saying in a calm tone, "Please, just take a look at the evidence on the cameras. They were set up in nearly every room in the house and recorded everything."

Beasley replied, "Hmm, it'd better be air tight to back up the story you all are telling."

Angelica lashed, "You weren't here! We all saw it! My dad isn't lying!"

The sheriff bit his tongue as he thought, *If I had a sassy kid like that I'd give her the back of my hand!*

Before he could reply, however, Edward said, "Angelica! You know you shouldn't speak to adults that way! Apologize to the sheriff!"

She could mouth the words, but couldn't suppress her glare. "I'm sorry."

The lukewarm apology was the best he was going to get. He decided to proceed with his duties. "Well, Mr. Barrister, I'm going to have to take some photos of the scene here. I'll need you to check to see if anything is stolen, and I'm going to need everyone else to wait outside. One question, though: What language is that on the walls? Spanish?"

Sara replied, "It's Latin. Father Anderson can confirm that."

The sheriff replied, "Any idea what it says?"

Sara answered, "You'll have to ask him. I don't speak Latin."

Beasley sighed. "Fair enough. Now, if you all wouldn't mind heading outside, I'll get started in here."

Nearly an hour later, the sheriff finally finished and approached the four standing in the turnaround.

Beasley said, "Okay, everyone, I've finished gathering the evidence I need. Just tell Roberta that I have her cameras and I'll give them back as soon as I review the footage."

Edward then asked, "What do you think happened to the windows?"

He sighed and shook his head. "That is a head-scratcher, Mr. Barrister. You say nothing of value was stolen, so it makes no sense to me why someone would steal three windows."

Sara spoke up. "It doesn't make any sense at all. Only a handful of us even knew we were coming up here."

Edward added, "I don't think I mentioned this before, but shortly before we all left, lightning struck near the house. The windows had weird images on them after that."

The sheriff asked, "Images? What kind of images?"

Sara replied, "Disturbing images. They should be on the recordings."

Beasley then asked, "And lightning did it? I don't recall hearing a storm yesterday. It was a clear night, all night, if I remember correctly."

Edward answered, "Exactly! We noticed the same thing too when we left."

Sara repeated a previous expression. "It's all on the cameras, I'm sure."

The sheriff replied, "All right then. I'll go and review the footage. You folks have a good day now."

The four were deeply dissatisfied with the encounter as the sheriff's car slowly rolled down the gravel scar and onto road leading back to town.

Seventy-two

Meanwhile, outside, Sara had a sensation come over her. Something was trying to pull her toward the woods on the Barrister property.

She had walked quickly down the path and soon found herself staring at the brown and yellow hues that plagued the forest now. The sensation seemed to wane, however, when she stopped. *What are you trying to tell me?* she thought to herself. She strained to see as far into the forest as possible. She knelt down and touched the ground… anything to try and establish a connection with the intangible force pulling on her.

After looking around for nearly a minute without a whisper, she suddenly felt very lightheaded. All at once, however, she saw an image briefly flash in her mind. It was a scene at night and one that took place near there area she was at, but a few decades in the past. She could barely make out details in the image, but what she managed to see was a young boy being dragged by his arm. The person pulling him seemed to be nearly ripping it out of the socket. The taller person was dressed in all black. She assumed it to be some sort of ritual clothing. The boy, whom she recognized as Timothy Harris, was briefly looking back at her in the still frame set in her mind.

She then heard a voice, Timothy's, speak quietly in her ear. *"I'm sorry for making you light-headed. I had to use your energy to show you that."*

Just as suddenly as the drive to walk toward the bridge had come over her, it was gone. Sara then felt in control of her faculties once more and shook her head from side to side. She spoke audibly to herself, "What were you trying to tell me? You were taken there by force, weren't you? Someone took advantage of your illness and brought you here. Why, though? Why would they bring you here?"

Sara nearly jumped out of her footwear as Angelica said from behind, "Who are you talking to?"

After hearing her voice it only took a few moments to catch her breath. With her heart still pattering away from fresh adrenaline, "Ange! Whoa, you scared me!"

"I'm sorry. I didn't mean to."

"That's okay, sweetie, I was just lost in thought there for a moment."

Tilting her head to the side she said, "Who were you talking to? I didn't see anyone around you."

"I was just talking to myself. I do that from time to time. I'm just trying to understand something that popped in my mind."

She knew Sara was withholding information, but didn't want to pester her. She knew her mentor would tell her the right things at the right time.

"Well, Dad and Grandpa are going to board up the window frames. Do you think you could take me to see my mom at the hospital? Dad said she wanted to see me."

"Yeah, I'll take you. Let's get going."

Seventy-three

Also at this time, Roberta was seated and waiting in the living room in her house. She was waiting alone for Ron to swing by and pick her up so they could go back and get there equipment to review the evidence. She held in her hand an old tintype photograph. It was rectangular in shape and upon it showed the image of an older woman dressed in 1800s clothing in line with the modest pioneer clothes at the time. Her thumb moved up and down the border of the tintype as she stared silently at it. The older woman's gaze glared back, seemingly reaching through the camera and time to harshly reproach anyone that dared stare too long. She was standing in front of a simple wooden house with her hands clasped in front of her. Her body language and eyes made it clear that she really didn't want to be photographed.

Roberta muttered quietly, "The only picture of you... so much I'll never know about you..."

She turned the tintype over. It read only: "Aunt Caroline. 1868."

The silence was suddenly broken by a horn honking outside in the driveway. Ron was there and it was time to go. She stood up and headed for the door while putting the tintype in a pocket of her cargo pants.

Father Anderson sat alone in his office looking over the Latin phrases he'd written down from the investigation. He read them to himself: '"*Potest, quod non corrumpetur. Necesse est quae possit expleri.*' We cannot be destroyed. We can only be satiated. '*Abyssus Sumus.*' We are the abyss. '*Puella decernet.*'

The girl will decide. Decide what?" He couldn't help but assume (or maybe at best, hope) that they were bluffing about their power. He was grounded and pious enough, however, to know it was best to overestimate their threat.

Something else was highlighted in his notes: "Things constantly happening in groups of three." He knew the tapping sounds came in groups of three thanks to Rosanna's attention to detail in her story. Angelica also remarked that three birds were found dead in the small tree. Three goats were slaughtered.... Whatever was perpetrating this "show" was really emphasizing the number again and again. It seemed to support the obvious: evil entities mocking the Holy Trinity by doing this. Only one thought, perhaps even smaller, a flicker of a thought made him uneasy: *Maybe they want me to believe it's that straightforward....*

Seventy-four

Sheriff Beasley had left the house on Holly Bush Road and back to his small office in town. As he opened the door to head into the building, his receptionist Blaire was seated at her desk and talking to one of the worrisome people out along the fringes of the rural community. Her hair was tied back in a modest bun that did little to hide her pudgy face. The dull polo shirt that bore the patch with her name and "Sheriff's Department" didn't help either. Beasley always thought of her as a reliable old warhorse and never asked why she never married.

As Sheriff Beasley removed his hand from the closing door, she said her goodbye to the person on the phone and hung up. Seeing her facial expression, he asked with a smirk, "Was that old Ms. Thompkins again?"

She sighed and smiled. "Yep, you guessed it. Take a stab at what the problem is now."

Her regular calls had obviously spawned this guessing game. "Let's see... teenagers drag racing in front of her house?"

"Not this time, no. Now it's ghosts! She swears she's seen her old grandpa rise from the ground, look in the side window, and then go back to rest six feet under. Imagine that!"

He shook his head, chuckling. "Well, that sounds like some kinda show to me! If she calls back, let me know and I might stop by there."

Sarcastically, "Yeah, I'll come running with every dementia moment she has." Beasley was walking toward his office and laughing when Blaire asked, "What was going on at," she changed her tone to faux-spooky, "*Holly Bush Road?*"

He stopped with his hand on his office's doorknob. "That's actually a weird one, too. I'll tell you about it after I make a quick phone call."

Blaire tittered as she said, "All right, I look forward to it!"

Her laughter stopped prematurely, however, as Beasley shut his door and closed all of the blinds. Even in the most chaotic of times (which weren't often in Miller's Run, for the most part), he always left his door open with only a handful of exceptions. She never questioned, however, what went on behind those closed doors and Beasley appreciated it.

Inside he quietly dialed a number on his phone. He didn't want to have to dial that number once more, but it was another "situation" as he put it.

The voice on the other end picked up. "Hello, St. Mary's. How can I help you?"

He leaned back in his chair and put his feet up on his desk. He then replied, "I'm sorry to bother you ladies but could I speak to Sister Francis?"

The pleasant voice of the younger woman then said, "Who, may I ask, is calling?"

"This is Sheriff Beasley over in Miller's Run."

The voice was familiar now. "Oh, hi, Sheriff Beasley, I didn't know it was you."

"Sister Gillian, right?"

"Yes, it is. How are you?" She had only been a teacher at the school for about half a year now, but was already familiar with the sheriff's voice. It didn't strike her as odd that he called so much in such a short period of time.

"I'm fine, thanks. But please, I really need to speak to Sister Francis."

"Oh, sure, no problem! I'll go get her now."

"I appreciate that, thank you." In the silence of his wait he couldn't help but think of what a lovely voice she had. Then again, hold on, she was a nun....

The nasally voice on the other end, that always managed to sound annoyed at every turn answered, "Hello, Sheriff Beasley. What is it, I'm very busy today!"

As apologetically as he could muster, "I hate to bother you, Sister Francis, but I've run into another *situation* at the old farmhouse."

She knew he was just stringing her along. "Well, what situation now?"

"Strangest thing happened there last night. I got called out there just now for some sort of vandalism. Three missing windows and graffiti on the walls. Do you have any thoughts on what might have happened?"

Her patience had run out before picking up the phone, but the aggravated tone in her voice was obvious. "With all due respect, Sheriff, you're wasting my time! I've got a whole school-full of snotty kids to get ready for and they'll be coming back in a few days! I would suggest you call Home Depot if you're at a loss on the windows!"

Not surprised at her tone, being perfectly normal for her temperament, he replied coolly, "Sister Francis, the windows were taken right out of the frames. The graffiti on the wall was written in Latin. Sounds a little strange for the average vandalism case, wouldn't you say?"

"Well, I don't know, isn't that your job!?" She paused for a moment and took her anger down from eleven to a healthier nine-out-of-ten. "Look... if you must, tell me what was written on the walls and I'll translate it for you. But make it fast, I have things to do!"

"Heh, I appreciate your help, Sister Francis. I can always count on you." He then picked up one of the camera cases he'd brought with him from the house and placed it on his desk. "You know what, Sister Francis...," popping each latch in turn, "I think there might be some footage on these cameras that you'd be keen on seeing. I don't reckon I could convince you to spare an hour or so this afternoon to help me review this evidence, could I?"

Understanding his obvious undertone, she sighed. "Very well, Sheriff. Stop by my office at around 5 P.M."

"I do appreciate your help, Sister Francis. I look forward to seeing your smiling face!"

Curtly, "Oh, please...." He wasn't surprised at her abrupt cessation of the call.

Seventy-five

Sara was holding Angelica's hand as they approached the front doors of the hospital. This was the quaint hospital that the small population of Miller's Run called their own. They could patch you up for the more mundane ailments, but for anything more than a heart attack or standard trauma, they would be shipped to the higher category hospital in the neighboring city of Cedar Hill. This was, of course, the same city in which Angelica went to school.

The front of the building was fashioned from plain white bricks and symmetrical, matching the layout of the rest of the hospital. All but a few of the windows had their curtains drawn despite the sunny day. They weren't treating many patients at that time and usually didn't. Despite being relatively small the capacity of the facility was never pushed beyond its limit.

Over the automatic sliding glass doors of the entrance was the only thing remotely attractive about the otherwise utilitarian architecture. A large sign, which was only recently bought no more than five years ago, displayed the name "Miller's Run Memorial Hospital" and an embossed old-style water mill with water cascading over the top. The metallic sheen of the golden colored signage glistened dully in the summer sun.

Not much was said as they approached the vestibule and walked into the lobby. A friendly older woman behind a receptionist's desk smiled and waved at them.

They waved back and walked down the hallway toward the visitors' elevators. Knowing the room number, Sara pressed the up arrow next to the elevator. Angelica was obviously not happy about being here again after a relatively short period of time. But there was also something else on her mind that made the situation doubly worse: she didn't want to see her mother right now. She could only seem to recall images of her from the night before, covered in blood and snarling and snapping like a crazed animal. Her imagination (and I'm sure another source) was filling her mind with awful imageries of her mother being deformed and perhaps looking like one of the foul shadow creatures in her nightmares. She had enough reason and sense at this point to know that was not going to be the case, but her fear-stained mind was relentless.

Sara could easily see that Angelica was uncomfortable. "You okay, sweetie? I know you're still shaken up after last night."

Without looking up, her eyes remained locked on an unseen target far off in the distance. "Do we have to see her?"

Gently, "Don't worry, Ange. Your dad said she's doing much better now. He told me that she doesn't have a single scratch on her."

A mild ding then sounded as the stainless steels doors of the elevator opened wide. They then stepped inside as Sara hit the number 3.

The elevator jerked initially but soon rose steadily in the shaft. Inside, despite Sara's words, Angelica's stomach was turning knots.

With her head down, the latter said, "Don't tell her I said this, but I'm afraid to be around her right now."

A motherly impulse rippled through her being. "Aw, sweetie, I know you're scared, but try and stay strong. Remember, Caroline and the shadow creatures *want* you to feel that way. Can you be the bravest eight-year-old girl I've ever met? Just for me?"

Still very uncertain, "I guess...."

The door then opened in front of them after the elevator came to a complete stop. They exited and started walking down the hall.

Sara said as she pointed at the door in the distance at the end of the hall, "There it is, room 333."

For reasons unbeknownst to her, the number was unsettling. Maybe it was because it was at the far end of the hall and gave her plenty of time to dread the entire walk. Maybe it was the fact that she didn't know exactly what lay on the other side of the partially closed door. Maybe she was just tired of the fixation on the number 3 over the past few weeks. Whatever the reason, she was being led by her hand down the hall. The force pulling her in that direction seemed to hold the tension of a steel cable despite Sara's gentle touch and barely tense arm leading the way.

They reached the door and Sara gently knocked a couple of times before saying, "Mrs. Barrister, it's Sara. Can Ange and I come in?"

Rosanna's voice was strained and sounded like she was trying to speak with vocal cords made of sandpaper. "Yeah, come in."

Sara smiled warmly and entered with her hesitant friend behind her. "Hey, Mrs. Barrister! I'm glad to see you're looking good as new!"

Her light mood and positive energy even brought a smile to Rosanna's face. It soon faded, however, as she saw her daughter still hiding behind Sara and looking at her very cautiously. The recently created dark circles under her eyes made her sad visage appear even more clearly. As warmly as she could say to her daughter, "Angelica, honey, I'm okay now, I promise."

Rose reached out her arms toward her daughter inviting her in for a hug. Angelica, however, stepped away even farther and instead shied toward the foot of the bed. She stared silently at her mother as if waiting for something awful to happen. Was this a trap? She wasn't willing to trust her again.

Sara then placed her hand on Angelica's shoulder and said, "Sweetie, it's okay. She's fine now."

Not budging an inch, "How do you we know it's not...." She had to think of the word again, but it quickly came to mind. "*Deception?*"

Rosanna's facial muscles relaxed and settled into an obvious defeated frown. She wasn't mad at her daughter, not by a long shot. Even though she couldn't remember most of what happened during the investigation, she knew enough by what the others had told her. Rosanna could actually feel not only the emotional pain in her heart, but also a strong stinging pain that seemed to radiate out like a several steel barbed thorns lodged under the muscle tissue.

Sara then placed her hand on Angelica's head. "This isn't deception, sweetie, I promise. She needs your support right now."

Angelica didn't dislodge.

The proverbial pain became greater as Rosanna said, "It's okay." She lowered her head. "After what happened, I don't blame her."

A long and awkward pause then ensued. Angelica had backed as far away from the foot of the bed as she could and leaned against the wall. Her eyes stayed glued nervously on her mother's face.

Sara then cleared her throat and said, "Well, Mrs. Barrister, I believe your husband told me you're probably going to get to go home this evening."

"Yeah, the doctors weren't able to find anything with all the tests they did. I was poked and prodded more than I care for last night. Well, I don't think they'd ever believe the explanation we would have."

With a reluctant smirk, "No, I guess they wouldn't."

"But don't worry, I didn't go into detail about what happened. I didn't want them locking me up in a rubber room or something."

Sara reflected a moment and snickered. "That was probably for the best. Oh, and I also spoke with the team over the phone this morning and they said they would review their evidence today. They would be more than happy to sit down with you and your husband to discuss what they found in their research and evidence tomorrow evening. Will that be okay?"

"Yeah, that should be fine. As long as we can have the meeting at the hotel. Ed and I talked and figured it would be best if we got away from the house for a while."

She nodded, then replied, "That'll be fine. Getting out of there for a while is a great idea. Until Father Anderson gets a response from The Church on the evidence he submits, staying there would be dangerous."

"Any idea how long that might take?"

"I wish I could say. I'm sure he will express the level of urgency first and foremost."

Sara and Rosanna continued to talk for several more minutes about the bizarre manner in which the windows were removed. Polite conversation, however, only lasted for so long. Eventually Angelica said she wanted to go back home and see her grandfather. She only waved to her mother before leaving, rejecting yet another attempt at a hug. The thorns dug deeper than ever.

Seventy-six

Later that afternoon, Sara had just exited her car and was knocking on the front door of Roberta's modest house.

"Come in, Sara!" was yelled across the nearby living room.

Tony and Ron were at their respective laptops listening to audio recordings from the night before. Even though the team was not happy with their camcorders being held up temporarily with the sheriff, they knew there wasn't much they could do about it. At least there were the audio files to review. They each looked up and nodded silently as Sara waved at them and grinned.

Before Sara could say a word, Roberta asked, "Hey, can I speak to you in private about something?"

She responded in a lowered tone, "Sure."

Roberta then led her out to the painted brown wooden deck at the rear entrance of the house. She closed both the screen door and the storm door behind her as Sara looked at her with a puzzled expression. The two of them leaned against the railing overlooking the edge of the deck and facing away from the door.

Roberta looked behind her before whispering, "Sara, I remember you mentioning a certain entity that you encountered at the Barrister house that seemed to be causing a lot of the trouble. What did you say her name was again?"

Even though Sara could sense a little bit of baiting in her question, she answered, "You mean the old woman?"

Roberta nodded.

Sara then continued. "Her name was Caroline, unless I'm mistaken."

She slowly nodded her head before saying, "And were you able to pick up on a time period? Roughly, anyway."

"Probably the 1800s. Mid to late 1800s, give or take."

Roberta looked back at the door again before whispering, "Can you keep a secret? I'm not sure if I want to reveal this to anyone else. Well, at least if it isn't completely necessary, and I don't think it is." She reached her hand down into her pocket and hesitated to show the object she held. "Look, I don't know a whole lot about her. But...," she then revealed the tintype and handed it to Sara, "is this who you saw?"

Amazed at the woman in the image staring at her, she stammered, "Y-yes. That's definitely her!" Roberta looked off into the distance as Sara turned the tintype over and read, "Aunt Caroline. 1868." She turned the image back over. As she locked eyes with the spite-filled woman glaring back at her, the mood went to uncomfortable quickly. Surely Sara's eyes were playing tricks on her. The eyes seemed to follow her no matter how she moved it around. This wasn't an oil painter's trick of the trade to give that illusion, this was a captured image. Maybe Sara's imagination was getting the better of her, as the reality seemed far worse. Perhaps the aborigines in Australia were right: maybe a piece of Caroline's soul was trapped there and sharing the contempt with the rest of her being.

Wanting to break the silence and the gaze, Sara said, "This picture belongs to you?"

Taking the tintype back and placing it in her pocket, Roberta responded, "Yeah, I nearly forgot I had it. It was in an old family photo box upstairs." She looked into Sara's eyes. "And you and I are cousins." She could see the tension and wanted to break it. With levity, "Of course, we're about sixth cousins five times removed, but blood is blood, I suppose."

Sara could hardly believe her eyes as she now noticed the vague hints of similarity in Roberta's facial features, mainly the eyes and mouth, compared to the image of Caroline. *"Blood is blood,"* despite being benign on its own, sounded unsettling in this situation. Regardless, Sara said, "Well, I can see why you would want to keep that a secret. Do you know anything about her at all?"

A light summer breeze caused her to squint a bit. "No, I wish I did. Other than this photograph, all my grandmother told me was that she was one of the first people to settle the area."

"And I'm guessing Tony didn't find anything in his research?"

"Nope, not a thing. Couldn't even find where her remains were interred. Of course, back in the day most people would just bury their family members on the property somewhere. No telling where that might be now."

Sara thought a moment, then replied, "Well, if that's all we know, I don't think it will be necessary to bring that up. I won't tell anyone if you don't want me to."

Roberta briefly smiled and said, "Thanks, Sara. I mean, *Cousin* Sara."

Laughing lightly, "No problem, cousin."

Seventy-seven

Around the same time at the Barrister house, the family Subaru was heading steadily up the driveway. Ed was driving and Rosanna was staring off into the distance with a forlorn expression on her face. Rosanna's father waved but only his son-in-law returned the gesture. Angelica had barely looked up from playing with her puppy. They were engaged in a tug-of-war with a piece of rope from the barn. She was genuinely laughing and reveling in this small glimpse of passing happiness and didn't want it to end.

Grandpa approached the car as it came to a stop. Rosanna smiled faintly at him as he opened the door for her. He spoke English fluently, but still had a thick Italian accent. He took her hand and helped her out.

"My sweet Rosy is home. Give Papa a hug!"

Angelica heard the "sweet" adjective used and shook her head briefly. *He hasn't seen her in a while...*, popped into her mind. She continued playing with Cerberus without looking up.

Edward saw this and called out to her, "Hey, baby girl, come on inside. We need to start getting packed."

She glanced up but said offhandedly, "I already did."

Edward then started, "Okay, well, come and help your mother pack."

She stopped playing for a moment and looked at him with a hint of annoyance crossing her face.

Rosanna, however, said quietly, "Ed, it's okay. She doesn't have to."

Her father had taken her arm and placed it over his shoulder as she walked away from the car.

She snickered, "Dad, I'm okay! I'm not crippled or anything."

The comment helped ease any uncertainty Edward might have been feeling about his daughter.

Grandpa then said in his friendly parental tone, "Now, now, Rosy, you shush! Let your father help you out! One day when I'm old you can carry *me* around if you want to!"

That afternoon, Sheriff Beasley and Sister Francis were inside the latter's office. Sheriff Beasley had transferred the data from the camcorders over to his laptop before arriving. He and Sister Francis each had one earpiece in and were looking on at the screen.

The sheriff was stone-faced as Sister Francis scoffed, "Those idiots have no idea what they're dealing with!" The blood had begun to cover Rosanna completely in the footage. "Look at that! Amazing!"

The sheriff seemed only partially uneasy with her response. He had watched bits and pieces of the footage earlier, but was just now seeing everything in real time. "Have you ever seen anything like that, Sister Francis?"

Still astonished, "No, I haven't! Can you even begin to imagine the level of power something like that requires? They're like putty in his hands!"

He could tell she was speaking with a hint of familiarity. The sheriff wasn't exactly sure who "he" was, but he had an idea.

Briefly pointing at the screen, "Now watch here... coming up...."

Moments later, the loud crash of thunder could be heard. The video feed from the cameras fizzled out for a few seconds before coming back on. They were then able to see the seared glass images left behind in the three windows.

Her eyes wide, almost frenzied, "Do you see that!? *That* is power! All of that in an instant! And to think, some people think seeing the Virgin Mary in a piece of toast is a miracle. *That*...," tapping her finger on the laptop screen, "is power!"

Silently he agreed with her, but said aloud, "So I take it this will be year we have to give something back. If that isn't a sign, I don't know what is."

Taking her earpiece out, "Yes, it certainly is. Tell Mayor Pinkerton and I'll get things going on my end." As they stood up, she added, "And of course, we can't have Roberta or Father Anderson seeing this."

He closed the laptop and put it in its satchel. "Absolutely. Oh, and don't worry about the footage of the window thieves getting out."

She could sense his somewhat reckless attempt at humor. "If that happened, I would hate to guess where a certain lawman's genitals might end up. Maybe flambéed and served with a nice glass of white wine."

He couldn't tell how far she was willing to take the joke. It *was* a joke, right? It wasn't worth taking any chances with her. Mildly uneasy, "That's not a game I'd want to play. No need to worry about anything."

Later that night, after having dropped off Cerberus at Sara's house, Angelica, her parents and grandfather were pulling into the parking lot of the Holiday Inn at the edge of town. They exited the family car and went to unload their luggage from the back.

Edward soon returned from the front desk with their two room keycards in hand. He took the first one and said, "Okay, Grandpa Leo, you're in room 210." He handed him the keycard. "And the three of us will be in room 212."

Almost cutting him off, Angelica said quickly, "I wanna stay with Grandpa! Please!"

He laughed and said, "That's fine with me! I have to warn you, though: I snore like a chainsaw!"

He did his best to imitate a chainsaw and Angelica laughed. "That's okay. I don't care."

Later that night, Edward and Rosanna were up late. It was around 1:30 A.M. and neither of them could sleep. The television was turned off an hour ago and the air conditioner in the room was making it quite comfortable.

Rosanna rolled over toward her husband and said, "Ed, there's something I have to do tomorrow morning."

"What's that, hon?"

"I need to go visit my mother. Will you three be okay with the truck at the house? I'll drop you off before I leave."

Concerned, "Well, yeah, we should be fine. Do you think it's safe for you to be driving such a long way by yourself? You just got out of the hospital today."

"I'll be fine, don't worry."

He then treaded into potentially dangerous waters. "Hon, is she even going to know you're there? I mean, in her condition...."

He lucked out. She wasn't feeling snappy in the least. "I know her condition. I... it's partly for me *and* her. It's something I need to do. I can't really explain it any better than that."

"Do you think you'll make it back by 9? Don't forget that the team wants to meet us here and go over the evidence. It's a five-hour round trip."

"I know. I'll be back in time."

Seventy-eight

Late that night, Roberta had finally fallen asleep for a couple of hours before she heard a continuous and regular tapping sound coming from the sliding glass door leading to her deck. She glanced over at her husband, who was still sound asleep before scooting over to the edge of the bed. She stepped onto the floor and gave another glance at her sleeping spouse before heading to the partially cracked door leading into the hallway.

Once in the hallway, she pushed the door so that it closed behind her. It was then that she heard a gentle voice calling in the distance. She couldn't make out the word being repeated at first, but after a few steps toward the door leading outside, she quickly realized that the voice was calling her name.

She was, however, at the door when she paused. Looking outside she could see nothing but pitch blackness. Even the light that normally burned all night in front of the shed in backyard was out.

As Roberta continued to stare into the blackness full of trepidation, she was startled to see a glowing non-corporeal orb begin to form at the edge of her lawn. Beyond that was the piney green barrier that eventually led to the greater forest beyond.

The orb then dove to the ground and transformed into a humanoid shape. The figure was lying on its stomach as its arms bent at ninety degree angles to push upward. The face of the entity then looked up and appeared distraught and helpless. Without moving her lips, the being spoke directly to Roberta's mind: "Please... Roberta! You have to help me! It's me, Caroline, your blood relation!" Roberta was hesitant to cross the threshold leading outside as the voice continued. "You must understand: The evil at the Barrister farm is holding me captive! It corrupts anyone and anything that lives there!"

The helplessness and pleading tone then caused Roberta to step out onto the deck. Hesitantly she replied, "We're still going over the evidence... and Sara said...."

Insistent but still gentle, "Sara can't see the forest for the trees! She can't find and fix the problem there on her own! You have to make sure that she and Father Anderson both drive out the evil within that cave! The evil comes from within the bowels of the earth itself!"

Roberta searched for the select words, but she stammered, "But... why me? Why are you warning me?"

"Because I know you're the only one who'll believe me. You're the only one willing to hear me out! And I've always been there for you, don't you remember?"

Roberta was confused for a moment, but then found brief memories (she wasn't entirely sure about their validity, but the memories were clear enough now). "Wait... so that was you that night? I saw you clear as day that night in the bathroom at the school gym! You told me to leave the guy that I was dating at the time."

Smiling as she steadied herself on her hands and knees, "Yes! He ended up murdering his wife and kid five years later! That could've been you, but I was watching out for you!"

"After all these years, you were the one. A shame I've only now realized who you are."

Caroline smiled as she rose to her feet. "Yes, and you know now where you get your talents from. In some ways you are not as sensitive as Sara, but you're so much better in other ways! I know why you go around haunted places and use your gadgets to try and get evidence. Deep down you want to validate the heightened intuition that's been rather quiet most of your life." She paused a moment, then continued. "Don't you understand? You shouldn't question the information being sent to you. The feelings you have are real and should be heeded."

Roberta then approached the bottom step of her deck and stopped. The ground and forest beyond were all still jet black save for the spot on which

Caroline now stepped and drew closer step by step. "I want to know more about you. Why aren't you mentioned anywhere I've looked?"

"Because, dear, our family and the 'proud folk' of this miserable town want to pretend I never existed! Look at our family's Bible, for instance. That smudged-out name in the family tree is me! They were superstitious and very much afraid of my abilities. Sometimes when I went to town to get things from the General Store they would go out of their way to walk on the other side of the road or even spit on me! All of this because of something I had no control over!

"And do you know that I had six miscarriages when I was alive? What do you think the 'kind folks' of Miller's Run village did? They blamed me for it naturally! Claimed I was cursed by God and that they wanted to make sure I didn't bring more 'abominations' into the world."

Roberta, her mouth agape, listened in near disbelief. She then said, "I would never have thought that people in this area would be so cruel!"

Caroline's brow furrowed as she said with disgust, "The worst part is how they took my life in the end! Blamed me for a year of bad crops and catastrophic livestock loss. Claimed I was a witch of all things! The 'respectable folk' of Miller's Run went on to track me down in a lynch mob and hang me! They even made sure to place the noose just right so I would die as slowly as possible! They wanted to make sure I felt the full heat of the fire they had built beneath me! It was agonizing! I screamed in vain and the last thing I saw before I closed my earthly eyes for good was the townspeople cursing and mocking through the flames that were licking up all around me! They were monsters far worse than their own imaginations had created!

"Several days after (I can't be sure at how many exactly), I once again felt very much alive but was obviously not in my body. They went out of their way to take my charred remains and dump them in the cave at the Barrister farm. I was trapped there in spirit, not being able to find my way out for some time. And that's when the evil started to corrupt me."

Astonished and wiping away a tear, Roberta said, "I had no idea you suffered so much! I wish you didn't have to go through that!"

Her tone was firm but kind as Caroline replied, "There's nothing we can do to erase the past. But you do need to get Sara and Father Anderson to bless and exorcise that cave! If they don't, things will only get worse for everyone involved!"

"Yes, of course, I'll do everything in my power to make sure they help set you free!"

"Excellent, my dear! Let nothing stand in your way!"

Seventy-nine

The next morning, Rosanna had just dropped off her family at home and was heading down the road away from Miller's Run. A feeling of distant but obvious dread started to come over her. She wasn't willing to engage it fully right away. The long drive to the *Sunny Acres Nursing Facility* would give her plenty of time to try and sort out that years-old emotional luggage. The radio in the car was only faintly turned up, just enough to hear the classical music from a local station. She hoped it would help sooth her mind, but it seemed to have a double-edge. It relaxed some of the extraneous concerns around her, but this in itself allowed her mind to roam the databank of memories tucked away neatly in her mind. "A place for everything and everything in its place." Her mind groaned at the burden of opening this casket-like compartment.

As she took a drink from her chilled water bottle a car behind her suddenly jerked itself into the left lane and blazed past her. He cut her off rather closely as he hurried along, obviously being the most important person on the road. She pulled the bottle away abruptly, spilling a few drops on her shirt. "Jerk! Learn how to drive!" The car payed her no mind as it cruised on reaching around 85mph and disappearing around the next bend. "Of course he doesn't get pulled over! But if I have an expired inspection sticker, look out!" She screwed the top back onto the plastic bottle and replaced it in the cup holder. She had fumbled a bit with the cap, but only noticed her hand trembling when she went to put it back on the steering wheel. Was it adrenaline from the traffic encounter? Perhaps, but....

Caroline's voice seemed distant, but was still able to be heard clearly: *"Oh, what's this? Seems you have a lot of fear burrowing around in there. Like a big old warble dug in and sucking the life right out of you!"*

Rosanna resisted the urge to lash out. The impulse was obviously less given her distance from the farm. She was expecting a drawn out mental skirmish like previous encounters, but Caroline's voice went silent. She looked into the rearview mirror, expecting to see a phantom passenger. No was there. She sighed. One thing did, however, stick in her mind rather ironically like its subject. She said aloud in a whisper, "What's a warble?" Despite having never encountered one or having ever been told what one was, the question sent a shiver down her back.

Rosanna had made it to the nursing facility in pretty good time. No major traffic, at least on the roads. As she pulled off the exit from the interstate and came to a stop at the stop sign, the car's deceleration began to make her mind wonder again. She was getting bits and pieces of the day when they diagnosed her mother with her current ailment: *"Acute encephalitis secondary to an auto-immune disorder."*

Her right turn signal blinked as she looked both ways before pulling out on the relatively rural highway leading to the facility. She and her father made sure that Emma Leone would be taken good care of within the limitations of their respective budgets. Despite her father's wishes, Enzo Leone would accept his daughter's contributions when she worked as a floor manager of a local department store in their hometown. It certainly wasn't Rosanna's first job choice, but it paid the bills after college. Once she met Edward and moved to the town of Miller's Run, however, the contribution decreased seeing as how she couldn't find a suitable job and wanted to focus on taking on the responsibilities of managing the home. Her father Enzo was more than happy to see her take on a more traditional role and he made sure to dote on her because of it.

The Subaru picked up speed and soon hit the speed limit of the rural highway: 55mph. Much like her efforts in spiritual matters, Rosanna went out of her way to always obey traffic laws.

"So far we can only speculate on how much damage this condition will do to her," the doctor stated plainly. *"She's lucky to be alive, but there is*

undeniable brain damage." Rosanna distinctly remembered the doctor's rapport being an expected detachment which bothered her despite knowing he had the best intentions and had probably diagnosed dozens of patients with the same exact thing.

About twenty minutes passed before Rosanna came to a near stop to turn into the parking lot of the small retirement facility. She pulled in and found a parking place amidst the nearly vacant asphalt. After turning off the car and activating the locks, she closed the driver's side door. She found herself stalling again, fidgeting with her keys and staring off into the distance.

"You hesitate when you are so close. Come on now, Rosanna, go and see your vegetable mother!"

The voice of Caroline had invaded once more. Rosanna only briefly looked around the parking lot before she regained control of her faculties. She sighed, then said quietly through gritted teeth, "Shut up!"

Caroline's small burst of laughter was followed by, *"You know, Rosy, if you aren't careful you may end up here one day yourself. Do you think sweet little Angelica is going to treat you any differently than you've treated your mother?"* Rosanna remained silent as Caroline continued. *"You know, since you all moved into my town I've gotten to know little Angelica. She may follow your orders, but she doesn't love you! Oh, no, she detests your presence entirely!"* Rosanna's eyes widened as she tried to stifle her reaction. Caroline continued. *"Yes! Please get angry! Please let your hatred for me bubble over! Give in to that rage that seizes you now!"*

Rosanna didn't notice the nurse dressed in decorative scrubs that approached her and asked, "Are you okay? You look like you've seen a ghost!"

She didn't see anything, but that wasn't the problem. "Huh!? Oh, I'm sorry! I was lost in thought there for a moment."

Rosanna's nervous laughter didn't completely convince the nurse as she asked, "Well, okay. Who are you here to visit?"

Her tone was grounded and sane now. "I'm just here to see my mother, Emma Leone."

A proverbial lightbulb went off in the young woman's head. "Oh, Mrs. Barrister, right? I thought I recognized you."

Rosanna looked more clearly at her. "Oh, right. We've met before, haven't we?" She looked down at the nurse's nametag on her top. "Susanne... right."

They both began walking toward the front doors.

"Haven't seen you up here in a while. How've you been?"

"Oh, you know, same old, same old."

Susanne's brown eyes couldn't help but see insecurity still written plainly on Rosanna's face. "Right. Well, your mother's been doing fine, all things considered."

"That's good."

Seeing the reluctance of Rosanna continue, "Okay then. This way."

She followed the nurse down the hall and toward the nurses' station. Rosanna couldn't help but notice that Susanne's dark blonde hair was tied in a braid almost identical to the one Angelica had started wearing. At first it was Sara, then her daughter, and now this random nurse at the facility. She detached her mind from the thoughts, however, as a corpulent nurse behind the desk greeted Susanne.

Susanne returned the greeting and introduced Rosanna. The chubby cheeks of the nurse pulled into a smile.

"Hey there, Mrs. Barrister! Good to see you again!"

Rosanna forced a smile in return. No ill will against the nurses, just the guest of the evening. "Hi, it's good to see you, too!" She looked back and forth briefly and decided to continue before having to draw out a conversation. She wanted to get this ordeal over with. Maybe stay and talk briefly after the visit. Her mother certainly wasn't going anywhere. "Room 137, correct?"

The nurse at the desk replied, "That's it! Just down the hall there."

Rosanna thanked them and started down the corridor. The evergreen color of the short carpeting did make the varnished wainscoting look attractive. There were also thick varnished handrails on the walls with a faux-gold strip running lengthwise. That gave way to the creamy-white walls and ceiling above it. It certainly looked better than the other nursing homes she and her father had researched. One thing that they couldn't avoid, however, was the inevitable smell of urine and various other secretions of the human body in its heavily aged state.

As she started to pass the patient's doors on the way down the hall, she briefly pinched her nose at a couple of the fouler smelling rooms. Most of the doors were shut or partially opened. Several steps in she could hear nurses in various rooms trying to negotiate with patients to get them into bed or take their daily prescriptions. They were courteous and gentle, but some of the patients certainly weren't.

Several steps later she looked up and could see the tag for room 137 extending from the wall above the door. She reached out for the door handle but stopped before she could grab it. A particularly strong whiff of fecal order was invading the hallway thanks to the open door directly across the hall. She covered her mouth and nose with her hand as she looked over and saw an elderly man lying in his bed. He was essentially in a catatonic state but they had managed to elevate the head of his bed and put a television on at the foot of the mattress. No one knew for sure if he was ever able to comprehend the programs on the screen, but they seemed to sooth him.

After taking a deep breath (and quickly succumbing to the smells she tried to ignore), she turned the knob and went inside. A mix of urgency from the odors and not wanting to confront her mother both chased her inside the room. She shut the door behind herself and was relieved to find that the stenches had not completely invaded that room. Her throat went dry abruptly as she carefully looked over at her mother. She was lying in her bed silently. Her head was only slightly elevated and she seemed to have no reaction to Rosanna's entrance.

It took her several seconds to muster the courage but she approached the bed. Rosanna didn't utter a word at first. She knew her mother's mind was riddled with dementia and that she was catatonic most of the time. Rosanna had gotten some of her good looks from her mother, but the evidence at this point in Emma's life didn't show those features very obviously. Her skin was wrinkled, crepe-like, and drained of the slight healthy hue it had in her younger days. She could see the dark veins running all through her arms and neck. Her mouth stayed agape as she breathed slowly. Rosanna had to double check to make sure she was breathing as the breaths were slight. The delicate wheeze in each comforted her somewhat. She tried to avoid eye contact with her mother's equally onyx-colored eyes but soon found it irrelevant as Emma stared at the ceiling.

Rosanna put her hand on her mother's and said quietly, "Hello, Mother...."

"Hello, Mother…," was repeated back at her by the otherwise motionless body in front of her.

Rosanna sighed in frustration as she nearly forgot a trait her mother had picked up after her disorder: echolalia. The same doctor that had diagnosed her with encephalitis had also mentioned that Rosanna's mother was simply having a secondary symptom to the dementia that now dominated. He explained it something to the effect of, *"Kind of like a parakeet, she will just repeat back what you say."*

Rosanna silently held her mother's hand for a minute or so before continuing. "I don't know if I'm being a good mom."

Emma replied in a heavily raspy voice, "I don't know if I'm being a good mom."

Rosanna knew her position was hopeless, but she continued. "Please stop repeating what I say."

"Please stop repeating what I say."

As the inept frustration built inside she heard, *"Did you really think you were going to come here and have some sort of touching conversation with her!?"*

Gritting her teeth again, Rosanna hissed, "Shut up, Caroline!"

Her mother replied, "Shut up, Caroline!"

Without thinking, Rosanna placed her hand over her mother's mouth. Caroline's tone was more insistent now. *"That's it! Suffocate that old hag! You know how much pain and misery she caused you growing up! Remember that time when she found out you were kissing that boy in school and she slapped you for it!? Right across your left cheek! You nearly fell down you were struck so hard! And you deserved it, too, you whore! Now strike her as she did you all those years ago! An eye for an eye, Rosy!"*

Rosanna's grip on her mother's face had tightened as she now looked back and forth frantically before locking eyes with her mother. Now Emma Leone was staring directly at her. In that moment, her stern gaze seemed to reach back through time and stir up unaddressed emotions which had been fermenting for years.

Suddenly, as Rosanna went to pull her hand away from her mother's mouth, Emma snapped at and bit her daughter's hand fiercely. She tried to pull it away, but Emma's yellow teeth were well dug in. Rosanna then stood up and tried to use her right hand to pull her left away. It wouldn't budge. She endured the pain for a few seconds before pulling her right hand back and ferociously slapping her across the cheek.

Emma's jaws unclamped and her hand went back to the pillow and staring up at the ceiling. Rosanna didn't believe what had just happened at first, but the bright red mark left on her mother's cheek confirmed that what had just taken place was all too real. She then retracted her hands and placed them over her own mouth. She began to whimper softly, "I'm so sorry...."

This time, however, her mother didn't echo back. She didn't say or do anything. Nervously, Rosanna looked up at the door. The slap had created quite a bit of sound, but no sounds outside could be heard. The heavy wooden door helped mitigate that.

As Rosanna's thoughts became clearer, she could hear Caroline laughing from inside the room. She then looked back down at her mother, only Emma's face was now Caroline's. Rosanna could distinctly see her visage and the cackling that ensued was surely loud enough to be heard. Rosanna's face then dipped down into her hands. *"Now doesn't that feel better, Rosy?"*

She quickly stifled her tears and looked up at her mother's face, which was now back to normal. Seeing her head laying lopsided on the pillow, she readjusted it and fixed up her mother's mildly displaced white curly hair.

As Rosanna started out of the room she heard, *"What would your father say about what you just did!? Elder abuse on your own mother!? Wait until Angelica finds out! What will your husband say!?"*

Rosanna decided to get out while the getting was good.

She quickly grabbed the door handle and headed out into the hallway, closing the door behind her. She wiped away the remaining tears the snuck out of her tear ducts and hurried past the nurses' desk. Seeing her obviously distressed, they tried to talk to her but she simply said a hasty goodbye and left the building. It would seem to her that her speedy retreat would never be fast enough.

Several minutes down the road the adrenaline had finally worn off. Her hands ached tremendously. This wasn't only from her mother's bite, but also the sheer force she'd exerted in slapping her.

Eighty

The afternoon sun was starting its decent toward the horizon at the Barrister farm. Edward was busy putting away the tools and leftover screws used to secure the plywood over the three affected windows. Sara walked by the barn, smiled warmly, and waved to Edward before heading toward Angelica and her grandfather. He waved back. He then stepped out a few steps from the barn door and looked up the path to see Angelica showing off her puppy and Enzo petting it on the head and smiling.

Without noticing at first, his eyes were drawn away and looking at Sara. Because of the heat that day she'd worn a breezy black dress with a matching formfitting top. He was then staring at her buttocks moving up and down underneath the fabric. Edward then heard the voice of Caroline whisper in his ear: *"What a wonderful ass. You could bounce a quarter off of those cheeks!"*

Edward then coughed nervously before heading back into the barn. He whispered aloud, "The hell?"

"Nothing wrong with sneaking a peek, Eddie-boy! No one will know but you and me."

He took his time putting the rest of the tools away.

Several minutes later, Edward stepped back out onto the turnaround and looked out toward Angelica and Sara sitting on the ground and playing with Cerberus. A grin came to his face as he saw daughter being genuinely happy. He knew it would only be temporary but they had to take what little peace they could get at this point.

As he went to take a step forward, however, he realized his right shoelace was untied. He bent down and began tying the strings. He completed the bow and looked up before standing again. Angelica and Sara had both gotten up, the former scooping up her dog. Sara had bent over to brush some pieces of grass from her skirt. Now he was staring at her cleavage that had now really caught his eye. He could clearly see she was wearing a black bra.

The moment passed but he heard, *"I bet her panties match the bra. I would even say she'd be willing to show you if you asked nicely. Just pull her aside and...."*

His concentration was broken as he felt warm liquid running copiously from nostrils. The liquid dripped onto the dirt beneath and then appeared a deep purple. He then knew it was a nosebleed and pinched the openings of his nose shut.

Seeing him doubled over and dripping blood, Sara and Angelica approached quickly. The former said, "Are you okay, Mr. Barrister?"

Still pinching his nose, "Yeah, it's just a nosebleed. I get them from time to time."

Angelica held her puppy in her arms and looked at him with concern as Sara went to her car and retrieved a small box of tissues.

She handed several of them to him.

As he plugged each nostril with a couple of the tissues, Angelica asked, "Are you sure you're okay, Dad?"

He patted on her the head and responded, "I'm fine, baby girl. Just the same old nosebleed."

Angelica then looked up and saw the family Subaru heading up the driveway.

In the car, Rosanna was looking at the small scene of Sara wiping blood from his mustache and around his mouth and beard. Sara looked concerned, but was also trying to be a little funny, which put Edward at ease. Despite having recently mended her relationship with Sara, Rosanna felt the tinges of jealousy still prickling away inside. The proverbial physician may have stitched up the wound, but it still stung inside.

Sara then waved to her and smiled. Rosanna waved but kept a rather stony expression. Then, sensing the rather cold aura of Rosanna, Sara excused herself to use the bathroom inside the Barrister home.

By the time the family car had made it to the turnaround, Angelica had left her father's side and was heading toward the bridge and stream area with Cerberus following dutifully along.

As she stepped out of the automobile, she clearly saw what was awry with Edward. She approached him with genuine concern and said, "Oh, honey. Another nosebleed? That looks like a real gusher!"

She reached out her right hand touched his cheek. He then noticed that Rosanna had her left hand in her pocket and was not taking it out. "Yeah, I was putting some stuff away in the barn, then bent down to tie my shoe and the fountain started."

"Do you need a paper towel? I can grab some from the kitchen."

Still noticing her hand buried in her pocket, "Nah, I think will do. Hey, what's wrong with your hand?"

Quickly, "What do you mean?"

"Your left hand. You've had it all the way in your pocket since you got here."

Her father then opened the back door and waved to her. "There's my Rosy!"

Quietly, "I'll explain later. Just back me up in the meantime."

Equally low in volume, "Okay."

Her father approached and embraced her. "How was your drive? Was Emma doing okay today?"

She had only used one arm to hug him. "Didn't run into any problems on the road. Mom's about the same as always."

As she put both of her hands into her pockets, Enzo asked, "What's wrong with your hands? Are you cold on a day like this?"

"Well, you know. Mother and I are known for our cold hands. Even in the summer we have them."

Chuckling, "Of course, of course."

Rosanna would never tell her father what had happened at "Sunny Acres." It would several days before she told her husband, and he would be the only one that knew besides herself.

Eighty-one

Just before 9:00 P.M. that night, the four members of the paranormal investigation team were holding their meeting with the Barristers in the hotel room that Rosanna and Edward were using. Enzo had decided that he would stay back at the farmhouse to make sure no one would try and break in or vandalize the place. Even after his daughter had begged him to stay with the group, he was insistent.

Angelica was seated on one of the beds along with Sara. Rosanna and Edward seated at the table where Tony had set up the laptop. Roberta had just taken a small stack of papers from the satchel she was carrying.

She started. "Okay, Mr. and Mrs. Barrister, we have found a decent amount of evidence that sheds some light on what *may* be happening on your property. Quite frankly, the entire town has a very," she paused, then continued, "troubled history. What we were able to find was often lacking any real details, at least prior to the start of the twentieth century. European settlers began coming to the area in the 1700s and would continue to do so for the next couple of centuries. As with most areas of the United States, this land was previously inhabited by tribes of Native Americans. The town itself, along with Cedar Hill, were once a part of the same territory and county. It wasn't until later that Miller's Run had broken apart from Cedar Hill, feeling that they no longer had much common ground on which to co-operate." She cleared her throat as she turned to a different page in the stack in her hand. "Now, the natives that were here were not like the other tribes in the surrounding territories. They were not accepted at all by the inhabitants of the region and were shunned by everyone. They labeled them the 'Eaters of Flesh'... human flesh. Their appearance was not like any natives we know today. Their facial structures were very different. They were typically seven feet tall or more in height and covered with noticeably more body hair. Their eyes, yellow or gold. Their skin color was even described by others as, 'a hue that bears the same gray color as stone itself.'" She turned the page and noticed Angelica's eyes wide in disbelief. Roberta continued. "They were so feared that no one dared approach their land. No other tribe would trade with them, and certainly not intermarry with them. This lead to a centuries-long practice of inbreeding that would ultimately make them weaker. Over time they showed more and more birth defects and a high mortality rate at birth. No official records of their numbers exists, but the neighboring tribes always noticed that their numbers never increased much."

Sara could see Angelica's uneasiness creeping up, so she put her arm around her and pulled her a little closer. Sara said quietly, "It's okay."

Roberta continued. "The 'Eaters of Flesh' would often try and raid the neighboring tribes because of their struggle to maintain a healthy supply of food. The area, back then, experienced a blight regularly for centuries. The tribe eventually started stealing children away to sacrifice them to the land in an attempt to please the angry spirits that lived under the earth."

She turned to a new set of papers that had black-and-white printouts on them. "Here, these are a few sketches that I was able to find from that time. This was before they had cameras, so it's the best we could do."

In turn, they each looked at the etchings and passed them around. One was a depiction of a tall and somewhat lanky "person" with shaggy unkempt hair, mostly on the head, some on the arms, legs, and chest as well (long for a typical person, but not so long as to make them apelike). The man's face was clearly deformed with severe asymmetry, one seeming to look in a different direction than the other. There was a certain wildness to his eyes that made Angelica uncomfortable. She picked up a similar (although lessened through the drawing) sensation when she saw the shadow beings on the property.

Another drawing showed similarly wild eyes and hair, but this one had a badly cleft palette, a very crooked nose, and a hand that seemed to always be contorted at his side. The angle at which the wrist was bent was painful to those who looked at it. One could also tell from the position in which he was seated that he had a horribly crooked back that met a similarly angled neck. This picture also showed what looked like a crude hatchet in his right hand.

The third depicted a female of the group. She clearly had a clubfoot and her breasts were so asymmetrical that one might think they were two halves to two different bodies meshed together. Her unkempt hair ran all the way down to her knees. Her face too was grossly off kilter and seemed to be in a constant state of rage. The curvature of her back also resembled the previous male.

The fourth was the most distorted looking of the previous. He had the same vacant and insane gaze but most of the teeth on the upper left side of his face protruded out at a grotesque angle that held his mouth permanently open. He barely had any hair on top of his head. His left hand had absurd misshapes which had two of his fingers veering off into one direction while the remaining two, and the thumb, went off in the other. His spine too was contorted and his skin was covered in what looked like welts and a multitude of pox scars.

The fifth and final drawing of the lot was only humanoid at best. The hair covering his body was far thicker and nearly black. His bare flesh could not be seen beneath any part of his body. His head, worst of all, was dog-like in appearance. To anyone looking at it by itself, it *was* the head of a dog. His body was not noticeably contorted like the rest of his ilk (I use that term extremely loosely). If anything he looked to be in prime shape. The eyes, much like the others, were golden in color. Angelica stared into them silently as did everyone else. Whoever the artist was, they did an excellent job of capturing the savagery of the fallen.

Roberta then said, "Now this one here. We believe he was the chief of the group. He was obviously the largest and strongest. He was the only one wearing the head of a wolf as a headdress."

Angelica quickly interrupted, "No. That's his actual head!"

Edward replied, "He's just wearing a pelt on his head, baby girl. People used to…."

Angelica cut him off as well. "No, that's his head! I've seen him before! I know that's his real head!"

Rosanna asked quickly, "When did you see him?"

"The night I almost drown in the creek! That's what I saw in my room!"

Edward remembered the dream. "That's what you saw that night?"

Angelica nodded as Sara quietly reflected. Sara, despite believing the initial assumption, could tell Angelica was telling the truth. She did see that "thing" in her room. Was this entity simply projecting this image to frighten her, or was it as simple as what was staring at her on the paper? Maybe that was its head, after all. She tucked the idea away as faintly recalled having perhaps read of something about before.

Despite being abhorred by the images, Angelica asked, "How did they get drawings of them if they were so violent?"

Impressed, Roberta answered, "That's a very good question. I don't have the best answer, but from what we've read, these drawings were made after they died."

Edward then asked, "Who killed them?"

Roberta answered, "A combination of settlers and natives, from I've read. The local tribes gave them permission to settle in the now Miller's Run and Cedar Hill area if they got rid of the Flesh Eaters. The natives figured that the land was cursed anyway and if the tribe was removed the European settlers wouldn't stay around long after that. It was a win-win situation for them."

Rosanna then asked, "So the settlers wiped them all out?"

Roberta responded, "It was a combination of the settlers and several of the natives that banded together and wiped them out. They were as thorough as possible, going as far as to burn the forests down and search the caves in the area. After this they incinerated the bodies and dumped them all into a cave. We're about 95-percent sure that it was the cave on your property."

Angelica then looked up at Sara. "So the shadow people I've seen are their spirits?"

Sara replied, "That's where it gets complicated, I think. From what I've seen and from what you've all told me, I think that the shadow entities have been there for many more centuries than we can fathom. When they 'acquire' a new spirit, they corrupt it and turn it into one of their own. Slowly they eat away at the essence of the spirit they bring in until it replicates their own level of corruption."

Ron then spoke up. "We all agree that this is the most probable explanation. It would explain why no one has done particularly well at your property since people settled the area."

Rosanna then said, "So what do we do about this?"

Tony answered, "Well, you three will have to make a decision. Father Anderson is going to proceed based on how *you* want to proceed. If you up and leave, there may still be spirits attached to you that would keep trying to harm you no matter where you go. On the other hand, if you decide to dig in and hunker down, Father Anderson will have to get permission from the Church to do a Minor Rite of Exorcism on the property."

Rosanna answered, "So basically we're taking a chance either way, correct?"

Each of the team members nodded their heads.

She continued. "Then I say we fight this! They're going to keep trying to wear us down no matter what! The Church is more powerful than any evil in this world!"

Roberta then said, "Well, I hope and pray for the best in your decision. It's going to be a tough road."

Rosanna continued. "My family has come here to live a better life and we're not going to let this corruption destroy us! Right, Ed?"

Edward had felt trepidation up to this point, but the fiery tone of Rosy inspired him. "Absolutely! We're in this together! Isn't that right, baby girl?"

Angelica was not so fired up. She responded equal parts frustrated and subdued. "Two-thirds majority wins...."

Sara then looked down at Angelica and said reassuringly, "Hey, come on now, we're all going into this together. I'm not going to cut and run. I'll help in every way that I can."

Ron added, "We all will!"

Angelica replied, "Okay, I'll fight, too."

The group then approved of her reply.

She, however, still had a big question on her mind. "But who's Caroline? You haven't mentioned anything about her."

Sara then looked blankly at Roberta, who sighed, then said, "You're right, Angelica, I almost completely forgot."

Angelica then thought to herself, *Liar!* Her instincts saw straight through that, but she remained silent.

Roberta then took the tintype from one of her pockets and handed it to Rosanna and Edward. Once they took in the image, they both knew right away that that was the same person. Angelica also made a quick and positive ID. They all looked at it again together as Roberta said, "We don't know much about her. We're not exactly sure how she fits into all of this."

Angelica again thought, *Liar!*

Edward then asked, "Was she possibly someone who lived on our land?"

Roberta answered, "Yes, that's a possibility. We're just not sure. She may be trapped there for all we know. Either way, the exorcism should free her if she's unable to move on."

Edward and Rosanna then began to ask other questions as Angelica looked up at Sara and said, "Sara, can we talk outside?"

It seemed like an odd request to the others, but Sara could almost hear the question now. She replied, "Sure, you all don't mind if we step out for a minute, do you?"

They didn't mind, and so the two of them went out onto the walkway and closing the door behind them.

Sara soon asked in a lowered voice, "Something's bothering you. What is it?"

Her young pupil replied, "Roberta knows more about Caroline but she isn't telling anyone. Why not?"

"Well, it's complicated. She's a distant relative of hers. She figures it would make things seem messier if she mentions that."

"Are you sure she really wants to help, then?"

Sara hesitated for a moment, realizing the weight of the question. "Of course. She wants what's best for you and your family."

Eighty-two

She was comfortable using the knife in her hand. It was all coming back to her quickly. The edge was sharp and true, slicing cleanly and easily through the flesh. No more postmortem twitches, no squirming. She knew where to cut and how deep. Maybe she thought her time doing this was over not long ago, but that was apparently a misconception.

Sister Gillian looked down at her blood-soaked hands only briefly before wiping her sweating forehead with her sleeve. It was hot that time of year in Miller's Run and the storage room at the Church's lake shelter was certainly not air conditioned. At least she had covered the floor with a tarp to keep the cleanup easier. Just hose it down afterward and everyone would be none the wiser.

A sudden waft of a familiar smell invaded her nose as she slung a handful of intestines into a five-gallon-bucket sitting across from her. At least she wasn't having to prepare chitterlings.

Suddenly, Sister Francis walked into the dimly lit room carrying a heavy black plastic bag over her shoulder. She quickly dropped the bag next to the guts bucket. The thud and squishy splattering sound was unappealing to say the least. She then noticed Sister Gillian turning her nose away from the handful of other miscellaneous pluck.

Raising an eyebrow, "What's wrong, Sister Gillian? I thought you grew up on a farm. You should be used to this."

Stifling a small cough before, she replied, "I did. Opossums always stink to high heck, though. They eat just about anything!"

Not willing to show any mercy, "Humph! I know what they smell like, believe me! I've done this plenty of times. The trick is to hurry up before they get too warm and start to bloat on you."

She tried to exhale the offending odor through her nose with a sharp breath, but it did nothing. "What are these for again? I don't think I understand."

"They're for a barbaric ritual that the hicks in Miller's Run do every so often. They make this gruesome effigy and burn it in times of peril. They say the people took to the ritual after settling the area after learning it from a local tribe of natives. It seems like a whole lot of pagan nonsense to me!"

Her eyebrows furrowed. "That is strange."

"That's one word for it. Now remember, you need to skin and gut thirty-six of these opossums in order to make the effigy. Once you're done with that I'll show you how to stitch them all together. Now work quickly! The parade is only a couple of days away!"

"Yes, Sister Francis."

She continued somewhat reluctantly. Despite the appalling amount of blood and guts to come, she knew this to be a form of hazing or simply doing work no one else would volunteer for.

At door leading to an adjoining room, Sister Francis stopped and turned back toward Sister Gillian. She knelt and picked up a pair of spare rubber gloves. After donning them, she scooped up the small pile of pelts her younger counterpart had made.

"I'll put these in the fridge so they don't spoil."

Surprised at this perceived act of kindness, "Well, thank you."

Sister Francis didn't turn back or acknowledge her smile as she left the room. Once out of sight and next to the fridge, she turned and looked back at the entrance way. Hearing Gillian cough and drop another pile of guts into the bucket, she placed the pelts on top of the chest freezer. Looking back once more and content with her privacy, she dragged her finger over the bloody inner lining of the fur. She then raised her finger slowly, looking longingly at the dripping crimson life fluid descending the length of her digit. The old nun then ran her tongue up the side of her finger before taking in the whole thing. The metallic tones of the iron-rich blood, the artificial taste of the rubber glove hiding underneath... it was rapturous. It was the closest thing to sex she'd known for decades. This wasn't the first time, oh no. This was a little delicacy she'd grown fond of over the years. The act, however, was not for an affinity for blood sausage or the like. The act was well known as sinful and taboo to her and perhaps that was what made it all the more exciting.

Feeling the chills running all over, she felt vulnerable and paranoid. Sister Gillian might walk in any second, and she certainly wouldn't like the consequences of that. The younger nun did not, however, do so. She remained in the room well into the evening before finishing the pile.

Eighty-three

Roberta and Father Anderson were seated in the waiting room of the Sheriff's Department building in Miller's Run. They had only been waiting a few seconds before Sheriff Beasley entered the room. He cut off their speech as they rose to speak.

"Now, Roberta, I've already told you that I can't turn those tapes over to you! They are evidence in a theft case and are not public property!"

Father Anderson spoke up in a calm tone. "Sheriff Beasley, I'm so sorry we've bothered you, but I simply wanted to make my plea in person. The evidence of what's happening at Holly Bush Road is key to gaining The Church's approval on how to proceed."

The sheriff lowered his voice again before saying, "Father Anderson, I respect you and your position, but I simply can't turn that footage over. It's being held as evidence in a theft case, as I've already said."

The priest replied, "I understand your position as well. I'm simply requesting the portion of the footage during the investigation. I haven't seen what happened after we all left, but I wouldn't think it would directly affect my case. The start of the investigation should be enough in itself."

Steadily, Beasley replied, "You were there. I saw you on the video myself. Shouldn't your word be enough for The Church?"

Subtly more insistent, "Yes, Sheriff, I was there. My own testimony only carries so much weight. As your bosses require hard evidence, so do mine. The footage will likely aid me in helping expedite this process. That family is in dire need of help!"

With some of the force in his tone returning, "With all due respect, sir, I don't come to your establishment and demand you tell me your parishioner's confessions. I would hope that you'd respect my line of work and not ask me to do something that would make me lose my job. Do you understand? I can't help you."

Roberta finally chimed in. "Sheriff, please. You and I both know the judge. Surely we speak with him and work something out."

The lawman replied, "And you know that the judge will not want to be bothered by this! He'll take my side and you'll have wasted everyone's time!" Regaining his composure, "Now, I'm going to ask you both politely to leave. There's nothing more that can be done. You'll have to wait for the judge's decision when he gets back from his vacation. Be glad I returned your spook hunting equipment as soon as I did."

With their proverbial hands tied, as with cuffs, the two left frustrated and without the footage they sought.

Eighty-four

It was partly cloudy on the day of the town's parade. Rosanna, seeing Mrs. Kelly, waved at her and watched as she returned the gesture from nearby in the crowd and soon approached her. Edward noticed someone missing from the usual members of the Kelly clan. He asked with a smile as they came within earshot, "Hey, Mary. Where's John?"

"Well, he's been selected to be in the parade this year. You'll see him soon enough."

John Jr. stood by his sister quietly as she gave a quick hug to Angelica. Edward continued. "Oh, yeah?"

Mary Kelly replied, "Yeah, every so often the parade changes its theme. When it's time for compensation, things are different."

Angelica looked puzzled as she asked, "What's that mean?"

Mrs. Kelly looked down at her, her face more solemn that its usual countenance, and said, "Well, we can't have everyone just taking and taking. At some point we have to give back. That's why it's called, after all, 'Recompense and Bounty.'"

The answer didn't really illuminate the situation for Angelica, but Rosanna was the first to speak. She presented the same wicker basket that the Kellys always left for them on their porch the past couple of years containing the family effigies. Their appearance this year, however, was different. Instead of the normal "blue for boys and pink for girls" outfits that usually adorned them, each wore a solid black outfit: Edward's in overalls and the ladies' in black dresses, respectively. The three dollies were also showing an obvious frown on their face instead of the accustomed smile. Their initials would be sewn on them with white cotton cloth later.

Still perplexed, Rosanna asked, "What do you mean? What do we give back?"

Mrs. Kelly replied, "It'll all make sense in the end, trust me."

Despite having known the family for three years and established themselves as part of the community, Rosanna was still feeling the "none of your business" tone leaking from around Mrs. Kelly's words.

Edward asked, "Do we do anything differently when the wagon passes by?"

Mary shook her head. "No, just follow what everyone else does. It's pretty much the same gesture on our part as the other years."

Not more than a minute passed when Edward heard someone calling his name from the nearby conglomerate of spectators. "Mr. Barrister? One second, I'll be right there."

Suddenly, Mary Kelly was eager to leave as she grabbed the hand of her daughter, who was talking to Angelica. The mother said in a hurried tone, "Well, Barristers, I think we left something in the car. We'll be back over in a minute, okay?"

Confused only a few moments by their hasty retreat, she turned to see the source of the greeting. The antique black dress, parasol, and round reflective sunglasses made it clear. Sara was approaching them. As always, she had mixed feelings when the people between her and her objective suddenly parted like the Red Sea. She rolled her eyes and let out a quick sigh before coming within easy speaking distance.

Edward smiled as Angelica said excitedly, "Sara!"

She smiled as she reached down with her hand and briefly caressed Angelica's cheek. Rosanna's smile was lukewarm, but genuine.

Edward shook Sara's hand as he said, "Good to see you again." He looked around at the crowd townsfolk lining the street and asked quietly, "Sara, why is everyone so much quieter this year? Usually everyone is smiling and having a good time."

With a straight face, "This is a year of recompense. Everyone is always more subdued during this form of the parade."

Without thinking, Rosanna extended her hand and placed it on Angelica's shoulder. Her unconscious attempt to pull Angelica back by her side, however, met brief resistance before she pulled away. She then asked, "How often does the parade change like this?"

Sara glanced down at Angelica, who'd moved closer to her side, before saying, "It depends, really. Usually it's about every three years or so, give or take."

Edward briefly scratched his bearded cheek as he said, "Well, I guess we still have a lot to learn about this place."

Sara then looked down at the heirloom silver watch around her wrist. She glanced over at the closest concession stand before saying, "I think I'm going to grab something to eat before the parade starts. Would you all like anything while I'm over there?"

Rosanna shook her head as Edward replied, "I wouldn't mind a hotdog, if it's not an inconvenience."

Sara replied, "Okay, it's no trouble... oh, wait, I forgot. They only have the blood sausage during a recompense parade. They do make smaller ones for hotdogs, though. Do you want one of those?"

He hesitated a moment, lost in Sara's alluring eyes that seemed to reach out beyond the reflect surface of her sunglasses. He quickly recovered, however, and said, "You know what, sure! You want one, hon?"

Rosanna's nose snarled obviously, "Ew, no thanks!"

Sara looked down at Angelica. "How about you, Ange?"

She thought about it for a moment before responding, "I will if that's what you're getting!"

Sara smiled. "Okay then!" She looked over at Rosanna and asked, "Do you mind if she comes with me? She can help me carry the food."

Both her parents nodded.

"All right, be right back. Let's go, Ange!"

Neither of them noticed that Mary Kelly and her kids were watching them from the other side of the street.

Rosanna then looked to Edward and said, "Don't expect any kisses from me until you get home and brush your teeth!"

Feigning surprise, he replied, "What? You mean I don't get to pretend I'm Vlad the Impaler tonight?"

Assuming he was making an innuendo, she slapped him on the arm. "You behave, Mr. Barrister!"

A few minutes later and Angelica and Sara were queued up to be next in line to place their order.

The latter turned and looked down at her friend. "Do you want a blood dog or just a sausage?"

She thought for a moment, then shrugged. "Whichever one you're having."

Sara smiled. "All right, two sausages and a bloody hotdog."

She grinned and replied, "Sara, where do you get your clothes? I haven't seen anyone else dress the same way you do."

"Well, some are antiques, but most I make myself." She essentially knew the answer to her next question, but asked anyway. "Do you dislike them?"

Angelica's eyes grew larger as she shook her head. "No, I love them! They're different and they make you look beautiful!"

She genuinely blushed. "Aww, thank you! Most people don't say things like that."

"Why not? It's true!"

Sara could tell that others around her were hearing her just fine, but were doing a bad job at pretending to not be listening. "Some people just have a hard time accepting things they don't consider *normal*."

A distant drum cadence now caught their attention as Sara paid for the food. She handed Angelica her vittles and hurried her back toward the sidewalk where Edward and Rosanna were waiting. Once beside him, Sara handed the blood dog to Edward. She silently rejected his offer to pay for it as the marching band's snare drummer continued playing alone. The tempo was noticeably slower and somber. Despite having not seen this version of the parade, the Barristers, and everyone else, were deathly quiet.

Several seconds passed before Rosanna looked over to see Sara's left arm half embracing and half shielding her. It was then that three flutes from the marching band began to play a solemn and haunting melody accompanying the drums. The melody being played in a minor key was accentuated by the black plumes (normally green) that adorned all the marching musicians.

Only the three flutes and percussion accompaniment played the rest of the parade which was far shorter than before. The second and final attraction was one that stunned the Barristers in its appearance. The wagon normally drawn by beast was there, but the "horsepower" was provided by fourteen men, one of whom was John Kelly Sr. Sister Francis and Sister Gillian were seated at the front seat. In the back of the wagon was a tall scarecrow-like effigy covered by a large tarp.

The Barristers looked on in disbelief as the men silently pulled the wagon on. Not sure whether to be more unsettled by that sight or the normalcy with which everyone else was accepting, they gawked. Their attention, however, was broken as a loud whip cracked from the hand of Sister Francis. She was only lashing at the air far above the men's backs, but it jarred the Barristers with each crack.

They didn't have long to stare, however, as they then saw everyone approaching and dropping off their individual effigies. They followed suit.

Only a few minutes later and the wagon had come to a stop in front of the town hall building. The men that were pulling the wheeled vehicle were given no rest after the haul. They removed their custom made harnesses and began unloading the effigies. Each was placed in a pile around a central podium, from which protruded a rod several inches long.

Once the corn dolly effigies were unloaded, four of the men moved the larger effigy from the wagon and placed it upon the rod via a hole in the base. It was then that Sister Gillian's creation, her Frankenstein's monster, was unveiled for the crowd to see. The shape was humanoid in general, but certain features were disproportionately larger. The arms and legs hung low along with ten fingers and toes made from opossum tails. The gray fur of the opossums comprised the "skin" of the ghoulish monstrosity, it being stitched and held together by thick black plastic thread. The eyes of the abomination were small amalgams of opossum eyes held together in a tiny, clear plastic bag. The head was vaguely canine in shape; as much as the crude wire mesh beneath allowed. This perversity of life looked appalling enough to anyone there to never come to life, but lively enough to dread such a thing possible.

As the members of the town formed a large circle around the soon-to-be-pyre, Mayor Pinkerton approached the pile of effigies and lowered his head. He waited a few moments, with Sheriff Beasley, Roberta and other members of the Town Council around him, before raising it again and spoke.

"Beloved people of Miller's Run, it is with a heavy heart that I declare this to be a year of want and recompense. Since the days of our first mayor, Silas Goodwin," he paused and looked up at Sara. He continued. "And the loss of Constance Goodwin, the good people of Miller's Run have sought peace and balance. May the Lord our God hear our cries for mercy!"

A small insight now made itself clear in Sara's mind. *They blame my family for this!?* She looked all around briefly. Only a few sets of eyes here and there looked up, but she could feel their energy radiating well enough.

The mayor then turned and nodded at John Kelly Sr. With his cue, he walked over to the pile of effigies and doused them heavily with the five gallon can of gasoline in his hands. Upon finishing, he produced a match tossed it onto the heap. It quickly went up with a "whoosh" and burned feverishly. The smell of burning hay, corn, and opossum flesh and hair soon saturated the air.

Everyone stayed to watch the fire burn into the evening until only embers and ashes remained.

Eighty-five

The last few days of Angelica's summer break went by quickly, as the last days of vacation always do. They took the advice given after the paranormal team's investigation and remained in the hotel on the edge of town, only going to their farm for clothing and such. The Church approved of the Minor Rite of Exorcism that was to be performed by Father Anderson several days later. Father Anderson would need time to prepare mentally and spiritually, and undergo fasting to purify his body for the task ahead. The wait seemed intolerable at times to the Barristers, but they were assured that there was no rushing in this matter. Not preparing properly could be catastrophic for the family, the team, and especially for Father Anderson.

On the last day of summer break, Angelica and Abby spent the day together at the Kelly farm. Most of that day was spent walking and talking in the patch of forest on their land. The two of them were a little surprised when John Jr. seemed really concerned about Angelica. He stayed fairly close to the two of them as they went into the forest. Despite Abby telling him to go away a couple of times, she soon relented and could tell that her brother was genuinely wanting to protect them. Angelica didn't mind, although most of her conversation time was spent with Abby.

As with every day, however, the time flew by and the next morning Rosanna was taking her daughter to school. She looked over proudly at Angelica, who was quietly staring out the passenger window. Her school uniform reminded her of her own time in Catholic school, although it was from a different area. She knew Angelica wasn't particularly fond of the garb as she tugged at the collar of the button-up white shirt under the navy blue vest bearing the school's seal. Smiling, "You look so nice in your uniform."

Angelica only glanced in her direction, neither making eye contact nor auditory response. She looked back out the window and now saw the sign marking the border of Miller's Run. She had seen the sign a few hundred times before. Angelica knew that the white text on the green wooden sign displayed: "Miller's Run Wants You Back!" Someone long ago, in the 1950s, decided that it would be a warm and thankful goodbye to any visitors or tourists (not that Miller's Run was ever notorious for tourists, then or now). As Angelica read the words out of habit, however, she noticed a difference in the text: "Miller's Run Wants You Dead!" She squinted her eyes in disbelief for a moment, but when she reopened them, they were already past the sign.

Rosanna glanced over at her daughter again but didn't want to force any conversation.

The rest of the drive was painfully uneventful. No words were shared between them. Angelica simply stared off into the distance never once looking toward her mother. The frosty aura given off by her daughter almost seemed so literal that Rosanna wouldn't have been surprised if she could see her breath fog up when she exhaled.

The Subaru came to a stop near the entrance to St. Mary's.

Rosanna said as Angelica opened the door, "Goodbye, sweetie. Have a good day at school."

Angelica returned a lukewarm goodbye.

Eighty-six

Later that morning, Angelica was sitting in the back row of her class. It was second period and time for math. She had her notebook and textbook out and open. Math always came easily to her, so even though this was technically "new material," it didn't take her mind long to start wandering. The regular teacher for her class was going to be unable to start until the third week due to a death in the family. In the meantime, Sister Francis would be substituting. This was the first year that Angelica would get to know more about her. Sister Francis carried a certain ironclad aura about her, made clear by her posture and body language. She would sometimes stand over her desk, leaning on her hands and angled arms which made her look like a despot shouting orders at her staff. Who knew third grade could be so militant. To deal with this intimidation, however, students would often make fun of her behind her back (granted her back needed to be about a mile away before they felt safe doing it). With her habit, the only feature visible would be her face. This made a key feature stick out even more than it would normally: a larger-than-usual nose. It wasn't particularly bulbous, but the angle at which it hooked over her top lip exaggerated its proportions in comparison to her face. The older students in the school, after maybe having several Latin lessons, referred to her as "Corvus in Christo" (Crow of Christ). No one, however, had the courage to ever say it to her face. Over the years it would trickle down to the younger students who would inevitably tell all of their friends and so on.

A few minutes into class, Angelica (who had already heard of the nickname in homeroom) was staring blankly at her as she wrote several numbers on the board and cawed. *Wow! That is a beak!* she thought to herself. As she stared forward, however, Angelica did not notice that her left hand had grabbed the pencil on her desk and was swirling around in odd directions.

Over a minute later, Angelica finally looked down at the unnoticed sketch she'd made. Staring back at her was the crudely etched face of a goat. Its tongue was hanging out of its mouth and there were X's drawn in place of the eyes. She didn't know how she'd drawn that without looking down even once. The fact that she was right-handed and had drawn this with her left hand baffled her even further.

She sat frozen in her seat staring at the image with a furrowed brow of confusion mixed equal parts with chilling uneasiness. Someone noticed she wasn't paying attention: Sister Francis.

The nun said in a scolding tone, "Angelica! Pay attention!"

Angelica apologized and went back to staring at the board. Someone in the front row, however, had briefly turned around to look at her down the aisle. She would soon come to know the name of this blonde-haired girl: Becky. Rebecca Probost looked at her arrogantly and raised her eyebrow briefly before turning about around to look at the chalkboard. She may have been the cutest child on Earth to her parents and any self-respecting member of the community would say the same. One thing that was never brought up to her otherwise cute face was her nose as well. It seemed to bear the same disproportion as Sister Francis' nose. But unlike the nun, however, she did her best to remain oblivious to this. Her parents would tell her that it made her unique in an attempt to boost her ego and counterbalance any shame. Anyone that knew Becky would state clearly that she didn't need a single ounce of ego inflation, as a single drop more would send her self-image into orbit.

Later, at recess, Angelica was tossing a dodgeball back and forth with a girl in her grade (she had just met her on the playground and already forgotten her name).

After a few throws she caught the ball and noticed a figure standing in one of the second story classrooms looking out. There was something different about that nun, something Angelica felt right away. She tossed the ball and caught it once more. She looked up and the figure was gone from the window. Angelica almost shrugged off the incident by the time she tossed the ball and caught it again. When she then looked over the figure of the nun was standing along a brick walkway that lined the playground. At that point she wanted to simply dismiss it as seeing two different nuns. After all, they all wore the same uniform. It wasn't until now, however, that she saw the nun's very pale blue eyes, almost gray. Immediately she made the connection to the story Sara had told her.

Angelica then looked over long enough to catch the red ball and toss it back. Upon catching it, she looked back toward the walkway and was astonished to see the nun glide straight through the thick dark green hedges bordering the playground without disturbing a single leaf. They were rigid and somewhat prickly leaves and dense enough that one wouldn't even be able to push their hand through without some pain. To this Sister, however, they'd might as well not been there at all.

As Angelica stared at the disembodied nun the flesh and blood nun overseeing the students blew her referee's whistle to let everyone know that recess was over.

The students began to file back into the nearby entrance of the school. Angelica stared at the spirit-nun as she walked toward the door. She then heard, *"Hello,"* in a calm voice. Angelica clearly saw the Sister nod her head and smile. What she didn't see, however, was Becky walking directly toward her. With a sudden thud Angelica hit the ground, her hair being the only thing that cushioned her head from the concrete. She was dazed for a second, but realized she'd just been body-checked by Becky.

Her large nose and face then loomed over her as she said, "Watch it, hayseed!"

Despite having seen Miss Probost walk against the grain of the students filing in to do this act, Sister Francis appeared over her as well. "Angelica, watch where you're going!"

The rest of the students went into the building around her as she strained to get up, her head still reeling.

Sister Francis' voice said once again before letting the door close behind her, "Well, come on, girl, you need to get to class!"

Upon standing the figure of the spirit nun was right in front of Angelica. The woman in her habit said, *"You're okay. Those two will give you trouble, but don't take it personally."*

Hesitantly she whispered, "Okay... thank you."

The spirit then vanished from sight. Without another word Angelica rose to her feet and walked back inside.

Later that day, most of the school was in the lunchroom. Angelica ate her food and took the tray back to the dishwashing window. She looked at the clock on the wall and realized that she had another ten minutes before she'd have to go to her next class. It was then that she looked over at Becky and two of her friends who were whispering something to one another before looking in her direction and giggling. She decided to go to the bathroom and hopefully use enough time to just make it to the next class.

After getting permission from one of the nuns nearby she headed to the bathroom.

It didn't take nearly as long as she thought it might, as she didn't want to have anything to do with Becky. As she washed her hands, however, she began to snicker and laugh. She'd just had an epiphany: "Beaky Becky." If Rebecca was going to continue to harass her, at least she'd have a clever name with which to fire back.

Content, she walked out into the hall to head back toward the lunchroom. In the hall, however, was the spirit of the nun she'd seen at recess earlier. *"Follow me, I want to show you something."* Despite being concerned about being found wandering the halls before her next class started, she silently agreed and followed her. The nun glided silently on the floor and then disappeared around a turn. As Angelica rounded the same she saw the Sister at the far end of the hallway. She was at a T-intersection and was pointing to her right. Angelica hesitated a moment, as she knew that was the area of the teachers' lounge. Sensing her apprehension, *"You'll be okay. There's something that you need to see."* She took a deep breath, looked all around and realized she was in the clear. She then began to walk at what she imagined was a pace that wouldn't arouse suspicion.

She approached the T-intersection where the nun was previously standing. Angelica looked all around once more and then at down the hall. The Sister was standing in front of a door and pointing to it now. *"In there."*

Angelica then realized that she was pointing at the teachers' supply room. She also knew that the door was kept locked and only the teachers had a key to get in. She looked over her shoulder and at the fogged-glass that was most of the top half of every door. She couldn't make out any humanoid shapes. She then said in a barely perceptible whisper, "I can't go in there! I'll get in trouble and it's locked!"

The spirit smiled and said, *"I give you permission to go in there. Here, let me get that lock for you."* The nun then vanished. All at once, the sounds of a key being inserted into and opening the lock were heard. The door then opened a couple of inches to the inside.

Angelica looked all around again before quietly stepping toward the door and opening it just enough to squeeze inside. Once there, she closed the door almost completely, leaving enough space to not have it abnormally ajar to a casual observer outside. Before her lay a relatively large room with stacks of papers, notebooks, boxes of pencils and pens, textbooks, and most everything a teacher could hope for.

Repeatedly she looked back toward the door as she walked among the shelves and tables.

After looking around the room for about thirty seconds, she whispered, "What am I looking for?"

"Over here." She could see the nun pointing to a room connected to this one. It was much smaller. *"Inside."*

Angelica then walked toward the adjoining chamber. Upon getting to the door she looked inside and found stacks of paint cans, varnish, and other various supplies that a person may need to do touchups on any job that may crop up at the school. The smell in the room was a musty odor combined with faint remnants of paint and wood coating.

She then whispered, "What's in here?"

"Look there...." A medium-sized drop cloth that was covering something leaning against the wall was tossed up and to the side by the apparently invisible arm of the nun. *"Do you remember?"*

Angelica quickly saw that they were three windowpanes. And they weren't just any old windows, they were the three from her house. She used the drop cloth nearby to carefully grip the glass and review each one in turn. These were no doubt the same windows that came from her own house.

She quietly reflected, but couldn't for the life of her figure out why they were there. Her concentration was broken, however, when she heard a feminine voice from outside in the hall. She faintly heard, "Who left this door open?"

Terrified, she covered the windows back up with the cloth. The spirit's voice then came through. *"Don't worry, you won't get in trouble. Just walk out into the open...."*

At first, Angelica thought it was crazy talk, but she slowly stepped out anyway. Immediately, one of the nuns at the school had walked in. In a calm voice she said, "Angelica, right? What on Earth on you doing in here?"

Sister Gillian, one of the nicest teachers she knew there. Unable to think of a good reason, Angelica just said, "I guess I got curious. The door was open and all."

She smiled. "Ah, okay. Well, as you can see it's incredibly boring in here. Now, let's get you back to class before you get in trouble. Don't worry, I won't turn you in. Just don't wander in here anymore, okay?"

"Okay, Sister Gillian, I won't."

That afternoon, Angelica was very glad that the first day back had come to an end. Not only that, she was getting to visit her new mentor Sara. She was picking her up for what she described as "some final preparations before the exorcism." Edward and Rosanna weren't really too sure about why she wanted to speak to Angelica alone, but they trusted her at this point and knew she was possibly the only local person that could help her. The latter of the two, however, still felt uncertain, but not enough to forbid.

Sara's car that was waiting for her when she left the building.

As Angelica approached the car she smiled and waved.

Sister Francis and Rebecca were looking on as the door came open.

The former immediately noticed Sara's face and remembered her. The nun then said to her grandniece in a hushed tone, "As I live and breathe! Their family is friends with Sara Goodwin!? I suppose I'm not surprised."

Becky looked up at Francis. "Who's she?"

The Sister replied, "Someone you don't want to have anything to do with. She was always a very headstrong student. There were even rumors among her classmates that she practiced witchcraft! May God have mercy on her soul if she's trying to corrupt that girl, even if that girl is a country bumpkin."

Angelica buckled her seatbelt after shutting the door. Sara looked down and smiled at Angelica before looking up and out the window. She made brief eye contact with Sister Francis. No malice, but also no kindness. Just a stony stare.

Smiling once again, "Are you ready to go?"

"Yep!"

Eighty-seven

Later that afternoon, the two arrived at Sara's house and headed inside. Sara then offered her friend something to drink before sitting down beside her at the small kitchen table. Angelica opened the bottle of water and took a drink.

Sara smiled and said, "So how was your first day back at school?"

"Not good."

"Oh, anything you want to talk about?"

She was ready to launch into a discussion about Rebecca, but that caused another thought to take first in line. "Yeah, I drew something in math class this morning." She opened her backpack and fished out the creepy drawing of the goat's head. "Here." She slid it across the table.

Sara looked it over and said, "Well, that's odd. Why would you want to draw something like this?"

Angelica replied, "I didn't know I was doing it. I was looking at the chalkboard at the front of the room the whole time! And besides, I drew it with my left hand. I'm right-handed."

Sara raised her head in understanding. "I see. You were probably experiencing automatic writing. Some sensitives have this ability in varying degrees."

Angelica, "So something was making me write this?"

"Well, in a manner of speaking, I suppose. Something may have been communicating with your subconscious mind. You said you were paying attention to the board and that you used your left hand. It may have been harder for it influence your right hand if you were in conscious control of it."

"What does it mean? What's the message?"

She briefly sighed. "That's the tough part sometimes. You may draw something like this that won't make much sense at the time. You'll simply have to keep your eyes open for something to follow. Do you remember if anything was looming around in your head right before or after you drew that?"

Angelica's eyes were suddenly wide with an epiphany. "Yeah! I was thinking that I would rather be at home playing with Cerberus! Then that made me think of my three goats."

Sara replied, "Hmm, well, that could be the beginning and end of the purpose. It could mean something more, however, so just watch for anything that might shed light on it."

A new thought jumped into Angelica's mind. "Oh! I saw the nun you were talking about at school today!"

Smiling, "That's wonderful! Did she speak to you?"

"Yeah. She figured out pretty quickly that I could see her. I saw her in a window upstairs, then she just appeared in the playground. She seemed really nice!"

"Great! I always felt her presence on the school campus."

"She even helped me up when Becky knocked me down."

Sara could easily see that that bugged her. "Oh, no. What happened?"

"We were going back inside from recess and she just ran into me! She did it on purpose, I know she did! Then Sister Francis yelled at *me* for it!"

"Oh. Are you okay?"

"Yeah, I'm okay. I had a headache after that, but it went away. I think Sister Francis and Becky are related."

"Why's that?"

"Because they both have the same huge nose. I'm going to start calling her Beaky Becky."

Chuckling, "I think you may be right. What's her last name?"

"Probost."

"Oh, then they *are* related."

Then, perhaps the most important event came into focus. Angelica then said, "I should've told you first thing, but I found our windows!"

The air of light gossiping caused a look of seriousness to overtake Sara's face. "Really? Where were they?"

"They were in a small closet inside the teachers' supply room."

Her eyebrows dropped and made her subtle frown more obvious. She paused before saying, "Wait, you found the three windows from your house at the school? Are you sure they were the same?"

"I'm positive! They had the burn marks and everything! All three were covered with a tarp and up against the wall. The ghost of the nun showed me where they were." She watched Sara's eyes lower and look side to side as she searched for an explanation. "Why would *they* have them? How did *they* know?"

Still baffled, "Ange, I don't understand it either. I mean, maybe one of the other team members found them and wanted them sealed away at the church. No one has told me anything about that if that's what happened. I'll have to call them later and ask."

Anyone could see the uneasiness on her face, but Angelica could feel it radiating from her like uranium. "Why are you so afraid?"

She finally made eye contact after a few seconds. "Because it doesn't make any sense. I feel like someone is trying to pull the wool over my eyes and I don't know who." She stood back up. "Come upstairs with me. I have some more evidence that I found in the family library that might help shed light on the situation."

They walked to the stairs and were soon on the second story. They headed down the hall to a door that was adorned with a brass metal ornament in the shape of a wolf's head. As Sara produced an old-fashioned skeleton key from her pocket, Angelica said, "That wolf's head is beautiful!"

She turned the key and the tumblers inside clicked. "Thank you! I've always liked it. Wait until you see inside!"

As Sara opened the door and stepped in, Angelica was overwhelmed by the sight of deep mahogany wood that made up the bookshelves, molding, and wainscoting wrapping every square inch of the walls. The smell of the old leather book covers and leather top cushioning of the chairs filled the room. On top of the mahogany desk was an old-fashioned quill pen next to a fountain pen.

Angelica's eyes were soon drawn to a large series of shelves to her right that contained a menagerie of statues ranging from inches to around two feet tall. She didn't recognize the different entities (most deities of various religions) associated with each sculpture, but knew many looked like Greco-Roman artwork from different classical art books her mother had at home. One immediately stood out to her: the statue of two baby boys underneath a she-wolf preparing to suckle. "Oh, cool!" she exclaimed. "I've seen that in a book before. What is it again?"

Smiling, "That is Romulus and Remus. They were said to be the brothers who eventually fought and that led to the founding of Rome. Obviously Romulus won. The myth states that they were raised by a she-wolf after they were left in the wild on their own as babies."

"Oh, yeah! I think Grandpa told me that story one night. He said he would take me to see Rome someday."

"You know, I haven't been to Rome either. Maybe one day if you don't get to go with your grandpa, I'll take you there."

Excited, "That'd be fun!" She looked back at the lineup and pointed to a sculpture of a figure wearing a pair of winged sandals and a winged cap. "I've seen that one, too. Isn't that Mercury?"

"Yes, or Hermes, depending on whether you prefer the Roman or the Greek name. He's the messenger of the gods."

She looked over a handful of other humanoid figures before her eyes locked onto a painted and decidedly different appearance. Besides being painted, unlike the previous statues, it was an amalgam of human and canine features. The uncanny resemblance immediately caught her eye.

She pointed. "Who's that, Sara?"

"That's Anubis, the ancient Egyptian god of the dead."

Thinking she had to jar her memory, "Doesn't he look a lot like that sketch you showed us?"

Sara's smile dropped a bit as she knew she couldn't slip anything past her friend's keen mind. "Yes, I noticed that myself. I wasn't sure if I should tell you and your family about it, as I didn't know if it would really help anything." She paused, but could see Angelica was very curious and not going to let it go without a resolution. "When I saw the sketch at the meeting, it made me remember something I'd read about years ago. Have you ever heard of the term 'cynocephaly'?"

Tilting her head, "Cyno... what?"

"Cynocephaly. I don't have any hard evidence to back it up, other than sketches and reading. Basically, in ancient times and all the way to the medieval period, there was a belief that dog-headed humans existed. They were like humans in most ways, except they had dog heads and were usually covered in thick fur. They were also described as being vicious and wild. They would usually act violently toward humans, although there were stories of people who traded with them. It was also mentioned that they communicated with barks and bays just like dogs. Now what they have to do with the whole situation at your property is something I'm just not seeing at the moment."

"Do you think they're real?"

She thought a moment before replying, "I don't know, Ange; I really don't. I might've said 'no' outright before, but I found a few sketches in my library here. They were similar to the one you saw that night, but they were all unique. From the looks of it, about six different ones were sketched altogether. It's hard to think the artist would make the same mistake that many times or intentionally try lie about it. They certainly didn't need any further motivation to wipeout the cannibals. It may sound crazy, but I suppose if they are real, there's no reason they wouldn't be on this continent too. But why...." She could see Angelica's eyes widening with creeping fear. She then shook her head. "I'm sorry, I was prattling on there. I'm going to do some more reading tonight on the matter. And don't worry, I doubt there are any living today if they are real."

"I'm not worried about the ones that are alive."

Understandingly, "I know what you mean. Stay strong, Ange. We *will* win."

"I hope so." She paused for a moment before abruptly asking, "I almost forgot, you never told me who Morrigan is."

Smirking, "You're right. In short, Morrigan was a goddess once worshiped by the ancestors of the Scottish, Irish, and other Celtic tribes in Europe. She was a goddess of war and death. She would often take the form of a crow."

Remembering that day clearly, "Oh, right. The crow landed on the car and stood there for a while staring at us."

"Exactly! I saw the crow and it made me think of her."

"So do you believe she exists?"

The discomfort was clear on her face. "Well, I'm not always sure of what I believe. Sometimes I get very confused. Life is slippery like that."

"I know what you mean. I didn't mean to snoop, I'm sorry."

Placing her hand on her shoulder, "Oh, it's okay! Trust me, life stays confusing as you grow up. You just have different puzzles to think on as you get older."

Sighing, "I was hoping things would get easier as I got older."

Laughing, "Oh, some things do, don't worry. Just don't get too comfortable with where you're at at any point."

Angelica's mood picked up slightly again. "You sure do have a lot of books here. Have you read them all yet?"

Turning to look at the collection, "There are, aren't they? I haven't even read half of them yet. That would take quite a bit of time, and I'm not *that* old yet."

Angelica chuckled and continued to look at the massive number of books jammed tightly into the shelves all around. Sara, however, had walked to the door on the opposite side of the room. As Angelica ran her hand over the smooth desk's surface, Sara pulled a second skeleton key from around her neck that was essentially invisible otherwise by being tucked into her top. As the lock on the door clicked open, she looked back at her approaching student. "Ange, will you close that door to the hall, please?"

She went over and closed the door before rejoining. As she approached the door Sara had just entered, she blocked further passage.

"Wait right here for just a moment. I'll be right back."

Angelica was confused, but waited anyway. She could hear Sara's shoes tapping gently on the floor with each step.

Several steps later Sara appeared at the door again and cracked it open. "Remember, don't tell anyone about this. Promise?"

Angelica was slightly nervous now but replied, "Yes, I promise."

"Good. You may come in now."

She opened the door and the room inside became visible. It was different than the other rooms in the house. For one, it had white marble tiled floors. Overall the walls formed a perfect square. Only a small rectangular window was found at the top of three of the walls, enough to let in some sunlight during the day. On the wall adjacent to the library wall was a fireplace that was back to back with the one in the library, sharing a common chimney. The center of the room, obviously designed to be the focus, was adorned for moderate braziers on pedestals. Behind each brazier was a white marble statue of four angels respectively. Connecting the four pedestals was a circle of red marble. In the center of all of this was a hefty mahogany altar that bore two untitled books. The altar was flanked by two brass candle holders that were about three feet tall. In each was a tall white candle. Angelica looked on in amazement at what was obviously, even to her at her young age, some sort of ritualistic room. Sara quickly got her attention again, however, as she knelt down in front of her. Angelica looked at her strangely as she noticed Sara's right hand was behind her back.

Sara then placed her left hand on Angelica's shoulder and said, "Angelica Barrister, do you trust me?"

She was going to respond "yes," but before the words could come out she pulled a small double-edged dagger from behind her back and placed it against Angelica's throat. She looked down at Sara's arm and muttered, "Why are you...?"

Sara's face was well composed and still gentle. "Angelica Barrister...." She paused and nodded once before continuing. She sounded out the next four words plainly and nodded in tempo. "Do, you, trust, me?"

Angelica gulped hard, but knew she always had trusted her and now was no exception. "Yes, I trust you."

Sara quickly took the dagger away and placed it on the altar. "Good. Now stand outside the circle and I'll sage you."

Angelica stopped and watched Sara open the two doors on the facing side of the altar. She produced a long lighter and two bags containing substances that Angelica couldn't recognize on sight alone. Sara then took a couple of pinches of the substance from one of the bags and tossed it onto the brazier before lighting it. The wooden sticks and shavings she'd placed in there, cedar, created a delightful smell in the air. After lighting all four she took a sage bundle from the altar's storage and lit it with the lighter. She then approached Angelica as she blew on the small embers to make them grow and produce wisps of gray smoke that rose lazily into the air. Sara then began to blow puffs of smoke in Angelica's direction as she looked up at the statues. Angelica soon recognized two of the figures. One was St. Michael, the archangel, depicted in the classic pose of standing with his foot upon the fallen enemy of The Church. The other she perceived as St. Gabriel, the archangel, posing with trumpet in hand and pointing it at the heavens. The other two, however, she didn't recognize.

Still amazed, Angelica said, "This room is beautiful! Are those the archangels there? Michael and Gabriel, right?"

Smiling now, "Yes, very good! The other two are Raphael and Uriel."

"Is this where you come to pray?"

"You could say that. In a way, this is a really fancy prayer room." She paused for a moment, then looked down at Angelica who was still showing some apprehension. Sara then knelt once again, placed her hands on the sides of Angelica's cranium and said, "I wasn't trying to scare you with the athame just now. It's just a practice you do before you invite someone into the circle. Do you understand? I would *never* harm a hair on your head."

Sara's eyes seemed greener and more genuine that she'd ever seen as they beamed at her from inches away.

Angelica replied, "I was just surprised, that's all."

She kissed her on the forehead. "Bravest little girl I've ever met." She then stood and opened one of the bags she'd gotten from the altar. "Now, stay inside this red circle until I say so. Do you understand?"

"Yes." Angelica tried figure out the meaning of the whole process happening before her, but she was fumbling around in proverbial darkness. She watched as Sara would drizzle enough salt within the red barrier circle and make cutting motions, as if into the ground, with the dagger in her hand.

After completing the pouring of the salt in a clockwise manner the entire boundary contained a clearly visible trail. She then looked down at Angelica and said, "Now, be silent while I send out my prayer." Lowering her head, she sent out a few silent words before raising the dagger in her right hand pointing it toward the heavens. With her left hand she tossed a bit of powder at the brazier and it flared briefly. In a loud and confident tone, she stood before the statue of the Raphael and said, "Blessed Archangel Raphael, guardian of the element of Air and watchtowers of the East, hear your supplicant's plea and be here with us now! Protect us from evil and darkness!" She then walked close to the edge of the circle toward the statue of Michael. There she repeated the same gesture with the dagger and the powder. "Blessed Archangel Michael, guardian of the element of Fire and watchtowers of the South, hear your supplicant's plea and be here with us now! Protect us from evil and darkness!" Sara then walked to the next statue, repeating the gestures and saying, "Blessed Archangel Gabriel, guardian of the element of Water and watchtowers of West, hear your supplicant's plea and be here with us now! Protect us from evil and darkness!" Finally she went to the last of the four statues and repeated the gestures once more. "Blessed Archangel Uriel, guardian of the element of Earth and watchtowers of the North, hear your supplicant's plea and be here with us now! Protect us from evil and darkness!" Sara then walked over to the altar once more, placed the dagger on top of it and returned the small pouches she'd taken out earlier. She then took out a small glass bottle of oil and another of water. After closing the doors she placed the bottle of oil on the altar. Still holding the bottle of water she knelt in front of Angelica again. She said quietly, "Okay, what I'm going to do now is ask that you receive a blessing to your sight. When I say sight, I mean your spirit eye, located here." She placed her finger on her forehead just above the midline between her visible eyes. "One of the most important things you'll need to develop as you grow is being able to see something or someone's true nature. Deception can cloud our ability to see clearly. Do you understand what I'm saying?"

Angelica nodded. "Yes."

"Good. Now, with your permission, I will pray to the Archangels and ask that they give you true sight. I have to tell you, however, that you may see more spirits after this blessing. Not only that, you might find that some people you encounter are not as nice as they appear. Do you understand the conditions?"

Angelica looked uncertain for a moment before saying, "You mean I'll see even more spirits? How will I be able to live at *my* house? Mom and Dad have decided that we're staying there."

The apprehension was ebbing from her and Sara could easily feel it. She looked down for a moment, trying to think of the best words. Engaging her eyes again, "Ange, I know it's scary right now, the position you're in, but if you don't have the ability to see things clearly, you're jeopardizing the lives of you and your family. It's imperative that your sight remains true. People with our abilities carry a heavy burden. Things will be difficult at times, but this will bring you a better understanding of how you can help yourself and others." Sara knew she was throwing a lot at Angelica in a short amount of time and so, gently, pulled her chin up which had dropped. "Hey, remember, I'll be there to teach you and we're all going to work together and take your property back to the best of our ability. One day you'll look back on this time and be stronger because of it."

Angelica sighed but now looked more confident.

"With that in mind, I'll ask you once again. Angelica Barrister, do you accept the blessing that I am about to pray for? I can only do this if you say you want the blessing."

She looked at her steadfastly. "I do. I accept."

Sara smiled warmly. "That's my girl!" She then turned and faced the altar once more. Raising her arms overhead and flattening her palms, she called out in a clear voice and said, "Hear the request of my heart divine angels above! I implore you to ready us for the battle that will take place at the property of the Barristers in the coming days! Keep the souls of those involved safe from the evil there and all around! And in your mercy I beseech you to give this girl, Angelica Barrister, the blessing of clear sight! Help her to discern good from evil, not only in others, but in herself as well. We petition the highest angels for these blessings!" Sara then took the bottle of water and dabbed some onto her finger. She knelt in front of Angelica and drew a star and circle on her forehead with it. She then turned around and repeated the gesture on her own forehead. "With this holy water we bless our mind's eye." After this she took the bottle of oil and repeated the symbol on Angelica and herself. "With this blessed oil we anoint our mind's eye." She then placed the oil and water back inside the altar and closed the doors. She took the dagger and held it above. "Blessed Archangels and divine guardians all over creation, we thank you for your blessings!" She then stepped to the edge of the circle, thrust the dagger over the salt barrier and made a cutting motion. "The circle is cut, but the blessings remain!"

As Sara smiled and placed the dagger inside the altar, Angelica felt the urge to turn around. Something suddenly stood out to her: a silver carving of a deer head on the top part of the door leading out. She said in an excited tone, "Sara, I just realized something!"

Placing her hand on her shoulder, "What's that, dear?"

Pointing at the door, "Look, a deer head! And on the door outside the library is a wolf's head!" She could see the confused expression on her face and continued. "Remember? The night you took me to Abby's house! A deer and a wolf stopped in the road!"

Sara was genuinely dumbstruck for a few seconds. "You know, you're right! The signs have been sitting right in front of my face and I didn't notice them! I've seen those carvings all my life and I guess I just stopped thinking about them. You see, I think the blessing is already working!"

"What does it mean, then?"

"I believe it means we're on the right track. Messages and signs like this can be cryptic at times, but I've always found if you just listen to your intuition, you'll find the reason."

As Sara stepped over to each brazier in return and began to cover them with their respective lids next to them, Angelica stared at the deer ornament on the door leading to the library. She then looked back. "Is it okay to step out of this circle now?"

"Oh, I forgot. I've closed the circle, so it's okay to walk out." She closed the lid on another brazier and said, "Hey, Ange, will you do me a favor? There's a broom and dustpan in the hall closet across from the library door. Will you get it for me, please?"

"Okay." She then opened the door to the library and exclaimed, "Sara, come look at this!"

As she approached the door she said, "What is it?"

Sara stepped in and saw Angelica pointing at the desk. On top of it was four neatly arranged large white feathers. They were even aligned to the cardinal directions.

Angelica then said, "This wasn't here before, was it?"

Sara replied, "No, it wasn't! That's an obvious sign if I've ever seen one!"

They both stood at the desk for a few moments, ogling the feathers.

Angelica then said, "I hope this is a good sign."

Smiling, "I believe it is...."

Suddenly a deathly cold and sharp gust of air scattered two of the feathers into the air. The air was cold enough to cause both of them to break out in goosebumps all over. The two dislodged feathers then slowly lilted to the ground, one after the other. Angelica then felt a tinge of anger, the peace and tranquility brought by the ritual suddenly waning.

"We're not scared of you, Caroline!"

Despite Angelica's brave statement, Sara became even more acutely aware of a larger and looming threat behind the hag in pioneer clothes. Trying to distract herself and Angelica from the unsettling scene, "Okay, let's go ahead and clean up the salt in the other room and I'll grab the books I wanted to show you and your family." Sara then went into the hall and retrieved the broom and dustpan from the closet. She paused at the door leading to the prayer room. "Just give me a second to clean up and we'll get going. Sound good?"

"Okay. Do you need my help?"

"No, I just need to sweep up the salt. Feel free to look around."

As Sara disappeared into the room, Angelica was quick to approach the bookcases. The first ones to catch her eyes were seven leather-bound books bearing the name *North American Wildlife*. She reached up and ran her finger down the leather spine complete with gold engraving. Close to that was a similar book series labeled *North American Botany*. She slid one of the books out and looked inside. Many of the painted images resembled plants she'd seen a million times back at the farm. She didn't dwell on the tome too long before placing it back into the ranks with the others.

Angelica continued to peruse the many books before her eyes fixated on a book that stood out from the others. Perhaps it was the lack of ornamentation that made it different. It was leather bound like the others, but the lack of effort put into any extraneous and aesthetic details was obvious. The title read, *Local Tribal Superstitions and Worship*. Beyond the visuals, Angelica felt a pull on her to grab it. She took a nearby stepstool and stood on the top shelf, reaching for and retrieving the book.

As she stepped back down, Sara entered the room. Closing the door behind her, "What's that you have there?"

Angelica felt embarrassed, as if she were caught doing something mischievous. "I was just going to look at it."

Sara smirked. "And you weren't going to read it?" Seeing Ange still a little uneasy, "It's okay, you can look at it." She then looked up at the clock on the wall and said, "Actually, how about I let you read that book next time you come over. We need to get going so I can present what I found to your parents."

Soon, the two of them were in the car heading back to the Barrister house where Rosanna and Edward were waiting.

As the car picked up speed on the main road, Angelica asked, "Do a lot of people pray the way you do? I've never seen anything like that before."

She glanced at the rearview mirror and said, "No, not many do. At least I don't know about it if they do."

Her curiosity was voracious. "Where did you learn how to do all of that?"

"Well, it was a combination of my mother and books."

"Can you teach me how to do it? I felt really calm and protected there."

"Maybe one day when you get older. Right now you're too young."

She rolled her eyes playfully. "Now you sound like my mom!"

Sara chuckled but couldn't help but feel bad about being compared to good old "Rosy Anna."

Eighty-eight

Not long after, the black BMW drew near the Barrister home. Angelica looked all around the visible expanse of their land still void of a single speck of life-filled green. As the car slowed down for the turn onto the driveway, she said with a mix of sarcasm and hopelessness, "I guess it's easy to figure out when you're on *our* land."

The car soon stopped in the turnaround as Edward came out to greet them. They stopped and got out of the car, Edward running over to pick up his daughter and greet her with a kiss. "Hey, baby girl! How was school today?"

She glanced over and didn't see her mother. "It sucked!"

Edward laughed but followed with genuine concern, "Well, what happened?"

As he put her down, "Becky happened! She knocked me down but I got yelled at for it!"

He replied, "Uh-oh! Who's Becky?"

Angelica suddenly ran toward the house and said, "I'll tell you in a minute. I'm going to go change!"

Edward then looked up at Sara who was approaching him. She said, "Becky sounds like a bully from what she told me. I know her family and they're not very pleasant people in general. Apparently she has a very large proboscis."

Edward laughed a bit louder than he anticipated. He then replied after his brief laughter begin to fall, "Well, I hope she keeps her big nose out of Angelica's business. If I know anything about Ange and her mother, you shouldn't try and push them around."

His spine ran cold as the familiar voice of his wife came from the opening screen door. "What's that, dear? Didn't catch that."

"D'oh, hey, hon! I was just telling Sara not to try and push the Leone women around."

She poked him hard in the ribs down low, causing him to wince in pain. "Is that right?"

Sara could see that Rosanna wasn't really upset, and decided to go for humor. With the leather books and a legal pad beneath her arm, she made a zipped-lip motion with her fingers. "I'm not saying a word! You're in trouble, Mr. Barrister!" She smiled and walked toward the backdoor, letting herself in.

Rosanna looked at her entering the house. *Just walking right in like she owns the place....* She quickly looked up at Edward and said with levity, "Remember, Ed, loose tongues sink ships!"

He laughed and kissed his wife on the forehead. *I wish she wouldn't call me "Mr. Barrister." It makes me feel so damned old!*

Inside the house, Angelica had darted out of her room having quickly changed into casual clothes.

Sara stopped her in the hall, however, and leaned in to whisper in her ear, "Ange, do you want to tell them about the windows you found?"

She just realized she hadn't really considered telling them yet. "I don't know... I guess if it'll help."

Still whispering as Rosanna and Edward came through the kitchen, "Okay. I'll bring it up after I give my talk. Sound good?" After Angelica nodded, Sara turned around and faced the Barristers. "Do you want to sit in the living room? We can start any time you want."

They looked at each other and nodded.

Soon enough, Sara was standing in the middle of the living room, her audience on the couch in front of her. She held the notes from the legal pad in her hands. She started. "Okay, Roberta already covered the basics of what happened here and in the town many years ago. In my family's personal library, I managed to find more intimate details related to the town and your property in particular. I'll warn you now that some of this is very unpleasant. If at any point you want me to stop, just say so. Understood?"

Edward, seated between his daughter and wife, looked at both of them to gage their reaction.

Sara continued. "If things become too graphic for Angelica's ears, I'll say so."

Rosanna and Edward looked more assured, but Angelica looked more annoyed than anything. Seeing her look, Sara glanced at her and sent a small amount of energy in her direction. It seemed to say, *"I said that for them, not you. I know you can handle this."*

Angelica's furrowed brow quickly relaxed as the words, although not heard, seemed perfectly crystal clear in her mind.

Sara began. "We already told you some things about the 'Flesh-Eaters,' or, 'Abominations' that lived here in the area when the Europeans first arrived. What Roberta told you was true, but there was more to it. You see, my family has been here in Miller's Run since the first days. The pioneers that came here first were led by my distant great grandfather Silas Goodwin. He, his wife, and four daughters all eventually built their first home near where my house is today. They were the first to establish a ferry across the river downstream. They were also the first to open a general store in town and he was also elected the first mayor of the township, but that's another lecture in itself.

"Anyway, the group was presented with the proposition by the local tribes to wipe out the Abominations, but not everyone was initially on board. From Silas' journal I was able to find out that it was a cold and crisp autumn evening when the settlers had all returned to their respective wagons to think about the vote coming up the next day. Everything seemed quiet and soon most everyone was asleep. The alarm was raised, however, when the two sentries who volunteered for the night's watch heard a girl screaming from the direction of the river. Then, several of the men grabbed their muskets and quickly got dressed. In the scramble, Silas' wife had managed to notice something. Their daughter, Constance, was gone. Silas had warned her not to go out alone, but apparently she had slipped away quietly to use the 'bathroom' area down river.

"When the men arrived at the banks, they saw her still lit lantern sitting undisturbed next to the taller weeds. They called out her name again and again through most of the night but couldn't find her.

"It wasn't until later, at first light, that they came upon the outskirts of the camp the Abominations had established. As they watched from the cover of the weeds, they could see a larger one, presumed to be an alpha male of the tribe, ordering a subservient male and female to 'hurry up,' with something, as best as they could tell. What they saw next horrified them. The two lesser 'things' ran off, each carrying a crude flint axe and a severed pale arm. Seeing this, Silas ordered the men to split up and surround the then grunting male that had distanced himself from the rest of the tribe. Silas then saw the bloodied sleeping clothes of his daughter hurled into the fire nearby. This caused Silas to fly into a fit of rage and run toward the alpha male with his musket in hand. When he rounded the crude mud structure behind which the Abomination was hiding, he paused only for a second. He never recovered from what he saw next." Seeing them waiting for the next line, she motioned to Edward to cover his daughter's ears. He did so, much to her chagrin. Sara continued, even placing her hand in front of her mouth as she spoke, "He was... *having his way with her corpse.*"

Rosanna's mouth dropped agape as she made the sign of the cross. Edward exclaimed, "Dear God!" Even though he didn't do it often away from Mass, he also made the sign of the cross.

Angelica looked at everyone in confusion. "What!? What was he doing!?"

Edward quickly replied, "Nothing you need to worry about, sweetie. Maybe when you get older."

Rosanna objected in scorn, "Older!? How about never!?"

Sara replied earnestly, "I'm sorry, but that's what happened. I didn't want it to seem like they just agreed to do it on the word of the locals and a lust for land."

Edward, still shaken, asked, "What happened then?"

"Well, needless to say, Silas was in an uncontrollable rage at that point. Nothing, not Heaven or Hell would get in his way. He charged the alpha male and bludgeoned him to death with his musket stock. The other men then started firing at the few Abominations that charged. They had never seen or heard a musket, so after the thunderous firing and dropping the warriors instantaneously, most of the others began to run away."

Savoring the vengeance now being read aloud, Edward said, "Damn right!"

Sara continued. "It took them several minutes to pull Silas away from the body of the alpha. He was covered in its blood and there wasn't much left of the head as he'd beaten it to a pulp. Even when his musket stock broke he picked up the shard remaining and stabbed its chest many, many times.

"When they returned to camp and explained to everyone what had happened, they bypassed the vote and all immediately agreed to follow him to wipe them all out. Some scouts of the local tribes also saw what was happening, and so they sent as many as they could to help. They took the life of every Abomination, young and old, male and female."

Rosanna felt a chill come over her as she asked with almost immediate regret, "How old was Constance?"

Sara glanced grimly at Angelica before looking at Rosanna and replying, "She was only eight years old."

Angelica felt a piece click into place in her mind, "The thing... I think it's the spirit of that...," she struggled, "Cynocep... thing!"

Rosanna looked at her with her eyebrow raised in confusion. "Cynuh... what?"

Sara wasn't really ready to share the idea with the family, but the cat had leaped out of the bag. "Cynocephalic. It roughly means 'dog-headed.' Remember the sketch we showed you? The one sketched was based on what Silas saw before he bludgeoned it death."

Edward looked puzzled and turned to his wife as she said, "Wait, you think the one with the dog pelt on his head was *actually* showing his real head!?"

Angelica jumped in. "Yeah, Mom! Remember, I told you all, that's what I saw in my room the first night we stayed here!"

Sara added, "I found some additional sketches of fallen Abominations. Here, take a look."

She presented the sketches and handed them to Edward and Rosanna. As they looked, the former said, "So they mentioned these things in the journal, too?"

Somewhat reluctantly, "Yes, they did. They claimed there were six of them in all."

Rosanna had found her boundaries of every reality stretched far in the past few months. This seemed to go a little too far for her. "Wait… you mean to tell me that the settlers claimed to have seen these things. They collaborated and stated this as fact? I'm sorry if this sounds rude, but I have trouble believing such a thing exists."

Sara responded, "Well, I'm not one-hundred-percent sure myself, but I'm just presenting what I've found. With Angelica's dream and the journal, it's worth looking at. Also, as I was digging through some of the old family books, I stumbled onto a rather interesting depiction that you may or may not recognize. It's a rare image, and not one that's officially accepted as legitimate, but it's worth looking at." She handed them a piece of paper with what seemed to depict a dog-headed person holding an older Eastern-Orthodox style cross in his hand.

Rosanna didn't recognize the image or understand the writing. "Who's this supposed to be?"

Sara answered, "That is said to be an image of St. Christopher. It was found in an old Eastern-Orthodox church. They believe he was depicted this way because of a mistranslation. He was reported to be a cannibal, gigantic, and bearing a canine head. After witnessing the Christ Child, however, he repented his evil ways and was given a human form. So goes the tale, anyway."

Rosanna replied with noticeable discomfort, "No, I don't believe that at all. I do not accept a Saint depicted as having a dog's head. That's blasphemous and absurd!"

Edward then said, "Hon, she said this is what she found and that's all. She's not trying to change our beliefs."

Rosanna shot an icy glance at Edward before Sara added, "Exactly. As I said, this image is not considered genuine by the Orthodox Church now. I did find, however, more references to dog-headed people throughout history. From ancient times, to the Classical period, all the way through the medieval era, they were referenced as fact. Obviously I only have the old accounts to show for it."

Angelica then said, "See, I told you I wasn't making it up."

Edward looked over at her and said reassuringly, "We didn't think you were lying, baby girl. Like you, we're trying to understand what's going on."

Angelica looked on, forlorn. "Now that thing is coming after me. I just know it!"

Edward hugged her and kissed her on top of her head. "Sweetie, don't worry. We're going to get rid of that damned thing. It won't bother anyone again. Sara and Father Anderson are going to help us through this." He looked up at Sara.

She understood the cue to reinforce. She paused only slightly (but long enough for Angelica to pick up on the hesitation she previously hadn't seen from her) before replying, "Right, Ange. We're going to take care of this." She could see the air in the room was still tense. "Well, how about a small break?" Seeing the adults nod in agreement, "Mr. and Mrs. Barrister, can I talk to you outside for a moment?"

They agreed.

Edward then said, "Just wait here on the couch, baby girl, we'll be right back."

She sighed. "Okay."

Once the three were out on the back porch, Sara said in a hushed tone, "I'm sorry I had to tell such a graphic story, but I think it's important that you hear it. I believe it's something we all need to be aware of. It's just another layer of the things that have happened here in the past couple of centuries, and this is just what we know of."

Edward asked in an unnerved tone, "You mean there's more!?"

Sara silently nodded.

Inside, Angelica had felt an uneasy pulling sensation that caused her to drift into the hallway. As she turned the corner, she was shocked to see the air around the door distorted. In the faint light she could make out what appeared to be black flames licking the door jam and flicking out into the hallway. As she heard the crackle and popping of the blaze, Caroline's voice came through clearly in her mind: *"Hell awaits, you little cunt!"*

She backed away slowly and nearly jumped out of her skin when Edward said, "Ange, you okay?"

She looked back at him and then toward her room once more. The flames were gone. Hesitantly, "Y-yeah. I'm okay...."

The three returned to the couch as Sara flipped a couple of pages on her legal pad. Seeing the correct line to on which to start, she began. "Now, I think it's imperative to address the *Caroline* issue. Yes, there was a woman named Caroline that lived near your property in the 1800s. Caroline Fleishhacker was a descendent of Silas Goodwin...."

Angelica interrupted. "*You're* related to Caroline!?"

Her mother scorned. "Angelica, don't interrupt her!"

Sara was anticipating the question but felt no easy way of saying it. She replied matter-of-factly, "Yes, she was a descendent of one of Silas' daughters and my relatives came from his son that he later had once they settled the area. Our connection only goes back to one split in the 1700s, so our relationship is not that close at all."

Angelica looked down. "I'm sorry, Sara."

She smiled. "It's okay, I understand." Sara looked back down at her pad.

Suddenly, time seemed to slow down for Edward. He was watching Sara's lips. He saw her tongue delicately touch her lips as she opened them and began to speak. She uttered a few words, but he didn't hear them. She glanced in his direction, simply addressing her audience, but he saw her pausing and looking deep into his eyes momentarily before continuing. He then heard his own voice in his mind: *"Just a kiss... dear God, just a kiss...."*

The moment was over quickly, however, and he turned to see something that blared in his mind now: Angelica staring at him, half confused and half upset. In nearly the same instance, he heard his daughter's voice: *"Dad!? What did you say!?"*

Sara had also stopped. It seemed the three had inadvertently just exchanged quick thoughts rather unintentionally.

Rosanna noticed and spoke up. "What's wrong?"

Edward froze inside. He prayed he didn't just say that aloud. And even if he didn't, he couldn't tell if Sara had heard him. He *knew* Angelica did. He looked at Rosanna and quietly said, "You didn't hear that?"

She responded, "Hear what?"

"Nothing." He looked back at Sara and Angelica in discomfort. He was at least partially relieved, but still apprehensive. Sara did look at him with her eyebrow raised momentarily. He then muttered, "Sorry...."

Rosanna still looked confused as Sara began to speak again. She started from the beginning again. "I was quite surprised to find that in my library, there was an old journal that Caroline had kept after she moved here. At first, most of it was simply going over how much she enjoyed helping set up her new home with her first husband. He (Thomas) and some neighbors had erected their log cabin not far from the stream and life seemed rather normal and pleasan.

"A few months after they completed work on the cabin, Caroline became pregnant with her first child. They were overjoyed that their family was starting in earnest.

"As time passed, however, Caroline began to worry more and more about her coming child. She wrote that in her nightmare she would see her baby falling from the sky. No matter how fast she ran she couldn't catch it and it would splatter on the ground before her. As she dropped to her knees to grab the pieces, the ground would open up and swallow the baby's body. She would then be pulled under herself. She had this dream for a month straight before the baby was born.

"When the time finally did come for her deliver the baby, they were relieved that the baby boy was born without a problem. She immediately began to think that it was just nerves and her friends assured her that all of their pregnancies made them terribly nervous, especially their first.

"Life went on as usual, but soon Caroline started having another recurring nightmare. She wrote that she find herself in their field running for what seemed like miles before coming to a dead end at a massive waterfall. As soon as she would approach she would see the body of her husband topple over the crest of the falls and be dashed on the rocks below before washing ashore. Each time she would pull his body to the shore only to see it decay at a horrid pace in front of her. She woke up screaming every night.

"Around a month after the baby was born, Caroline awoke one morning and started feeding the baby as her husband went out to chop some firewood. It was getting toward the end of summer, so she knew he'd be out most of the day.

"Later that afternoon, however, Caroline became worried as her husband hadn't returned yet for supper. She took the baby and walked out to the edge of the woods calling his name, but he didn't respond. Until nearly nightfall she walked up and down the stream calling his name and searching, but she never found him.

"The next morning, Caroline set out early and made it to a neighbor's cabin around dawn. She told them about her husband disappearing and they agreed to send a few of the men out to look for him.

"They searched for a day before finding his axe in the forest. The day after that they found his body face down in the stream. He didn't have any obvious wounds that they could see, so they never figured out how a man of his age and vigor could simply drown in a stream that wasn't more than a foot deep where they found him.

"Needless to say, Caroline was overwhelmed with grief. Not only that, she was stricken to near panic at what to do with her life. She had just had a baby and her husband died. They were living in relatively wild territory, so she didn't have many options. The only thing she could think to do was try and remarry, but in such a small community it seemed a difficult process.

"Now, not long after her husband had died, she was awoken one morning by her dog barking. Not sure if it was a threat, she grabbed the musket from over the fireplace and went out the door. There, at the top of the hill near her house, stood two natives from the friendly local tribe. One of them was an older man wearing many beads, well-worn leather bottoms, and feathers in his hair. Clearly he was a man of great importance. Next to him was a middle-aged woman bearing a basket filled with corn, berries, and other food items.

"Still deeply mourning and unsure as to how her husband had died, she raised the musket and pointed it at them. She yelled, 'If you killed my husband, you'll have to try a lot harder with me!' The man stood silent a moment.

"The man then raised his hand in a calming gesture. He then said in accurate but awkwardly paced English, 'Peace. Your people call me Owl of the Sun. Our people have traded with yours peacefully for many years. We heard of your loss and are deeply sorry.' He then motioned to the woman next to him, who stepped forward with the basket. 'We bring this to you to pay our respect.'

"Caroline immediately suspected that they knew something. She pulled the musket up again and demanded, 'What do you know of my husband!? Did you kill him!?'

"The man seemed hurt, but must've known she was still in shock from the situation. He said calmly, 'Please, we have no quarrel with you or your people. We do know who killed your husband. Please, lower your weapon, we have brought none with us.' The woman quietly backed away after placing the basket of food on the ground as Caroline lowered the musket.

"Caroline then said, 'You know who killed my husband? Who was it?'

"He replied, 'The *spirit* of the, you call them *Abominations*, killed him. They lured him to the stream and drowned him.'

"She said, 'Abominations? They were killed years ago!'

"He attempted to make it more clear. 'No, the *spirit* of the *Abominations*. Not living like we are.' Caroline was confused, so he continued. 'I am the Medicine Man of my tribe. I know you have the gift of sight. I have seen you in a vision and I have come to warn you. Do not go to the cave of the evil spirits. They are, what your people call, *damned*. It is, as you would say, a doorway to Hell. You will be tempted to go there, but you must not. They will *consume* you! Their kind ate the flesh of other people and they continue this in death! They will consume your spirit for all time!'

"Caroline was dumbstruck and said, 'What cave? Which one? There are many caves here!'

"He replied, 'You will see in your dreams. You see much in your dreams. You would be wise to listen to them. You knew your husband was going to die before it happened, did you not?' She nodded and he continued. 'Then you know of other things that *may* happen. You have to learn the difference between what you *can* prevent, and what you *cannot*. It is a hard lesson.'

"Caroline replied, 'I knew my mother was going to die a month before it happened. Several weeks before my father died, the same. How will I know what I can change?'

"He then said, 'As I said, you will have to learn the messages of your own mind. The spirits will speak to you and you will grow to know the difference. Whatever you do, do *not* listen to the spirits of the cave! They will try and deceive you any way they can!'

"Caroline then said, 'Thank you for the warning. I'll do what I can.'

"The Medicine Man replied, 'Go now and grieve in peace. When the time comes for harvest, we will help you until you are able to remarry if your people do not. But remember, you must always keep your mind aware.' He then said something in their tribe's language that she didn't understand before leaving with the woman who came with him.

"Several days after the Medicine Man left something drastic happened. Now this should sound familiar: Her land dried up in a blight similar to your own. All the plants died, including the crops they had planted. Now Caroline, only twenty years old at the time, was in dire straits. Here her husband had just died, she had to care for her baby, and now the crops she was looking to rely on were all withered. One of her neighbors was kind enough to let her move in. The night before she left, however, she had another nightmare. She described it as running through the dead fields, hearing the faint voice of her dead husband, Thomas, calling in the distance. She would occasionally see him far away, but wasn't quite able to reach him. That's when she came upon the cave: the cave we believe is on your land. When she got to the entrance, she saw her husband just beyond what she described as 'iron gates.' He looked very disheveled and terrified. He said to her, 'Caroline, my dear, they've trapped me here! They are holding me ransom, as well as killing our land! They won't let me free from here unless you make a choice! Please, Caroline, I'm in Hell!'

"She cried back, 'What choice!? What do they want!?'

"He replied, 'They want our baby! They want it or they'll devour me day and night for all eternity!' She then heard him scream an inhuman sound as a large solid black humanoid shape with glowing yellow eyes kicked him in the head from behind as another gnawed at his leg. He screamed out, 'You can't raise the child yourself! No one will buy tainted land! Please, for the love of *God*, set me free from here!'

"The next morning Caroline woke up screaming and in tears. The baby was also screaming. The image of her husband in the dream the night before was still seared into her mind. She kept seeing his face over and over, and kept hearing his cries, again and again. It became too much for her and she dropped to her knees. She looked at the land around her and heard her child screaming from inside the house. Despite her maternal instincts, despite knowing she may stand a chance roughing it with neighbors a while, she couldn't be sure that would work. Her mind kept pounding away with the idea of the blight spreading to other land and killing off everyone. She also knew that raising the child by herself now was virtually hopeless. And Thomas... the thought of him in Hell crushed her more than anything. They were regulars at the local Protestant Church and pious, but neither scripture nor sermon seemed to make anything better.

"She then went on to say that something in her mind just 'clicked' out of place and she saw the situation from a very detached point of view. She was compelled to take the child to the cave, forgoing her love for it and the lack of knowledge of what would happen at that cave.

"She went on to write that once afternoon had rolled around, her mind became very fuzzy. She recalls walking a great distance across many hills, through a large swathe of pine and oak forest, and nearly half a mile of swampy ground. Once she finally made it to the cave, it was nightfall. As she walked closer to the cave, the baby began to cry more loudly, but she hardly noticed. She then described walking into the cave, unable to see anything, but somehow knowing where to go.

"She eventually made it to a large and mostly empty room, from what she could perceive somehow, and found a large out-of-place rock in the center of the floor. She then said that a stern and deep voice, far deeper than any man, commanded her to place the child on the rock. She did so. It then instructed her to take another rock from nearby and raise it overhead. She did so. She was then instructed to smash the child's head with the rock. She did so. She didn't know how many times she had hit the child, but when she came to in her bed the next morning, she was covered in blood and her feet, ankles, and dress were soaked with mud and caked with vegetation. She'd hoped it was only a nightmare, of course, but the confirmation of the baby being gone from the crib made it clear that it wasn't a dream. She ran out the front door screaming and weeping, but was surprised to see that the vegetation all around had returned to life. The crops were restored as well as the trees.

"In her next entry, which was about two weeks later, she wrote, 'I made my choice. My land has been restored and I've met a new man in town. I don't know what else to say about this.'

"Caroline went on to marry that new suitor, but a little over year after that, her husband hung himself and the blight returned. Sadly, she took her newborn daughter to the cave and she met the same fate. This pattern repeated itself until she died a widow many years after a total of six husbands met an untimely death and six children were 'offered.' In the later years of her life, she was referred to as the 'Siren of Miller's Run' for her string of unfortunate marriages. No one ever caught her in the act or found the children's bodies, so she was never suspected. After the first husband's death, she simply started telling everyone that the children died of a disease or were stillborn."

Rosanna suddenly felt a tinge of sympathy, perhaps trying to understand what would drive a mother to do that sort of thing. She crossed herself.

Edward then said, "I can't believe she did that to her own children."

Rosanna then said, "May God have mercy on her soul."

Angelica suddenly became irate. "What!? She killed *six* of her children! *She* made that choice *six times*!"

Rosanna sharply replied, "Angelica! It's not our place to judge! Only God can judge!"

Angelica was still flustered as she looked to Sara, who said, "Yes, Angelica, she *did* make many, many wicked decisions and we should learn to avoid making the same mistakes. Hers in a cautionary tale."

Edward could see that the sunlight outside was waning quite a bit and he was wanting to get his family moving back to their hotel room before dark. "I'm afraid to ask, but what else has happened here?"

Sara said plainly, "Many people have come and gone to this property over the years, never quite able to secure a living. You already know the story of Amos Harris. Back in the sixties and up until a few years ago, teenagers would sneak up to the cave after hearing about it at school. They would hear ghost stories and go up there to do witchcraft or devil worship, as if they knew how. You know, basic stuff that lots of dumb teenagers do when they're bored in a small town like this."

Angelica suddenly noticed what seemed like a small pinprick touch her mother's mind and a tiny bell in her own mind rang with a message she'd almost forgotten but couldn't quite remember. Something touched a nerve in what Sara said, but Rosanna was hiding it well. Angelica only glanced at her as she said, "Well, it's a good thing that cave is boarded up now."

Sara nodded then said, "Well, that's all of the extra information that I had to include. I know it was gruesome, but it needed to be mentioned. I can't stress enough how unsafe it is on this property."

Edward said, "Thanks for all the information, Sara. We're lucky to have your help."

Sara replied, "You're welcome. Now, I believe Angelica has some news to share with you."

She nodded at Sara and said to her parents, "I found our windows."

They both looked at her with piqued curiosity as Edward said, "Really? Where?"

Angelica replied, "At school, in a closet in the teachers' supply room."

Edward was gob-smacked, but Rosanna replied after quick consideration, "I wonder if Father Anderson found them and moved them there?"

Sara responded, "I don't know. Angelica told me before we got here and I've yet to contact him. No one from the team has mentioned anything about it to me."

Edward looked at his daughter. "And you're sure it was...."

He was cut off. "Yes, I'm sure! I *know* what they look like!"

Rosanna peered over at her daughter and said, "Why were you in the teachers' supply room? How did you know they would be there?"

Angelica, even now after all that had happened, was reluctant to tell her mother, "A nun there showed me. A spirit, not a live one."

Sara added, "I saw the same nun in spirit form when I went to school there."

Rosanna still wasn't quite ready to let go of her beliefs of distrusting ambiguous spirits, even if they appeared very benign. "How do you know she was a nun? What if she was *deceiving* you?" She felt a bit proud for a moment, throwing a word back at her daughter that had been used painfully against her recently.

Angelica and Sara both picked up on it as the latter said, "The same way you *know* that's your daughter and that you *know* you pray to Mary and Jesus."

Edward could sense a flare of tension and slid into the role of moderator out of habit and looked at Angelica. "So they were sitting out in plain sight?"

She replied, "No, they were in the closet covered up."

He looked around at all three of them and said, "We really need to contact Father Anderson about this. This just doesn't make any sense."

Rosanna looked down at her watch. "Well, he *should* still be at his office. I'll hurry and see if I can catch him." She walked to the kitchen and picked up her cell phone before heading outside onto the porch to call.

As Rosanna began to speak outside, Angelica asked, "Does Roberta know that you have Caroline's diary?"

Sara shook her head gently. "No, I haven't told the team. I'm really not sure how she'd react."

Edward asked, "Why's that?"

Sara replied, "She's also a descendant of hers. No surprise in a small community like this. Go back far enough and people are bound to be related."

Seconds later, Rosanna came back into the room. She put her phone in her back pocket and said, "I talked with Father Anderson and he had no idea that the windows were at the church. He said he'd call the team members and ask around the clergy."

Sara closed her eyes and shook her head. "Something's just not right about all of this. What am I missing?" She was noticeably stressed on the last sentence. She then looked outside and said, "Well, I'd imagine you want to get going soon. I'll be heading out. Mr. Barrister, Angelica, can I see you outside, please?"

Ed replied, "Sure."

Rosanna raised her eyebrow and said, "Thank you for the information, Sara, we appreciate it." She then politely told her goodbye, Sara returning the same.

Outside, the two stood in front of Sara at her car as she said in lowered tone, "Ange, Mr. Barrister, remember: *Anger* and *fear* are not the only tools they'll use to sabotage your family."

Edward felt and heard the inflections and knew without a doubt that she'd heard his thoughts earlier.

Eighty-nine

Angelica suddenly found herself in the driveway leading to the turnaround between the two barns. It was nighttime in this dreamscape and the full moon
overhead showed the surroundings with relative clarity. Nothing seemed terribly out of place compared to the nightmares she'd been having recently.

Suddenly, however, the silence was broken by a window being opened
fully at the back side of the house. It was coming from the direction of
her bedroom. She then noticed that different windows were on the house,
the kind that were there when she first moved in. They were replaced by
her father.

She then noticed a human figure step out of the opening and fall somewhat clumsily to the ground. It soon corrected itself and stood up. She could
then hear something coming from the boy approaching the turnaround: a
heavy breathing sound. He was struggling to breathe and shambling toward
her. As the moonlight overhead caught on his features more, she recognized
the form as Timothy Harris.

She backed away a few steps as he approached, readying for some sort
of confrontation. Strangely he seemed not to notice her.

Timothy then simply came to a stop in the turnaround and breathed
heavily. Confused, Angelica walked toward him. He still didn't move.

Slowly she crept to within two feet of him. Still nothing. A foot closer
and still nothing. She then stuck her hand out and found it go straight through
his form. This caused her to then quickly realize that she was watching

something that happened in the past. A memory of the farm, the land, and the dwellers thereupon was playing out like a movie.

She looked closely at his face and saw that his eyes were still closed. He seemed to be conflicted in his mind and groaned now and then as he played an invisible tug-of-war with an unseen force.

Angelica then heard a car approaching the driveway from the road. She turned to see its headlights briefly before the driver turned them off and pulled off onto the gravel drive.

The driver of the car was then creeping up the gravel road, obviously trying to minimize the noise they made.

She dashed toward the house and looked into the window where her parents' bedroom was positioned in the present day. Inside she could barely make out the silhouette of Amos Harris lying face down on the bed and snoring loudly. Clearly the alcohol he'd been consuming all day was keeping him in a deep stupor.

Soon enough, she heard the car pull to a stop and two doors carefully open. Out of instinct she ducked behind the closest corner of the house to her and watched the scene unfold. Two individuals around five feet tall and dressed in long black garments walked toward the boy. Once in reach they each grabbed one of his arms. As he began to mumble in protest, still seemingly sleepwalking, one of the figures put their hand over his mouth.

He was then coerced to go up the trail leading from the turnaround toward the stream. Angelica immediately had a strong suspicion on where they were taking him.

She shadowed them up to the point where the bridge began. At this point she'd managed to run slightly ahead of them. As they stepped near the bridge and into the full moonlight she was shocked at what she saw. The black robes were simply the back side of their habits. This was seemingly two nuns, wearing a black handkerchief covering the bottom half of their faces and they were taking him to the cave.

Angelica followed. She tried to get closer to see their faces, but she was unable to make out any details. The only detail she could discern were that one of them was somewhat portly, especially compared to the other.

At the mouth of the cave, one of the nuns produced a large metal flash-light and shown it inside. The thinner one went in first. The rotund nun then followed, pushing Timothy in front of her. Angelica was then close enough to see the thinner nun turn around and have the only part of her face visible stand out: her eyes. She had what most would think of as bug eyes. They were large compared to her face with brown irises. It was also safe to assume that most who saw her eyes might assume she was partially insane. You don't forget those kind of eyes.

The corpulent one then turned to see if anyone was coming toward them. Angelica, of course, couldn't be seen. The nun's face, however, revealed squinty eyes resting atop plump cheeks.

With the images of the eyes burned into her subconscious she approached the mouth of the cave. She watched them walk inside and drag the boy along with them. As she went to cross the threshold, however....

Angelica awoke breathless in her bed in the hotel room. Her grandfather was snoring away on the other bed as she blinked her eyes to fixate on the parking lot lights barely skirting the edges of the curtains.

She would try and sleep the rest of the night, but was being constantly awakened by the faces of the two nuns in her dream staring back at her.

Ninety

Later that morning at school, Angelica, still exhausted from the lack of sleep, was tossing a basketball up from close range trying to net it. She was having moderate success and was at least partially distracted.

Suddenly, from behind, a dodgeball struck the back of her head with enough force to make her stumble and lurch her arms out in front of her. She didn't even have to look behind to know it was Becky, as she was already calling over to her, "Angelica, throw the ball back!"

Angelica was ready to throw it back, but not with friendly intent. She grabbed the ball and spun around, heaving it sidearm with all her might at her target. It went over Becky's head, however, and flew to the opposite side of the playground.

Seeing this, Angelica approached her. "Why did you hit me, Becky!?"

A smirk came to her face as she replied, "It was an accident, I promise."

"You're *lying*! I heard you all laughing about it!"

As Becky's friends came to her side she said, "Oh, I get it." Looking to her two friends in turn, she continued with a smug face. "Angelica is possessed! I heard that she needs an exorcism!"

As Angelica's eyes suddenly filled with rage, one of Becky's friends laughed, the other looking more shocked than anything. The two friends, however, backed away as Angelica said through gritted teeth, "Shut up, *Beaky*!"

Becky opened her eyes in shock. "You take that back!" She then shoved Angelica.

The gesture was returned with twice the force, causing Rebecca to fall on her backside. She started crying as other children on the playground began to form a crowd around them.

This was when Sister Francis also made her way toward them. She cawed out, "Angelica Barrister! What on Earth were you thinking!? You had no reason to do that! You're staying after school, young lady, and I'm going to have a talk with your parents!"

The "wounded" Beaky then called out, "I didn't mean for the ball to hit her!"

The Sister put her arm around her comfortingly as she walked her from the playground. "I know you didn't, sweetie. Come on inside and try and calm down."

On the way in, Becky briefly turned around and stuck her tongue out at Angelica before turning and stepping into the school.

That afternoon, Angelica was sitting in her last class of the day: Social Studies. She was eager to end the day, but didn't look forward to the potential punishment after school. She had been feeling a strange feeling of dread all day. It was as if something were following her around but not revealing itself. She desperately hoped her father would pick her up today.

The room was a little warm given the older air conditioner used to cool the room down. Suddenly the girls in the back of the classroom started to smell something. It was faint at first but soon became stronger. It was the unmistakable smell of flesh decaying. Angelica scrunched her nose as the girls in front of her did the same. Soon it made its way to the front of the class and into Sister Francis' ample nostrils. It was she that said, "Where is that coming from!?" As she looked around for an answer, one of the girls sitting next to Angelica shrieked out as she looked down at Angelica's backpack in the aisle. She could see a deep red liquid beginning to seep through the gray cloth and into the floor. In an instant everyone got out of their seats and backed away.

Sister Francis walked toward her pack and said, "Angelica, what are you carrying in there!?"

The smell was bad enough, but Angelica looked on in horror, speechless, as she knew it was something horrible, something beyond the smell alone.

She bumped into the girl behind her as she tried to back away farther, but was unable to do so. As Sister Francis then reached down for the pack, she rather crudely picked it up and placed it on Angelica's desk, causing some of the dark blood to splatter on the surface. She then opened the bag and was nearly knocked off her feet by the smell and site within. Angelica and the girls nearby only caught a brief look at what was waiting obscured from view. A severed goat's head with coffee-colored fur and solid red eyeballs stared blankly into the air.

Becky then said over the murmuring class, "I told you she was possessed!"

The girls each looked at Angelica in horror as Sister Francis said, "Class, calm down! Everyone into the hall, now!" As they filed out, Angelica was stopped at the front of the class. "Is this your idea of a joke, young lady!?"

Her face showed profound disbelief. "Why would I do something like that!? I didn't carry that to school with me!"

Raising her tone further, "Well, you are going to have think of the reason this happened before your parents get here!"

The smell was now overwhelming in the classroom, which made Angelica dry heave. "Can I please leave? I'm going to be sick!"

Frustrated, she took Angelica by the arm and led her into the hallway. "Let's go, then!" In the hallway, the crowd of girls parted abruptly as Angelica made a beeline for the bathroom down the hall.

Angelica had nearly thrown up in the bathroom, but was mostly concerned with the tears that were streaming down her cheeks. Her eyes were puffy and pink as she sat in the front office area of the school looking up at the clock. The bell had just rung and school was out. She knew her ride home would be on time, as it was 99-percent of the time. As the dread inside her mind and stomach tried to meet in a lump in her throat, she looked around the office and saw several black and white and color photos of past faculty, nuns and priests. She hadn't really had a reason to be here before, so she looked around with fresh eyes. Angelica was looking for confirmation of the faces she'd seen in the dream from earlier.

Her eyes scanned the walls for a couple of minutes before she locked her eyes onto a promising photo. A black-and-white photograph showing a lineup of nuns from the 1950s caught her eye. On the end of the lineup of twelve nuns were the two faces she'd seen, no doubt about it. The eyes were exactly the same. She strained a bit to see any further details and was compelled to leave her seat for a closer look. She knew she wasn't supposed to get up, but the need be 100-percent sure was stronger now. She looked back and forth with each step before she stopped and stood on her tiptoes.

Suddenly she heard Sister Francis speaking in the hall and saw her silhouette and another approaching the door. She darted back to her seat and managed to sit back down just as the door was being opened. In stepped Sister Francis and, thankfully to Angelica, Edward. At least it wouldn't be as bad a tongue lashing. Before the two of them could speak to one another, however, Sister Francis was taking them straight to her office.

Once inside, the nun sat down at her desk as Edward and his daughter sat down in front of her. She began. "Thank you for your time, Mr. Barrister. As I was saying on the way in, two rather unsettling things happened today. First, Angelica pushed one of her classmates and knocked her onto the ground because she accidentally hit her with a dodgeball!"

Edward looked down at her, but she didn't respond. Her face was scowling and looking away and down at the floor. He put his hand on her shoulder as the nun continued.

"And the most disturbing thing I've witnessed at this school happened just a few minutes ago! We were in Social Studies class and everyone started to smell something rotten! We quickly found out that she, your daughter, had a severed animal head in her backpack!"

He had remained silent on the shoving part, but this was beyond the limits. "What!? Honey, why would you do...?"

She snapped her head around in his direction before he could finish. "I didn't put that in there! Why would I put a goat head in my backpack!?"

Sister Francis sighed in frustration as Edward looked back at her. "Now wait a second. I drove Ange to school this morning. There's no way she smuggled in a goat's head! We've been staying a hotel the past few nights. Someone else had to have put it there!"

The nun responded with some heat, "Mr. Barrister, I wouldn't be accusing her of something like this if it didn't happen!"

They were interrupted by a knock at the door. She was expecting some-one and here he was.

The janitor stepped just into the doorway. "Sister Francis, I left the backpack out in the tool shed. It stank way too much to bring inside." The haggard and wrinkled man in the jumpsuit, who'd no doubt sprin-kled a lifetime's worth of sawdust on kiddie puke, was clearly disturbed by what he saw.

Sister Francis then stood up from the desk and said, "Thank you, Mr. Sanders. Mr. Barrister, Angelica, follow me."

They followed the nun and janitor outside to a small building on the edge of the grounds. There he opened the locked door as everyone was al-ready clamping their noses between two fingers. He then took a five-gallon bucket from the corner of the room and brought it to the entrance. There he opened the black plastic bag in which he'd put Angelica's backpack. It was left open just long enough for Edward to see the hornless head inside.

He recoiled in disgust. "Wow, that's strong!"

He dry-heaved once as the janitor now fished a small piece of paper out of his coveralls pocket. "Oh, Sister Francis, I found this piece of paper in its mouth. It was just sticking out."

Mr. Sanders placed the simple piece of yellowish brown paper in her hand. From the discoloration it looked as if the paper were inserted while there was still saliva and blood in the beast's mouth. It bared only two words: *"Puella elegit."* Sister Francis understood the words but not their meaning. No one could really decipher it, but the translation made Angelica feel more uneasy than ever. *"Puella elegit…. The girl has chosen."*

In the car ride on the way to the hotel, Edward was still flustered. He looked over at Angelica not far from the school and said in an even tone, "Hon, did you by any chance see anyone messing around your backpack be-fore that happened?"

Her scowl had already left minutes ago, she seeing that her father didn't really care about the dodge ball incident. He clearly didn't think she perpe-trated the goat's head. She thought for a moment before replying. "No, I had it with me almost the whole day. The only time it wasn't next to me was at recess."

Baffled, "Who would do something like that?"

Seeming to make a connection in her mind, "It was probably Caroline! And it was Coffee's head, I know it!"

It had just hit him that the resemblance was uncanny, "How in the... I buried those goats the same day. You were there, you saw it." She nodded as he continued. "If Caroline did this... I don't know how she did." Angelica could sense her father was deeply disturbed, even afraid. "I don't know what we're going to do. This is getting insane! Father Anderson did say it might get worse before the exorcism. I guess we should've expected this."

Angelica knew he was correct, but didn't want to image *how* it could for a second.

Later that evening, after getting nowhere on the explanation brainstorming pertaining to Angelica's odd gift in her backpack, Rosanna stepped out of the hotel room and dialed up Father Anderson. He answered quickly and she replied, "Hello, Father Anderson, it's Rosanna Barrister. How are you today?"

In a pleasant tone, "Well, hello, Rosanna. I'm fine, and how are you?"

"I'm hanging in there. I was calling to see if you had found out anything about the windows Angelica saw."

Still puzzled himself, "You know, I asked just about everyone at the church and school and no one had any idea what I was talking about. I have to admit that what Angelica described is strange."

"That is odd. I don't know, I can't shake the feeling she made it up."

"She did make it all up...." Rosanna tried to ignore the old hag's words.

"Well, I don't why she would do something like that either. I did hear about what happened at the school today. No one imagined that, I saw the evidence for myself. Whatever infernal forces are working at your property are clearly trying to scare us. We can't... no, we *won't* give in!"

"Absolutely, Father! What time should we expect you tomorrow?"

"I should be there around 8:00 A.M. to begin preparations, if that's a good time for you."

"That sounds fine, Father Anderson. We'll see you tomorrow." Rosanna then hung up the phone and walked to the door next to their own. She knocked and soon her father answered.

He smiled and opened the door for her. "There's my Rosy!"

"Hey, Dad. Can I speak to you outside for a minute?"

"Sure, sure...." He stepped outside.

Rosanna peaked inside long enough to see her daughter quietly reading a book on the far bed. She didn't look up as her mother said, "Be right back with Grandpa."

Angelica said nothing and simply glanced in her direction.

As Rosanna closed the door she said, "Dad, I don't think you should come tomorrow."

Surprised, "What? I came all this way to be with you! I want to fight alongside you!"

She sighed uncomfortably and looked down at the ground. Looking back up at his face, "Dad, I just don't think a man of your age needs to be involved in this. It's been very nasty at the farm for a few weeks now."

"Rosy, are you serious!? Your dad is only sixty-three years old! How old is your priest?"

Smiling, "He's fifty-eight, I believe."

"So us old guys have to stick together!"

Her face went stone serious. "Dad, please. I mean it. I have a bad feeling about this. I think the best thing you can do for us is pray."

"What do you mean? I always pray for you, Rosy!"

"I know, Dad, but I mean go to the church in town while Father Anderson is doing the rite." He started to say her name again, but she cut him off. "Dad, please! Please do this for me! I don't want you getting hurt!"

He then let out a long sigh of frustration before kissing her on the forehead. "Just like your mother, stubborn as a bull!" He hugged her. "I'll go and pray for you like you ask. Promise me you'll be careful, Rosy."

"I will, Dad."

Ninety-one

Edward was driving the family Subaru down the road leading home. He had told Rosanna that he had to go back to the house for something, but he wasn't clear on what. When he finally convinced her to stop worrying, he got in the car and pulled out of the hotel parking lot. *I just need to get some things from the house...,* kept going through his mind, which was rather cloudy and dull the entire trip back toward Holly Bush Road. As he robotically applied the brakes to slow down for the turnoff, however, the voice in his mind melded with that of Caroline's. *"Not this house, Mr. Barrister. You know which house you're going to and what thing you're going for. Go get what you've wanted for so long now. Go and take it!"* His foot slid slowly from the brake and mashed on the accelerator as he then sped past their driveway.

The trip passed quickly in his muddled mind. Only pure desire was dragging him along as if he were being dragged by a wild horse. The car bumped rather sharply as he crossed over the threshold to Parris Road and up to the side of house, the Subaru dragging to a stop at the sharp application of the brakes.

Inside, Sara knew he was coming. The thoughts were pecking away at her mind for the past twenty minutes and the haphazard approach of the car outside confirmed her fears. Before the car door quickly opened and slammed sharply behind Edward outside, her three wolfdogs were already growling with a deep and guttural tone.

As he rapped on the door forcefully outside, Sara approached the wooden barricade and paused. Her heart was racing at optimum pace and she found it difficult to focus. The three canines continued to snarl and growl as she nervously reached into the drawer of an antique table next to her. She took the slightly heavy metal object in her hand and placed it behind her back. *BAM, BAM, BAM.*

She tried to control her breathing, but adrenaline was making it difficult. *BAM, BAM, BAM.*

A familiar voice came from behind. *"He's not in his right mind. Snap him out of it!"*

"I know, Mother. Please help me."

"Always...."

BAM, BAM, BAM.

Sara jerked the door open as he still pulling his hand away. She looked into his eyes with a scowl on her face the likes of which he'd never seen from her before. He said nothing. Edward's eyes blankly stared at her own as her palms began to sweat. She raised her voice to speak over the sound of her growling guardians. "Mr. Barrister, you're not in your right mind! Go back to your family!"

His face dragged itself into a scowl of its own. He angrily flared his eyes at the dogs. "Shut... the fuck... UP!"

In an instant she tried to flood his mind with horrific images. The gray matter in his skull spraying with blood from the back of his head, his limp body falling to the floor. The three wolfdogs leaping past the threshold of the door and tackling him and tearing his throat out. They managed to get through, but his control was still in the minority.

What came to her mind was a simple, distant, and paltry cry from Edward's mind... *"Help... me... please...."*

Hearing this, she quickly produced the nickel-plated snub-nosed .38 caliber revolver that had been behind. She placed the muzzle barely an inch from his forehead as the canines growled and snapped louder than ever. "Wake up, Mr. Barrister!"

Suddenly he felt the color drain from his face. He nearly lost his footing as he came to staring at a loaded pistol in his face. As he began to shake uncontrollably, the dogs calmed down once again. He stammered, "Where... how did I get here?"

The dogs were quietly panting now, but Sara's guard was still up. "I knew you were coming! You weren't in control of yourself!"

Edward's mind was suddenly flooded with more images, disturbing ones. He saw himself forcing Sara to do his every sexual whim. He saw himself loving every second of the promised expedition to the very ends of dark frenzy and Bacchanalian rapture. The voice of Caroline came through at full volume: *"Mr. Barrister... such a disappointment. There she is; no one else around for miles. Take her! She doesn't have the guts to use that gun! Look at how it shakes in her hand! FUCK HER! DO IT, YOU DICKLESS BITCH!"* He suddenly felt naked and cold. He also wasn't able to regain his footing before stumbling to the floorboards of the porch.

Sara kept the gun in hand, but let it fall to her side. She cautiously walked toward him. That comforting voice came through with a warm ring. *"He's fine now. He resisted."*

She tried to calm herself with a sigh before saying, "Are you okay, Mr. Barrister?"

He looked all around as he returned to his feet. "I think so. What the hell happened just now?"

"Something was controlling you, manipulating you. You have to learn to protect yourself from that sort of influence. It preys on those who are sensitive like us."

Still unsettled, "Right... I should get going now. I'm sorry for coming here like this."

"I can show you the same thing I'm teaching your daughter." He nodded and started to walk toward the car as she said, "And Mr. Barrister, I won't speak of this unless it is necessary. Are we clear?"

"Y... yeah." He calmly returned to the car and drove away. Mercifully for him, this time, no one drove by to see this incident.

Sara returned to her house and shut the door behind her. Her three companions looked on and whimpered as she felt hot tears now welling up in her eyes. The strain was too much and soon she slid down the door and sat on the ground, unable to control her weeping. The voice of Caroline then slithered into her mind: *"Is it too much for you? I understand... I understand all too well. Go on, wrap your pretty lips around that pistol and blot out that burning light of yours."*

Her face red and hot, she looked down at the revolver still in her hand. For the first time in her life she actually thought about it. An image, however, suddenly appeared to her right and broke her concentration on the machine of destruction in her hand. It was her mother, kneeling next to her and shaking her head. *"That's not the way. You know that."*

Her mother's gentle words snapped her out of the sudden despair. She then tossed the revolver onto floor where it hit a large ornate rug and clumped with a dull thud. Caroline hissed again, *"You can't win this fight... you know that!"*

Suddenly emboldened with a flash of anger, "Go to hell!"

Caroline chuckled. *"Too late, you little bitch!"*

Ninety-two

Several miles away at the lake where Angelica learned to swim not long after arriving in Miller's Run, Lake Albert, Sister Francis was pulling a white van up to a modest concrete building. The sun had just dipped below the horizon and the van bearing the church's name went dark as the headlights turned off. She then stepped out with two younger nuns filing out of the sliding door on the side.

The three then met up at the back of the van as Sister Francis grabbed the handles and opened the rear door. The overhead light in the back came on and shown down on top of a tarp covering a stack of alternating layers of glass and particle board. Sister Francis looked all around for any observers as she ordered her assistants to begin. "Hurry up and be careful! Those are priceless!"

The windows were not tremendously large, just five feet by three feet. Gingerly the two younger nuns slid the first window sandwich out of the truck. With one of them at each end, Francis led them to the backdoor of the concrete building. A reflective white sign with red lettering read "Maintenance" overhead. The key from Sister Francis' pocket quickly opened the lock on the blackened iron grate doors and they were inside in seconds.

Once inside, the two paused in the center of the room which held various gardening utensils, basic tools for simple repairs, breaker boxes for the lights outside, and a plethora of spider webs and victimized and desiccated insects therein. Sister Francis then produced a keyring with three keys from around her neck that was hidden beneath her habit. She opened the two large padlocks on an otherwise barely visible door. The two younger nuns approached her as she clicked on the lights on the concrete stairs leading underground.

When they reached the landing on the bottom area, a third locked door made of heavy steel blocked further progression. Sister Francis unlocked the last padlock and opened the door. Inside was a polished gray stone-tiled floor at the base of a room exactly ten feet in height. The rectangular chamber was lined on the long sides with statues of iconic figures unfamiliar to the standard Catholic faith. Over each statue was a red electric light that shed crimson and black shadows on the menacing forms. They were human in appearance, anyway.

Near the entrance to the room, Sister Francis suddenly said to her assistants, "Leave the window here on the floor and hurry back with the other two before we're seen! And I don't have to remind you of what happens if you damage them one iota!"

They quickly bowed their heads and said in unison, "Yes, Sister Francis," before placing their load gently on the floor and darting out afterward.

Once they were gone, Sister Francis walked up the aisle leading to an unseen altar shrouded in thick darkness. She placed her hands together and bowed her head for a moment while uttering a small personal prayer. "Oh, Lords of the Void, oh Dwellers of the Abyss, you have blessed me with this gift. Angra Mainyu, the malignant destruction, you showed me the true power. Great Herald of Anubis, Caller of the Dead, you blessed me so generously all those years ago in my bed. You watch over me every night and keep away the weak and useless. I will continue to feed you, continue to be for you. Your meal is coming soon—open wide!"

The sound of the younger nuns shuffling down the stairs toward the room caused her to stop before she was heard.

The other two windows were left in the dark environs and the locked doors were returned to their original shape. No living soul saw them come or go that night.

Ninety-three

Meanwhile, at Sara's home, she and her three wolfdogs were readying themselves in the marbled prayer room. Sara had lit the four braziers and went through the start of the ritual she had performed. She sat on a black cushion with her legs crossed in a meditative posture. As she closed her eyes and focused on her student who slept in the hotel on the edge of town, her three guardian canines were lying in a triangular arrangement around her, one at each point.

After nearly an hour of meditation she managed to connect with Angelica....

Angelica found herself in a familiar place: the dreamscape of her property. The land had taken on a more frightening appearance than ever. The remnants of the vegetation covering the ground was a deep shade of gray. The sky was red with fast moving thunderous black clouds flying overhead. Their speed was far greater than natural, but no wind or rain seemed to accompany them. The thicket of thorn bushes was also as pervasive, but the thickness of the vines were greater along with the accompanying thorns.

As she looked about cautiously she heard what sounded like two or three people talking and giggling. She ascertained the direction of origin and followed it toward the area she knew to be the stream.

She approached and the voices of the young ladies seemed to be right in front of her. At first she couldn't see hide nor hair of anyone, but something pulled her toward the stream. She stood at the bank and looked down at the water. The water now, however, looked more akin to mercury flowing. On this liquid silver screen of sorts she saw what she guessed as three teenage girls seated around a board on the floor. On the board was the alphabet, yes, no... all the trademarks of a talking board. Angelica didn't know what it was, but she watched as one the girls asked a question. "How many kids will I have?" The question didn't hit her nearly as hard as the questioner: a younger version of her mother.

Angelica watched carefully as the number one was selected by the planchette the three girls had their fingers on. They started to laugh as their hands flew off of the triangular piece of plastic that held the circular plastic lens in the middle. The girls then, however, heard a door open and close downstairs and they quickly tucked the board away into a cardboard box and under the nearby bed.

As she tried to understand the significance of the images she'd just seen, another started to play out. Now she saw her mother just a couple of years older. She was with a man she didn't recognize. The two of them were beginning to walk toward what looked like an office of sorts. Her mother was very distressed and stopped before opening the glass door on the brick building. She then heard her say, "Gary, I'm not sure about this. My parents would kill me if they found out!"

He answered, "Rosanna, it's okay. We didn't plan on this happening. It would be worse to bring it into the world. We wouldn't be able to support it and your parents would resent you for the rest of your life! They won't find out, trust me...."

The scene then transitioned to another that was just a few days later. Rosanna was in her room at her one-bedroom apartment crying heavily. In her hands she held a picture of her and her boyfriend taken not long ago. It was the last time she'd see Gary and the baby promised by the spirit board years prior was not the one they'd visited the doctor about. The loss of her companion, the abortion of the pregnancy, and the deep scarring and burning of her betraying her faith caused her to spiral out of control with depression.

The scene then showed snippets of information shortly after revealing Rosanna speaking to a different doctor in a different type of office. She also *saw her mother crying heavily in a confessional and unloading the details on her parish priest.*

This too faded.

Angelica did not see anything for several seconds and so she leaned forward to try and look closer. What she saw staring back at her, however, caused her to freeze solid. The reflection closely resembled her but with one major exception: Her corneas were black and her pupils and iris were white in both eyes. This inversion of her normal eyes caused her to tremble as her mouth dropped open.

She wasn't able to stare long before hearing from behind, "I see you've wanted to see the truth! Be careful what you wish for! That mother of yours got rid of the first baby and now she wants to get rid of you!"

Angelica turned around and saw a far more hideous version of Caroline than she'd ever seen before. Her skin was now mostly black, green, purple, and brown from decay and barely holding on to the frame of her skeleton. Caroline's eyes were solid black with a glowing yellow center. The clothes that still clung to her form were heavily deteriorated and covered with thick fungus. Black fluid slowly dripped from her eye sockets and down one corner of her mouth.

Seeing her hideous form, "You're lying!"

Caroline lurched forward and stood inches from Angelica's face. "Like hell I am!" The smell of her breath was nearly enough to knock Angelica down as Caroline continued. "By the way, did you like the little present I sent you?" Her voice then distorted into a growly mimicry of a goat bleating. She then began laughing maniacally.

Clearly enraged, "You bitch!"

Caroline suddenly clasped the back of Angelica's head with her left hand picked her up to face level. Her voice gurgling and crackling and full of malice, "I've had enough of your lip, you little cunt!" She placed her right hand over Angelica's mouth and turned her toward the other direction. A strange rumbling in the ground sounded as a portion of the thorn branches started to part. The dirt soon gave way to a nude female form, that of Rosanna, pushing through the ground. Caroline continued with sarcasm. "But since I'm such a compassionate and forgiving person, I'm going to make a peace offering. Here you go: two flowers from me! Watch them blossom!"

Angelica looked on in horror as a nude form of her mother and another nude form, that of her father, pushed its way through the dirt. As they were fully exposed their chest cavities began to crackle and open slowly. The two cried out in absolute torture as their intestines and other organs pushed up and flowed over the expanding gap between the ribs and the rest of the torso. Soon the only thing left in the cavities were their respective hearts, each beating frantically. This then went in a crescendo to a grand finale of a bloody explosion. Always end with a bang! As the bodies twitched and stared vacantly off into space, Caroline exclaimed, "Oh, look! Fireworks at the end!"

Angelica had opened her mouth to scream, but found no outlet. Only Caroline's index finger slipped into her mouth. Despite the vile taste and smell she bit down hard and gnawed away at the putrid flesh. Caroline growled in pain as she pulled her hands away. Angelica fell to the ground with a souvenir in her mouth: the distal part of the rotten finger. As she started to run she spit out the half-digit. She felt immediate revulsion and was barely able to continue egressing as a thin line of coal-colored fluid trickled from in her mouth.

Caroline, meanwhile, was grabbing her own hand and gnashing her teeth. The pain soon dissolved into laughter, however, as she cried out, "That's it, Angie-bear, run! Give Aunt Caroline a good chase!"

The black fluid spread out in a starburst like pattern from the edges of Angelica's lips as she frantically ran down a long and tenebrous trail surrounded by thorns. What she couldn't see, however, was that the trail was essentially just a circle where she was. Huffing and puffing, she ran continually down the leftward path.

Angelica suddenly stopped in her tracks, however, as Caroline was standing in front of her laughing and walking steadily toward her. She cackled, "You can't get avoid your fate, Angelica!" As Angelica turned and ran back in the other direction, Caroline continued to laugh.

As she came to an opposite point in the circular path, however, she heard a familiar voice call out from above, "Angelica, stop running...."

She slowed but didn't stop. "Sara!?"

Caroline then shouted, "Fuck off, witch!"

At this sound, Angelica began to run once more until she ran up on Caroline again. She was waiting and then approaching her once more with a sneer. Angelica shot off back in the opposite direction.

Angelica then quickly realized the true shape of path. She looked up as the voice of Sara came through once more. "Angelica Barrister, do you trust me?"

Not willing to beat back her fear completely, she now saw a small opening in the thorns below that led off the main path and farther in. She dove to the ground and crawled under the barbed barrier, tearing her flesh on the thorns. Gritting her teeth, she pushed on and out of sight. From her vantage she could now see Caroline walking by and apparently not noticing her. She then said, "There's no point in hiding!" Caroline, however, continued on around the path and out of sight. Seeing this, Angelica turned around and now saw another path opening up that she didn't notice initially. Several steps on in, however, she quickly realized that the path was decreasing in width drastically. It soon disappeared around a corner.

As she turned the corner, she was horrified to see that it led straight to the cave on her property. The briar vines that choked the surrounding area now led back to and extended out like the arms of a giant squid, the cave its rock-hard beak. Sara's voice came through again, this time more firm. "Angelica, stop running from her!" Angelica wasn't willing to chance the cave and so turned around. Blocking her way back, however, was the blackened form of Timothy Harris squared up like a lineman ready to prevent further passage. The voice came through again. "Angelica Barrister, do you trust me!?"

Looking briefly into Timothy's yellow eyes before turning hers skyward, "YES!" Angelica then lowered her shoulder and charged straight at Timothy. Growling and donning her scowl she ran square into him, knocking him to the ground. Were it not for being eight years old, she might've had a football career then and there.

Timothy's form lay splayed on the ground, moaning and twisting. Angelica then continued to back away from the cave, but was knocked on the ground by a loud crash. The deafening crackle and boom was a heavy bolt of lightning hitting the ground nearby. The golden energy blast knocked a huge swathe of the thorns blocking the path in front of her. Scrambling to her feet, she looked back long enough to catch a glimpse of what looked like black root-like tentacles slowly rising from the ground. They only protruded a few inches before wrapping themselves around Timothy's form and pulling him underground. A new and much larger form, however, began to rise up in its place. She didn't wait around to see what it was.

After turning and heading in the opposite direction, Angelica heard the sound of panting coming from all around. A few steps in and she saw Caroline clumsily attempting to get up after being clearly hit by the energy blast from before. "The witch brought friends...." She coughed up and spat out a large swathe of her infernal blood and screamed, "I brought a friend too, you fucking whore! The big dog is here to play!" Angelica, as Caroline said this, noticed for the first time that something was coming from underneath the hag's long dress and extending into the ground. The great black tentacle then disappeared somewhere up Caroline's skirt in her groin area. As the old woman in decayed pioneer clothes finally got to her feet, she looked directly at Angelica. "Your little hussy friend can't save you now!" Angelica then felt the ground vibrating in successive thuds. As she turned back around, she now saw the form of an Abomination lumbering forward. His solid black form and yellow eyes made her immediately aware of his intent: His canine head made his identity clear. Caroline then gleefully said, "He wants that pretty pink pussy of yours, Angelica! He likes 'em young! He's going to fuck you, eat you, and spit out the bone!"

As the lecherous and gurgled breathing coming from the monstrous humanoid grew louder, a massive crashing sound came through once again. It wasn't the lightning, but instead the sound of the remaining briars being parted by an unseen force. Three large black wolfdogs suddenly ran through explosively. They went past both Caroline and Angelica and quickly ganged up on the Abominable Herald of Anubis. Each took their own spot and clamped down. First an arm, then a leg, and finally the throat respectively.

Feeling safer on her vulnerable flank, she turned around and faced Caroline once again. The hag was stepping toward her steadily. Out of instinct, Angelica threw her arms up in front of her. She now noticed, however, that the nearby briars extended out and took on the shape she was making. They weren't attached to the ground, but by some exertion of her own will they ripped from the ground and flew toward her arms. They then wrapped themselves all around her body, the thorns digging into her flesh and tearing the skin. She cried out in pain momentarily as Caroline paused in her tracks.

A fourth figure now emerged from behind the old hag. It was a form Angelica recognized: the albino deer. It was not docile or skittish like most deer, instead snorting loud puffs of air from its nose and mouth and digging its front hooves into the ground. Caroline turned to face the doe as her challenging posture became more aggressive. "You can't fool me!"

Seeing Caroline turn and face away from her, Angelica had already become aware that the briars were responding as extensions of her own body. Her arm encased in a wrapping of thorns, she raised it over head and struck out in a sidearm gesture. A viciously loud crack was heard as the length of briars lashed hard against Caroline's back. As she screamed out in pain, her shredded top slid down over one shoulder. Her jet-colored blood oozed heavily down her blistered and rotting flesh. Angelica raised her left arm overhead and struck her back again. Caroline cried out in sheer agony again, falling to her knees and bleeding even more heavily. Angelica, seeing her more vulnerable than ever, lashed out her right arm and wrapped the vine of thorn around Caroline's throat. As she struggled to breath, Angelica lashed out her left arm and wrapped it around the inky tentacle that rose from beneath the ground. With both ends now seized, Angelica pulled in opposing directions with all her strength. Caroline's neck was ripped open wide and spurting black fluid heavily like a hydrant. The tentacle soon shot back into the ground as well. She watched as the form of Caroline slowly twitched: violently, then softly... then quiet. Angelica then turned to see that the wolfdogs had brought the Abomination to its knees as it now howled in pain as well. As the monstrosity dropped, the wolfdog attached to the throat jerked its head to one side a final time, tearing a gushing gash out of the throat.

The albino doe quietly stepped up behind Angelica. As she turned, the briars quickly retreated from around Angelica's body. Much to her dismay, however, she felt the extreme pain consume her body like fire again. As she dropped to the ground screaming with blood coming from every inch of her body, the albino deer looked down and into Angelica's eyes: "Angelica, wake up!"

Angelica awoke in the hotel room crying out in pain. Her grandfather was quickly awakened as she stumbled to get out of the bed. He asked, "Angelica, dear, are you okay!? What happened!?"

She ran into the bathroom and quickly turned on the lights. She was expecting to be covered in blood, but it was only sweat. Her eyes had also returned to their original colors. When she looked down at her arms, however, she saw dozens and dozens of tiny straight red cuts that extended all around her arms, though they were not on the surface. They appeared to have been made a few layers deep.

She wept loudly and cried out, "It burns! It burns, Grandpa!"

He was dumbstruck. "Santa Maria!" He crossed himself.

Ninety-four

The next morning at around 8:00 AM, Father Anderson, Sara, and Roberta were pulling up the driveway as the Barristers were all waiting for them on the back porch. Edward quickly went out to greet them as Rosanna stayed behind with her daughter. Their mood toward one another was still very frosty at this point.

Initially Rosanna was glad when her daughter looked up at her and said, "Mom?"

"Hmm, what is it, honey?"

Her face blank, eerily so as well as her tone. "What's a spirit board?"

She was reflexively suspicious about the question, clearly. "Where in the world did you hear about those? Was it Sara?" Unconsciously she had a desire for that to be true.

Angelica responded, "No, this doesn't have anything to do with Sara. Do *you* know what a spirit board is?"

The insolent tone of Angelica's voice almost crested in her mind above the blunt question, but not quite. She looked down quickly before meeting her eyes. "It's nothing you need to worry about. All I can say is: *Never* use one! They're forbidden by The Church!"

Sara soon stepped out of the van and walked toward the back porch. She could see the marks all along Angelica's arms as she smiled and ran toward her. She threw her arms around Sara as the latter said, "Ange! What happened to your arms!?"

Angelica looked up at her with a smile and said in a lowered tone, "You were there. You saw what happened."

Sara grinned and winked. "Yes, I was, dear. Yes, I was." She looked down at Angelica's arms, nonetheless. "Well, it doesn't look like you bled any. That's a good thing at least, right?"

She replied, "Yeah, I guess so."

Father Anderson was also now looking at her arms. "My goodness, Angelica, you've been through quite a battle! Here, let's not waste any time." He took a bottle of holy water from his pocket and blessed her.

A few minutes later inside and everyone was gathered in the living room. Father Anderson had performed the communion rite with everyone and was ready to start the ritual. "First off, I'd like to thank Roberta here for volunteering to be my assistant today. Father Cooper was supposed to be my assistant but he came down with a sudden flu. His fever was so elevated when I asked to speak to him that he wasn't able to form coherent words."

Rosanna replied with great concern, "Oh, no! Is he going to be okay?"

"They have him stabilized at the hospital. They told me that as long as they can keep his fever under control he should be fine. Worst case of flu they'd seen in decades. Keep him in your prayers but also know that this may be a sign. Whatever is here clearly doesn't want this rite to take place. We must proceed with courage and faith." He then opened the leather-bound book he was carrying in his arms and said, "We are here today to call upon our most holy God and his divine servants. We are here to aid the Barrister family in regaining their home, property, and lives. Let us now pray to St. Michael, the Archangel: In the name of the Father, and of the Son, and of the Holy Ghost. Amen.

"Most glorious Prince of the Heavenly Armies, Saint Michael the Archangel, defend us in our battle against principalities and powers, against the rulers of this world of darkness, against the spirits of wickedness in the high places. Come to the assistance of men whom God had created to His likeness and whom He has redeemed at a great price from the tyranny of the devil. The Holy Church venerates you as her guardian and protector; to you, the Lord has entrusted the souls of the redeemed to be led into heaven. Pray therefore the God of Peace to crush Satan beneath our feet, that he may no longer retain men captive and do injury to the Church. Offer our prayers to the Most High, that without delay they may draw His mercy down upon us; take hold of the dragon, the old serpent, which is the devil and Satan, bind him and cast him into the bottomless pit that he may no longer seduce the nations."

During the brief pause, Angelica spoke up. Her voice, however, was an equal mixture of her own and the voice of Caroline. Caroline's voice, however, did not sound as deranged as in Angelica's dreams. It was her voice from her mortal time. "This won't work, you know...."

Everyone looked at her aghast. Father Anderson, however, maintained a calm demeanor as Rosanna said in a scolding tone, "Angelica! Don't say that!"

She replied blankly, "This isn't the first time this has happened and it won't be the last."

Her tone more elevated, "That's enough, Angelica! Stop talking!"

Her voice still bifurcated, "What are you going to do, Mother? Are you going to kill me like you did my sister?"

Rosanna's eyes widened to the point that they resembled headlights on a car. She was speechless as Angelica continued.

"You know you can only have one child, right? You and Edward keep trying but it won't work."

Rosanna replied in horror, "Wha... what are you talking about!? How did you...!?"

Still calm, the partially manipulated Angelica replied, "I was there that night, Rosanna Leone. You and your little Ouija board game got a little too real, didn't it?"

Rosanna was starting to tremble, visibly shaken and starting to get angry.

"Well, come on then. I know you don't love this little cunt here, so why not kill her? Just strangle her and get it over with."

Unknowingly, Rosanna had raised her hand but managed to stop it from striking the cheek of her daughter. "You monster! What the hell are you!?"

The voice coming from her daughter then burst into existence over both Angelica's and Caroline's younger voice to become the nightmare tone. "Go ahead, Rosy Anna, you bitch! Hit me! Hit this little cunt for talking back to you! Hit her like you hit your mother!"

Rosanna was completely overtaken by fear and started to back away.

The voice became louder. "You always were a coward, Rosanna! A damnable bitch who has to push her kid around to feel good about herself! Do it! Hit me, you bitch!"

Angelica was advancing toward her mother but was abruptly stopped by Father Anderson aggressively splashing her face and body with the holy water from the sprinkler he had with him. He then said in a commanding tone as Angelica recoiled and screamed, "In the Name of Jesus Christ, our God and Lord, strengthened by the intercession of the Immaculate Virgin Mary, Mother of God, of Blessed Michael the Archangel, of the Blessed Apostles Peter and Paul and all the Saints...."

Angelica was now shrieking in agony and fell to the ground writhing. In her own voice she cried out, "You're hurting me! Stop it!"

Edward, seeing the holy water covering her arms and feeling for himself a fraction of the great pain she was in, started toward her. He was stopped, however, by Father Anderson as he blocked his path.

"We must continue! The enemy will try and deceive us all!" He picked up where he had left off. "And powerful in the holy authority of our ministry, we confidently undertake to repulse the attacks and deceits of the devil. God arises; His enemies are scattered and those who hate Him flee before Him. As smoke is driven away, so are they driven; as wax melts before the fire, so the wicked perish at the presence of God."

Angelica soon stopped writhing as Father Anderson continued the prayers nearby. She looked around for a few moments in confusion before becoming very much aware of the current events once again. Partially soaked with water, she got to her knees and looked over at her mother staring back at her. Edward was standing between them but she could see her face. Her eyes were as big as saucers and she looked positively frozen. She didn't feel the same anger coming from her now. The emotion she radiated now was deep and abysmal fear.

A few moments passed and Father Anderson felt comfortable going into the other areas of the house with Roberta following behind him. Sara helped Angelica to her feet as Edward helped his wife.

As the priest approached the door to Rosanna and Edward's bedroom, he made the sign of the cross with the holy water before entering. Roberta, however, noticed something unsettling about the water he was throwing. As it landed, he continued to look down and read from his book, but she was seeing red stains appearing wherever the water touched.

Shocked, she said, "Father Anderson, look! It's turning to blood!"

He was only momentarily shaken by it, but continued reciting with force. "We drive you from us, whoever you may be, unclean spirits, all satanic powers, all infernal invaders, all wicked legions, assemblies and sects! In the Name and by the power of Our Lord Jesus Christ," he made the sign of the cross, "may you be snatched away and driven from the Church of God and from the souls made to the image and likeness of God and redeemed by the Precious Blood of the Divine Lamb!"

He continued to sling blood spatters all over everything the water touched. When he stepped out to bless the doorway to Angelica's bedroom, a darker and thicker red blood began to splatter and ooze down the white door.

As he recited the next parts of the prayer inside Angelica's room, she was watching from the hall with Sara close behind her.

Angelica then said, in her own voice, "You don't understand! It *wants* blood!"

Sara looked down with concern and pulled her closer.

Edward continued to comfort Rosanna in the living room as the team and Angelica headed upstairs. She watched as the rooms were blessed one by one with the now viscous blood sprinkler.

She pleaded, "Father Anderson, it won't go away! It wants blood!"

Father Anderson heard her and responded, "I must finish the rite, Angelica! You must have faith!"

As he continued, Roberta looked at Sara with mild agitation hoping she would do something about the distractions. Sara nodded and escorted her back down the stairs.

Once at the bottom, Angelica said, "I know what it wants! Why doesn't anyone believe me!?"

Sara got down to eye level. "I know, sweetie, but we have to let Father Anderson finish the rite! Be strong!"

Frustrated, "But we shouldn't go...."

She was cut off as Father Anderson and Roberta came down the stairs right next to them. Father Anderson then said, "We must head outside so I can continue to bless the property."

The five followed Father Anderson outside as he continued his prayers and approached the drab barn to his left. He made the sign of the cross at the doorway before Roberta flung it open. The smell of decay was enough to almost cause him to fall to his backside. He kept upright, however, only to see a huge swarm of large warble flies zip loudly from the environs and suddenly surround and ground Edward and Rosanna. They aggressively latched to their skin as the two began to panic and try to slough off as many as they could.

Edward screamed, "Get 'em off me!"

The others rushed over to try and shoo them away, but they only left on their own accord after nearly half a minute. Rosanna and her husband thrashed and cried out with each invasive maneuver. The holy water flung on them seemed to help, but the now red liquid made their appearance even more unsettling.

They stopped for a moment as Roberta went inside the house and brought out two towels for the bloodied parents. Father Anderson, however, was insistent as he went toward the barn once again.

"Christ, God's Word made flesh, commands you," he made the sign of the cross, "He who to save our race outdone through your envy, humbled Himself, becoming obedient even unto death; he who has built His Church on the firm rock and declared that the gates of hell shall not prevail against Her, because He will dwell with Her all days even to the end of the world.

"The sacred Sign of the Cross commands you," he made the sign of the cross.

At this, they all heard a thunderous gurgling sound coming from inside the closed well at the back of the barn. A powerful stench, resembling feces and decaying flesh, gushed out and once again nearly knocked Father Anderson over.

He stood, however, and continued. "As does also the power of the mysteries of the Christian Faith!"

Meanwhile, outside, Rosanna and Edward were now scratching feverishly at small pink marks all over their forearms and legs. They were also experiencing massive sensory overload as the smell was smashing them in the face at the same time. They scrambled to put distance between themselves and the drab barn.

As the bubbling fluid from inside ceased to flow out, Father Anderson turned his attention back to Rosanna and Edward. He stepped toward them and said defiantly, "Be gone, Satan, inventor and master of all deceit, enemy of man's salvation!"

The sprinkling of the blood seemed to only agitate the gnawing sensation at their flesh.

Angelica, shielded by Sara now, saw her mother scream out, "Make it stop, Father! Please!"

As he cast more of the red holy liquid in her direction, small cylindrical masses began to form and puff up beneath their skin. The inch-long lumps began to then sear their flesh with pain. They then felt the pulsating masses under their skin plump up and poke through their epidermal cocoon. All six of them watched in disgust and terror as dozens of warble larvae each undulated its way out of the small holes they'd made in the Barrister parents' flesh and drip to the ground like raindrops. Each larva then subsequently dissolved into the ground before their very eyes.

Father Anderson continued the prayer and splashed them again and again. Roberta and Sara then went over to them to try and wipe the blood away that was seeping from their skin.

When he reached a new paragraph in the text he paused and looked down at the Barristers, who were trying to rise to their knees. He then said, "It is imperative that we continue! Mr. and Mrs. Barrister, can you stand!?"

Rosanna coughed as Edward summoned the courage to growl. "Yes! Finish it! We can't stop now!" He looked at his wife and helped her to her feet. "We have to do this! I need you, Rosy!"

Despite wincing in pain, she stood up with him. "Yes! We finish this together!"

Sara brought Angelica closer and held her hand as she looked up at her mother. Sara then said, "Come on, Angelica! We're going to win come hell or high water!"

After blessing the normal barn uneventfully, they headed down the path leading to the bridge.

Several steps later as they approached the bridge, Roberta suddenly said, "The cave, Father! I believe that's where the source is!"

She then turned around and briefly glanced at the Barristers and Sara. Angelica didn't like the face that looked back. It looked more and more like Caroline than ever.

Angelica then said in a hushed tone to Sara, "We can't go in there! It's a trap!"

Sara was perplexed for a moment, but as Roberta called out to them again, she and the three other headed toward her.

Once they arrived at the mouth of the cave, Father Anderson approached and made the sign of the cross at the doorway.

Before he could begin his next line, however, Roberta said, "We have to go in there, Father! We have to drive it out completely!"

Angelica then looked up and noticed that there were a lot more brown briar-covered vines thickly surrounding the closed portal. She then saw a terrible image in her mind: Sara blossoming like the sick "flowers" Caroline showed her in the dream from the night before. Angelica began to panic as she saw her father open the lock on the door and step aside to open it for them.

Frantically she ran at Sara and clamped her arms around hers. "Sara, you can't go in there!"

Roberta, however, called out and said, "Sara, we need your help in here!"

She looked their way and tried to walk forward, but Angelica was hanging onto her arm now with all of her weight. She then said, "Ange, please! They need my help!"

Rosanna then said with some annoyance, "Angelica, let her go! They need her!"

Edward turned to face the tussle as Father Anderson and Roberta were well into the cave. As Angelica clung desperately to Sara's arm, they all heard the door to the cave slam shut violently by an unseen force. The vines that were surrounding the doorway now quickly covered it completely. Inside they could hear the muffled sounds of Roberta and Father Anderson screaming desperately. Angelica then looked on in terror as a large boulder broke loose from the rock face and fell in front of the door and landing on Edward's left leg. It was crushed. He screamed in agony as the three women rushed toward him.

Sara and Rosanna then tried to move the large rock, but were unable.

Rosanna then looked to her daughter and said, "Angelica, my phone is back in the kitchen! Run! Run and get it and call 911! We have to save Daddy! Run!"

Angelica, at 100-percent adrenaline, turned and blasted away back toward the house. She ran faster than she'd ever thought possible. Once at the bridge, however, she saw that the water level in the creek, which was fairly low on the way in, was now cresting up to the banks and starting to leap up onto the wooden planks. She only paused for a microsecond before splashing across and bee-lining it straight for the house.

Once there she went inside and sure enough the phone was lying on the kitchen table. She quickly dialed the emergency number.

"Hello, this is 911. What is your emergency?"

"My dad had a big rock fall on him! He needs help now!"

Having tracked the call immediately, "Okay, you're on Holly Bush Road, correct?"

"Yes! Hurry!"

"I already have an ambulance on the way. Please wait there at the house so the paramedics will know where to go, okay, honey?"

Angelica desperately wanted to run back to her father, but she knew the best thing to do was wait for help.

Epilogue

Edward survived his leg being crushed by the boulder on the property. It would take three surgeries in total before he would be able to walk without a cane. The slight limp would remain indefinitely.

Angelica would unfortunately bear the name of "Goat Girl" from her more mean-spirited classmates. Her relationship with her mother improved somewhat, but wouldn't get much warmer than chilly on most occasions.

The vegetation did return to its normal green hue the very next day after the Minor Rite of Exorcism performed by Father Anderson and Roberta. Despite the valiant efforts of volunteers and paid rescuers, they never found the bodies of Father Anderson or Roberta.

Christmas Eve night following that summer, Angelica was seated on the edge of her bed looking at a framed photo taken not long after the day of the rite. In it was her dad in a hospital bed with his leg in a cast. He looked mildly happy giving the thumbs-up, thanks to the morphine drip next to the bed. Rosanna, Angelica, and Sara were all leaning in to show their smiles and thumbs-ups as well.

She then put the picture down on her nightstand and walked to the window in her darkened room. As she looked outside she intensely enjoyed the thick snowflakes beginning to fall. This was the first time she would experience a snowy Christmas and it made her feel all warm and fuzzy on the inside. Peace seemed to have finally descended on the house and property. Perhaps the rite had worked after all.

Comforted by that thought she walked over to her bed and turned off her lamp.

Angelica awoke in the field of fresh snow with a golden sky in the background. It wasn't cold like regular snow. In fact, it seemed quite warm and smooth beneath her feet. She ran and laughed through the powdery playground, chasing her wolfdog Cerberus. He barked merrily in front of her, indulging in being pursued. The golden sky then seemed to rain auric, angelic voices. "Come here, my dear...."

As she looked skyward in awe the ground suddenly opened up and sucked her down like a canister in a bank teller tube. She slipped down a long slimy slit in the earth until she flew out abruptly into a cesspool of the familiar black liquid.

Gradually she rose to her feet and began to trudge through the muck and into an odd hallway lit by haphazardly positioned shafts of yellow light coming from above. Jagged rocks made up the walls in the corridor she now tentatively walked down. She looked up several times, but was not able to tell how far down she was, as the cracks in the Earth seemed to stretch up unnaturally high.

Waiting for her at the end of this long stony corridor was what initially appeared to be just a massive wall of rocks nearly sixty feet high. She paused and stared, trying to figure out what she was supposed to infer from this.

Suddenly, from behind, she saw scores of dark gray and black humanoid forms shamble from the corridor and into the main chamber. The figures were mostly made up of individuals around three feet tall and slightly more. They clearly appeared to be children and seemed to pay no attention to Angelica as they filed into the large wall and disappear one by one.

She gazed for almost a minute before she felt a massive blast of energy, visible in the form of a massive yellow orb expanding, knock her back and squarely to the ground. Her mind suddenly raced feverishly as stacks of information flooded her mind. What she felt deep down, however, was unsettling. Consciousness. Sentience. Awareness. Whatever it was, it was alive and ancient. To it, a century felt more like a week. This bored in deeply, making her feel especially miniscule compared to its grandiose scale.

Suddenly, the information became too much, far too much for her mortal mind to comprehend. It was also causing her intense pain as she dropped to her knees, feeling that her head would explode at any second. She looked up and cried out in agony....

Christmas morning. She woke in her bed with a sharp breathless gasp. Looking down at the foot of her bed, she saw the completely desiccated form of an old woman on her knees and reaching out for her. It wasn't moving, however, as Angelica recognized it to be Caroline, or what was left of her. She then heard Caroline's voice clearly in her mind: *"Replace... me...."* The eyes... the eyes seem to still possess their familiar insanity. Was it possible she was still alive?

Angelica screamed.

Hearing this in her bedroom, Rosanna jumped to her feet and came down the hall. She opened the door to Angelica's room and flicked on the overhead light. Angelica glanced over at the door, then back at the foot of her bed. The remains of Caroline were then gone. Seeing her gasping for air and her eyes as big as hubcaps, she stepped to her bedside.

With genuine concern, "You okay, sweetie? Another nightmare?"

She could hear her father struggling to get up in the next room over. Slowly she got her breathing under control, "Yeah...."

"Aw, I'm sorry. That's the first one you've had in a while, isn't it?"

"Uh-huh...."

Slowing her own breathing down to demonstrate, "That's it, Ange, deep breaths. You're okay now."

Angelica looked out at the snow that had accumulated from the night before along with the pink sky heralding the arrival of the morning sun.

Edward, using a crutch, stepped into the doorway now. "Hey, baby girl, you okay?"

Looking at her father, "I'm fine. Just a nightmare."

Her mother then said to her, "Well, since we're up, we'd might as well start opening presents. But first, my sweaty daughter, you need to go and take a shower. Remember, Sara is coming over later."

Sara later came over and presented her with what was probably Angelica's favorite gift. She had personally made a black dress for her that was distinctly Victorian in style and anachronistically perfect. Rosanna would occasionally call her Wednesday Addams in jest, but was somewhat disturbed by how it somewhat resembled the style of dress her mother used to wear in her younger days.

Reader, you are probably left with a few questions and I understand. It's clear that *they* will only let you see what *they* want you to see. On the same coin, I suppose I'm doing that, too. Such deception mixed with truth is infuriating and a tangled mess to understand. Just know that most creatures get used to their favorite toys and eventually want a new one. A cat may stop playing with a mouse toy it has grown tired of over the years, such as a dog gets tired of the same chew toy. Are entities of higher levels of consciousness any different?